For Amy,

Be healthy!

Ryn Pitts

Deadly Benefits

Ryn Pitts

Author's Note

This novel is a work of fiction. The author has created characters, organizations, events and circumstances within this book for the reader's pleasure, and intends no connection to real people, living or dead.

Three great mysteries:

Air to a Bird

Water to a Fish

Mankind to Himself

A Hindu proverb

Prologue

January 16, 2002, evening

He'd been more or less drunk since New Year's Eve and that was two weeks ago. Slumming with the tourists along Soi 33 on that sweaty tropical night, cheap booze at 150 baht, he and Gilly had toasted farewell to 2001, the year of freaking terrorists, and welcomed 2002 with beery optimism. Let the Feds crack down on this cranked up world. Better them chasing down Arabs than snooping in our drawers, right, Gilly?

Giggles across the bar from a pair of Thai girls in body-hugging black silk. Mister? Mister? Three thousand baht for good time?

Why not?

Hormonal logic coaxed him up the stairs. You had to let down once in awhile, right? Take a chance. Money and risk nuzzled in the same sack; that much he knew. And what were the odds of snagging a twofer the minute one year rolls into the next? Lucky omen. Had to be.

An hour later, the girls—gone, and so were his 14k gold cuff links. No problem; it's only money. Screw it as long as the windfall runs. And it would. Then as he pulled on his trousers, he reached for his Blackberry. Gone, too. Shit! Money can't fix that!

Now he was stinking sober. From the twenty-fourth floor of his penthouse overlooking the Bangkok skyline—banks, embassies, hospitals—he waited among Asian antiques, state-of-the-art computer technology and a sky-high putting green along the south terrace. The spectacular balcony garden, well-tended by the house staff, blazed in a lush lime green of tropical plants, fruits and spices that he couldn't begin to name except for the occasional spikey fingers of cannabis growing among them.

Another two weeks in this damnable paradise before he could go home. Minnesota ice and snow never looked so good.

He looked up to catch the last of another bruised purple sunset when his chief house servant, Bao, approached with an envelope of rich vellum bearing his name and Sukhumvit address. He brushed Bao away and the servant vanished like a puff of smoke. No postage stamp. Must have been hand-delivered to the building's security guard. He slit open the seal with a breakfast knife. On the card, the message read:

TROUBLE on CNN

The plasma screen TV blossomed into American talking heads reading from TelePrompTers. American Taliban fighter John Walker will be brought back to the United States to stand trial on multiple charges, including conspiracy to kill U.S. nationals abroad, the Justice Department said Tuesday. . . . . British police have refused to rule out taking action against Prince Harry over his cannabis use and underage drinking. . . .

What was Gilly worried about: some Brit smoking a little pot? He chuckled. No one, not even a royal prick can stay off good grass. Couldn't be our weed unless somebody'd been careless and crossed the wrong ocean. Another laugh. Then he saw the trailer inching along the bottom of the screen.

US Coast Guard raids Thai fishing vessel in Pacific ocean . . .13 tons of cocaine hidden under frozen squid . . . .

If he'd been drunk he might have missed the significance but now, clean and clear-headed, all synapses were firing. He lunged to his computer and clicked his way to the CNN web site in search of the news posting.

During the raid of a Thai fishing vessel in the Pacific Ocean, US Coast Guard officials may have found the largest shipment of cocaine ever intercepted at sea. Investigators now believe they have tapped into a complex money-laundering ring operating in Bolivia, Colombia, Chile, Ecuador, Nicaragua and most recently, Thailand. The drug cartel under investigation is suspected of moving millions of illegal drug dollars through an elaborate network of brokers into unregulated US insurance investments that are being used as sanctuaries for dirty money.

Worse than any freaking hallucination was the story unfolding on the screen. He needed gin. No, he needed gin and a lude.

Officials at the Securities and Exchange Commission would not comment on their pending case against the Maryland-based Eastern Shore Life Settlement Company, now in receivership, except to note that "a trail of cash led to the doorstep of Eastern Shore's corporate offices."

He pounded his fist on the glass table with enough force to topple a vase of exotic flowers. While he figured out what to do next, Bao had slipped silently into the room carrying a broom. With him, a roomful of ghosts took up residence. That he had always feared being found out made the news story worming across the bottom of screen seem like some kind of doomed Midwestern destiny. He thought of calling Danny. Or his sister in Fargo. No time for that. The program was ready, the files encrypted. Get a grip, man. With a few strokes on the keyboard, the hard drive would be destroyed. Completely unrecoverable, even by the freaking government, after fifteen minutes of continual erasure. He entered the code. The program complied. It was that easy.

From the hollow of a cloisonné vase, he pulled out bundles of cash and stuffed them into a duffel with a change of clothes and three bogus passports. He swept the room for other evidence and saw the envelope. With a touch of his cigarette lighter, the fire licked away at **Trouble** until every trace of paper was gone. Bao said nothing as he shuffled away with the still-smoldering ashes.

He looked about the room one last time at the wealth that surrounded him. It was as much an illusion as the ghosts that haunted him. That much he'd learned after three years in the business. Fear made leaving it all behind easier than he'd ever imagined. No time for regrets. No time to waste.

The ghosts followed him as he hurried through the penthouse door. When the elevator finally arrived on the 24th floor, he stepped in and surrendered to the closing doors. How long might it take to reach bottom?

Saturday, April 1, 2002

One

The basement stairwell was somber as though Swedish Hospital were already in mourning. Heli Harri glanced at her Timex: 7:04 PM. Whatever sliver of peace this moment offered, she knew it was about to end. Summoned by her pager to a code blue in the ICU had, by necessity, reordered her next hour of work because somebody's life, now measured in minutes, was on the line. Back in the pharmacy, IV orders from Med-Surg and Oncology were piling up hopelessly. Agitated outpatients with prescriptions at the in/out window would pace longer. Heli tightened the laces of her Reeboks with a quiet grunt. Five flights to climb before reaching 503. She imagined the code team assembled, waiting for her, always last to arrive from the drug cave buried deep in the bowels of the old building.

Drug cave. Two months as a temp pharmacist on weekends, and already the hospital slang came easy—easier than its new drug protocols, old computer systems and bewildering hospital acronyms, not to mention dodging the in-fighting festering among hospital employees. Heli drew in a deep breath. This was no time for distraction. No excuse for fatigue despite starting a second night shift after a landmark day's work at Corner Drug. And no room for failure. Adrenaline kicked in and *Suomi* resolve rising from her deep Finnish roots powered her up the steps, two at a time.

A crowd had already gathered around the bed when she entered 503. From the corner of the room, beeping monitors, a crash cart, the oxygen tank, suction and defibrillator were already in place. She opened the top drawer of the cart for a ritualized check of the med tray in the sickly overhead lighting that made it nearly impossible to check expiration dates. Vasopressin, epinephrine, lidocaine, bicarb—ready like soldiers to be deployed.

Across the room from the ICU bed, someone had written on a white board: TODAY IS SATURDAY, APRIL 1, 2002. April Fool's Day. Heli took a quick breath and refocused. Heroes were needed tonight, not fools. While God and doctors took credit for good outcomes, patients survived their stay at Swedish only when the long chain of hospital care remained unbroken by human error. Drug protocols cycled through her mind. Fingers sought the dosing guide in her pocket. Bodies came in all sizes, and the margin for error was slim. When a code was called, fear tightened the knot in her stomach every time.

A stout nurse named Roxy, with alert eyes and a bad

complexion, drew back the sheets and loosened the patient's gown. A gum-snapping respiratory therapist and a CRNA in baggy green scrubs jostled for position near the monitors. Behind them, a second year resident checked the defib paddles. When a medical student leaned forward, a sliver of space opened and only then did Heli catch sight of chief resident, Dr. Sandeep Venkata, standing at the foot of the bed with chart in hand.

The events of the past two hours swirled in Heli's mind. Had Venkata been called back to the hospital tonight because of *this* patient? She studied the contour of Sandy's face, as grave now as it had been intimate earlier this evening when some magical life-twist of fate had brought them together for dinner at the Jade.

Roxy began chest compressions, a hundred per minute, on the frail chest. "One... two. . .three. . .four. . . ."

"Out of the way! We have to bag her." The respiratory tech slapped a mask over the patient's face and squeezed an Ambou bag to ventilate the lungs.

Roxy nudged between two RNs and leaned kiss-close to the patient. "Come on, Chris, we're gonna need some help from you this time."

Heli winced. Christopher, Christy, Christine. How many times had she typed this Scandinavian variant on prescription labels at her drugstore? Kristian, Kristiann, Kristine. It was not so much the familiar name that gave her pause as the coincidence. Finns mistrusted coincidence. She hoped this Chris was a stranger. Someone passing through Fargo. *Not* Christine Runyan. In her eye-line, a v-fib rhythm rippled across the monitor. She twisted in her cashmere sweater—a cautious choice for the first date she'd had in years—but now ridiculously hot under her smock. Stay on task, she resolved. Made wiser by twelve previous codes (all successful), she rearranged the ampoules and syringes per protocol.

Venkata studied the cardiac tracing on the monitor, slowly turning the pages of the chart, with an apparent indifference to the chaos around him. "A Crohn's patient in septic shock," he noted, his words arcing in Heli's direction.

She drew a quick breath. No. Held it, as if exhaling might make this real. Christine Runyan, the young Crohn's patient who'd been in her drugstore yesterday with her daughter—now lying in the ICU bed. No. Christine—buying Little Mermaid Band-Aids for Anya, dropping off another roll of film for her scrap-booking obsession. No.

Venkata's nod confirmed the worst.

Silence thickened like an emulsion.

"Please call Dr. Lavelle," Venkata's tone was urgent.

"For Pete's sake, Dr. V., it's Saturday night," Roxy puffed. "You know Lavelle ignores pages on the weekend."

"Call Dr. Lavelle *now*." Tension coated the chief resident's voice like last night's winter ice bearing down on telephone wires. "Alert the family."

"Her husband's right outside the door, raising hell with the ward clerk. You know paramedics. He insists on being in here."

Heli heard Trevor Runyan's rant. 'Why's a resident running the code? Where's Lavelle? Christine. . . .' Gradually his bluster grew fainter, as if someone—Security, probably—were leading him back down the hall. The cramped room grew warmer with trapped heat as Heli's thoughts cycled stubbornly back to yesterday afternoon. Why? How? Despite being fed through an IV line in her chest, Christine had seemed chipper at Corner Drug. Now, just 24 hours later, why was she in code blue status? Heli wiped a bead of sweat near the scar on her forehead as she steered through the possibilities. Another infected catheter? Typical with indwelling lines.

"Careful on the compressions, Roxy. Do not break a rib. Mrs. Runyan is very fragile." Venkata pushed through a drove of nurses. "A wide QRS complex on the monitor. What is her rhythm?"

"V-fib, Doctor."

"We will shock her immediately. Paddles are charging. Everyone stand back. All clear?" Venkata looked around. "Two hundred joules, now."

Poo. . . oo. . .ft!

Eyes blinked in unison. A throat cleared; gum snapped. The medical student winced, leaned in closer. A tiny muscle twitched near Heli's eye.

"What are we getting?"

"Still v-fib." Roxy stepped in. "Stay with us, Chris. We're all here to help you, hon, but you gotta work with us."

Without waiting for the order, Heli removed the epinephrine injection from its sheath. She assembled the lidocaine syringe, threading the vial into its injector until the needle penetrated the rubber stopper.

"Have we heard from Dr. Lavelle?" The lines across Venkata's brow radiated growing alarm.

"Believe it or not, he's on his way."

"We will shock her again. All clear?" Venkata looked around. "Three hundred joules. Now."

Heli bit her lip, closed her eyes.

The door opened and Dr. Mark Lavelle shoved his way to Venkata's side. He glanced at the paddles in the chief resident's hands. "Did she get a rhythm?"

"No, Sir. Do you wish to take over?"

"Keep going." Lavelle eyes darted from the monitor to his patient. "Why hasn't she been intubated?"

"Airway is too small for the adult tube," the respiratory tech muttered. "The small endo-trach tube was missing from the cart. Peds is sending one up."

"Typical for this place," Lavelle snapped.

The green wave on the monitor's screen was a choppy erratic line like a badly bruised saw blade.

"Administer 1 milligram Epinephrine through the line."

Heli handed the pre-filled syringe to the nurse.

"Move it if you want to help her!" Lavelle bellowed over his shoulder.

"Epi, 1 mg IV in the central line. Time: 7:41."

"What's the rhythm?"

"Still v-fib."

"Administer Sodium bicarb, 1 mEq/kg IV."

Heli held the bicarb syringe at eye level to verify the dose, silently cursing the pathetic light as she glimpsed the tiny graduations. Noise streaming in from the corridor had intensified with tall tales of last night's storm—extra shifts, cars buried in snow, EVAC heroics. No longer could she hear the soft whir of the IV pump or the monitor's steady beeping. A deep breath steadied her hands.

The sudden crash of metal—an oxygen tank rolling across the floor—provoked a new round of pandemonium.

"What in the name of God is going on back there?" Dr. Lavelle spun around, his eyes wild. "Hurry up with that bicarb or we'll lose her!"

As a burly nurse scrambled to retrieve the rolling tank, Heli rushed forward with the syringe. Without an immediate bolus of bicarbonate, Christine might die. The possibility lurched inside Heli's chest, harsh and violent, like a fish snagged by a hook. Then she felt a hit—real, this time—a sharp blow from the side. Her right arm jerked up in a lunatic salute. The syringe flew from her hand, squirting bicarbonate solution into the air, while the barrel struck the cart's metal frame and shattered, producing a rain of glass shards at her feet.

"Klutz!" The nurse glared red-hot.

Under her jacket the cashmere sweater, now plastered to Heli's back, felt like a transdermal patch. Let it pass: an inner voice sounding much like her father's advice. Every trout is tempted by bait, but the wise ignore it. Much later, the scene would play out a hundred times in her memory: the nurse with the tank of oxygen in outstretched arms, oblivious to anyone in her path, crashing into her from behind and knocking the syringe from her hand. In time, she would reflect on the finger-pointing, blame-game hospital culture at the kitchen table before her collection of mayflies, but now was a reset moment. All that mattered was that bicarbonate reach Christine's bloodstream stat.

"Bicarb, 1 mEq/kg," she said with a steadying breath. "Sorry."

"Try telling a dead patient how sorry you are," Lavelle growled. "This isn't a soda fountain. Seconds count here!"

"Bicarb administered. Time: 7:46."

"Rhythm?"

"Still v-fib, Dr. V."

"We will shock her again. Everyone, stand back. Clear? Three hundred sixty joules, now."

"No pulse, Dr. V."

"Another amp of epinephrine. Now!"

Heli handed the syringe to the nurse. Only three remained in the drawer.

"Epi pushed through central line. Time: 7:51."

The room quieted. The wave on the screen collapsed to a single flat line. Only the *whoosh* of the Ambou bag and the rhythmic compressions broke the silence.

"Check the leads once again, please."

"Leads are in place and functioning, Dr. V. She's gone straight-line."

Venkata turned to Dr. Lavelle. "Sir, we are at the end of the protocol, and we have no rhythm. The patient is in asystole."

Lavelle shoved him aside. "Giving up, Sandy?" He smacked the bedrails. "She's not even thirty years old. This was not supposed to happen. What will you tell the family? How will you explain your failure?"

"Back off, Lavelle." Roxy stepped forward. "Talk like that doesn't help."

"You, an LPN, speaking to me in that tone? You don't belong anywhere near a critically ill patient."

"Please," Venkata implored.

"You, Butterfingers! Give me another amp of epi with a long

9

eighteen gauge needle. Can you manage to do that without dropping something?"

Heli's cheeks burned rage-red. There it was on the tip of her tongue—the words Lavelle so needed to hear. *Better than your dirty fingers, Doctor.* You'd have to be in a Versed coma not to know that this pompous East Coast snob was too cozy with pharmaceutical reps. Strutted regularly through Fargo's better restaurants with a Pharma sycophant trailing behind to pick up the tab. But the words dissolved on her tongue like a nitroglycerin pill: bitter but lifesaving. What she needed now, more than to win a squabbling match, was to establish Corner Drug's financial health, and this part-time job at Swedish was paving the way.

"Dr. Lavelle, please," Venkata interceded. "Intracardiac administration is beyond the protocol. It will do her no good."

"Maybe if you'd called me in earlier tonight this wouldn't be necessary. You've been second-guessing me all along on this case, Sandy. Are you satisfied? You'll have to live with this the rest of your life." He shouted over his shoulder, "Where's the epi?"

The syringe was ready but Heli hesitated. She'd never before seen epi work in a situation like this.

"I gave you an order!" Lavelle glared. "Are you deaf, incompetent, or both?"

He seized it from her hand and attached the six inch needle to its hub. "Prepare the area around the xyphoid process." A nurse quickly painted the chest area with antiseptic. With a gloved index finger, Lavelle palpated the space at the bottom of Christine's sternum and advanced the tip of the needle directly into her chest, angling it slightly in the direction of her left shoulder. He pulled the plunger back until reddish black blood blossomed into the barrel. Then he pushed epinephrine directly into a chamber of her heart.

Every eye fixated on the monitor's persistent flat line.

Prairie flat.

The hospital chaplain entered the room with a tattered Bible, its gold ribbon marking the page of the twenty-third Psalm.

Peacefully flat.

Roxy took Christine's hand and sandwiched it between her own. "Let her go, Lavelle. Let her go."

"She is right, Sir. We must stop." Venkata looked around at each member of the code team who rustled in a moment of awkward silence. "The code has ended. Mrs. Runyan has died."

Lavelle backed away and slumped against the wall. A solemn nurse disconnected the defibrillator and removed the endotracheal tube from the dead woman's mouth.

Muscle memory pushed Heli through follow-up duties. Close the drawer of the crash cart. Gather up used syringes and drop needles into the red sharps container. Her mouth was dry as gauze. For the first time, she stared at the emaciated body, entwined by IV tubing and electrodes, lost in a sea of white. The soft-bird heart, now stilled. The pallid face she would never forget.

The chaplain prayed while the medical student yawned. A nurse disconnected the cardiac monitor. Another tidied the floor of spills and neutralized the air with a fresh sanitizing scent.

Roxy placed one lifeless hand over the other and drew a sheet over the body. "Good-bye, Chris," she whispered. "You were a real trouper. Safe travels, girl."

"Leave the central line in place for the autopsy," the salty house administrator directed. "We'll need the family's authorization. Tonight, if possible."

Lavelle sprang back up as if he'd been electrified. "*I'll* determine if we need an autopsy and there is absolutely no need for one on this patient. She died of septic shock from an overwhelming infection of her central line." He slammed the door shut and toggled on the overhead lights. "Nobody leaves this room."

Activity quieted under Lavelle's sweeping scowl. "My patient just died less than ten minutes ago. Why? Because this hospital is a dangerous place. I'm surrounded by incompetence everywhere I look. It starts at the top and ends here in a room where another patient died because of your mistakes." He clenched his jaw. "Do you know what your problem is?"

No one answered.

"Let me be very clear. It's your pathetic Midwestern attitude. Good is good enough. You don't aspire to anything better. I trained in a world of the best, and you settle for mediocrity. I demand excellence, and all I get from you is 'good is good enough.'"

"Sir," Venkata implored, "perhaps there is a better time. . . ."

"Stay out of this. How many more patients must die before this intolerable care is addressed?"

The door opened quietly and a woman with smoky eyes stepped in. She wore an ID badge that swung from a lanyard: *Alayne Ludemann, Manager, Emergency Room.*

"What are you doing in here?" Lavelle barked. "No wonder this hospital is falling apart. People are never where they're supposed to be."

"I'm a friend of the family."

From the corner of her eye, Heli watched as Roxy's eyes rolled.

"And you!" Lavelle turned on Heli. "What are *you* doing at a code?"

Heli felt the heat of his glare.

"I demand that pharmacy send me experienced professionals. You're just hired help." Lavelle cleared his throat but it sounded like a snarl. "I expect people to follow my orders without hesitation. If you can't rise to that, you may as well be counting pills. Your entire department could be replaced by a robot."

Robots, who don't know fatigue, Heli thought, or feel shame. Maybe Lavelle was right. Robots aren't driven by money. Robots don't grieve the dead.

"Sir, the family is waiting."

"You disgust me, all of you. Your dull stares, your colorless food, your tedious lives, your dangling prepositions. Inept, miserable cretins who dim the intellect of anyone—" He broke off abruptly as Alayne Ludemann reached for the wall phone.

"Send Security to 503," she said calmly.

"I will not be evicted from my patient's side!" Lavelle hissed. "I *will* be dictating my own summary of this incident—every blistering violation—for the Joint Commission, Medicare, review boards, *and* the insurers." He flung open the door, and added without turning: "If you doubt me, read the headlines Monday morning."

Then he stalked out, his white jacket billowing behind like a cape.

With a heavy sigh, Venkata turned to enter a final note in the chart of Christine Runyan, MRN: 996784-2:

At 6:25 PM, 1 April, patient became hypotensive at 80/50 and failed to respond to fluids. She was transferred to the ICU at 6:50PM with a dopamine drip. All respirations and pulses ceased at 7:21PM, and a code was called. Patient was in ventricular fibrillation. CPR was performed and treatment initiated per protocol and beyond. Patient failed to respond and became asystolic. She was pronounced dead at 7:48 PM.

Sandeep Venkata, MD

Two

"Tell me about the little sparrow. One more time, Sita?"

Venkata heard his own voice from the past. A child of five, he'd been too young to understand a word like carcinoma. His beloved Amma was lifted from her bed and laid on the terrazzo floor of their home in Mumbai. Relatives gathered. No more medication, his father had pronounced, dipping a leaf of sweet basil in water from the Ganges to place on Amma's lips.

Death. *Aum Namo Naraya Nama Sivaya.*

Thirteen days of grieving followed. He remembered the shimmering oil lamp, the solemn Brahmin priests, the Sanskrit and pungent scents from the kitchen fire. Nothing had soothed his broken heart but the lulling voice of the housemaid, Sita.

"She has become a little sparrow, Deepa. But she will return and bring everything that is required for you to grow into a fine man. Be still; listen for her wings. Watch for her, always."

The chief resident closed his eyes in a prolonged squint and pinched the bridge of his nose. Time to collect his thoughts and to rid his mind of boyish ruminations. He was a man now, a physician, and the death of a patient did not imply that his duties were over. A family waited. The timing was most inauspicious. Dr. Lavelle had behaved badly with the code team, coming unglued, as the American residents liked to say. They had attended dozens of deaths together, but Venkata had never seen his mentor behave like this. He hoped for an explanation but doubted it would happen.

When he saw Dr. Lavelle trudging down the hallway, Venkata hurried to catch up, lagging the proper two steps that defined his rank as a resident. The waiting room off the Intensive Care unit had once been a laundry storage closet. A single table lamp barely lit the room. So terribly small and dark for anxious families, thought Venkata, hoping Dr. Lavelle would not erupt again about administration's poor judgment, overcrowding, the sickly green vinyl walls or the insipid border of swaying sunflowers intended to brighten the outlook of worried families.

Trevor Runyan leapt from the sofa. "Is she all right?"

The chief resident glanced at the oversized clock on the wall: 8:01 PM. He turned off the television to silence Rex Harrison in a rerun of *My Fair Lady.* An empty coffee carafe sizzled on a burner, filling the room with an acrid scent.

Lavelle straightened his shoulders and drew a long deep breath. "Trevor, we lost her. We . . ."

"No. . . . " Trevor lurched back.

"We did everything we could for her. She. . . ."

"No!" He stumbled backward, falling weak-kneed onto the couch where his young daughter nestled under her pink parka.

Venkata averted his eyes from the shell-shocked husband. This stoic Midwestern culture seemed to dictate a quiet reserve from families at such times. No piercing screams or doleful wails. No high pitched ululations. Only dry silence and a stricken husband, numbed by grief.

"We did everything we could to bring her back, but she was . . . is. . . . gone."

"Daddy?" Anya moved from her side of the couch and put a small arm around her father's shoulder. "Is Mommy okay?"

The door opened, sending in light from the corridor and a frantic woman who filled the door frame.

"BG!" The child ran across the carpet into the bearish arms of her aunt.

"Come here, kiddo. Come to Brigid." The woman hoisted the child up and kissed her forehead. "Oh my God, Trev, I got here as fast as I could." She looked around the room of white coats. "What happened?"

"Ask him." Trevor shot up from the couch and pointed at Lavelle.

"Trev, no! I swear to God Chrissy wasn't that sick when I brought her in this morning. No sicker than before."

"It's okay, Daddy." Anya chewed the ribbing of her sleeve as tears welled in her eyes. "Mommy will get better. She always does."

"Didn't they give her the medicine same as before?" Brigid stroked the child's matted hair.

"I don't know but I'll find out." Trevor glared at Lavelle. "Everything. Do you understand?"

"Pull yourself together, Trevor." Lavelle checked his beeper. "We'll deal with your questions later."

Venkata felt his toes curl inside his loafers. Dr. Lavelle's response would have ranked low on the Jefferson Scale of Physician Empathy.

"The chaplain is waiting. Someone can stay with your daughter."

Trevor clamped his neck, stared at the floor muttering, "No. . . no." Minutes passed. Then he glanced at the clock. "Brigid, take Anya home and put her to bed." He reached for the child's jacket and boots. "You stay with BG, honey. Daddy will be home soon; I promise."

When the door closed behind them, the house administrator clicked her pen and closed her notebook. "The body, Mr. Runyan. We will need to . . . "

Venkata watched Trevor stiffen and fix an icy stare at Lavelle. "What happened to Christine? Give it to me straight."

"You know as well as I that Crohn's finally claimed her life. She was immuno-compromised from the drugs we used to treat the disease, and when she became septic, her ninety pound body wasn't capable of fighting off the infection. She would have starved without parenteral nutrition. TPN was a risk we agreed to take to keep her alive."

"I don't believe you." Trevor shook his head. "She was getting better—felt well enough to go out yesterday. This had something to do with the TPN." He covered his ashen face with both hands. "My god, Christine, what have we done to you?'

"Trevor, you're upset and. . . ."

"Upset? Upset?" Trevor gasped. "My mistake was listening to you in the first place. Your fancy talk and your money. Christine is dead, god dammit, and this is on your back." The air seemed to chill around Trevor, forging a determination that preempted grief. "Listen to me, Lavelle: if the TPN had anything to do with her death, you'll pay. You won't get away with killing my wife."

Venkata bristled. Anger was a common reaction to an unexpected death, but he'd not anticipated this outburst from the husband. To insult an esteemed physician like Dr. Lavelle was most improper. The chief resident swallowed the quiet outrage building in his throat. The husband must be excused. He is delirious with grief.

"Dr. Venkata and I did absolutely everything we could for her," Lavelle repeated.

"Tell it to the jury, Lavelle." Trevor's voice cracked. "The next time we talk will be in a courtroom."

Venkata felt a pinch to his adrenals. Four months away from starting an Infectious Disease fellowship at Duke, might his record now be marred by malpractice? Reported to the National Practitioner Data Bank, noted on every application for medical licensure, disclosed to malpractice insurers, a blemish on every credentialing form, not to mention the toll on his psyche and the shame he would bring to his parents in Mumbai. And Heli. What would she think of him now, so disgraced?

Had he done everything medically possible for Mrs. Runyan?

No one would challenge his clinical judgment more than his own superego, not even the most critical Dr. Lavelle. His conclusion was the same every time he'd revisited the details of her care. He would have changed nothing about the decisions he'd made. Yet the death puzzled him, made him uneasy, desperate to reach the hospital library and to burrow through medical journals to find answers to this most puzzling case. Yes, that is precisely what he must do.

***

Heli Harri sought refuge in the public restroom just beyond the swinging double doors that barricaded the ICU. Her heart was racing, beating so loudly she felt pounding in both ears. She leaned against the locked door to steady herself. Christine Runyan, dead? She closed her eyes and saw the once apple-cheeked elementary teacher now lifeless under a sheet in 503. Yesterday at Corner Drug, Christine had reported that the TPN was doing its job and so were the drugs that tamed her bowel, slowed the inflammation, dulled the pain and quelled her anxiety. Life seemed reasonably normal—more time with her daughter, even sipping clear liquids like egg drop soup with her sister at the Jade.

Trevor was another matter. He was probably getting the bad news right now. It would be awkward for her to offer condolences when she had just sent Trevor a dunning message last week on his overdue account. Yet she needed to talk to him, find some words to convey how sorry . . .

The code scene replayed in her mind. Each time, the haunting sounds magnified: mechanical breaths of the ventilator, *poo-shuk.* . . . . *poo-shuk.* . . . . *poo-shuk.* . . . ., the *clank-clank-clank* of the oxygen cylinder rolling across the floor, the *spla.aa..a. . .at* of the glass syringe shattering against the cart's metal frame, Lavelle's scalding voice.

What would Sandy think of her now? Clumsy with the bicarb, slow with the dosing, a loose grip on the syringe that flew from her hand. *Was* it her fault? Were these warning signs of burning the candle at both ends? Leaning close to the mirror, she traced the scar over her left eyebrow, a remnant of the accident. Sean, dead, their unborn child denied its first breath. Was keeping busy not just economic necessity but some sort of psychological dodge? Now she and Trevor had loss in common. Heli dried her hands, tossed the paper towel in the trash and trusted the right words would come when needed.

She left the restroom and stood in the shadows a respectful distance from the family room. The door was closed. She waited ten minutes, hoping to catch sight of Trevor and Anya and knowing that with every passing minute, IV orders were piling up in the pharmacy. When the door finally opened, Brigid Olander marched out with Anya scrambling behind. Minutes later, Trevor Runyan followed, slamming the door behind him.

A noisy crash cart rumbled by, restocked for the next arresting heart. A conversation with the family seemed unlikely. Hospital life marched on. So must she.

"Is Lavelle with the family?"

The question floated from a plume behind her invoking Heli's inner Linnaeus. The scent of Narcissus was sweet and slightly irritating like wild daffodils to her botanical nose. She turned to find Alayne Ludemann, ER Manager, dragging a tapered red fingernail down a clipboard in her grip.

"You've just missed Trevor." Heli said, concentrating on Alayne's perfectly manicured hand. Of course the nails were fake—a differentiating marker between paper-pushing administrators like Alayne and clinicians—*real* workers who cared for patients and who were forbidden to wear artificial nails because bacteria harbored under acrylic layers.

Alayne made a sweeping line across the page with a yellow highlighter and closed the folder. "It's too bad about Christine, but frankly, I'm not surprised. When I heard the code called, I thought it might be her. She was on a first name basis with everyone in my ER. Four visits in the past three months. That's frequent flyer status with us. One more, and we'd have pinned wings to her gown."

Heli said nothing. Silence is comfortable for a Finn. For hours, if necessary.

"Not quite used to hospital humor yet?" Alayne made a pout of mock disappointment. "New, aren't you?" She put a long finger to her lips. "But I've seen you around. The Jade Garden?"

"My second home. I'm Heli Harri," she said, offering a reluctant handshake. "The Jade and I are neighbors." She couldn't remember ever seeing this woman there. "I own Corner Drug across the street."

"Who knew? Well, good for you, Heli. We need more bohemians like you to resurrect that struggling part of Fargo. No risk; no reward. Isn't that the business mantra?"

"Actually," Heli hesitated, "I'm Finnish. We're too stubborn to walk away."

"Mm," Alayne smiled with a tilt of her head. "Then why are you at Swedish on a Saturday night? Trolling the hospital wards for a social life?"

"I'm a catch-and-release angler, not a troller. I've been working weekends here for a few months."

"In that case, shouldn't you be back in the hospital pharmacy, falling farther and farther behind?" Alayne placed a red-tipped hand on the pharmacist's arm. "It was a joke, Heli. Hospital life can be very difficult if you take everything too seriously. I can help you. If you expect to survive the day-in, day-out stress around here, you'd better lighten up."

Heli glanced at her watch. The night was slipping by and she was falling behind, way behind. "Speaking of stress," she said, following an impulse to end this hallway counseling session, "I'm waiting for Dr. Lavelle."

Alayne twisted a gold linked bracelet. "You're a friend of his?"

"You were in 503. Did we look like friends?" Heli bit her lip. "He and I have some unfinished business."

"Really." Alayne's eyelids dropped to half-mast. "Ah, Dr. Lavelle, our in-house contrarian. The hospital's leading terrorist, according to our CEO. When I phone Mr. Bohley later this evening, he'll be very interested to learn of Lavelle's involvement in the Runyan case. There *will* be consequences."

"Mistakes were made."

Alayne flashed a tight smile. "Discreet, aren't you? Here's my advice: be very careful around Dr. Lavelle. You can get run over by the politics in this hospital."

Telling a Finn to be careful is like reminding a calendar that its days are numbered. Heli paused longer this time. Silence unnerved most people, especially those with agendas.

"You're looking at a hardened survivor of many political wars here at Swedish," Alayne added, lowering her voice to a therapeutic level. "Just between you and me, clever girls with a stubborn streak, especially those who don't fit the mold, fall the hardest. Consider yourself warned, Heli."

With her clipboard as armor, she pivoted on slender heels and click-clacked down the hall with an authority that turned heads.

Three

When Anya awakens on the couch at 3:30 AM on Saturday, April 1, *The Little Mermaid* has ended. The television screen is a bright shade of electric blue. Ariel and Eric have sailed into the sunset with King Triton's rainbow arcing overhead. Humans and mer-folks are by now living happily ever after.

She sits upright on the sofa's edge and rubs the sand from her eyes. On the carpet a cold pizza crust dries on an oily paper plate. The yellow light of the city's snow plow shines through the curtains of her family's garden-level apartment, reminding her of the storm outside. Maybe tomorrow BG will make snow angels with her in the front yard. Still sleepy, she draws up Grandma Olander's quilt with the turkey red center in every block. Grandma O said red stood for the hearth of the home where once-upon-a-time prairie families gathered to be warm in their log cabins. Although Anya has never seen a real hearth, or a log cabin for that matter, she imagines such a place on a blustery night like this, where her entire family, Mommy, Daddy, BG and Grandma O, might be all together, safe and sound. Since Mommy got sick, there aren't many happy times anymore. Like most nights, she is home alone with her mother, who is sleeping soundly, hooked up to a machine that pumps medicine into her chest to make her well.

In pink fuzzy slippers, Anya scampers through the unlit hallway, dragging Grandma O's quilt behind, past the bathroom where she thinks of peeing, but does not stop because she's freezing to death. Instead, she darts into bed and pulls the quilt over her head to keep the bats away.

"No bats anywhere, kiddo. I checked out every closet, under the bed, in the utility room, behind the furnace. No bats." That was BG's promise, and her auntie could be trusted. "Even if there were bats out there, they sure won't be flying around in a snowstorm. Radio says I-94 is already closed. No travel advised. Everyone in Fargo's hunkering down with pizza and videos just like you." That's what BG had said right before she left the apartment. "Gotta get to work at the Jade. I'm locking the door behind me. No bats. Hear that, no bats! Nothing to be afraid of, Ana-banana. I'll be back tomorrow afternoon. Be brave, now."

But Anya is scared. Bats: big-eared, sucker-footed, naked-backed, ghost-faced bats with huge wings flew regularly into her dreams. Fanged bats whose laser eyes burned with hunger. Black furry vampire bats that frightened children by licking their cheeks in the middle of the night. Sometimes, a thousand bats swarmed around her, pulled her up by her silky blonde hair and carried her away through the night to a dark cave where she was left alone, very alone, away from her sick Mommy, away from Daddy, and away from BG who always looked out for her.

Anya lets the quilt slide down over her face to test the darkness. The apartment is quiet except for the blast of the old furnace and the hum of a refrigerator that have become old friends. An occasional slap of the pump machine in her mother's room drifts across the hall. She puts a small hand over her heart and feels its pounding. Ever since Daddy had placed the thin, drum-like skin of his stethoscope on her chest and stuck earbuds into her ears, she's been fascinated with the sounds a heart makes.

Lub-*dub*. Lub-*dub*.

"When people die, like Grandpa O did last summer," her daddy explained, "the heart gets real tired, gives out and finally stops. No more sounds. Sometimes death is a blessing."

Lub-*dub*. Lub-*dub*.

Then another noise. Not scary. The familiar creaking of the front door. Anya swallows her fear as she hears the knob twist slowly and the door rub against the threshold. Seconds later the door closes quietly, and the latch clicks shut. Probably Daddy, Anya convinces herself. He sometimes comes home in the middle of his shift from the ambulance place to check on "his girls." It's hard to be brave so much of the time, especially at night, when she has to come up with reasons for noises. Her daddy once promised that when he could afford a house with a fence, Anya might have a puppy to play with. She would choose a Sheltie like the long-haired pup she'd made friends with at the pet store. A dog in the apartment at this minute might run to the front door to welcome Daddy home from the storm.

But there is no puppy, Anya knows, as she listens to the padding of footsteps moving through the carpeted hallway dividing the apartment's two bedrooms. At least no flurry of batwings, and for that Anya is relieved. Rather, the noise sounds like shuffling heavy boots, and the *swoosh* of a winter jacket brushing against the walls. Strange that Daddy doesn't turn a light on. He'd get into trouble with BG for not taking off his boots and tracking in all that snow.

It occurs to Anya that she might call out to her daddy to tell him the good news. No bats flying tonight and so far, no accidents on her sheets. That would please him, maybe make him smile.

But she doesn't utter a word.

The sounds move closer to the bedrooms and Anya, peeking above the quilt, sees a flashlight beam move through the darkness toward her mother's bedroom. She watches the stream of light turn into her mother's bedroom and disappear.

Why hasn't Daddy stopped in to check on me?

Shivering inside flannel pajamas, she nudges deeper into the bed covers, drawing her knees to her chest to stay warm.

Lub-*dub*. Lub-*dub*.

Maybe this isn't Daddy after all. Could this be another new nurse? Is Mommy sick again? Has she missed hearing her mommy's call for help? BG promised that her mother was getting better.

Lub-*dub*. Lub-*dub*.

Darkness again. Minutes pass with no sounds at all. It occurs to Anya that she might be dreaming, just imagining the sounds she'd heard, but a pressing bladder and the possibility of an accident make her realize she is very much awake. Someone is rustling paper now, like tearing open a bag of Cheese Curls.

Then another noise, not from her mother's bedroom, but far off, in the direction of the front door. Anya hears a key turn in the lock, and the sound of the creaking door opening a second time. This time the door bangs against the doorstop. Who could this be if Daddy was already here? Anya is confused and frightened and barely able to control her brimming bladder.

Lub-*dub*. Lub-*dub*. Lub-*dub*. Lub-*dub*.

From across the hallway, Anya hears a plop, like something dropping off a table, and the same *swoosh* of fabric against the door frame. Someone is leaving her mother's bedroom, running through the back door that leads to the room where everyone in the building washes clothes. From there, it's an easy way to get outside.

A pager beeps. Anya traces the noise to the front door. Someone says a bad word. "Shit!" A jacket rustles, a zipper slides. After a long pause, the second somebody moves through the hallway to her mother's bedroom, following the same path as the earlier one. Anya hears a closet door glide along its track in her parent's bedroom before slamming shut. Not even this racket seems to wake her mother.

Someone is in her parent's closet; Anya is sure of it. Most of Mommy's clothes don't fit anymore since she's gotten skinny so the closet is nearly empty and it's become her favorite place to play. Once she'd built a secret cave by moving aside her daddy's cowboy boots, and throwing a blanket over the boxes of mail-order medicine stored on the closet floor. It was there in her own underwater cave that she sometimes cried.

Minutes later, Anya hears the front door close. Any fear she once felt yields to her bladder that is about to spring a leak. She scrambles over the carpet, wet with melting snow which tickles her bare feet, to the bathroom where she pees with tremendous relief. From the bathroom she moves to her mother's bedroom and peeks inside.

"Mommy, are you ok?"

When there is no answer, Anya steps inside and switches on the ginger lamp on the bedside table. Mommy is very still. The water bag hangs over the bedpost, and the machine continues pumping medicine into her mother's chest just like before. The closet door is open.

"Mommy. Mommy, please wake up. I need to talk to you."

Anya's eyes move from the nightstand to the small waste basket filled with Kleenex tissues, day-old newspapers, and three scrap-booking magazines. Something else too—a syringe with a pointy needle—like the old nurse, Donna, used last night when she stopped in to check on Mommy. And one more thing. Pretty, it is. A smooth round ball of glass the size of a crab apple. It has a hole in the middle and a cap that twists off. Anya has never seen anything quite like it.

"Mommy, please say something to me so I know you're all right."

Slowly, her mother rolls over on her side. "Oh, Honey, . . . what time is it? Why are you up so early? Goodness, . . . the cartoons don't start for hours. Go back to sleep, baby. I'm fine. Just so very . . . tired."

"I'm glad, Mommy. I thought I heard something in your bedroom. I'm dry, Mommy. Did you hear that? Another dry night."

But there is no response from her mother who has already drifted back to sleep.

"G'night, Mommy. I'll take care of you. I'm your little doctor, remember?"

Now that Mommy is okay, Anya returns her attention to the waste basket. She cups the glass bottle in her hands and holds it up for a better look in the room's dim light. For a minute, she is Ariel with a nautilus shell in her hand. Inside the bottle, tiny painted orange fish swim in a pond of clear blue water among pink lilies and flowing green seaweed. The scene is the prettiest thing Anya has ever seen. When she turns the bottle in her hand, it seems as though the fish, like Flounder, are floating inside, but of course, she knows better. It's as though she's holding the bottom of the sea in her hand. Anya removes the stopper and squints inside the hollow chamber to find a few drops of watery liquid. She puts her nose to the chamber, thinking it might be perfume, but it doesn't smell like anything.

No longer is Anya worried about bats, noises or wetting the bed. She sorts through the remaining stuff in the wastebasket to find the syringe. If someone threw it away, it must mean Mommy no longer needs it. Same with the glass bottle. Finders, keepers. Like Ariel, she carries the syringe and needle into her bedroom and squirrels away the pointy thing and the glass bottle in her Fischer Price medical bag next to a plastic stethoscope and a toy thermometer. She hides the toy bag in her own secret underwater grotto behind the ruffled bed-skirt.

When Anya returns to her mother's bedroom, she kisses the pale flesh of her mother's sunken cheek and strokes an arm that is not much bigger than her own. "I've been very brave tonight, Mommy," she whispers. "Whoever came to visit you left something behind for my doctor bag." She hesitates. "Finders, keepers; right, Mommy?" When her mother doesn't answer, Anya shrugs, "Losers, weepers." She falls asleep with a smile on her face.

Friday, March 31, 2002

Four

He stood ramrod-straight in a starched white coat gazing from his office window at the gathering snowstorm beyond. Some matters like the extremes of nature were simply beyond his control, and this maddened him.

"Excuse me, Doctor."

The staid voice of Phyllis, the office receptionist, interrupted his Friday afternoon reverie. He turned around slowly, carefully, as though the stew of his turmoil might somehow spill over into the exchange. "What is it?"

"Your waiting room is empty."

Mark Raymond Lavelle, MD, consulted his TAG Heuer. "At 3 o'clock in the afternoon?" he asked incredulously. Dread and delight crossed paths in his mind. Another empty waiting room meant his patient billings would be down for the third consecutive month. On the other hand, with no more patients to see this afternoon, the chance for an early start to a cozy, snowbound weekend without his wife was appealing.

"I'm sure it's the storm, Doctor. Patients are canceling, afraid to go out in this weather. Even if it is the last day of March."

"I see." His gaze returned to the window. Heavy snow covered the parking lot and blanketed the stark landscape for as far as he could see. Lavelle closed his eyes, trying to imagine the great Laurentide Ice Sheet covering this stretch of land twenty thousand years ago, depositing glacial debris in its wake. He opened his eyes and with sorrowful clarity, realized that he, Mark Raymond Lavelle, with a tinge of blue in his blood, a Princeton degree, and stiff alimony payments, had also been transported— scraped, gouged and abandoned on the beach of this ancient lakebed—mostly against his will, but with the hope to practice medicine with a fresh start.

"Did you know, Phyllis," he asked, less interested in her answer than in placing intellectual distance between them, "that Fargo was once the southern lakeshore of the great Lake Agassiz, the largest body of fresh water on the globe?"

"How very interesting." After a respectful pause, she continued, "there are two call-backs that came in after lunch, and I have another stack of correspondence for you to sign. The letters must go out this afternoon."

Lavelle left the window and approached his desk. Its size commanded most of the space in the room and its disarray betrayed the neat and controlled image the forty-three year old physician liked to convey. He thumbed through a stack of insurance forms tagged for his signature and repositioned piles of medical charts from one side of his desk to the other. A dog-eared copy of the *New England Journal of Medicine* lay open to an article on infectious cellulitis. A gold paperweight bearing the insignia of the American Medical Association rested on his latest financial statement that disclosed an eroding net worth. Wasn't it the AMA's job to look out for his financial security? To negotiate favorable payment for medical services? To fight ridiculous governmental rules and regulations? Why wasn't their lobby as strong as those damn lawyers?

"About the call-backs, Doctor. Shall I call for the charts?"

"No more charts!"

The stack of medical records teetered on his desk, threatening an avalanche of paper. What was the AMA doing about the oppressive paperwork necessary to get paid by insurance companies and their obstructive audits? How had it happened that medicine had become a game where well-intentioned physicians had to scheme to survive or perish under the weight of invading regulators, for-profit conglomerates and special interest politics?

Lavelle glared at Phyllis but checked his biting anger. Not exactly her fault, this mess on his desk. Unlike so many other women in his life whose demands had penetrated his solar plexus (not to mention his bank account), this inconspicuous soul listened, served, defended, ignored and forgave without asking for much in return.

He smiled at the ageing matron. "Who is sounding the alarm for medical attention on this Friday afternoon? Let me guess." Mentally, he scrolled through a list of usual suspects. "It must be Mabel Gelling offering me another organ recital. Is it her ulcer this time, or a nasty cough? Perhaps a bout of indigestion? A touch of Reynauds, now that the weather has turned chilly? Bursitis?"

"Right again, Doctor. Mrs. Gelling complains of shoulder pain. Change of weather, she imagines. And, you are also asked to call a 'Donna' at Swedish Home Health services about the Runyan woman."

The smile dissolved from Lavelle's face. "Oh?" His forehead creased. If Mabel Gelling played a lead role among his troupe of hypochondriacs, Christine Runyan, the young Crohn's patient, was an entirely different matter. Leaning forward in his chair, he asked, "is there a problem?"

"Something about her lab results and a new order for TPN

therapy."

"Very well, Phyllis. I'll return the calls and wrap up here somewhat earlier than I anticipated."

"The correspondence, Doctor? The dictation? Your mail?"

"Gather it up and place it in my briefcase. Anything in the mail that requires immediate attention?"

"Yes, you should be aware of a certified letter from the Eastern Shore Life Settlement Company. Also, the pharmaceutical rep from Averill asks that you complete a speaker registration form for their medical meeting in Switzerland next month."

Lavelle squirmed slightly. The boondoggle was payback for his arrangement with Averill, and very likely, Phyllis knew as much. Had she ever, even briefly, escaped the Midwest?

"And the Phase IV clinical research data on Exvantium are due. Actually, the reports are past due. The Averill rep asked that I remind you."

Lavelle glanced to the far corner of his desk where the charts of those patients on Exvantium awaited his review. At $250 per record, his participation in this pharmaceutical marketing scheme would easily net him an untaxed, unreported four thousand dollars for merely switching his patients to Averill's new off-formulary block-buster drug for hypertension.

"There is also a letter from Mr. Bohley at Swedish Hospital. It was hand delivered and marked 'confidential.' Of course, I didn't open it."

"Thank you, Phyllis. Efficient as always." He winked at her, trusting in his coy ability to overcome her insistence about the paperwork.

"One more thing," he added, avoiding eye contact as he gathered up journals scattered about his desk. "Would you be so kind as to start my car so it will be warm when I leave in fifteen minutes?" Lavelle tossed the keys to his Escalade SUV across the desk. "And take the rest of the afternoon off. You should arrange to be home before the storm hits." He had no idea where she lived, how she lived, if she even had a life beyond the curved reception desk that barricaded the hallway to his exam rooms.

"Certainly, Doctor." Phyllis closed the door behind her without a sound as she slipped out of the room.

The Runyan case was fresh in Lavelle's mind. Christine Runyan's name often flashed before his eyes on prescription pads, insurance forms, discharge summaries and pink telephone call-back messages. Now his patient's name was indelibly linked to a phone call he'd gotten from Eddy two weeks ago. Eddy, his closest friend from residency, had called to boast about his latest leap into entrepreneurial medicine. The memory, still fresh and provocative, surfaced at the mention of the Runyan name.

"Mark, old boy," Dr. Pierce Eddington, a successful oncologist practicing in New Orleans, had inquired, "an internist like you must treat patients with home IV therapy in your practice all the time. Hemophilia? Chemotherapy? Pain control? Crohn's?"

"Why do you ask?" Lavelle felt a visceral tug when he heard 'Crohn's.'

A shared history, mostly of deconstructing western movies and comparing investment strategies continued to bind them despite geographic distance. Eddy had been a shrewd source of business advice on optimizing the profitability of a medical practice. Review your billing practices, he'd recommended, and step up the number of colonoscopies you perform. It's a good and profitable screening test for cancer, and who isn't worried about the big C? Limit the number of Medicare and Medicaid patients you see; reimbursement is too low. Give your patients every insurance benefit they're entitled to. Order anything they want. Advocate for your patients, and they'll love you forever. Loyalty you can take to the bank.

"There's some easy money in the home infusion business, my friend," Eddy professed that bleak wintry day with the assurance of a rainmaker. "My partners and I discovered we were leaving profits from chemotherapy on the table for hospitals and pharmacies to lap up. At our expense, I might add. Same is true for antibiotics, narcotics, parenteral nutrition—anything you can push through a vein in the home setting. Why should hospitals make money off the work we generate? Just isn't right, Mark. So, we got smart and launched a start-up mail-order pharmacy business, GEM Pharmacy Services, in Baton Rouge."

Eddy explained the business model in the soulless jargon of an MBA student: new market niche, referral networks, exclusive contracts, pricing spread, third party agreements, distribution channels and cheap labor. A very scalable and profitable venture. Win-win-win.

With the phone cradled ear to shoulder, Lavelle remembered coating his lips with an aloe lip balm. Unlike Philadelphia, the northern plains were dry in January. While Eddy rambled over the phone line, Lavelle reached for a pencil and doodled idly across a notepad:

CHRISTINE

"The patients, Eddy; is it safe for them?" Lavelle asked with a perfected tone of righteous indignation. How did they do in this latest get-rich strategy from his enterprising friend? For all he knew, Eddy's pharmacy might be operating out of a Baton Rouge basement with chimps holding test tubes.

Eddy's voice surged. "That's the best part. Insurance companies are tickled pink to pay our charges because home therapy keeps people out of the hospital. Patients love the convenience of having the stuff arrive in their mailbox. They never see a bill, even for co-pays, because everything slides through the computers of insurance companies without any human review."

At the time Mark recalled Phyllis's frequent telephone struggles with customer service clerks. The rules embedded within the fine print of managed care contracts were indecipherable to him, but Phyllis seemed to understand the game well enough to battle the insurance companies with their well-crafted set of roadblocks meant to interfere with the free-flow of payment for his medical services.

"You're on your hospital's Pharmacy and Therapeutics committee, aren't you, Mark? If you can steer some referral business our way, we'll see to it that you're rewarded for the effort. Quietly, of course; you know how Medicare is about referral practices."

Lavelle's doodling stopped and he was silent except for the tapping sound of his pencil on the desk. Eddy was proposing a kickback. Federal laws specifically prohibited such practices, and the penalties were steep. But Eddy went on.

"Don't worry, Mark. We're small potatoes-- way under the radar of the Justice Department. They go after bigger fish like Tenet and HCA: big violator get big fines. No one is greedier than the Justice Department. Anyway, state regulators in Louisiana haven't got the time, the staff or frankly, the brains to figure out what we're doing. I doubt they're any smarter up in South Dakota."

"It's North Dakota," Lavelle corrected him. Already he'd become as sensitive as the locals to the Dakota comparison.

"You want in, Mark? Easiest money you'll ever make. Haven't we all got practice expenses to cover, overhead to consider? The insurance companies have been stealing from physicians for years, cowboy. Remember Lon Chaney in *High*

Noon? The public doesn't give a damn about integrity. A town that won't defend itself deserves no help."

Lavelle had folded the sheet of paper and placed it under desk blotter as a reminder the next time Trevor Runyan complained about the costs of his wife's therapy.

The wait was not long. On a chance meeting in mid-February, Trevor confronted Lavelle in the ER, acknowledging that while his wife's chronic disease was stabilizing, the cost of the TPN therapy was breaking the family budget. "It costs $300 a day!"

"Come now, Trevor." Lavelle said. "You certainly don't pay that amount yourself, do you? You must have insurance."

"Sure, but I still have co-pays and co-insurance, and the bills are piling up. Christine isn't able to work any longer," the husband said with a trace of embarrassment. "I'm trying to pay off the hospital . . ."

"Trevor," Lavelle interrupted.

"But Corner Drug's another story. Could be a collection agency in my future if I don't pay up soon. I don't know what to do. Any way we could try something else, or back off on the TPN?"

"Trevor," Lavelle bristled, "if you want a second opinion on Christine's care, you're entirely free to do so. I shall turn over her case immediately if you desire. However, as long as I'm managing her care, I'll not be second-guessed by you, or anyone else. Do you understand?"

"No. Yes, I mean—just wondering if there was something less expensive."

"Trevor, let me be the physician, you be the husband, and Christine will be well served by both of us," Lavelle replied, placing a paternalistic arm around the younger man's shoulder. "With Christine as ill as she is, you're going to have to play the insurance game like the rest of us if you expect to survive financially. I have an idea."

"Like what?" Trevor asked, shrugging off the arm on his shoulder.

One week later, the first box of TPN solution and supplies from GEM Pharmacy Services reached the mailbox of the Runyan apartment.

Lavelle was genuinely pleased to help the financially strapped family. When the first five thousand dollar payback from GEM reached his desk, he paged Trevor, inviting him to his office. Upon arriving, the physician handed him an unmarked envelope containing five hundred dollars in cash.

"What's this?" the paramedic asked.

"Some sort of company rebate for the TPN," Lavelle answered. "GEM Pharmacy Services appreciates your business," he replied, failing to acknowledge payment for his recently acquired role as medical director for GEM's Midwest expansion.

Trevor counted the bills, his eyes, round as silver dollars. "Thanks, Doc. This is incredible. Guess I owe you, huh?"

"Don't mention it," Lavelle leaned forward. "Don't mention it to anyone."

Five

Sandeep Venkata walked into the residents' lounge with the purposeful gait of a Rhodes scholar. He was exhausted, hungry and homesick for Mumbai, especially for the street food: rich curries, spicy chutneys and buttery naans. The good people of Fargo craved comfort food during a snowstorm, and so did he. His was just different from theirs.

The spring snowstorm had created staffing problems for the medical wards. Several residents were already working hundred hour weeks, an issue that some of them were actively protesting. Truck drivers were limited to eleven consecutive hours on the road. Airline pilots flew only eight hours in a twenty-four hour period, and no more than thirty hours per week. Why should residents, who held lives in their hands, be expected to make life and death decisions in an exhausted state? Of course, the arguments had fallen on the deaf ears of hospital administrators who were unwilling to increase operating expenses by hiring additional physicians.

Venkata yawned. Sleep was not in his immediate future. Rather than leave the hospital, he stayed on for another thirty hour shift. Sugared donuts and coffee from the physicians' lounge across the hall might keep him awake. Mercifully, no one was there to witness his plunder.

When he returned to the residents' lounge, the single computer was free. Perhaps he would send an email to his parents eight thousand miles away. Friday night, 7:40 PM in Fargo and halfway around the world, 7:10AM in Mumbai. Since Saturday was a full working day in India, his father, an internist and his mother, an obstetrician, would already be at the small private hospital they owned on the Pune-Mumbai industrial belt. Later in the day his father would watch a cricket match on the telly with medical journals strewn about the settee, while his mother, elegant in a flame sari, would be sipping coffee on the divan.

Dear Mum and Dad, tonight a snowstorm threatens Fargo. No matter how long I live here, it is difficult to get used to everything white—the people, the food, the landscape. Even though it is springtime, I still wear a goose-down jacket and heavy boots. My car will be under a snow bank by morning. The sight of this would make you laugh.

Most days he logged on to the global weather network to check conditions in Mumbai. Today, his parents would endure temperatures of ninety degrees Fahrenheit with 90% humidity. Thoughts of Sita spiking potatoes in the kitchen with green chilies and cilantro for their late dinner piqued his hunger and reminded him how very far away from home he was.

Hospital is busy, and I have been called to interesting cases. Father, your advice to choose USA over UK for my residency seems to have been very wise. Even in this remote Midwestern area, the research opportunities and technology available to treat patients are far superior. I wish there were more hours in the day to learn all there is to know.

He considered whether he should share the potential news with his parents but it wasn't definite yet, so he decided to wait until the National Institute of Health formally approved his pending grant application. Last week a panel reviewer in Washington, DC had sounded very optimistic. Antibiotic therapy of nosocomial infections in hospitalized patients with hematologic malignancies was worthy of funding, the reviewer had said.

Just like Dr. Lavelle predicted, Venkata recalled. Such a remarkable physician. His diagnostic skills are second to none, and he knows the medical literature better than any attending at Swedish. If only his personal habits—avoiding call, not answering his pager—were not so problematic. A difficult man, but I am lucky to have him for a mentor. He made a mental note to thank Dr. Lavelle for guiding him through the rigorous application process. "I have a nose for finding money," Dr. Lavelle had said, peering over his tortoise framed bifocals, "I know how the system works."

The attending physicians at this hospital are very demanding, but in turn, they have rewarded my hard work by opening doors at the highest levels in research funding. I may have some good news for you, but it is too early to speculate, yet I hope to soon make you very proud.

Venkata finished a second sugary donut and automatically reached for the beeper clipped to his belt. Had he missed a page? The ER might be calling any minute now.

The e-mail to his parents was nearly complete, although silent about the embarrassing designation recently bestowed upon him by the ICU nurses. An enlarged photo of him hung over the caption: *Dr. Sandeep Venkata, Most Eligible Bachelor, Swedish Hospital, 2002.* The poster had been widely circulated throughout the hospital: employee lounges, surgical locker rooms and the bulletin board in the residents' lounge. When Venkata first saw his photo a week ago, he removed the poster, but within an hour another appeared in its place. He closed his eyes in embarrassment. No, this must not reach his parents in Mumbai. At the moment, nosocomial infections in hospitals seemed less contagious than the sexual aggression of American women.

Every day in hospital brings a new surprise. New technology to make precise diagnoses. New methods of treatment for curing infectious diseases. Best of all—the patients. They are hard-working and truthful with no inclination for cunning. They accept me as their physician, and I do what I can to adapt to their culture.

His beeper vibrated. Four digits appeared: 2187. He did not recognize the number as ER or any other hospital department that frequently paged him. Mildly curious, he punched in the number, and completed the email to his parents while waiting for a response.

Just now paged so I must go. Thank you for sending photos from Oxford. They evoked fine memories of my studies there. I send my love to you, to Arundhati and to Sita whose sweet pal payson *I am sorely missing.*

"Pharmacy, Heli Harri speaking." It was a female voice— strong and crisp.

"This is Dr. Venkata. You've paged me?" Why was pharmacy calling?

"Sorry to bother you, Dr. Venkata, with . . . a compliance matter about an order you've written."

At the mere suggestion of a problem, this woman with the clear voice and the semi-familiar name had Venkata's full attention. A problem with an order he'd written? It had been a long day, and he knew the outcome statistics of overworked residents. Six times as many diagnostic errors when compared to a control group, and 36% greater medical errors. Often, incorrect medication dosages. His defenses rose. Mistakes were incompatible with his self-image and intolerable in his role as chief resident. And if he were to be chastised, even mildly, by a female, this would be an insufferable rebuke. An insult to his status.

"According to the latest hospital rules, I'm required to call you—any physician—who uses a dangerous abbreviation in a medical order."

"A dangerous abbreviation?" Venkata's fear that he might have inadvertently overdosed an unsuspecting patient vanished. For that, he was relieved, but now he was confused if not incredulous at this interruption. "Your name, again? Slowly, please."

"My name is Heli Harri." She spoke each syllable with exacting clarity. "I'm the night pharmacist on duty this weekend."

Her explicit enunciation enabled Venkata to recall when he'd first heard that name. Soon the specific memory of the woman with the clear voice washed pleasantly over him. Tall. Pale. More distinctly Nordic than most women of this region. A pair of intelligent blue eyes marred by that unfortunate scar above her left brow. Amenable to plastic surgery, he'd assessed, when they'd first met a few months ago at a party hosted by the surgical nurses. Venkata had enjoyed her no-nonsense conversation about the preservation of historic buildings. She lived in such a building downtown above the drugstore where she worked. Knew the order of planets and their average distance from the sun, the winning answer she provided to the championship round of Trivial Pursuit. She drove a blue Saab with a vanity license plate, SISU, whatever that meant. Left the party early; drove home alone.

"But I thought you were the owner of Corner Drug? What are you doing here at hospital?"

"So." The silence that followed made him uncertain if his question had crossed some cultural line. "Before moving to Fargo, I was a staff pharmacist at a Minneapolis hospital. Weekend relief work keeps my inpatient skills current." She paused. "Actually, my accountant thinks it's a good idea."

She must be as tired as I am, Venkata thought, realizing he'd moved off focus in this professional interaction. "I see. Yes, very well." Her pale face lingered in his memory. "Tell me; what is this dangerous order I have written?"

"Technically speaking, one of your orders has violated a hospital rule."

Venkata lowered his dark lids and shook his head. Was there no end to hospital rules, interruptions, paperwork? In parts of India, physicians relied solely on what their patients reported without any written medical records whatsoever.

"According to our Patient Safety officer, I must personally

speak with the ordering physician anytime a dangerous abbreviation or confusing handwriting appears on an order."

"And what dangerous abbreviation did I use?" Venkata might have been more irritated if this interaction were not charmed by the woman with the clear voice.

She took a deep breath and continued. "You wrote 'D/C gentamycin' in a patient's chart. D/C is considered to be a dangerous abbreviation, or so the Joint Commission on the Accreditation of Health Care Organizations believes. The hospital requires you to write out the word 'discontinue' so there is no uncertainty regarding your intention as the ordering physician. D/C could mean *discontinue* or it could mean *discharge*. See what I mean?"

"This makes no sense to me, no sense at all! I wish to discontinue the gentamycin, yes? How could that be any clearer? Did you think I wanted to 'discharge' the gentamycin? This is ridiculous."

"Actually, I agree with you on this one, but other abbreviations I've seen have been open to multiple interpretations. Errors have resulted." She paused again. "I don't want to hurt someone because of a misinterpretation. We all share responsibility for the safety of our patients."

Patient safety. Venkata thought it had become a feeding frenzy of lawyers, an easy headline for journalists, job security for nursing administrators, a bully-pulpit for politicians and an indelible stain on the profession of medicine.

"And," she continued, "I'm sure as chief resident, you'd demand nothing less of your interns."

"Of course you are right." Venkata flinched at the safety lecture he didn't require, remembering his training in southern India where he'd treated twenty thousand people with limited health resources, often with no medical records at all. So much more detail he might have shared, but, with her waiting on the phone—performing her job as she was expected to do by the hospital—he curtailed his tendency to be pedantic.

"In parts of the world beyond Fargo," he said, "patient safety is linked to desperate poverty—malnutrition, raw sewage in canals, lack of vaccination, not dangerous abbreviations. It is sometimes a difficult transition to make."

"There is that to consider, yes. But here, in a complex medical system, we can't ignore the Hawthorne effect: we change our performance in response to being observed."

She is persistent, Venkata thought, as the line grew quiet. He wasn't sure what he'd say if she pressed on. The silence grew into mild tension. Later he would marvel at how much was at stake during that pause.

"Dr. Venkata, are you always this decent?"

Not entirely certain what her question implied, he was, at the very least, relieved that she had not been put off by his remark, grateful that their debate seemed to be over and amused that she thought him to be "decent" which, on his value scale, was far superior to the superficial designation bestowed upon him by the critical care nurses.

"We do not disagree on the importance of keeping patients safe, Heli."

"Then I'd better hop off my bureaucratic high horse, get back to the IV room and do my real job."

As their conversation waned, Venkata remembered the good-natured cajoling of the house physicians about the importance of becoming Americanized. "You must know the capital of every state in the union. You must have at least three sweaters in your closet with American logos. You must be able to quote from the Lewis and Clark journals. You'll be accepted in this part of the country when you know the name of the third baseman for the Minnesota Twins, when you believe in at least three conspiracy theories, and when you can interpret every vanity license plate along I-94."

He took a deep breath. "I have a question for you, Heli. A question about another abbreviation." Flirtation seemed so easy for the other residents. "Tell me, please, what does *sisu* mean?"

"Sorry?"

"SISU, your license plate. I have wondered about it ever since I saw you drive away from a party we both attended."

"SISU?" Her voice softened, mellowed as though he'd struck a deep chord within her. "It's Finnish. So . . .it means . . . what must be done *will* be done . . . regardless of what it takes. And, typically, the hard way, like raking leaves into the wind or shoveling a sidewalk during a snowstorm. You might say that Finns never give up. Or, you might say that we just love to be miserable."

Just then, Venkata's pager chirped. Very bad timing. "ER is calling, Heli. Will you be around hospital later this evening? Perhaps we can talk more over a coffee."

"I'll be working straight through the night, and opening Corner Drug at 8 AM sharp tomorrow. See what I mean about misery?"

"Perhaps another time, yes?"

"Patients first, coffee later."

Her voice conveyed what the chief resident thought must surely be a smile. He pondered his next move as he waited for the ER to answer.

Six

The Escalade performed handily on the snow-slick streets of Fargo as Dr. Lavelle drove home from his office that Friday evening. To mark the onset of the weekend, his beeper was switched off. He navigated the winding street along the river to Fargo's toniest residential district. Located on a ridge overlooking the Red River of the North, the prime real estate (dubbed Pill Hill) had become a medical magnet for wealthy radiologists and orthopedic surgeons whose stately brick manors rose above the community below.

"A man of your status belongs in a neighborhood like this," the attractive realtor had persuaded him three years ago. A week later he owned an expansive two-story brick colonial in the emerging Main Line of Fargo. A month later, he married the newly divorced, capillary-thin realtor with the hurricane hair who'd sold him the property. Together he and Claudette Hegge formed the portrait of prosperity he hoped to transmit to his adopted community. Love at first *site*, she often said when asked about her conquest.

The house was mercifully quiet at 7PM. Lavelle passed from the large vaulted foyer with its rose marble floor to the main living area. Following a Christmas shopping trip to Hong Kong, his wife had stuffed the room with Asian reproductions: porcelain vases, cross-legged buddhas and shelves heavy with expensive knick-knacks. A cloisonné peacock with emerald eyes in the corner of the room dared him to enter. The room looked like a design war between the Ming and Tsing dynasties. He shook his head and sought relief from the chaos at the bar. Two shots of Booker's from the Waterford decanter and he retreated to the library, the only space in the home untouched by Claudette's decorating excesses.

He gathered dry wood from the timber box and sparked a fire in the fireplace, rubbed his hands together before the radiating warmth, then browsed the cherry shelves that flanked the fireplace. Medical texts, biographies, and a collection of leather-bound classics. His illustrious ancestor, Francis Hopkinson, a United States District Judge and signatory on the Declaration of Independence looked down disapprovingly from the portrait over the mantle. Fargo was a long way from the Eastern Establishment where his family had long prospered.

***

"Venkata? This is Petterson in the ER. Look, fella, I know you've put in a long day, but with the storm brewing, it's a friggin' zoo down here and I need some help. Chest pain. Fractures. Twenty or thirty hot ears, by the looks of it. And the usual crop of hypothermics and sidewalk sleepers. Hang on a minute." The chief resident overheard the ER physician being told about a snowmobile accident . . . something about barbed wire. "Get a trauma surgeon, dammit." Petterson yelled in the distance. "I don't care if you have to send EVAC out to get him. Venkata, you still there? I've got a carbon monoxide poisoning, frost bite, a howling meth addict and three hypochondriacs clogging up the treatment rooms."

"What do you need?" Adrenaline now removed any trace of fatigue in the chief resident.

"Get down here fast as you can. I'll try to find an orthopod. Can't be golfing in this weather, can they? We could use Lavelle too. He cleans out an ER faster than any doc I know." Petterson's voice moved in and out of range. "Have you seen him tonight?"

"No, Sir. Should I page him?"

"Nah. We'll find him, although it'll be like chasing a fart in a blizzard."

The chief resident raced through the hospital corridors, bypassing elevators in favor of stairwells, past the lab, pharmacy and radiology, reaching the Emergency department in record time. Seconds counted in matters of life and death. Dangerous abbreviations did not.

Seven

Lavelle opened the stainless door of the Sub-Zero on Friday evening and found three Chinese take-out boxes delivered by the Jade Garden the night before. Szechuan lamb for him, a respectable approximation of his favorite entrée at Susanna Foo's in Philadelphia. Kung Pao chicken with cashews for Claudette. Scant portion of Moo Shu pork, shrimp fried rice, one greasy wonton and two fortune cookies bearing hidden exhortations for the future.

As the lamb revolved in the microwave, Lavelle studied his reflected image in the glass cabinet. He was generally satisfied with the contours of his face. No need for rhinoplasty or chin reshaping; the skin under his jaw was still taut while most men his age struggled with turkey wattle. He pulled the lazy skin back from the corners of his eyes and acknowledged the eventuality of eyelid tightening but that was years away. Right now, the problem was his thinning hair. He could cover the gray with tint, but nothing would conceal a receding hairline.

The lamb, fragrant with red peppercorns, came out of the microwave and Claudette's leftover chicken went in.

After reading a recent article on a rare but life threatening *staph aureas* infection following a hair transplant, hair plugs were definitely out. Propecia was a wonder drug for male pattern baldness but his first attempt to obtain the drug had gone badly. An image of that oddly attractive but impertinent pharmacist rose in his mind. During the holidays, Heli Harri had refused to fill his prescription at Corner Drug. "Not a good idea, Doctor," she'd said. "Self-prescribing is a red flag for auditors. Maybe someone could call this in for you? It avoids problems for both of us."

The scent of garlic wafted from the sizzling chicken. He slid the Moo Shu pork into the microwave for the final blast.

Better to avoid this Heli Harri altogether—those self-righteous types are dangerous. Not at all like Claudette. Aside from his wife's robust spending habits, like this opulent kitchen whose Viking range had never been used in three years of marriage, she was easy and relatively low maintenance. A compatible partner in their shared ambitions.

Lavelle balanced his dinner on a teak tray with the two fortune cookies and a notable pinot noir from the Russian River valley. He moved from the kitchen, past the formal dining room, down a long hall beyond the great room to a home theatre at the far end of the house. He'd redesigned the room to assure maximal darkness. The windows were double-shaded with blackout blinds, and the ten by six foot viewing screen hung on a blackened wall. Foam board covered the walls and ceiling to minimize the vibrations of seven speakers and two sub-woofers.

Reclining in the Spielberg lounger, Lavelle used a touch-pad remote to start a digitally re-mastered version of his favorite movie. He was instantly transported to Hadleyville, 'a dirty little village in the middle of nowhere.' High shots of the western ghost town rolled unhurriedly before him: a barren sky, a lone tumbleweed along a vacated main street, a desert rat escaping from the town saloon, the Ten Commandments hanging askew in the white wooden church. No matter how many times he'd seen *High Noon,* he never tired of watching heroes like himself, men haunted by their past.

Fifty-one minutes into the film, as Will Kane listened to the monologue from the cynical ex-marshal, Lavelle felt his cell phone vibrate. He smiled at the caller ID.

"Eddy," he answered, hitting the pause button to freeze the actors in still life poses, "you're interrupting Matt Howe," and here Lavelle convincingly imitated the old sheriff, "'If you're honest, you're poor your whole life, and in the end you wind up dyin' all alone on some dirty street. For what? For nothin'. For a tin star.'"

"Sorry, old boy. I always wondered what you northern barbarians did in all that snow. The reports on the weather channel are amazing."

Since moving to the Midwest, Lavelle had learned to expect phone calls whenever the national news called attention to stormy weather in Fargo. His friends along both coasts never tired of chiding him about living in the land known for record-breaking snow and bone-chilling wind.

"Maybe I've been here too long, Eddy, but I'm starting to enjoy these storms."

"A bad sign, Mark, a very bad sign. When you pick up the Fargo accent, it will be my obligation to pry you from that godforsaken part of the world and return you to civilization."

Lavelle bristled. He'd earned the right to deride the Midwest but he resented when outsiders did so. "There must be a better reason for your call than to insult the good people of Fargo," he said as he sipped the earthy wine.

Dr. Pierce Eddington paused. Lavelle maneuvered a bite of lamb with chopsticks as he waited for his friend's response. He imagined Eddy dining at Commander's Palace or some other *haute cuisine* establishment in the Big Easy while he was freezing his ass off in Fargo.

"Eddy? Are you calling just to gloat about the weather?"

"A few problems here . . ."

"Problems? You and Jennifer? Too bad, I always liked her."
Still smarting from his own brutal divorce, Lavelle had ready advice
on the tip of his wine-stained tongue. "But nevertheless, I advise you
to get yourself the meanest attorney in the South and . . ."

"No, my marriage is fine. At least I think we're fine." Eddy
paused again. "It's GEM Pharmacy. I'm afraid we've been inspected
by the state and the surprise visit didn't go well. There is a quality
problem, it seems."

Considering the blistering financial fallout of Lavelle's divorce to
Kathy, a mere quality problem sounded like a bargain. "Tell me more,
Eddy." Mark swirled the pinot in the glass to oxygenate the wine.
Crimson velvet tears formed on the inside of the crystal goblet. He
held a small amount of wine on his tongue and waited for the tannins
to bite the roof of his mouth.

Eddy continued. "I've told you what I know at this point—
haven't had time to pore through the reviews, but they've shut us
down, Mark. GEM is out of commission, temporarily, at least. "

"How can they do that?" Lavelle asked incredulously.

"I'd rather not go into the details until I get a better understanding
of the situation. But for now, all business activity at GEM has been
suspended. I wanted to tell you first thing since you're now involved
with the venture."

Instantly Lavelle became uneasy. Less than a month ago, he'd
suggested to the hospital's Pharmacy and Therapeutics committee that
a mail-order alternative might be a low-cost alternative for patients on
home infusion therapy. He'd even mentioned GEM by name. A few
oncologists seemed interested. Had anyone acted on his suggestion?
He might have to backtrack with his colleagues. And he'd have to
change the Runyan woman's therapy. The incompetence of others
vexed him. It seemed that even Eddy couldn't be trusted to execute a
deal smoothly.

"Go back to Hadleyville, Mark, and let me worry about this,"
Eddy said. "I've got a few connections that can make this problem go
away before the snow melts in Fargo."

Lavelle tapped the mute button, and the stoic Will Kane unfroze,
assuming his desperate role of saving an apathetic town from itself.

Twenty-nine minutes later, his cell phone rang again at.

"Eddy, what is it now? How many times am I going to be
interrupted tonight?"

"Mark, the GEM problem . . ."

"Tell me it's solved and I'll buy you dinner at Galatoire's next
time I'm in New Orleans."

"Unfortunately, things are heating up a bit. My partners and I just met, and we've decided to do a quiet recall until this thing settles down."

"A quiet recall? What the hell is a quiet recall?"

"We need you to retrieve any unused medication, infusion, syringes, tubing, other supplies, anything sent from GEM to its customers. Just in case."

"In case of what?" Mark answered with a growl. "And for the record, here in no-man's-land, they're still called patients, not customers. Am I to break into homes and raid their medicine cabinets? What exactly is going on, Eddy?"

"Slow down, cowboy. It's merely a precautionary measure. Probably unnecessary."

"Why don't you simply issue a recall alert to GEM's patients and have them return their shipments? Wouldn't that be simpler?"

"Simpler, yes, but we're attempting to do this quietly, without arousing suspicion. Get my point? And we no longer have the names and addresses of GEM's patients." Lavelle heard Eddy take a deep breath. "They confiscated our computer systems."

"Good God, man! I thought you said you'd handle this!"

"It *is* being handled, Mark, and you'd be wise to fall in line and help us out. We need the goods back in our office by tomorrow. It's considerably easier to put out a small fire than a big one, understand? Once we clear up this little problem, we'll be back in business."

While he was being lectured, Lavelle considered how he might approach Trevor Runyan about the change in plans. The nervous paramedic would no doubt question why and how much it would cost him and where was he supposed to get new TPN solution. This 'quiet recall' was merely a euphemism for somebody's slapdash mistake. Lavelle knew he had some shoveling to do to dig himself out of an embarrassing mess.

"Eddy, we've got a storm raging here in North Dakota. Nobody is able to go anywhere. I'll do what I can tomorrow if the weather cooperates."

An icy tension filled the line. "I'm disappointed in you, Mark," Eddy finally replied in a distinctly patriarchal tone that reminded Lavelle of a condescending schoolmaster from his boarding school days. After a hollow pause, he continued, "I let you in on this deal, assuming that you were a player on both the risk and reward side of this venture. If I'm wrong, Mark, let me know, because a weak link breaks the chain and we're of no mind to . . . ."

"You'll have the merchandise as soon as roads open and vehicles can transport it," Mark said. 'Don't shove me . . . I'm tired of being shoved.' Hadn't Kane said that in the movie?

"Hold on, Mark." Lavelle heard bits and pieces of muffled conversation in the background. Finally, he returned to the phone. "If the weather is really that bad, just get the compounded pharmaceuticals—the chemo bags and infusions, and destroy them. Forget about shipping. Promise me that you will personally oversee their destruction?"

"Right." Lavelle was damned if he'd run errands for his Southern friend on the worst night of the season. "Good night, Eddy."

He left the darkened theatre and trudged to his home office, now chilly, as though the walls were pervious to the frigid winds blowing from the north. Smoldering embers still glowed in the fireplace. He threw a log on the ashes. An excellent fire resurrected and crackled lustily, breaking the silence in the deserted house. The mahogany mantel clock read 10:44 PM.

The GEM situation is manageable. Eddy always had a slightly paranoid tendency, even during residency days, and this was just another over-reaction. Collapsed in his desk chair, he saw the CEO's unopened letter. This night was already a sleigh ride to hell. Why not read what the simpering idiot has to say, then call it a night in hopes that matters, especially the weather, might improve in the morning. That bastard Bohley had been a barb in his flesh ever since the Hellenbolt matter in December. What a preposterous day *that* had been! Summoned to the CEO's office one afternoon shortly before Christmas, he was confronted with what Bohley called a 'medical complaint.' Yes, he'd hospitalized Sonia Hellenbolt, a sixty-three year old female, for a gastrointestinal disorder. No, he did not know that she happened to be the wife of Swedish Board Chair, Wendell Hellenbolt, the largest sugar beet farmer in the region. Yes, Lavelle had made a spontaneous trip back to New Jersey for the holidays while Mrs. Hellenbolt was in his care. Yes, he'd left her in the care of chief resident, Dr. Sandeep Venkata and . . . yes, . . . perhaps. . . without communicating his departure to the Hellenbolt family.

Hellenbolt had considered his actions to be a medical oversight, and was especially displeased that his wife's care had been relegated to a resident, and a foreign resident at that. On that December afternoon, Bohley reminded Lavelle that he'd been there long enough to know how to navigate hospital politics.

The reply was vintage Lavelle.

"I am a physician, a very good physician, not a politician. I'll thank you to limit your attention to running this troubled hospital and to deal with a blatantly bigoted Board Chair while I practice the art of medicine without further excoriation from you. Be reminded that I am revered by my colleagues and by grateful patients. Such is the metric by which I agree to be measured."

He'd stormed out of Bohley's office, leaving the little ferret cowering behind his desk.

Yes, he'd regained the upper hand with Bohley that day, Lavelle thought smugly, as he retrieved the new letter from its envelope.

Dr. Lavelle,

I have been asked by the Chief of Staff at Swedish Hospital to notify you to appear before the Medical Staff Executive Committee in response to a complaint about your behavior.

On January 9, 2001, I was informed by the Director of Pharmacy that you have been prescribing Exvantium, an off-formulary angiotensinogen converting enzyme inhibitor (ACEI), for your hospitalized patients. According to the complaint, even with patients who are admitted on an appropriate, formulary-allowed ACEI, you are regularly switching them to the far more expensive Exvantium. I was also informed by the Director of Pharmacy that the ACEI you insist upon using has no therapeutic advantage over the three ACEI's that are on the formulary. On the five occasions the pharmacy director has discussed this practice with you, you have failed to offer any scientific, evidence-based rationale for your choice of ACEI.

Lavelle bristled. The cheeky Director of Pharmacy had a lot of nerve questioning him, a physician with a superior knowledge of drug therapy, on his choice of medication.

On February 3, 2001, I was informed by two members of the medical staff that they had been approached by the pharmaceutical representative who sells Exvantium to participate in "Phase IV Clinical Trials" of that drug. They alleged that the representative had offered them $250 for every patient they switched to, or started on, Exvantium, for which they completed a brief questionnaire after their patients had been on Exvantium for sixty days. These members believe that the clinical trial proposed by the representative was a marketing ploy, not science. They refused because this activity would constitute an explicit violation of the code of ethics at Swedish Hospital.

Dammit! He'd warned the Averill rep that he must be careful when soliciting other physicians. "Not everyone is as trustworthy as I am, Nick. Research should be left to those of us with experience in this field. Don't let sales quotas drive you to bad decisions. Greed is a terrible thing, Nick. You must not become a slave to it."

I refer you to Section VI of the Medical Staff Bylaws regarding ethical relationships between members of the medical staff and vendors of medical devices and drugs:

"It is inappropriate for a member of the medical staff to accept payment of any kind in exchange for agreeing to utilize a specific product or service in the hospital. Such payments include, but are not limited to, money, tangible gifts of any value, entertainment, travel, or food –for himself or for any member of his/her family or staff. Any member of the medical staff who engages in such activity will be called before the Medical Staff Executive Committee and subject to the disciplinary procedures outlined in Section III of these Bylaws."

So this letter wasn't about Sonia Hellenbolt's rotund belly after all. He inhaled deeply, bringing his shoulders up to his ears. Oxygen permeated the recesses of his lungs. If, like actors and musicians, he was to perform under excessive pressure, he must slow his racing mind.

The knowledge that there is a significant financial inducement for prescribing Exvantium casts your non-scientific insistence upon using it in a highly suspect light.

A listing of all of your hospitalized patients given Exvantium over the past 18 months is available in the Medical Records Department for your review. Please be prepared to discuss these cases at the next meeting of the Medical Staff Executive Committee on April 15, 2002.

Sincerely yours,
Byron R. Bohley, FAMACG, CEO

Lavelle felt his anger grow hotter than the fire that flared before him. To be upbraided by Bohley, a mere administrator—a charlatan in a silk suit—was something he could ignore. But facing a conspiracy of colleagues, all jealous of his superior clinical skills, his grasp of the medical literature and his enviable financial position, was a real threat. Someone must have intentionally scheduled his 'hearing' precisely when he planned to be in Switzerland at the Averill sponsored meeting.

Dwarfed by the towering problems that now surrounded him, he walked the hallways of his home, oblivious to the ringing phone in the hallway. When he reached the kitchen, he turned on the television. Weather warnings dominated the local stations. Oddly, he was still hungry. He dialed the Jade Garden on the kitchen phone and placed an order for Kung Pao Chicken, extra garlic, to go.

"Are you serious?" a youthful voice answered.

"I'm both serious AND hungry," Lavelle growled.

"We don't have a delivery service, man, and if we did, we sure as hell wouldn't be going out on a night like this. You could try Dominos."

Lavelle no sooner hung up the kitchen phone when his cell phone vibrated again. The chrome kitchen clock read 11:55PM. Eddy was on the line.

"What is it *now?*" Lavelle foraged the cupboards for something, anything, to eat.

"Our GEM problems are intensifying. Mark, listen to me very carefully. You must get any chemotherapy solutions, any TPN mixtures, any compounded IV products back to us ASAP."

"Now? I told you, Eddy, we've got a goddamn white-out here. I can't see the row of elms at the end of my property! People go out in a blizzard like this, and they die. They freeze to death, crawling on bleeding hands and knees, trying to get from the barn to the house. Their cars stall in snow banks and they die from carbon monoxide poisoning or hypothermia." Lavelle recounted every exaggerated weather story he could remember. "Do you think I'm going to risk my life in this weather because you can't manage your anxiety?"

"Mark." The voice was steely cold. "I don't have time for your protestations, and frankly, neither do you. Get to your office now. Clean your files of any correspondence with GEM—checks, invoices, any records you might have in your office. Shred the evidence, and do it now. I don't give a rat's ass if the fucking world is coming to an end in Fargo."

The clock was a minute away from midnight.

Saturday, April 1, 2002

Eight

Donna Wadeson reclined in a Lazy-Boy rocker in her apartment on the dreary west side of Fargo. It was her favorite spot to reflect with a cup of strong coffee, early in the morning before the city came to life, on how far she'd come during this disastrous year. After a week on her aching feet, her swollen knees would finally get some relief. Without call or obligations to home-bound patients, she'd finally earned a day off from the nursing job at Swedish Home Health Services she'd begun just a month ago

A farmer's wife for thirty-seven years, Donna found the habit of rising before dawn hard to break. At 5 AM, the first pot of coffee boiled on the range in her galley kitchen. She craved a hearty breakfast and scanned the refrigerator for possibilities. A carton of organically grown eggs was just the ticket.

No one fries eggs better than my Donna, her husband Jerry had bragged. Fried in sizzling hot butter, crispy brown around the edges, the yolk basted softly by steam during the final minutes. Removed from the frying pan, just so, and set upon a thick slice of homemade bread lathered in more sweet cream butter. No one should marry a woman who can't fry an egg, he'd said, without any awareness of how the world around him had gone politically and nutritionally correct. That was Jerry, she smiled fondly, the man who had loved her for forty years.

Now his empty chair faced her as she looked across the round oak table that once dominated the kitchen of their 1910 farm house forty miles southwest of Fargo. Jerry had taken over the family farm near Prosper while Donna worked as a charge nurse at the local community hospital. They'd been together all those years, husband and wife, square dancing partners and business mates in the rugged, unpredictable business of farming.

Not a story-book ending, theirs. They weren't the only ones struggling to make a decent living on the farm. Most of their neighbors had reluctantly moved to Fargo to take on whatever jobs might be available. After a tough meeting in the spring of 2001, their banker had finally said: "You've lost money farming this land for the past nine years. Cut your losses, try something different."

Old Doc Kundert, the cigar-smoking general practitioner who claimed he'd brought over fourteen hundred Prosper babies into the world, said the same. "You may be broke, but you've still got your skills. Hell, I hate to lose you over at our little hospital, but you're a damn good nurse. And one who still knows how to take care of patients."

She'd flinched when Doc said that. Despite years of experience in every department of their community hospital—lifting mutilated victims of farm accidents onto gurneys or running down shabby halls to rooms with blinking lights, Donna was still intimidated by the new ways of medicine. Nursing had changed so much over the years. All the new miracle drugs, special procedures, and complicated technologies required professional skills she lacked.

A move to Fargo: that was their plan but, as they say, life threw a curve. She'd been at the Prosper hospital the day when Jerry needed her the most. Donna could only imagine how it might have happened. On a scorching afternoon in July, when the last green and yellow John Deere combine pulled away from their farm, Jerry stood by the kitchen sink, watching from the window, sweating. Not a cloud in the big Dakota sky. Instinctively, he would have worried about the prairie drought. He would run the faucet and fill a jelly jar with cold water, pure and quenching, that traveled from the cool deep well his homesteading grandfather had dropped to the aquifer below. The same land Jerry had now lost to creditors. Then, at the age of fifty-nine, he must have collapsed and died on the linoleum floor, his heart quivering like a sack of angle worms, then quieting to a final stillness. Donna came home from her hospital shift to find his lifeless body sprawled amidst the shattered glass.

Doc Kundert called it a massive heart attack but Donna knew differently. Her faith and the wisdom of Ecclesiastes said there was a time for everything. Jerry had died from despair and defeat and it was her purpose to carry on, whatever that meant.

Enough self-pity! She adjusted her legs on the footrest and turned on the TV at 5:30 AM. The local public television station was airing old episodes of the Lawrence Welk show. Bobby and Sissy dancing across the screen. Guy and Ralna in nasal harmony. And Welk himself, the North Dakota native son who'd made it in the fickle world of music.

Rrrrring. The telephone, at this time of morning? *Rrrrrring. Rrrrrring.*

"Hello? Hello, who is this?"

"Is this. . . Donna?" a faint voice asked. "I'm calling for my home health nurse, Donna Wadeson. This is. . . um. . .Christine." Her diction was slow and slightly slurred. "Are you the one who. . . . came over. . . last night. . . to hang. . . . my TPN bag?"

With champagne music in the background, fear bubbled up inside Donna. She muted the sound, leaving only Welk's waxy smile on the screen. Of course she remembered the frail young woman she'd met a week ago—all ninety-five pounds of her—looking like a plate of quail bones stripped of meat.

"Yes, yes, Christine, this is Donna. What's wrong? My goodness, it's early for you to be awake."

"I'm sorry. . .to be, uh, calling you on a Saturday. But you said I could call, right? I just. . . um, . . . there might be a . . . problem.

Of the thirty patients assigned to her by Swedish Home Health Services, Donna thought Christine Runyan, the twenty-eight year old Crohn's patient, was her most worrisome case. According to Dr. Lavelle's notes, Christine had been doing well on home total parenteral nutrition or TPN, another of those blessed medical acronyms in the alphabet soup of health care. Food in a plastic bag—carbs, protein, fats, electrolytes and vitamins—flowed through plastic tubing into a catheter implanted in Christine's chest and began its journey throughout her starving body. Every evening at 8PM, the programmable infusion pump pumped continuously over a ten hour period until the bag emptied at 6 AM the next morning. This nightly TPN cycling enabled patients like Christine to live a nearly normal life during the day.

"Christine, are you home alone? Is there anyone I can talk to?"

"Just Anya, my daughter. She's sleeping now. She had a bad night too."

"What seems to be wrong?"

"I'm feeling. . .kinda warm. . . and sweaty. . . like I have a fever or something."

"Do you feel bad enough to go to the emergency room? Shall I call an ambulance?"

"No! My husband, Trevor, works there. . . and. . .I don't want. . .to get him. . .all upset."

Donna mentally scrolled through her last visit. Friday morning she'd drawn blood for a kidney function test, delivered it to the lab and made sure that the results be faxed to her by 2 PM. They were normal, expect for a low potassium, so she'd phoned Dr. Lavelle's office at once about the abnormality. According to his snotty receptionist, the doctor was not available, but Dr. Lavelle returned her call at 4:45 PM and Donna, with practiced deference, reported the lab results and suggested an adjustment in Christine's next TPN solution. In a typical Friday afternoon physician voice, Lavelle agreed, and dictated a new order, which she phoned into the Swedish hospital pharmacy at 5 PM. It had already been a long Friday, and now she had to wait for the order to be prepared so she could pick it up and deliver the bag to the Runyans.

"Christine, are you having trouble with the infusion pump?"

When hanging the new TPN bag at 7 PM last night, Donna struggled to program the battery-operated infusion pump. A series of unrelenting beeps and error messages would not be silenced. This was Donna's abiding belief—that when it came right down to it, beeps and dials and programmable functions failed according to their own bad nature.

"Let me help," Christine had offered. "I'm good with computers." A few keystrokes from her fragile hands, and the beeps stopped and the infusion pump functioned properly. Awed and grateful for a computer-literate generation, Donna replied, "S'pose you could help me with my VCR?" Together, they'd had a good chuckle. Laughter *was* the best medicine.

"No, it seems . . . to. . .be infusing. . . fine. I just . . . I don't know. . . I feel sick. Not good."

"Is the catheter site red or sore?"

"Don't know . . . it seems all right."

"Have you taken anything? Are you feeling weak? Have you been out of bed yet this morning?"

"Just to the bathroom. I took a sleeping pill last night. Terrible dreams. Worse than being awake."

"Any cramping, pain, nausea or any. . ."

"I don't know what to do. I was doing so well. Now, this. I just got out of the hospital a month ago . . . and I don't want to go back there. Trevor is still at work and I. . . . don't want . . .oh, I don't really. . . know what to do. Maybe I'm just . . . you know. . a little scared."

With Christine's disease flaring, Donna's day off seemed iffy. Febrile and lethargic, at least that's how her patient sounded on the phone. Infection was always a risk with TPN therapy. The changed order: was it warranted? And there was the fuss with the infusion pump. She worried how this might reflect on her reputation at the agency, on her nursing career, on her new start in Fargo. Life was handing her one new problem after another and she felt wholly inadequate. The reassuring voice of Doc Kundert echoed in her mind. "You're a damn good nurse, Donna. You know that you can't treat a patient over the phone. Gotta look at 'em, examine 'em, watch 'em react to your touch."

No, it probably wasn't a life-threatening situation. It could probably wait until Christine's husband, a paramedic, got home. The agency wouldn't be reimbursed for her services. Health plans would pay for an ER visit, but not for services their bureaucrats considered to be an "unnecessary" home visit. Doc Kundert again: "forget the bull; just do the right thing."

"Christine, I'll be over in a few minutes. Don't you worry. Soon as I get my car shoveled out, I'll be there." The snow storm had blanketed the west side of Fargo with the kind of heavy snow that filled the ER with middle-aged men who'd overestimated their stamina and shoveled their way into a heart attack. On the farm, Jerry would have attached a snowplow to the front end of his tractor and cheerfully plowed a path from their garage to the county road, spreading snow like Moses parting the Red Sea.

"Will you be able to let me in?" Donna asked, remembering that she was no longer in Prosper where residents rarely locked their doors.

"Um, . . . I'm so. . . tired. There's a key. . . right under the rug. . .just outside. . . the apartment door. Can you . . .let. . . yourself in?"

"Sure can."

"Please. . . hurry." Her voice ended in a whimper.

Nine

One hundred ninety-seven emails appeared in his mailbox on Saturday morning. Not so bad, Byron Bohley reckoned, considering that on Friday he'd attended a management seminar in Minneapolis called *Leadership for Turbulent Times*. He'd intended to return that evening but a sudden snowstorm in the valley had caused the short flight back to Fargo to be rescheduled on Saturday. After landing on the snow-cleared runway at 9 AM, he'd called his wife to tell her that he'd be dropping by the hospital to check his messages.

"You're paranoid," Betsy yawned. "What are you so worried about?"

"I'm paid to worry. Paid well enough for you to hob-nob at the Country Club." He snapped his cell phone shut. *I'd like to see you pay the membership fee on your salary as a Pilates instructor,* he thought.

What *was* he worried about? The question was another jab at his self-esteem. At the recent Chamber of Commerce roast, the mayor of Fargo chided, "The CEO of Swedish Hospital seems paranoid about everything. He's had a rear view mirror installed on his stationary bike." That evening, after a string of jokes about his Hobbit height, his pelican waddle and his perpetual tardiness, a member of Bohley's board called him the loneliest man in the hospital. "His best friend is a fire hydrant."

"And I know what a fire hydrant feels like!" Bohley retorted, later reminding Betsy how much applause his line had prompted.

Near the end of the fundraiser, Dr. Andy Thorson, the hospital's chief of staff, presented Bohley with a ribboned package from the medical staff. The fifty-five year old CEO tore off the foil paper before a watchful crowd. "Not quite heavy enough for a golden parachute," he'd said, wrestling with the stubborn tape until a framed poster was released from the wrapper. It contained an enlarged photo of Bohley with the Board of Directors snagged from the hospital's latest annual report. Under it, a caption read: *None of us is as dumb as all of us.*

The physicians in the crowd convulsed with laughter.

Let the sons-a-bitches laugh, Bohley thought, remembering that never-ending night of abuse. The hospital was *not* having a banner year. Most hospitals weren't. That bit of sorry news might sober all of Fargo once the implications were understood. Medicare cutbacks stymied further expansion plans and capital spending in the city. Just wait until the bankers, building contractors, consultants and developers who fed like parasites off the hospital's growth figured that out. Frozen salaries for employees meant less money circulating in the local economy. Fewer Mercedes, smaller diamond rings, more shopping at Walmart instead of the mom-and-pop businesses that had been part of the community for decades. Six law suits were pending against the hospital with another three in settlement. Watch the malpractice rates soar and the bottom line erode. The revenue trends were no brighter. Medicare was headed toward insolvency.

Bohley hoped the goddamned system would somehow survive for the ten years he had left before retiring. For now, he simply tried to manage the moment; the future was north of hopeless. His Board was sticking their uninformed noses into operational matters, but if he'd learned anything over thirty years in this business, it was how to confuse a Board. Produce enough charts and graphs to overwhelm their ego-inflated minds, and watch eyes glaze over in boredom. Flood them with industry jargon, impossible acronyms and technical information, and then watch them pretend to understand. Failure was easy to explain if you had some clever underling prepare the right Power Point presentation.

As for the rest of the hospital, every day produced some 'crisis' like changing the operating room schedule or the brand of coffee in the physician's lounge. Nurses were trouble too. Money and promises were the grease he applied to buy favor with their monoculture, peppered, of course, with speeches on their critical role as front-line providers, the soul of the organization. All this he could handle. But the latest challenge was new: making sure people felt that the hospital was still a safe place for patients.

Bohley scanned his inbox for bad news. There it was: an email with a "priority" flag from Wendell Hellenbolt, the Board Chair, requesting the CEO "pull a few strings . . . and get his case moved up on the waiting list for elective surgery." Always some favor for the Board Chair, but it could be worse. No mention of Bohley's travel expenses, not after Hellenbolt and other Board members got that free hospital-funded winter meeting in Maui.

The rest of his mailbox was junk. Endless minutes from the medical staff meeting, the Finance committee, the Board's nominating committee and a special task force evaluating employee insurance benefits, a progress report on the cancer center project. A note from Public Relations reminding him that next week was "Practice Kindness" week. Daffodils would be sold in the lobby. The Hospital auxiliary issued an e-vite to their spring tea. Would Mr. Bohley say a few words of commendation to the volunteers? A day in the life of a CEO. He deleted most of the messages without opening them.

Then he saw the name of Mark Lavelle on his screen and his heartburn flared. The message had been sent at midnight, March 31, with a screaming red exclamation point. Why was medicine's original leech writing emails on the weekend?

***

"Praise God," Donna shrieked as her laptop hummed, then chortled, gasped, and finally signaled a successful transmission. Download. Upload. *Over*load, as far as she was concerned.

Like magic, Dr. Lavelle's discharge summary of Christine's February hospitalization appeared on her screen. Donna smiled. Maybe Jerry was up there pulling strings for her just now.

> *Patient:Christine Runyon*
> *MRN:996784-2*
> *Date of Admission: February 2, 2002*
> *Date of Discharge: February 6, 2002*

Christine Runyon is a 28 year old white female with a history of Crohn's Disease, multiple small bowel resections, and short bowel syndrome requiring TPN for nutritional support admitted on February 2 because of fever and chills.

Christine was healthy until 1996 when, at the age of 22, she developed cramping abdominal pain, alternating bouts of diarrhea and constipation, intermittent fever, and weight loss. She delayed medical attention until the diarrhea became bloody and her weight had dropped 20 pounds. I worked her up at that time and made a firm diagnosis of Crohn's Disease.

Seeing Lavelle's name, that bow-tied horse's pa-toot with the gold cufflinks and fancy education, made her wince. He might need to be phoned about Christine's status, or "bothered," as he'd once sniped.

Christine was treated medically with poor control of her symptoms until 1998 when she was admitted with severe abdominal pain and a small bowel obstruction. She underwent surgery by Dr. Blackman who performed a bowel resection. Postoperative recovery was complicated by a wound infection and by great difficulty reestablishing oral food intake. Since that time

Christine has had five further hospitalizations – three for bowel obstructions requiring surgery for lysis of adhesions and for bowel resections and two for catheter-related sepsis. Christine has been on home TPN since November of 2001.

With the exception of these 2 episodes of catheter related sepsis resulting in visits to the ER, Christine has been doing fairly well for the past two years. She drinks water and eats jello with good control of her abdominal pain and diarrhea on Remicade. Her weight has increased from a low of 78 pounds two years ago to 94 pounds. Although she is no longer able to remain employed as an elementary teacher, she has resumed a number of her normal activities, including caring for her active young daughter.

Christine was at baseline until the morning of admission when she developed chills, sweats, and a temperature spike of 104 F. Her husband brought her to the ER where a temperature of 104.5 F and a BP of 90/60 were measured. She was diaphoretic and lethargic. The site of her central catheter was reddened and tender, and she was admitted with a presumptive diagnosis of catheter related sepsis.

Poor thing. No wonder she doesn't want to go back to the hospital. Donna scrolled through the discharge summary until she came to the problem list.

Catheter related sepsis
Severe malnutrition secondary to short bowel syndrome
Crohn's disease

The patient was discharged in good spirits on the fourth hospital day on home TPN and the above noted medications with an appointment to see me in the office in 7 days. She will be followed at home by Swedish Home Health Services.

Mark Lavelle, MD, Internal Medicine
Cc:Dr. Blackman
Swedish Home Health Services

Donna thought about the difficult situation to which Christine had been discharged. Living with a chronic disease like Crohn's was a full-time job. Medication schedules, physician visits, constant trips to the drugstore, the special care involved with home TPN therapy, chronic economic stress. The disease drained so much physical and mental strength that it left no energy for rest of life—family outings, school carnivals, church programs, shopping at the mall. Did physicians understand this? In Dr. Lavelle's case, she doubted it. He knew disease well enough, but he sure had a lot to learn about life.

***

With an ochre sunrise unfolding in her rear view mirror, Donna drove her rusting S-10 Blazer the short distance to the Runyan home. The sickly yellow apartment building was located in a 1970's development that was becoming Fargo's newest ghetto.

At 6:20AM, the sidewalk had not yet been shoveled, so she dusted off the snow that clung to her Sorel boots before descending the half flight of stairs to apartment #3. She bent down slowly on stiff knees, wincing in pain, and lifted the black rubber-backed floor mat to locate the key. Then she heard voices on the other side of the door.

"You should have called me. I tell you, you should have called me." A female voice, husky and insistent. Probably a smoker. She could barely hear Christine's thin response.

"I told Mom and Dad I'd take care of you. How come you get sick, and you don't call me. Now we gotta pay for a nurse visit."

Donna's formidable knock interrupted the conversation. A tall, coarse woman in her mid-thirties opened the door and without any exchange of pleasantries, said in the same throaty voice, "Chrissy said you'd be coming over."

"I'm Donna Wadeson with Swedish Home Health Services. And I'm afraid I've brought some wet snow in with me that I can't shake from my boots. So sorry. Unbelievable weather." Everyone in the Midwest talked about the weather. It filled that big empty space between strangers.

"Yeah, sure."

"And how is our patient, Christine? Are you her. ."

"Chrissy's sister, Brigid."

"And she's my Auntie BG," echoed a small voice from around a corner.

"Anya, honey, you up already, pumpkin? After that big day we had yesterday, traipsing around downtown? I though you'd sleep 'till noon today. Come here and give me a big hug."

The child, dressed in red twill pants and a faded pink cotton sweatshirt, threw herself into the arms of Brigid. With mussy morning hair falling across her face, she reminded Donna of Cossette, the pitiful orphaned child in *Les Miserables*. Three times

Donna had watched that show on public television, enduring the series of membership breaks at the show's most tearful moments.

"Well, kiddo, you're a colorful sight. Anyone made you breakfast today?" Brigid moved into the sparse kitchen with Anya trailing behind. "Same as before?" BG asked. Captain Crunch pellets poured into a yellow plastic bowl as Anya fetched milk from the refrigerator. A foul smell escaped as she opened the door.

"Whew! Smells worse than my Daddy's bait shop over in Muskee. Remember, I was telling you. . . ."

"I hate to interrupt, but I should see Christine. Is she still in bed?"

"Bedroom's still where it was last night, and Chrissy's been waiting for you. Called you at 5:30 this morning, didn't she?"

Donna moved through the hallway toward Christine's bedroom and found her resting. She backtracked to the small bathroom, retrieved antibacterial soap from her nursing bag and scrubbed her hands while humming the entire stanza of Yankee Doodle. Satisfied that her hand-washing technique complied with published nursing standards, she reached for a frayed blue towel.

Christine looked especially small and shrunken in the queen-size bed, huddled under a generous blue and white lone star quilt. A small lamp by her bedside emitted a dim stream of light. Someone, Brigid probably, had refreshed a glass with ice chips and a straw. The TPN bag was suspended over the right bedpost and the monitor on the infusion pump read "empty container" without any error messages on the read-out. Donna sent a second prayer of gratitude to the patron saint of computer-aided drug delivery systems. A wicker basket by the bedside overflowed with used tissues, scrap-booking magazines and yesterday's newspaper.

"Christine, how are you feeling? Any better since we talked?"

"Oh, hi. . .Donna." The patient's eyes opened slowly and her voice was shaky. "Thanks for coming . . . on a Saturday. I probably shouldn't have called. My sister came over. . . after I hung up the phone."

"Nonsense. How do you feel now?"

"Still kinda hot. . . and I've got the chills, . . . even under this quilt."

Donna was not surprised. Christine looked 'pale and punk,' a catch-all phrase she learned from Doc Kundert. "Let's take your temperature."

Christine nodded, used to the routine.

With the thermometer placed underneath her patient's tongue,

Donna resorted to yes-and-no questions. "Any cough?"

Headshake, left to right. No cough.

"Any pain or burning when you urinate?"

No pain or burning.

"Headache?"

No headache.

"But you're weak and still tired?"

Christine's eyebrows rose as if to ask, "isn't that obvious?"

The thermometer reached 103.2 degrees, higher than Donna had expected when she first placed her hand on Christine's forehead. She pulled aside the sleeve of Christine's cotton gown to examine the catheter insertion site near the sternum—a problem area for bacterial growth. But the catheter site looked normal— neither red nor any evidence of pus formation—and yet Christine simply did not look well.

"I think you need to be seen by a physician," Donna advised as Brigid and Anya entered the room.

"Oh, no. . . no. . . no," Christine moaned, her bird-like frame quivering beneath the sheets.

"We should have you seen in the hospital ER today. I can phone ahead and let them know you'll be coming."

Brigid turned abruptly and mumbled something about more bills. "I'm calling Trev."

Donna reached for Christine's hand and squeezed it sympathetically. Scopes and sticks. Pokes and pumps. Injections, invasions. If anyone knew what happened in hospitals, it was this vulnerable young woman. Mistakes, malfunctions, mishaps.

"You've been through a lot, haven't you, Christine? You'll be better off in the hospital."

"Will Dr. Lavelle. . . ."

"Someone will notify him," Donna nodded as she removed the empty TPN bag that hung over the bedpost and packed the shriveled plastic container in her go-bag. It would come in handy later as she recorded the changes made to the TPN. Documentation was so important, wasn't it? If *it's not documented, it didn't happen*, she thought, mimicking the home health trainer during her orientation session. Back in her apartment, she'd be spending the better part of Saturday keying all of this into the blessed computer. So much for her day off, but it couldn't wait until Monday.

"It's settled, then," Brigid announced as she re-entered the bedroom, carrying the portable phone as some symbol of authority. "I'll be taking Chrissy to the ER. Trev will meet us there. You can go now, Donna. Everything's set. The family's taking over."

"What about me?" Anya asked, pulling the thumb from her mouth just long enough for the question to escape.

So embarrassing was this family oversight that Donna, ever attuned to the need for rescue, hesitated for only a moment. "Well, now, why don't I stay with Anya until you return? I still have my paperwork to do. I can just as well finish it here." She patted the laptop in its bag.

"That ok, kiddo?" Brigid asked without so much as a grateful nod in Donna's direction. "I'll be back soon as I can."

Ten

Dr. Sandeep Venkata inhales a deep breath of medicinally scented air as he glances at the ER clock: 0700, Saturday. Everywhere, patients growing anxious with an overworked staff. Priority cases moved to the top of the treatment list in the aftermath of the snowstorm. Everyone wants to be first.

"Venkata! Over here!" Petterson roars above a swarm of screaming children, parents rocking, pacing, bouncing, shushing, anything to quiet them. "You had any pediatric experience? Kids are driving me nuts. Gotta be a saint to go into pediatrics. If we get the red eardrums treated and the meth addict settled down, we'll at least be able to see the rest of them."

Before Venkata can answer, Petterson's flight of ideas lands elsewhere. "You know, I haven't had any goddamn luck finding Lavelle, and he's got a hot one in room #5. Young woman with Crohn's. A TPN patient. Most likely an infected catheter. Probably a hit. She's a regular here; been in a couple of times already this year. Ever seen her in clinic? Seems like Lavelle is always pulling you in on his cases."

"I would have to see her chart." Venkata does not recall such a case. Perhaps if he were not so tired he might remember. "What is the patient's name?"

"Runyan. Twenty-eight year old white female spiking a pretty good temp. Referred by home health. See what's going on with her, Venkata, then help us out with the rest of the crowd. Hope you don't have anything planned for the rest of the weekend. No hot dates, or anything like that." Petterson grins broadly displaying a fine row of capped teeth. "Say, haven't I seen photos of you around the hospital? Mr. Most-Eligible-Bachelor-2002? By the way, how many hours you been working this week?"

"I am fine, Dr. Petterson."

"Go on, then. No point waiting for Lavelle. If I know him, he's poring over his investment strategy, looking for some third world country to buy."

The chief resident moves to the tall counter that encloses the nurse's station, the master control center for all ER activity. Before he has time to ask, a male nurse whose name tag reads "Reuben, RN," slides a metal clipboard with the ER sheet bearing the intake information on Christine Runyan. Demographics, insurance coverage, chief complaint, vital signs and medications. Venkata reviews the data. A blood pressure of 90/60. In American ER slang, she is definitely a *keeper.*

In treatment room #5, the small frame of Christine Runyan appears lost under a warmed blanket that falls over the side of the gurney. She is alone in the room. Her eyes are closed.

"Mrs. Runyan?" The chief resident places a gentle hand on the bed to rouse her. "Mrs. Runyan, I am Dr. Venkata. You are not feeling so well?"

Her eyelids open slowly to his call. "Where's Dr. Lavelle? I . . . want to see. . . Dr. Lavelle." Her voice is faint and plaintive.

"We have a call in to him, Mrs. Runyan. I am certain Dr. Lavelle will be here very soon. The snowstorm has presented problems for people getting to hospital. Meanwhile, I will examine you—try to understand why you have a fever."

His patient has already lapsed into sleep. Venkata washes his hands and examines the emaciated white female who is somnolent and wifty. Difficult to arouse; diaphoretic and tachypneic. Appears acutely ill. Her dissipated body reminds him of his experiences in the most impoverished regions of India. Venkata warms the drum of his stethoscope on his palm before placing it over her lungs to listen for rales or rhonchi. He listens to the heart for murmurs, and to the abdomen for bowel sounds. The abdomen is soft and non-tender with no masses or organomegaly. He returns to the sink on the far wall of the treatment room to scrub his hands once again. Then the chief resident puts on latex surgical gloves.

"Mrs. Runyan, now I must examine your catheter site. I will need to loosen your gown. Can you pull your arm out of the sleeve? Good, very good. Thank you, Mrs. Runyan."

There are tears in her eyes. Why is she all alone, he wonders? So frightened, and no family member here to comfort her. Venkata returns his attention to the four-by-four inch square of gauze dressing taped to her chest. The paper tape bears the date of the last dressing change, 3.27.02, and the initials of the caregiver, DW/RN. Gently, he removes the gauze for an unobstructed look at the insertion site. He sees a wide area stained a bright orange from Betadine antiseptic, and the plastic catheter tip under the skin. No pus or inflammation around the hole. Good, a healthy healing process in place.

Venkata calls for a nurse and, minutes later, Reuben, RN, appears in #5. "I have just examined Mrs. Runyan. If there are any family members waiting, I would like to speak with them."

"Haven't seen anyone around, Doc. She was brought in by her big sister; that much I know. The sister provided all the insurance information—knew that as well as her own name.

We've seen this family in the ER before. Her husband is a paramedic with Lake Agassiz Emergency Services. You might recognize him; he's around here a lot. Word is that he was in earlier this morning transporting a case. I can probably find him."

Reuben is known as the butterfly of ER society; Venkata now understands why. Little escaped his scrutiny.

"Not now. Please re-dress the site of Mrs. Runyan's central line. I removed the dressing to examine for possible infection."

"*Staph* again?" Reuben raises his Boris Karloff eyebrows with suspicion rather than compassion. "Three admissions already this year. Infected line every time."

Venkata moves into the hallway, speaking to Reuben who follows. "Mrs. Runyan is quite ill. Something is going on in her belly or in her central line. Most likely, a catheter related sepsis. I will order blood cultures times three, complete blood count, chemistry panel and arterial blood gases. Also, a urinalysis, chest x-ray and both a flat plate and upright of her abdomen. I will need a lumbar puncture to understand her mental status lapses. After the blood cultures, I will order Vancomycin IV."

"You call it, Doc. Just like before, right?"

"Has Dr. Lavelle been located?" Venkata believes the attending physician's involvement is very important just now.

"Far as I know, he hasn't answered multiple pages. No answer at his office or at his home. Someone ought to implant a GPS device in that guy so we can map his whereabouts."

The chief resident purses his lips at the disrespectful comment.

"You writing orders for TPN too?"

"Yes, yes, the TPN." Had he almost forgotten to write orders for the infusion that surely had kept this young woman alive? "What formulation has she been on?"

"Well, that's the thing, Doc. The chart's kinda confusing. The last order documented on 3/05/02 was sent to some mail-order pharmacy in the south. GEM Pharmacy. You ever heard of that?"

"Did you check the home health agency records?"

"Nothing documented there but progress notes, the latest being Thursday, 3/29/02."

"Then I will confer with hospital pharmacy on a standard formulation. In the meantime, please recheck Mrs. Runyan's blood pressure while I write the orders."

Venkata checks his watch: 7:25 AM. Heli, that pharmacist with the clear voice who has been on his mind all night, is probably gone by now. Downtown at her drugstore, he thinks wistfully. He wants to see Heli again. Not another brief, chance encounter. Something more. How to make this happen? He imagines more conversation; he fantasizes, connives, then reprimands the distraction he has permitted, actually invited, into this moment.

"I'll try a pediatric cuff this time. She's got a damn small arm."

"Excellent."

Venkata leans against the corridor wall, mentally weaving together the medical facts of the Runyan case. The odds favor another central line infection, worrisome in a compromised patient, but treatable. If the source of the fever were intra-abdominal, he might order a CT scan. For now, he will have to wait for the first lab results, a full twenty-four hours away. The next ten patients will occupy some of that time, with maybe a few hours of sleep thereafter if he is lucky. That is, if he can sleep at all.

"Doc, her blood pressure is still low, but holding, 92/65."

He thinks about the low BP. Is she dehydrated? Or is she developing septic shock? He decides to wait for her chart to look at prior blood pressures. Meanwhile, run a liter of normal saline in case she is dry. Septic shock. Venkata knows the 50-50 survival statistics for sepsis of unknown origin.

Dr. Lavelle may not be answering his pages, Venkata realizes, but he will most certainly respond to a call on his cell phone. The private number, he once explained to the chief resident, was reserved exclusively for incoming calls from his tax accountant, his investment advisor and his medical school friend in Louisiana. "Use it only in extreme emergencies, Venkata. That's a warning, not an invitation."

Venkata punches in the cell phone number that he has committed to memory for just this purpose. It rings once, twice, three times. The chief resident learns that he likes waiting no less than the crowd in the ER lobby. *You must answer this call, Dr. Lavelle.* He rolls a felt tip pen between his thumb and forefinger. *You are the best diagnostician I know. You have information I need to treat this woman. Your patient is calling for you. I will you to answer this call.*

The phone rings a fourth time. A fifth. On the sixth ring, Venkata drops onto a rolling stool by the counter as he hears the erudite voice of Dr. Mark Lavelle.

"Eddy, is that you?"

The interrogating tone reminds Venkata of the consequences he will face if this call is considered superfluous by the authoritative voice on the other end of the line.

Eleven

Trevor Runyan paced the ER waiting room early Saturday morning. Five hours ago, he'd moved easily throughout the ER with full privileges. Now he waited like a civilian among other families with old magazines and caffeinated slurry in the overcrowded room. He knew that on the other side of the swinging double doors, head traumas, resuscitations and overdoses held priority status. Where was Christine's place in the queue?

In a corner of the waiting area, a silent television displayed a national weather map. A perky blonde in a tailored suit pointed to the country's midsection while Fargo's temperature and wind chill trailed along the bottom of the screen. A hospital janitor leaned on the handle of his mop to watch before he resumed mopping the gumbo—half snow, half mud—from the floor.

"Got a minute?"

A vague feeling of dread washed over him as he turned to the familiar voice. "What are you doing here on a Saturday morning?" he said.

"You couldn't keep me away from this kind of action." Alayne Ludemann's eyes threw off light like sparks. "I love storms. We tested every ER response system last night, and we passed with flying colors." She moved in closer and said softly, "Mr. Bohley will be very pleased with me."

Her blue fleece vest and designer jeans did little to erode her reputation as the toughest and best manager in the growing bureaucracy of Swedish Hospital. Under her supervision, the ER now ran like clockwork and exceeded every quality standard imposed by accrediting organizations. Administrators liked her firm, consistent style. Employees thought her demanding but fair.

"I looked for you when I was here a few hours ago," he murmured. "Where were you?"

"Here, there—everywhere. Management-by-walking-around. Do you really expect me to recall every minute of the busiest night we've had all year?" She glanced at Katie Couric on the television. "Look at her, Trevor. Lots of *woo* in that woman. Do you know that she makes more than Matt Lauer?"

"Why don't you answer my pages anymore?"

"Trevor, drop the questions! What are *you* doing here? Taking a double shift for time-and-a-half?"

"I wish." He looked around the room that now included a

family with a set of wailing twins. "Waiting; that's what I'm doing. Waiting for someone to look at Christine. Waiting for the resident. Waiting for that jerk, Lavelle. Probably waiting for a bed to open up on 6 Main." Trevor felt his anger rising. "Have you ever had to wait like this, or is it just some statistic to you?"

"You know damn well I've done my share of waiting. You know it, and you've done nothing about it. Nothing. If you want to get into this, let's talk in my office."

He followed her to a small windowless room at the end of the hallway. Being with Alayne Ludemann used to throw him into testosterone storm. Once the attention had felt as good as money in the bank, but lately it was deflating in value. The lying and sneaking away were no longer worth great sex. In fact, he'd come to dread it. Yet this morning he followed her like a dog.

She closed the door and hit him with the burnt-sugar tone he'd been dreading.

"What's wrong with Christine *now*?"

"Fever again. Probably just another catheter infection. Some antibiotics and she'll be good to go. Same as before."

"Does that mean we have some time today?"

He stepped back. "Jesus, my wife is right down the hall in *your* ER. What's wrong with you?"

"What's wrong with *me*? Nothing at all as long as it's convenient for you. When it comes to your pleasure, Trevor, time or place have never posed much of a problem. On the gurney. In your ambulance. The supply room over the noon hour. Even in the laundry room of your own apartment when Christine was asleep in the next room. Quite a shock for your sister-in-law, wasn't it?"

Trevor backed away until his heels hit the wall. He was no match for Alayne. She outranked him, outclassed him, outwitted him. What had she ever gotten out of their sexual antics except one more conquest in a round of power games? One afternoon when he was supposed to be sleeping on the couch (where he'd been reassigned since Christine started TPN), he'd watched some chick-chatter on Dr. Phil. Three women bragged about their addictions to sex, power and control. How they'd do anything, even slum around just to satisfy their desires. Maybe that was Alayne. Could that be her reason for their eight month affair? And what drove him? Lust. A big ego from screwing the most powerful woman in the hospital and, damn it, a break from a bleak life, and a wife who could no longer stand his touch. He'd been losing Christine to Crohn's for years. And Alayne had become more demanding. The fact that he was broke, single-parenting a child and nursing his wife meant nothing to her. It was like having two wives and he felt inadequate to satisfy either. He was trapped.

"I'm sorry, Trevor. Really sorry. It's just that I thought we'd grown closer, maybe a chance that we could . . . but it's always about *Christine*."

At times like this, he could almost believe her. Need him for what? To be there on her climb to the top just in case the air went out of her tires along the way? Maybe under that vinyl exterior was a woman almost as insecure as he. Her apology nearly struck his heart, but saying Christine's name in that hateful way had tightened the vise around his head. Christine—down the hall, frightened and alone.

"Keep her out of this."

"How can we do that, Trevor? She's been at the center of everything, the core of every problem you have. And you, taking on this battle alone. I want to help. I know the medical bills have stopped you from doing what you really want to do."

"All I ever wanted from you was some understanding of what it's been like, maybe a few laughs, not a running commentary on . . . ."

"But you got more, didn't you? You've got problems and I offer solutions. Don't deny it. Haven't I pulled strings around here for your benefit? Didn't I line you up with an important insurance contact?"

At the mention of that incident in February, Trevor relived the humiliating experience as if it were yesterday. He'd been paged at work for a call from Jack, no last name, just a friend-of-a-friend who wanted to talk insurance.

"Got something you might be interested in," Jack had said. "No obligation. I understand you've got a tough situation on your hands. Wife is pretty sick, right? I might be able to help. I don't mean to be in your business but, hey, who couldn't use some extra dough at a time like this?"

Trevor's interest had stirred. He owed Swedish Hospital $27,000 and Corner Drug another $3500. Heli Harri was on his case. The last pharmacy statement threatened him with a collection agency unless he paid her in full. Friends at the ambulance company had learned of his predicament and suggested a spaghetti fund raiser to defray his expenses. Jesus Christ, how had it come to this?

He remembered Jack's quick-paced voice entirely too clearly. "Trevor, can you meet me downtown tomorrow, say 10 AM at

Latte Da? Love that place, don't you? Double-shot espresso, that's what I always have. Bam! Bam! And I'm good for the day. We'll have a talk, man to man."

On a crisp Thursday in February when the hoarfrost clung to the elms, he met the mysterious Jack. The thin-lipped middle-aged man whose yellow fingernails revealed a serious smoking habit, drank his coffee in successive gulps. "I know quite a bit about your . . . situation," Jack began cautiously. "Damn tough, that Crohn's. Heard your wife's not working any more."

"She's a school teacher," Trevor said, "but too weak now to. . . ."

"So money's a problem. Did you ever think you'd be in this kind of situation? Nobody does. Saddled with health problems and no money to pay the bills you never dreamed of having."

Trevor moved uncomfortably in the booth with one eye on the steady flow of coffee connoisseurs lining up for their caffeine fix at Latte Da. The rich, bittersweet aroma of freshly ground beans seemed to him a luxury. A kerchiefed barista behind the coffee bar took orders for Caramel Macchiato, Meriweather Blend and Dakota Delites. He longed for a life of such sweet choices.

"You got your co-pays, your deductibles, your non-covered services," Jack the Ripper continued, "experimental therapy, psychotherapy, assisted living, this and that, the list goes on and on. You probably got childcare expenses too?"

Trevor studied the *faux* wood tabletop.

"You know, Trevor, ok if I call you Trevor? I mean, 'Mr. Runyan' sounds a little formal between two guys like us, right?" Jack's sweaty hands were now moving companionably in the tight space. "There was this scientific-type study that tried to figure out what was the worst thing about having a . . . what's the word, a . . . catastrophic illness? You know what these guys found? Not the diagnosis; nope. It was the financial drain of the damned disease. That's right. It's out there on the Internet. You can read it yourself."

Trevor didn't need a study to validate the findings. Jack's eyes darted about the room like a rat's.

"So," Jack continued, his words racing to a climax, "some guys designed a financial tool back in the late eighties to help people like you and Mrs. Runyan. It's called a viatical settlement. V-i-a-t-i-c-a-l. Money in your pocket just when you need it before. . . well, you know what I'm getting at."

"No, I don't know what you're getting at," Trevor shot back, not even trying to hide his agitation. Steamed milk hissed in the background.

"Ok, ok, ok. Here's how this thing works. People who own life insurance may be entitled to a viatical settlement if they have a catastrophic illness like cancer or AIDS. Ever seen AIDS, Trevor? Now that's worse than Crohn's."

Trevor remained silent.

"In simple terms," Jack explained, "you sell the life insurance policy of the person with a catastrophic illness to a third party, and in exchange, you get an immediate, tax-exempt payment. That's right; you pay no taxes to Uncle Sam." Jack's voice had the pitch of a vendor on the Home Shopping Network. "And, since you don't own the insurance anymore, you don't pay any more premiums, but . . . you get the immediate cash benefit of the life insurance. I kid you not!"

"What's the trade-off?" Trevor asked suspiciously.

"The trade-off is that you give up the future cash benefit of the life insurance, in return for a smaller-but-immediate cash benefit when you need it most—now."

"This is legal?" Trevor asked incredulously. "Buying and selling a death benefit? Gambling on someone's life? Jesus Christ."

"Ab-so-lute-ly! The viatical settlement industry is regulated by the state's Department of Insurance."

Trevor took a deep breath as Jack's fingers twitched, searching for a phantom cigarette. This sounded morbid, sinister, crooked.

"How much money could I get?"

"Course, that depends, doesn't it, on what we call the variables. But you might be able to get anywhere from 45% to 85% of the face value of the policy."

Applying this formula to the life insurance policy he'd taken out on Christine in 1997, the year Anya was born, that meant between $45,000 and $85,000. Enough to pay off Swedish Hospital, Corner Drug and maybe even a down payment on a small fixer-upper where Anya could play in the backyard with a dog. Living essentially debt-free with only a small mortgage would solve nearly everything that stood in the way of his happiness.

"What are these *variables*?"

"A little paperwork—a viatical settlement qualifying worksheet that we'll have to fill out on your wife. Age, sex, medical condition, policy type, smoking status. Were you ever a smoker, Trevor?" Jack shook his oily hands. "Quitting's a bitch. These patches are worthless; take my word for it. Ah, life

The snowfall was heavier now and the wind was gaining speed in the valley. Lavelle opened his briefcase and shuffled through the mail that Phyllis had carefully categorized. The top letter, stamped *confidential,* was from the hospital's CEO, Byron Bohley. He grimaced. He wanted to relax, not to aggravate himself by reading impertinent edicts from a hospital administrator. He tossed it aside and picked up the next letter from the Eastern Shore Life Settlement Company. He slid his sterling letter opener through the crease of the envelope and scanned the letter. An unfamiliar name at the bottom of the page expressed effusive gratitude for the physician's role in assisting Mrs. Christine Runyan in her pursuit of an insurance settlement. Enclosed was a copy of a letter attesting the clinical facts of her case, signed by Mark R. Lavelle, MD.

Lavelle cast the letter aside and tapped his fingers across the surface of the Brazilian walnut desk that had accompanied him to this place, the middle of nowhere. His gaze drifted to the window where outside, the wind produced small spiral funnels that danced like delirious ghosts. "Hmmm," he muttered, trying to remember exactly what he'd done to accommodate the Runyan patient that merited this follow-up, but without reaching the resolution he searched for.

Feeling skittish, he craved the soothing influence of classical music. Something light and playful to temper the austere weather and his own deteriorating mood. Perhaps Schubert before the young composer had succumbed to syphilis, maybe Opus 114, the Trout: exuberant, lyrical, inspiring. It was spring, after all, the season of rebirth and redemption. The sounds of Yo-Yo Ma's affecting cello filled the room. Lavelle leaned back in his blood-red leather chair, fingers laced behind his head, drinking in the youthful innocence and happiness which Schubert had captured, something he seemed to have lost along the *basso continuo* of his own life.

The telephone in the hallway rang once, twice, then insistently. Claudette, perhaps? The hospital? Mrs. Gelling? Maybe his psycho-invading father, the psychiatrist from New Jersey? His ex from Philly?

Lavelle ignored the intrusions. The weekend had arrived, a storm raged and ice crackled in his crystal tumbler. The world could wait, even be avoided, in a snowstorm. The sedating effects of short chain hydrocarbons eased his escape. Once again, the slippery trout had eluded the hook.

expectancy: that's a variable too. The insured, in your case—your wife—must be terminally ill with a life expectancy of less than two years. We put this information out for competitive bidding. The purchase by the winning viatical settlement company takes place when, like I just said, the terminally ill person is expected to live twenty four months or less. So we'd need a physician to certify that your wife . . . omigod, . . . I know this must be tough for you, but we'd need a letter from your wife's doctor that she'll very likely be . . . .dead, within two years."

Trevor slid from the booth and bolted for Alayne's office where she was waiting for him. Before he hurled a string of objections to the viatical idea, she handed him a prepared letter on Swedish Hospital stationery, dated February 28, 2002. The letter was addressed to the Eastern Shore Life Settlement Company. The body of the letter certified that Christine Runyan, MRN 996784-2, a Crohn's patient with multiple small bowel resections, was seriously ill and who had, at best, a prognosis of less than two years to live. The letter was signed by Mark R. Lavelle, MD.

"This will sail through an insurance company without a pair of eyes ever seeing the signature," Alayne said. "Some computer will scan the letter and automatically spit out a payment."

"Don't even think of sending that letter. I'll find the money somewhere."

"Trevor, this is nothing to worry about. I know how the system works," she said, chuckled, "or doesn't work."

He swallowed hard. The sour taste didn't go away.

"You wouldn't be the first to hoodwink an insurance company. This is chump-change for them. Who needs the money more than you?" She paused. "Believe me, Trevor; I want to help."

"And if Lavelle finds out?"

"Trust me, if I know Lavelle, he'll play along with anything that gouges an insurance company."

"Don't mail the letter."

"Do you have a better idea?"

"I'll find one."

Alayne curled her hands over the arms of her ergonomic office chair. "I'm disappointed in you, Trevor. And when I'm disappointed, everyone loses."

***

The shave-and-a-haircut knock on Alayne's office door

startled Trevor. Wordlessly, she motioned him to hide behind the door. He glanced at his watch: Saturday, 7:21 AM. How long had he left Christine alone?

"Shhh, I'll handle this," she warned, resuming a stiff administrative posture before opening the door just far enough to see who was on the other side.

"Hello, Ma'am. Am I disturbing you?"

"What do you want, Reuben?"

"Well, Ma'am, I was wondering if by any chance you might know the whereabouts of Trevor Runyan."

"If you're looking for Trevor, why don't you page him?"

In the background, Trevor cringed at the sound of his name. What if his beeper went off right now? He slid the control to 'vibrate.'

"Now, why didn't I think of that?" Reuben smacked his forehead with his palm. "Of course, just page him! I'll do exactly that, Ma'am. Don't suppose you might know his pager number?"

"Why are you looking for Trevor?"

"Mrs. Runyan is in #5 and Dr. Venkata will be admitting her to 6 Main." His heavy clog tapped on the floor. "Poor thing is scared stiff. Seems like a husband might want to be with his wife at a time like this."

"Is that all, Reuben?" Alayne gathered a file from her desk. "I've been reviewing last night's stats and I really should get back to work."

"By all means, Ma'am. What a night! Tough cases, every one of them, and nobody went out the back door toes-up, if you know what I mean. In and out before we could hurt them. Ha-ha!"

"Thank you very much, Reuben. You're a credit to this department." As she closed the door, she added, "I'll remember this when I write your performance review."

The jaunty nurse turned to leave, whistling as his hands found the oversized pockets of his white cargo pants. "I always say, Ma'am, a good storm sure brings out the best in people, don't you think?"

Twelve

April. What other month makes a fool of us on the very first day, Lavelle muttered to himself, as he fed documents into his office's paper shredder. Within seconds knife blades diced the incriminating paper trail, spewing confetti, weightless as snowflakes, into a plastic container. The shredder's groan obscured the sound of a key turning in the lock of the office suite's outer door. When the bay of overhead lights flashed on, Lavelle whirled around.

"Phyllis! What in God's name are you doing here so early on a Saturday morning?"

Dressed sensibly in a tired woolen coat and a close-fitting felt hat, she walked behind the reception counter and placed a large shoulder bag on the ledge. "Good morning, Doctor." Lavelle's overcoat draped the back of her chair. A jumble of papers, file folders, a staple remover and a pizza carton littered the space left tidy when she'd closed the office Friday afternoon. "I might ask the same of you."

"Come now, Phyllis. This is *my* office and you, of all people, know how my paperwork piles up."

A red light blinked on the paper shredder.

"Trouble?" she asked. "It overheats sometimes when it's been heavily used."

Lavelle moved in front of the shredder to block the view of paper stuck in the machine's throat.

"It seems Claudette's endless receipts and credit card statements are too much for our office machine," Lavelle drew his eyebrows together. "A very interesting documentary on identity theft aired on PBS last evening. Alarming, really. Happens quite easily unless one takes proper precautions." He smiled. "Of course, in Claudette's case, it might be *less* expensive for me if somebody actually stole her credit card. No one could possibly outspend her."

Phyllis smiled dutifully.

"You didn't answer my question." Lavelle persisted. "What are you doing here the morning after our storm?"

"I work every Saturday morning, Doctor. The only way I stay on top of the demands of this office is to work when the office is closed and the phones are quiet." Phyllis removed the oily cardboard pizza box from her counter and tossed two Dr. Pepper cans into the wastebasket. "At the risk of drawing attention to myself, this office runs efficiently because of my weekend efforts,

"May I see the letter again?" She studied the document. "See the garish green logo of Swedish Hospital at the top of the page?"

Lavelle nodded. The **S** enclosed by a three-sided shield had always reminded him of a coiled snake, trapped in a corner and ready to strike.

"So what?"

"The letter was obviously prepared in the hospital. Perhaps you dictated it there."

Lavelle crossed his arms. Hospital dictation was another matter that raised his dander.

"As you know, I always include my initials on your letters. I don't see my initials, or for that matter, any initials on this page. It leads me to believe that the letter is likely the work of some younger, less experienced clerk in the hospital's Patient Accounts department. It certainly is not my work." She pointed to storage cupboards on the far wall. "You won't find any stationary with the Swedish letterhead on those shelves."

Lavelle stroked his chin, considering the information.

"And if I may be so bold, Doctor, the signature does not appear to be yours. The lower loop of the **L** is very uncharacteristic of your hand and so much thinner than your usual swoop. Your **L** looks like it was lifted from the Eli Lilly logo."

The physician grabbed the letter from her desk. The font was so small he had to extend his arms an embarrassing distance to read it.

"Nor is the proportion right between the taller letters like the l and the smaller e. Unless I'm mistaken, you always sign your correspondence with a Mont Blanc fountain pen, not the felt tip used for this signature."

Amazing! She's right, thought Lavelle. How many times a day does a physician sign his name, he wondered? Chart notes, prescription blanks, lab results, letters to patients, insurance forms, legal attestations, do-not-resuscitate orders, death certificates. Scribbled hurriedly, occasionally undecipherable, yet rarely challenged. Nothing more potent than the physician's pen, his favorite medical school professor had once said, where all healthcare begins and ends.

Who had the temerity to forge his signature? Why, a criminal offense had it been on a prescription blank! One more violation of his professional status. And to think that a mere receptionist, not he, first suspected the forgery completely unnerved him.

"I hadn't realized that in addition to your office competencies, you are also a skilled graphologist. What else don't I know about you, Phyllis?" He scratched the stubble on his chin. "What more do you know about me?"

When his cell phone rang, he headed to his office and closed the door. "Eddy, is that you?"

"No, Dr. Lavelle." The mellifluous voice on the line needed no identification. If signatures had markers as Phyllis seemed to believe, so did voices, and this one was distinctly Dr. Sandeep Venkata.

"I am very sorry for troubling you so early on Saturday morning, but I have just now hospitalized your patient."

"And you couldn't rouse the internist on call?" Enough on my mind already, he thought, massaging his neck muscles with a free hand.

"The patient is Mrs. Christine Runyan." The chief resident paused momentarily as though he expected to be chastised again. "She is not well, and I felt you should be notified."

With a sinking, punch-in-the-stomach dread, Lavelle slumped into his chair. My God, what next? The desk calendar lay open to Saturday, April 1, 2002. T. S. Eliot was right. April may become the cruelest month of all.

"I believe you should know, Sir, the patient is asking for you. I have done what I can. She seems very sick. Perhaps with your superior understanding of the case, you may want to personally oversee her care."

Lavelle took a deep breath and slowly exhaled, willing the tension out of his body. This was not a time for poetry, for superstition, or self-doubt. If Venkata made the effort to track him down, this patient must be seriously ill, and he needed to be fully in control of the unfolding situation.

"Tell me what's going on with Christine," Lavelle asked, assuming the role of inquisitive professor before a trembling student.

The chief resident reported details of Christine Runyan's early morning ER visit and his decision to admit her to the Medical Surgical ward of Swedish.

"How does the central line site look?"

"Clear, not red."

"That doesn't preclude a line infection and you know it," Lavelle snapped.

"Quite right, Sir. I've ordered blood cultures."

"Is the TPN bag still hanging?"

"Sir?"

"Is she still on the TPN infusion?"

"No, only normal saline to rehydrate her."

"Did she come in with a TPN bag?"

"I. . . don't recall, Sir."

"You don't recall, Dr. Venkata?" Lavelle's voice grew shrill. "A starving eighty-five pound patient, and you can't recall whether she was being infused at the time you examined her?"

"Yes. No." Venkata flustered. "I am quite certain the infusion was not running when she came into ER."

"Then somebody must have removed the bag?"

"Yes. . . I mean, I cannot confirm that. . .possibility."

"Find the infusion bag now! Do I make myself clear?"

"I will check with the ER nurse immediately." A cautionary pause followed. "Will you be coming to hospital to see her, Sir?"

"I'll be in." Lavelle drew a breath for credibility. "As soon as I finish my paperwork." He ended the call and opened his office door, shouting, "Phyllis? The hospital called and I have to go in."

"Would you like me to start your car, as before?"

"No, I'll need a ride." He offered no further explanation. "Are you prepared to drive me to Swedish?"

"Certainly. Your car? Is it . . . .? May I ask how you got to the office this morning?"

"No, you may not." Rarely did her meddling instincts get so out of hand. Racing past her toward the door, his mood was falling faster than the sea of paper that scattered in his wake.

"Hurry up. It's the Runyan woman."

Thirteen

1 April 2002
To: Byron Bohley, CEO, Swedish Hospital
From: Mark Lavelle, MD
Cc: Wendell Hellenbolt, Chair of the Board

Having read your letter of March 20, I am given little choice but to state emphatically there are gaping holes in your understanding of the Formulary issue, but I shall refrain from discussing the practice of medicine with a lay person.

Lay person, bean-counters, suits, peckerheads. Typical cattle-branding by the medical staff. Bohley felt a fiery pain at the back of his throat. The sons-a-bitches have no idea what it takes to keep a hospital going. Used to be like running a motel. In and out. No questions asked as long as the food on the tray stayed hot. A third-party picked up the tab, never quibbling if a three cent aspirin billed out at five bucks. Now the government was stepping up its control, and doing it badly. The fat-cat insurance companies chiseled away at profits. Bad debts rose. The uninsured crowded the ER like squatters on frontier soil. And the media had infiltrated the building like lice, chasing every patient safety story they could flame into a headline. Bitter juices seared his throat. He chewed a Rolaids tablet from a half empty bottle in his desk drawer.

There was so little left under his direct influence that his job had become expensive babysitting. It required that he work long hours rearranging problems, socializing in the physician's lounge, and heeding the sage advice from Betsy. "Smile, and wear a white shirt." During seven years at the helm of Swedish Hospital, he'd become a colorless well-paid bobble-head. Not bad for an accountant who'd never passed the CPA exam.

Your problem is that you are ignoring the real issues that substantially increase risks for our patients. Specifically:
Your decision to outsource medical transcription services to India is shortsighted. I have always depended on the hospital's on-site personnel to prepare my dictated notes. Their work was superb. Now dictation comes back for me to sign with blank spots and misspelled words. You may be saving money, but you are wasting my time and threatening the lives of patients.

The outsourcing, a savings of $7 million to last year's budget, was a no-brainer. Sure, there were kinks to work out, but the American labor market in this specialized niche was no longer competitive and the Asians were eager for the business. Disruptive technology changed a lot of professions. The day was coming when radiologists in Seoul might be reading hospital-generated x-rays on-line. Good, Bohley thought. Fewer moles in dark rooms here at Swedish.

An unhealthy nursing bureaucracy has flourished under your tenure. Do not try to hide behind the irrelevant fact that the hospital's nurse-to-patient ratio meets national standards. Blinking call buttons go unanswered. Why? Because RNs are at meetings, "visioning, empowering, or teambuilding." Such silliness is costly and does little for acutely ill patients.

Bohley chuckled. After years of abuse from physicians, nurses had finally discovered strength in numbers. Hell, this hospital is a sea of estrogen. Keeping the girls happy may cost this hospital some money, but it sure quiets their talk of unions.

It is a well-known fact in this hospital that certain surgeons do not wash their hands between seeing patients. Dr. Semmelweis called attention to this peril in 1865. Hand-washing is the cornerstone of infection control and has been proven beyond a doubt to prevent the transmission of infections. Yet compliance with hand-washing in this hospital ranges between 28% and 44%, with orthopedic surgeons being the worst. It is indefensible that you do not demand a fastidious adoption of the hand-washing practice. Analyze the infection rate of every surgeon and you will appreciate the grave danger that exists for many patients if hand-washing is not practiced de rigueur. If you and your Board will not manage this problem, perhaps the media will.

Bohley slumped back in his chair and threw two more Rolaids into his mouth. He knew the surgeons Lavelle was talking about: Schneider and McCord, the two busiest surgeons on his medical staff. Without them, hospital OR revenues would drop like a stone. The Surgery department chair wouldn't touch the issue. The medical director had cowered, "I'm only a family practitioner; they'll laugh me out of the room." The OR nursing director threw up her hands at the problem. Was it really a CEO's job to remind surgeons to wash their hands between patients? And take the risk of losing their cases to the other hospital in town?

The restrictive drug Formulary of this hospital prohibits access to life-saving drugs for patients. The process for adding or deleting drugs to this list is largely driven by pharmacy in the name of cost-savings. Personally, I cannot recall the last time a pharmacist's decision impacted the health and well-being of a patient. Their count-and-pour role in the health system is relatively simple in contrast to physicians who bear the responsibility (and the liability) for life and death decisions. You are placing handcuffs on the medical staff by restricting the drug Formulary. It is nothing more than a professional tactic by pharmacists to wield power away from physicians.

By God, this time he had Lavelle in his crosshairs on the Exvantium kickback. The CEO imagined Lavelle squirming at the upcoming Medical Staff Executive Committee where the situation would be considered by physician peers. This *lay person* in the room will enjoy every minute! Time is always your friend; good advice from his neighbor, a criminal defense attorney who represented child molesters, white-collar criminals and meth addicts. "Remember, you don't have to be the brightest, just the most patient." Patience was paying off when it came to Lavelle.

Regarding your invitation to appear before the Medical Staff Executive Committee on April 15, you may consult my attorney, Mr. J. Edward Mancino, Esq., of the Mancino, Barnes, Gaynor & Nigrelli Law Firm, 4 Federal Square, Philadelphia, Pa., regarding this summons.
MRL, MD

Bohley felt a dull pressure spread across his chest. Was this gastric reflux or a full- blown heart attack? And was there a physician in this hospital who cared that he, a stressed-out overweight man in his fifties who hadn't been near a health club in ten years except to pick up Betsy, might be coming up on the Big One? He felt his pulse: rapid. He loosened his tie and unbuttoned his starched shirt collar. Jesus, this office was hotter than hell.

Lavelle was getting out of hand. The email was one thing; copying the message to the Chair of the Board, quite another. Now he'd have Hellenbolt's endless questions to deal with. What's the meaning of this, of that? It was an affront to executive authority. How could Bohley be expected to lead if he didn't address

Lavelle's blatant insubordination? It's turning into a contest; who can piss higher on the barn wall?

Maybe this was a situation where action trumped patience. Bohley punched the familiar four numbers on his phone. As it rang, he calculated the days until retirement: 2,237. A helluva long time before he could follow his dream to open a pet shop in a strip-mall on the outskirts of Fargo. Plenty of dogs, cats, gerbils, gold fish. Nobody talks back in the pet business. Play with the puppies and let them slobber love all over his face while cash walked through the door. No government involved. No health insurance. Maybe buy a plot of land and start a pet cemetery.

"Alayne Ludemann speaking. What can I do for you, Mr. Bohley?"

The CEO chose his words carefully. "When we talked at the Christmas party about a little problem I was having within the medical staff, you assured me you could fix it."

"Exactly. I have a plan and it's unfolding nicely."

"I'm not so sure. Wednesday evening I asked you to speed up that plan." Talking to this woman made him feel better than any drug on the market. He shifted in his leather chair.

"Indeed you did. I'm very reliable, Mr. Bohley. And loyal. Are you asking for something more?"

The CEO twisted the diamond ring on his pinky finger, a gift from Betsy for their twenty-fifth wedding anniversary. It was a full carat, bezel-set in gold. "Meet me in our usual place. Fifteen minutes. Be careful."

Bohley peed a dribbly stream into his personal toilet, the perk he valued most among all others now that he was becoming an old man and had to piss every damn time he turned around. Prostatitis, was it? He buttoned his shirt, tightened the knot of his Burberry tie and slid into an overcoat, 44 short. He locked the door to the executive suite as he left, and removed the security card from his wallet. With four flights of stairs before him, he hoped his heart was up to it.

She was waiting on the landing, looking poised and properly apologetic for being the first to arrive, watching as he—huffing and puffing like a bulldog—climbed the last three steps to the hospital's mechanical penthouse. It was his oasis on the prairie, the only place where he could escape the phone, the constant medical staff interruptions and the festering problems that clung to him like barnacles.

Fourteen

From the kitchen window of the Runyans' apartment, Donna watched Brigid's rusting Ford van pull away from the curb onto the snow-crusted street with Christine, lost in a bundle of blankets, secured in the passenger seat. The nurse noted the time: 6:35 AM, and wondered how backed up the ER might be on a Saturday morning.

Across the room, Anya sat slack-faced at a card table cluttered with scrapbooking supplies—acid-free paper, glue sticks, crimping scissors and *Alphadotz* stickers. A shoebox held several hundred photographs with a few snapshots, marked and dated, set aside.

"What have we here?" Donna peered through bifocals over Anya's shoulders. "Is that your daddy?" She studied the younger image of Trevor, bulked up in a football uniform with his arm around a dimpled Christine in a cheerleading sweater. She turned over the photograph and read someone's careful printing: **Homecoming, Muskee High School, 1989**. "So your mom and dad were high school sweethearts, just like Jerry and me."

Anya said nothing.

"Will you look at this?" Donna reached for another snapshot of Christine, this time lost in layers of white lace next to Trevor, bow-tied and grinning from the window of a Chevy Silverado truck. **Just Married, 1996**. "You were just a sparkle in their eyes then, Anya."

The little girl looked up but kept silent.

"Here's somebody you might recognize." Donna studied a photo of Brigid holding a newborn blanketed in pink. "What a beautiful baby!" She turned over the photograph. **Anya, 4 days old, 1997**.

The last snapshot made Donna smile. **Anya fishing with BG, 2001**. "A sunnie that big had to come out of a Minnesota lake."

"What's wrong with Mommy? Is she really sick this time?" Anya's bare legs fidgeted under the folding chair. "Is she gonna die?"

"Goodness, no. Is that what you've been thinking? We just need to do everything we can for your mommy, and that means a doctor's look."

"What will he do to her?" The child squinted.

"Oh, maybe some blood tests. Things that can only be done in a hospital."

"Mommy hates being in the hospital. She told me so. Says she's scared." Anya's voice lowered to barely a whisper. "That makes me scared."

"It's only scary because it's unfamiliar. Not at all like being at home, that's for sure." Donna knew her assurances did little to convince a child, or adults for that matter. The media was making such a fuss about hospital safety. Just the other night an ABC news reporter said that one person in California dies every hour from an avoidable hospital error. Donna wondered if the young reporter had ever been in a hospital. Ever seen human tragedy in its rawest form? Ever walked in the shoes of hardworking staff who pulled patients from the jaws of death? You never heard such outlandish hype from the tongue of Jim Lehrer!

"Anya, do you know what most hospital patients complain about? I mean, besides missing their family?"

The child peeled back the adhesive on an *Alphadotz* sticker and stuck it on a card.

"It's the food. *Nobody* likes hospital food." Donna chuckled. "Too bland, too cold, too late, too much, too little. Too. . . healthy."

"Mommy doesn't get to eat any food. Except in bags."

"Uh huh." Donna shifted her weight from one foot to the other, embarrassed that a child had to remind her of Christine's solid food restriction. "And what's more, they complain about people in and out of their rooms at all times of the day and night. Doctors they don't always know or like."

"Mommy likes her doctor."

"Well, isn't that a good thing?" Donna wasn't about to challenge the notion of someone liking Dr. Lavelle. Takes all kinds to fill a world. She supposed everyone had a good side. Even a rascal like Lavelle.

"Will you play with me?"

"Well now," Donna put her hands on hips. "What would you like to play?"

"We could play 'doctor.' I have a doctor's bag. Daddy found one for me."

"Did he now? Well, I'd like to see that special bag. Maybe there's something in there I can use."

"There is!" Anya's voice bloomed with enthusiasm. "Little Mermaid Band-Aids from the drugstore. And a pointy thing like you use. And something really, really pretty. I'll show you." Anya scampered off to her bedroom.

How quickly a child's fancy can change. Donna pursed her lips as she took stock of the room, with her *cleanliness-is-next-to-godliness* principle in mind. The place was near disaster. Piles of dirty laundry. Nauseating smells from Christine's bedroom. Probably rotting food in the fridge. How can people live like this?

Anya reappeared with a small plastic doctor's bag and a pleading look. Donna recalculated. The medical documentation could wait. Just a little tidying up was definitely in order. Doing the bare minimum wouldn't take long and it would make everyone feel better.

"Let's pick up around the house first, make it nice for your mommy when she comes home. We'll make a game of it, and when we're all done, we'll play doctor or nurse or whatever you call it."

"O----kay," the child sighed. "But I get to be the doctor; you be the patient. I know where your heart is. Can I listen to it?"

"Work comes before play, Anya." Not that there was any evidence of that rule in this apartment. "Work hard, play hard; that's what we'll do for the rest of the morning."

In the haste of the morning's activity, Donna realized no one had removed the rechargeable battery pack from Christine's infusion pump. She plugged the battery pack into a wall outlet, amused at the new disciple of technology she was becoming. When Christine returned home, the pump would be ready to go for the next infusion. She closed the sliding closet door in the bedroom where boxes of TPN solution were stacked. Before turning off the light, she gave the bedroom one last critical look. How gratifying an ordered room could be once it had a proper woman's touch.

"Where do you suppose I should throw this?" Donna asked, pointing to a Hefty garbage bag of waste she'd collected from every basket in the apartment.

"Daddy puts it downstairs where the washer machine is." Anya motioned Donna to follow, leading her to the apartment door. "My new bike's down there, too. I'll show you. BG bought me a purple bike with pink streamers."

As the door opened, a wave of stale air drifted upward. Donna's nose twitched as she dragged the garbage bag without noticing the dark form that appeared in the doorway. A split-second later, her eyes locked on the stranger. Instinctively, she wrenched Anya away from the door.

"Hi, Buddy." Anya wrestled free of Donna's grip. "He lives across the hall."

Donna swallowed audibly and studied the stranger. He wore navy sweatpants and a purple sweatshirt with "Vikings" stamped across his vast chest. The hood nearly concealed his deeply-set eyes. He said nothing as he rocked back and forth on his heels and toes. Back and forth. Back and forth.

"Did you know we had a really, really bad storm last night, Buddy?"

"Where's Brigid?" Buddy moved a few steps forward and rubbed his thumb and fingertips together.

"Not here." Anya reached for the doorknob as if to signal it was about to close. "Come back when Daddy gets home."

His Spock eyebrows seemed sad rather than menacing but it was Buddy's lip-smacking that finally enabled Donna to put two and two together. The same sounds, repetitive movements of Doc Kunkel's son—the one who spent most of his life in the state hospital. She loosened her grip on the garbage bag and let it collapse on the floor.

"Need my pills." Buddy said. "Need my pills."

"Gotta wait for BG. She's got your pills. You go back down the basement and wait," Anya said sternly as though she were the adult in charge. The door closed and Buddy was out of sight. "C'mon, Donna, let's play." She took the nurse's hand and led her into the kitchen. "Buddy is, you know, kinda . . . um. . . ." She pointed a finger to her head and made a circular motion in the universal cuckoo gesture. "Don't be scared. He won't hurt us 'long as he takes his pills."

Let's hope so, Donna thought as she stepped around the garbage bag to lock the apartment door. Her aching knees could use a sit-down and her courage, a cup of strong coffee. It was 8:40AM and already she was exhausted. But the best way to beat a case of nerves was to stay busy. With Anya's help, she changed the bed sheets, straightened the quilt and wiped watermarks from the night stand in Christine's room. She dusted and polished, scoured and swept. Someone had apparently traipsed into the apartment during the night, soiling the carpet with winter sludge from the entry all the way to the bedrooms. She pushed the old Dirt Devil across the threadbare carpet while Anya followed on her heels, swinging the cord as if it were a jump rope.

Just then Brigid stormed through the front door. In her bulky jacket and Sorel boots, she looked like a Himalayan Sherpa guide from a PBS special. Anya ran to her, burying her face in the soft folds of her aunt's jacket. The worried look on Brigid's face signaled bad news, and Donna knew that her nursing instincts had been on the mark.

"Your mom's in the hospital, Kiddo. Your daddy needs to stay there for awhile. I'm here to take care of you, Baby." Brigid carried the child into the tidied living room and did a slow 180 degree scan. "What's happened to this place?" She turned toward Donna. "You've been cleaning? I don't believe it! What's the matter; don't we live well enough for you?"

"Well, I was just trying to be helpful. Anya and I . . . I'm sorry if I've appeared to be. . ."

"Snooping around in other people's business, that's what you were doing."

"I'm sorry, really, I thought with all this family has to deal with, I might help out with . . ."

"You can leave now. We do the best we can, Trev and me. I'm here. I'll look after things. We don't need you anymore. Go. I told Chrissy she shouldn't have called you in the first place."

Anya shoved a thumb into her mouth while Donna quickly gathered up her nursing bag and coat.

"Good bye, Anya. I'm sure your mother will be home before long, dear. Thanks for all your help this morning."

"We didn't get to play doctor. You promised. You promised." Anya turned her back and curled into the sofa.

"Another time, Anya. I'm so sorry." Donna turned to Brigid. "You can reach me through the agency if I can be of any help. I'm sure everything will turn out just fine for all of you."

By 8AM, Donna had skimmed over the compacted snowy streets back to her apartment where she collapsed in her La-Z-Boy rocker. The medical documentation she ought to be doing lingered in her mind like a snowdrift waiting to be cleared. But she was tired and her knees hurt. Rock-and-roll Buddy made another appearance in her mind. He'd certainly scared the dickens out of her. Remember to ask the pharmacist at Corner Drug what kind of medication caused this kind of movement disorder.

She didn't take many pills for just that reason: the side effects. For goodness sakes, she could use some relief for her aching knees, especially in this cold weather. Her joints had crackled like dry firewood earlier this morning when she'd knelt down to fetch the key under the floor mat where Christine had told her it would be. All that pain and effort, only to find the key wasn't there.

One *more* thing out of order in a household that seemed to be losing its grip. Donna snuggled deep in the chair, closed her eyes and waited for some blessed sleep to come.

Fifteen

Dr. Lavelle passed through the historic front doors of Swedish Hospital via the old red brick building, avoiding other options that were usually under construction. Nearly a century earlier, the original structure had been a sanatorium for tuberculosis patients, mostly Swedish immigrants. Since 1907, the core building had metastasized in every direction. The Jenny Lind Women's Pavilion unfolded to the north opposite an outpatient surgery center to the south. A state-of-the-art laboratory and Imaging Services spread to the west. The most recent building project, rumored to be a monument to Byron Bohley's legacy, was a seven-story cancer tower which the local newspaper regarded as "an architectural disaster and an insult to the pocketbooks of uninsured North Dakotans."

The wheels of medicine were already in motion. Gurneys, IV poles and wheelchairs rumbled by supply carts and mobile kitchen trolleys in noisy hallways. Docile patients said little, pale and disgraced in immodest gowns, as they were driven to their next conscription. *Any questions? None? Very well, let's get started then.* Family members waited passively, yearning for a word from the doctor, any doctor, on a weekend. Waiting for discharge orders and take-home medications. Fearing further delays. Hoping for better news than the last story shared by a stranger over bitter coffee in the family room. Fates compared. Best of luck, wished. Magazines discarded. Bibles opened. Life and death bridged by the work of mortals, elevated to the role of ministering angels in white.

Lavelle approached a central bank of elevators. He planned to reach the surgical lounge where he would shower, shave and slip on green scrubs before dealing with the Runyan situation on Six Main. With his pager on, his cell phone off, he waited for an elevator. It was slower than usual this morning. Elevators should be reserved for busy physicians, he silently argued, not for the general public. Not even for hospital employees. Is it any wonder that America is the fattest country on earth? Elevators were a health hazard, forcing doctors to mix with the sneezing-sick in one tight incubator of germs. He intended to blister the administration on this very matter in his next email to Byron Bohley.

When the heavy door eased back, Lavelle confronted an onslaught of hospital staff darting out as if *Flight of the Bumble Bee* buzzed in their ears. But he did not expect her—an apparition in Polartec, leggings and gaiters, sporting a long red scarf curled twice around her neck. A backpack slung over one shoulder. Her face beamed with a healthy glow.

"Dr. Lavelle." She seemed surprised to see him. "Good morning."

"Ms. Harri." He felt the few hair follicles on his scalp constrict as he uttered the name. "I expect to find you behind a drugstore counter, not dressed for . . . an Iditarod run."

The backpack began a slow slide off her shoulder and she repositioned it with an insouciant shrug. "Actually, I'm working weekends in the hospital pharmacy. Temporarily, of course."

"Pharmacy can certainly use the help." His eyes rolled back before his gaze washed over her, tip to toe. That she glanced down self-consciously had been so far his most satisfying pleasure of the morning.

"With a storm advancing, better to ski along the river than to trust my Saab on these roads."

"Adventurous of you," he said, checking his watch. *Skiing* during a snowstorm?

"Finns are born on skis. At least that's what my father believed. Flat-footed and fearless."

"And occasionally foolhardy, it seems."

A pause reigned as though she were measuring the angle of his insinuation. "Whatever it takes." Then, a slow nod. "Remember the Winter War of 1939?"

His own winter war was building around the Runyan case and clouding his interest in mindless chatter. He let her question drop and elbowed his way into the elevator, indifferent to etiquette where exiting trumps entering. As they passed across the threshold, her backpack brushed against him, knocking him slightly off balance. He watched as the sliding door attempted to close in her path before she foiled it with a hearty push. The door receded like an unworthy opponent.

Her don't-mess-with-me-shove was not lost on Lavelle who saw in himself the same purposeful tenacity. He wondered if the same pluckiness had anything to do with the scar that marred Heli Harri's inscrutable face.

***

Reuben Welle never seemed to tire of his ER job. On Saturday morning, Venkata understood why. He found the charismatic nurse holding court in the break room among a female contingent whose rapt attention he'd clearly captured.

"Excuse me for interrupting." Venkata opened the door slightly and nosed in through the sliver of space.

The room hushed.

"What's up, Doc?" Reuben wisecracked amid a backdrop of laughter.

"May I speak with you privately, Reuben?"

Reuben left the round table littered with Dunkin' Donut boxes and Styrofoam cups. "I'll finish the story later," he promised, rolling his eyes back in exaggerated suspense.

As the two stood in the ER corridor, Venkata wasted no time. "Christine Runyan is hospitalized on Six Main. I have located Dr. Lavelle and. . . ."

"Holy moley, if you found Lavelle on a Saturday morning, you deserve a better tag than 'Most Eligible Bachelor.'"

"Please be serious." The chief resident paused. "Do you remember if Mrs. Runyan came into hospital with a TPN infusion this morning?"

"Nope."

"Is that *no*, you don't remember, or *no*, she did not arrive with a TPN bag?"

"Christine Runyan," Reuben emphasized, "did not. Come. Into the ER. With. An infusion bag. Period."

"My memory as well. Thank you. You may go back to your . . . ."

"What's the big deal with the bag?"

Venkata dreaded any question for which he lacked an answer. "It is unimportant now. Had she come to hospital with a TPN bag, Dr. Lavelle wanted to see it. He must have his reasons."

Reuben looked around the hallway as though on the look-out for peeps. "Doc," he asked, closing in on Venkata, "about her admission. . . ."

"Yes?"

"I may be way out of line here, but people around the ER think there may be something funny going on in that household."

"Funny?"

"Not funny, *ha ha,* but funny like maybe something shady."

"Come to the point, please." Venkata expected Dr. Lavelle to arrive at any minute. There was no time to waste.

"Listen up, Doc. People around here are wondering why this woman has so many infections. One right after the other: January, February, March, and she's admitted every time. Always an infection of the central line. Kinda makes us wonder what's going on in that home."

"Do you mean her home health care may be inadequate?" Venkata still hadn't found the latest progress notes uploaded to the agency's medical record. Did such laxity extend to hands-on nursing care?

"Maybe, maybe not," he shrugged. "What about the family? They spend more time around her than anyone else."

"According to the chart, the husband—a paramedic—is the principle caregiver. Surely he knows the importance of sterile technique with an in-dwelling catheter."

"Sure, Trevor knows how to dress a wound, but what if . . . "

Venkata stared at the nurse and felt himself drawn into a tangled web of speculation spun by Reuben.

"Look, I'm just repeating what others are saying. Maybe having Christine in the hospital with a low-grade infection every so often is a benefit."

"What could you possibly mean—a benefit?"

"Think about it. She's never *that* sick, right? Just sick enough to get hospitalized so the insurance kicks in. After she's admitted, we load her up with spendy antibiotics and she gets better in a day or two. Everything's paid by her health plan: 24/7 care, TPN solutions, supplies, and two weeks' of take-home meds. Meanwhile, the husband, as they say, is 'free to pursue other opportunities.' "

"You cannot possibly be suggesting that the infection has been induced by Mr. Runyan?"

"I'm not suggesting anything, just telling you what everyone is saying. Her husband may have good reasons for wanting her admitted from time to time. It's less expensive for him when she's *in* the hospital than when she's home. No point having insurance if you don't get anything out of it."

Intentional cruelty was beyond Venkata's imagination. Too often in his career he'd encountered the darker side of human nature. Abuse sickened and confused him—innocent children, defenseless women, vulnerable adults, even patients who self-mutilated. His every waking hour had been devoted to keeping people alive at any cost while psychopathology drove others to inflict harm. It was this appalling irony he could not reconcile. Human motivation was vague territory better left to psychiatrists.

"Our attention must focus on the best care we can offer Mrs. Runyan. A proper assessment, detailed history, thorough examination and careful interpretation of her lab results. Your speculation is not helpful to that process, Reuben, and I suggest . . . ."

"Hey!" Reuben threw up his hands and backed away. "I'm only. . . ."

"I know," Venkata turned to leave, "you are only repeating what everyone else is saying."

The chief resident walked toward the stairwell with Reuben following close behind. As they turned the corner, Alayne Ludemann appeared with a clipboard cradled in one arm.

"Hello, again, Ma'am," Reuben brightened. "Doc and I were just consulting on the Runyan woman."

"I see." Alayne thumbed through several pages on the clip board. "According to my report, she's been admitted to Six Main. How does her case concern you, Reuben?"

Venkata stepped in. "I required his corroboration on a small detail." To the male nurse, he added. "You've been very helpful."

"How is she this time around?" Alayne asked the chief resident.

"I will know more when the lab results are back," he answered, reaching for his beeper. "I must go to her now. Dr. Lavelle is paging me."

"Dr. Lavelle, here on the weekend? An April Fool joke, right?"

Tired and annoyed, Venkata turned to leave. Six flights up, Dr. Lavelle waited. The chief resident took the stairs to compose himself for the inquisition.

***

"Christine, do you know where you are?" Dr. Lavelle asked softly as he leaned over the bed in 604.

She nodded, tears flooding her sunken eyes. "Where's Anya?"

"She's home with Brigid," Trevor said from the vinyl chair by her bedside. "Don't worry about her; she'll be just fine. When you feel better, I'll get her on the phone. She wants to talk to you."

"Don't leave me," she whispered to her husband, "bad dreams in the night. . . scared." Her eyes rolled back deliriously.

"Let her rest for now," Lavelle instructed Trevor. "I've examined her and I'm quite certain we've got another infection of the central line. I want to confer with Dr. Venkata," he explained to the husband who cracked his knuckles without making eye contact. "I'll speak with you again shortly."

In the corridor, Lavelle asked, "Have you located the TPN bag, Sandy?"

"No, sir."

"And why not?" Lavelle crossed arms over his chest.

"Mrs. Runyan did not come into hospital with an infusion bag. According to home health notes of last week, her TPN typically runs for ten hours, from 6 PM to 6 AM. Her cycle would have been completed before arriving at the hospital."

Lavelle considered the chief resident's explanation. "And so you never saw the bag, not even the empty bag?"

"I did not. Is it important? Perhaps the TPN bag remains in the home."

"Yes, well . . . ." Lavelle ran a hand through his hair still damp from a recent shower. "The patient is certainly ill, even incoherent. Odds are it's another *staph aureas* infection. You've started her on vancomycin?"

Venkata nodded at the conventional choice for treating gram positive infections.

"I want a CT scan of the abdomen."

The chief resident continued nodding.

"And I'm adding gentamycin for a possible gram negative infection from the urine," Lavelle paused, "and clindamycin for any anaerobes in her belly."

Venkata raised his eyebrows. His nodding stopped. "Before the cultures come back? Should we not wait to see precisely what microbe we are treating, Sir?"

"And have some nursing bureaucrat come by with her mumbo jumbo admission criteria, challenging us on why the patient is occupying a hospital bed without a comprehensive treatment plan?"

"But Mrs. Runyan is very sick! Certainly no one can think she should not be hospitalized? By tomorrow, the blood cultures will be read and we will know the specific pathogen."

"I will not wait twenty-four hours." Lavelle shot back. "I intend to cover all the bases on this case."

Maybe I am overtired, Venkata thought, mentally counting the hours he'd gone without sleep. Dr. Lavelle's aggressive approach eluded him. Such potent antibiotics seemed premature at this point. He looked directly at the senior physician and asked, "what am I missing, Sir?"

"You're thinking like a family practitioner. Simply treating the obvious. We're internists, you and I," he said like an older fraternity brother. "We're trained to think more broadly, to consider multiple causative agents."

When you hear hoof beats, think horses, not zebras. The

diagnostic aphorism drilled into the head of every first-year resident echoed in Venkata's mind. In disease, first look for ordinary explanations. Eliminate the simple explanations before grasping for elaborate ones. I'm hearing horses, Venkata concluded, not zebras. Is he testing me?

"Sir, with all due respect, you have cautioned me about the side effects of these drugs in the past. Very toxic. Renal failure, ototoxicity, severe colitis. Can we take such risks with Mrs. Runyan? It seems that in this case, waiting for the lab results is in her best interest."

Lavelle's face flushed with color. "Wait, Dr. Venkata? Did you say, wait?"

The chief resident swallowed, appreciating at that moment that the full consequences of disturbing Dr. Lavelle earlier in the morning had not been avoided, only delayed. Now was his trial by fire. Not a good time, he realized, to suggest an infectious disease consultation.

"Imagine this, Sandy. You're on the witness stand in a courtroom here in Fargo. Your patient, a young mother with a preschool child has tragically died while in your care. Some reptilian lawyer for the prosecution presents a tender photo of the once happy family at Christmas, and enlists the sympathy of every juror. Then he turns to you and asks if you did *everything* you could to save the young woman. You stammer and protest. The sleazy attorney screams, 'Answer the question.' By now, the jury is convinced you're a serial killer. Then he asks the question again, 'Did you do everything you could to save the woman,' and you say, 'No, I decided to wait.' 'A pharmaceutical arsenal of life-saving medicine at your disposal and you decided to wait?' 'But, your Honor,' you beg, and he says sternly, 'Answer the question,' and you admit, barely audible, 'Sir, I decided to wait.'"

It occurred to the chief resident to object, but he did not. He is treating a zebra, Venkata concluded, and I do not understand why. Defensive medicine, perhaps, but not without some risk for the patient. The two additional antibiotics might be indicated at some point, he could agree, but not now. If Christine Runyan's kidneys shut down or she goes deaf while on these medications, the case will surely come up for peer review before the hospital's Quality Committee. Horses and zebras would be an integral part of that discussion.

Lavelle rolled on. "After the jury rules for the plaintiff, the news of your incompetence is above-the-fold, headline news. Suddenly, your malpractice premiums double, and your career is essentially over. Your marriage fails, and financially, you barely scrape by conducting physicals for some life insurance company. You'll never see a real patient again. Why?" Lavelle paused. "Because you waited. Waited too long on one case that will haunt you for the rest of your life."

A worm of self-doubt burrowed through the usually keen mind of the chief resident. He thought of his parents in India and the shame that he might bring to them.

"Sandy," Lavelle directed, "write the orders for clindamycin and gentamycin, stat. Stay on the case; call me if her condition worsens. I'll explain the situation to Trevor."

Venkata removed Christine Runyan's chart from the wall rack and slowly thumbed through the pages to the last entry in the progress notes: his. He probed every corner of the Runyan case for a solid reason to avoid ordering the medication. Oblivious to the hallway commotion of morning rounds, he leaned against the wall with his head thrust back and closed his eyes. What am I missing in this case?

***

Lavelle returned to room 604 where Christine was sleeping. The vertical blinds on the window had been drawn tightly closed and the room was unusually dark for ten o'clock in the morning. Trevor had positioned his chair near her bedside, and he leaned forward, elbows on his knees, chin cupped in his hands, watching the rapid, shallow breathing of his wife.

"Dr. Venkata briefed me on the events of this morning," Lavelle said. "The home health notes haven't been recorded yet, which is par for this hospital," he noted with a trace of sarcasm, "so I've had to rely on the chief resident for the facts."

Trevor didn't turn away from Christine.

"Although I expect this is yet another infection of the central line, we're not taking any chances with your wife's health. We'll be adding some more antibiotics, and if pharmacy surprises us by actually getting the IVs prepared quickly, Christine should improve markedly."

"Does this have anything to do with the new infusion bags?" Trevor asked.

"Certainly not." Lavelle closed the door of 604. "Absolutely not."

"Then why the recall? The big rush? Your middle-of-the-night call?"

"Come now, Trevor," Lavelle approached him. "You know the government. Probably a misspelled word on the label or something equally ludicrous."

Trevor said nothing, watching Christine's delicate rib cage rise and fall in quick, gauzy breaths.

"There have been too many of these infections, Trevor. Can you shed any light on this?"

"What do you mean?"

"I'm simply asking you to consider the frequency of Christine's infections and whether you might have anything to say about it."

"Sounds like an accusation. Like I'm not taking good enough care of her."

"Trevor, Trevor," Lavelle's tone warmed, "control yourself. We're on the same side. We both want Christine to get better, don't we?"

The husband looked as though he were fighting back tears.

"You did take care of the GEM infusion bags as I instructed?" Lavelle asked quietly. "You destroyed them, right?"

"I said I'd take care of it."

"Go home, Trevor." Lavelle advised. "Let Christine rest. Get some sleep yourself. We'll call you if anything changes."

Sixteen

A rough-hewn pine slab wobbled on the wall of Corner Drug as Heli Harri slammed the back door into the dispensing area: *One's own home, one's own master*. It mattered to her, this Finnish proverb.

"Hey, Jayson, thanks for coming in early." Heli wiggled out of her polar fleece and unlaced her boots. "I had no idea when I'd be able to leave the hospital."

"Busier than a squirrel on speed," the part-time pharmacist grinned, shaking a prescription bottle filled with pink bubblegum liquid.

His smile was generous like the happy hippo's from Heli's Moomin storybooks. Working odd shifts, tackling software glitches, charming blue-haired ladies who wanted a man-druggist: that was Jayson. Hiring him might have been the best decision she'd made since opening Corner Drug in 1997. By fall, he'd be gone, on his way to Michigan for graduate work in medical informatics. A quick outie, he called it, before returning to North Dakota.

A line of amber vials waited on the high counter. Migraine meds for Mrs. Wallace. Valproic acid for Theresa Upton who'd had a grand mal seizure in front of the vitamin display less than a month ago. Prenatal vitamins for Becky Hager who'd spent three years and fifty-five thousand dollars on infertility treatment. Viagra for Mr. Cameron, the school superintendent.

"Better living through chemistry." Jayson shrugged as he moved to the computer to prepare a label for the pink suspension. "How come every kid in town is named 'Emily?'"

Jacob, Joshua, Samuel or Tyler if a boy; Madison, Hannah, Sarah or Emily if a girl. Heli wondered how many times she'd typed those names onto pediatric labels. Her own child, had she/ he lived, would not have been given such a prosy name. Maybe a *Liisa*, or a *Jussi*. Strong Finnish names from the legends of the Kalevala.

The telephone rang. Heli reached to answer but Jayson intercepted. Liberated from the call, she flipped through the morning mail searching in particular for an envelope from her accountant. Clyde Erickson, CPA, held the answer to the question that dogged her day and night: how much longer must her weekends of moonlighting continue to keep Corner Drug open? "A troublesome negative trend," he'd reported after reviewing the store's financials at the end of last year. "Revenue is up but your gross margin is eroding. You'll have to live without a salary for awhile longer, and if business doesn't turn around, you'll need an infusion of cash to sustain operations."

"We'll have it ready by the time you get here, Mrs. Danielson. Remember to bring your insurance card. *Eeeeyup.* We need to see it ev-er-y time." Jayson dropped the phone in its cradle. He lifted a large bottle of Prozac in a *cheers* gesture, and poured green and white capsules onto the counting tray. "You pharming at Swedish again tonight?"

"Unless I find a passport out of debt, and I don't see one in today's mail."

His shoulders tossed a 'whatever' expression as more pills rolled joyfully across the tray.

She paused to read the headlines of *Pharmacy Times*: average prescription costs rise by twelve percent. "With any luck, I'll get off to a better start tonight now that the storm has passed. I was backed up on IVs from the get-go. Same with the chemo infusions. Loads of ER scripts." Stifling a yawn, she continued sorting through the mail. Drug invoices, pharmaceutical promotions, FDA recalls. A few envelopes containing customer payments. Hardly anyone paid their bills on the first of the month anymore. Still nothing from her overdue accounts. Erickson had specifically inquired about the Runyan balance. With any luck, the accounts receivables would be down by the tenth, and Erickson's projections, up.

"You look totally fogged." Jayson poured red cough syrup into a four ounce bottle. The scent of wild cherry bark drifted across the room. *Prunus Serotina:* the smell of bitter almonds. "Time for some serious shut-eye, Boss. Murlene will be here any minute." He turned a child-resistant cap on the bottle until it clicked. "A question before you head upstairs. Should I put Murlene on the St. Urho display or have her check in the cosmetics order?"

Heli rubbed her forehead gently. In her mind she pictured Murlene—her Southern belle clerk who'd been transplanted from Georgia to North Dakota forty years ago by an Air Force husband—teetering on a step stool in the storefront window where purple and green streamers framed the hero of Finland, St. Urho. The display lampooning the Irish had actually drawn curious traffic into the store. But customers walking along Devine Street would expect an Easter display now that March 16 had passed. Soft bunnies and fuzzy baby chicks should be replacing frogs and grasshoppers. Heli smothered a yawn. The cosmetic shelves were full of holes and needed restocking.

"Empty shelves don't sell. Ask Murlene to tag the merchandise." Another yawn. "St. Urho and his frogs have center stage for a few more days." She glanced at the clock. "If I'm not downstairs by 4 PM, call me."

She left through the back door of the prescription area and climbed one flight of stairs to her apartment over the store with her new key ring in hand. Last summer, all of the locks in the turn-of-the-century building had been changed and wired. Although seven months had passed, she hadn't completely adjusted to new security habits or the monitored surveillance of the building.

"Is the expense really necessary?" she'd asked Officer Tim LaDuke the evening of the break-in last August.

"Look," the investigating officer had said firmly, "a single woman sleeping alone over a half million dollars of bennies, ludes, percs, z's, not to mention the barbs, the bulls, the speed, the XTC, . . . a good lick for every gutter junkie in this town. A druggie's Disneyworld. Understand? Once violated," he'd said in a cocksure voice, "you'll learn to think like a criminal. You'll be watching for signs of B & E, any evidence of intrusion."

The key turned stubbornly in the lock. When the door creaked open, the taffy scent of over-ripe bananas welcomed Heli home. Sunlight poured into the small living area from two east windows overlooking Devine Street. The room was quiet. An imitation leather loveseat and mismatched side tables—cast-off furniture from Murlene's latest divorce—were undisturbed. A Formica table with chrome legs near her tiny kitchen still held fly-tying equipment: a sturdy vise, tying bobbins, her father's bodkin, hackle pliers and the giraffe neck lamp she required for her exacting hobby. The single small closet was more than adequate for her sparse wardrobe. Books, mostly botany texts and medieval prose, remained in the order she'd left them with a heavy layer of dust intact. In the small bathroom, she drew back the shower curtain surrounding the claw-footed bathtub. No bloody bodies. Satisfied, she closed the slatted blinds on the windows to darken the room.

LaDuke had been the first officer to arrive on the scene that warm summer evening after the drugstore's security alarm, wired into the police station, had sounded shortly after midnight. Heli waited, terrified, as the tall, intense officer prowled the aisles panther-like. She followed, barely able to match his long strides. A crow bar lay in a puddle of glass where the perpetrator had entered by breaking a side window. He inspected the rear steel door that opened to an alley. "All exterior points of entry into this building should have sensing contacts." LaDuke looked up to the sign over the prescription counter. "Where do you keep the narcs?"

An old bank safe in the dispensing area housed the Schedule II controlled substances. LaDuke seemed impressed by the massive vault with its two locks, one key, one combination. When activated, it released an elaborate bolt mechanism sending out steel rods in all directions, securing every side of the door. He'd dropped to his knees to study the lock mechanism, turning the dial clockwise, then counterclockwise, listening to the clicking mechanism. "Damn," he'd exclaimed, "no one's gonna haul this beast out of here anytime soon." Then, he'd leaned his ear toward his shoulder to catch a radio report: a 10-15, prisoner in custody.

"The second officer caught our perp near the river. He'll be spending some time as a guest in the county hotel. We'll want a statement from you, Heli. About the security matter, here's the thing. Bad guys don't like lights, and security systems cut down their interest in B & E. Show me the apartment; show me the basement."

So she'd complied with the advice of LaDuke, not because she could afford the additional expense of security monitoring. Not because she was one to take precautionary advice from an insistent, albeit handsome policeman. Not because he'd been the first man in her apartment since moving to Fargo. It was because Sean had demonstrated, at such great cost, what an addict will do for his habit. By mid-September, an updated electronic intrusion detection system was in place. Alarm buttons near the computer terminals, the cash registers and under the prescription counter were linked directly to law enforcement.

Heli shed her work clothes into a wicker hamper and pulled a cotton sleep shirt from the bureau. She needed sleep desperately, to reach REM stage as soon as possible. She opened the closet doors and a Murphy bed catapulted onto the floor. She propped feather pillows against the headboard and crawled under the soft duvet. A tray with buttered toast and herbal tea—a blend of chamomile and hibiscus—balanced on her lap. To the steaming tea she added tincture of valerian, precisely fifteen minims. Sleep would follow reliably.

The phone rang twice downstairs followed by the remote sound of Jayson's hello. A busy phone was a good sign; perhaps her business was turning around after all.

She always knew she'd open a pharmacy someday, be the

master of her own house, without the corporate edicts, politics, the merciless bottom-line mentality of the chains. The charming two-story brick building on the corner of Front Street and Devine in the gentrified area of Fargo had enticed her when she'd first arrived in 1996. The Jade Garden, Latte Da, The Hungry Mind—an independent book store, and Second Time Around, an upscale consignment shop, had already opened. Swedish Hospital was less than two miles away. And there was no drugstore in the immediate area. Downtown beckoned her.

Eight months later, after miles of paperwork, credit reports and meetings with loan officers, the green neon sign that hung over the entrance to Corner Drug was finally illuminated. The first dollar bill from the Chamber of Commerce, framed and ceremonial, had come easily. Every dollar since had been a struggle.

Heli yawned. She rolled over in bed, turning her back from the sliver of light that penetrated the blinds. The valerian root extract had made her drowsy, but anxiety floated freely in the slim middle space between waking and sleeping. Another Wal-Mart expansion in West Fargo with 24-hour pharmacy service. Legislative cuts to Medicaid payments. Mail-order pharmacies eroding her business. Busloads of patients motoring to Canada for cheaper, untested drugs.

She drew the duvet over her head like a child hiding in a cloister of goose down. In another seven hours she'd be back in the hospital pharmacy, preparing IVs and filling in-patient orders, with the ever-present possibility of being summoned to a code. And now it seemed that her job included scolding physicians for using dangerous abbreviations. What a warped use of her time! Still, the liquid chocolate voice of Venkata sweetened the thought. *Will you be around hospital later this evening? Perhaps we can talk over a coffee?* Venkata. Before leaving the hospital pharmacy this morning, she'd logged onto the hospital's website to read about Sandeep Venkata. Chief resident. Medical school in India. Rhodes Scholar. Fetching smile capable of bending the will of a wary Finn.

Thirty minutes since she'd last checked the clock, and still no sleep. Heli closed her eyes and resorted to her usual sleep-inducing tricks. No wooly lambs jumping over fences in springtime. Mnemonics instead. Word games learned at her mother's knee. *Kingdom, Phylum, Class, Order, Family, Genus, Species.* Kids Prefer Cheese Over Fried Green Spinach. *Mercury, Venus, Earth, Mars, Jupiter, Saturn, Uranus, Neptune, Pluto.* My

Very Easy Method: Just Set Up Nine Pumpkins. As she'd sailed from high school through pharmacy college, the devices matured. Moh's hardness scale, from soft to hard. The twelve cranial nerves. International Classification of Hazardous Substances. Geologic Time Periods. Heli pulled the pillow over her face, unable to corral her mind from code protocols and emergency drugs on the crash cart. Maximum dose of Bretylium? Thirty five milligrams per kilogram over twenty four hours. Conversion from pounds to kilograms? . . . Drip rate? . . . The last code at Swedish had been a gunshot wound and . . . .

She bolted upright in bed, turned on the lamp and opened the drawer of her bedside chest. It was still there, her Glock .40 Model 27, hidden in a nest of black lace from Victoria's Secret. So far, neither had been essential to her life in Fargo. Still, master of one's home required measures beyond locks and sensors. One had to be prepared for every possibility. Satisfied, she doused the light and nestled under the duvet, sliding deeper into the bed. Her eyes finally closed without the need for more word games, and her lips settled into an impish smile.

***

Venkata imagined a luxurious sleep like the carefree slumber of his boyhood in Mumbai, when all the troubles of the world fell upon the shoulders of adults, and his child's soul was free of temporal burdens.

He made the long walk from Six Main to the backwater area of the hospital in hopes of finding an unoccupied sleeping room reserved for exhausted residents. If he were lucky, #5 might still be available. Although all six windowless rooms were generically equipped with a single bed, a small television and a standard issue bedside table, #5 contained the thermostat that controlled the temperature of the other rooms.

The door to #5 was closed and the raspy snore of another resident, a western North Dakota native who preferred a sixty degree sleeping environment, left Venkata with few choices. He entered #4 and braced for the stone cold floor under his feet. Shivering, he crawled under the blankets.

Details of the Runyan case bounced around in his mind like the Brownian motion of suspended particles. Unable to sleep, he sat up in bed, pulled a hooded sweatshirt over his head, and reached for Harrison's *Principles of Internal Medicine* that someone had left in the room. He read Section 2, "Basic considerations in infectious disease" and Section 4, "Approach to therapy for bacterial disease." Finally he reviewed Section 6, "Alterations in gastrointestinal function."

Unsatisfied, he threw back the bed covers. Eleven AM: too late for breakfast in the cafeteria, too early for any lab results, too frigid in this room for sleep.

He bypassed the residents' lounge, teeming with people and their personal weather testimonials, and headed for a study carrel in the hospital library to scour journals for articles pertinent to the Runyan case. To know what he did not know. To reach beyond his present level of understanding. Only then might he sleep.

The library was unusually quiet. Venkata logged onto the National Library of Medicine and searched for articles on sepsis in patients with indwelling vascular catheters. Three hundred sixty-nine hits appeared. He scrolled through the abstracts, clicking his way to relevant articles. He reviewed the drug monographs of gentamycin and clindamycin in the *Physician's Desk Reference.* He searched WebMD for new information reported on Crohn's disease. An hour later, the screen became a spectacle blur. How did Dr. Lavelle stay on top of this staggering amount of information? He marveled at a mind that seemed to process information like a Pentium chip.

One last detail. He logged into the home health agency's medical record system. Would the documentation be there on his third try of the morning? The blinking cursor waited for his password. He entered - s a m b h a r - pigeon pea with vegetables—the spicy stew of his youth. Something he would never forget.

The screen opened to a medical chart format. Venkata typed in Christine Runyan's name and verified her date of birth. Seconds later, his patient's chart appeared. A new entry dated 04/01/02; excellent! His breathing quickened at the prospect of new information.

One click, and the nursing progress notes of Donna Wadeson, RN, appeared, describing in clear detail her early morning visit to the Runyan home. The note had been entered in a standard medical SOAP format: a brief history of the illness as told by the patient, followed by details of the nurse's physical exam, her assessment and her plan to refer the patient to the ER. DW's assessment was entirely consistent with Venkata's impression of Mrs. Runyan as she'd presented in the ER. The nursing notes included this observation: "the TPN bag was empty and I removed it."

"The bag; did you discard it? Do you know where it is at the moment?"

"Sure do. Right here in my go-bag." Venkata heard the ruffle of papers and a zipper slide along metal teeth.

The chief resident heaved a sigh of relief. Maybe now he'd be able to sleep. "I will need the bag."

"This shriveled old bag? Sure, I was about to toss it in the dumpster."

"If you please, I will need it today." Venkata was overreacting and he knew it, but the desire to please Dr. Lavelle was strong. Any chance to restore lost credibility was irresistible.

"You seem like a pleasant young man, not an egomaniac like some I could name, expecting nurses to drop everything when they call. I suppose I can make a special trip," she hesitated. "Tell you what. I was shoveling so I could drive over to Corner Drug to get something for my sore knees. I could bring the bag to the hospital later this afternoon." Donna paused. "If you don't mind me asking, why do you need the TPN bag?"

Before he could answer, she blurted out, "Did I make a mistake?"

I'm asking myself the same question, Venkata reflected, but avoided an answer because his mind was suddenly alive with new possibilities. "I will meet you at Corner Drug at 4 PM."

For the first time in the day, Venkata smiled as he nestled under the covers in the chilly sleeping quarters of room #4. A most interesting day unfolded in his mind. Later, he would wait in a drugstore to receive a parcel from a woman who sounded old enough to be his *maamoo*. It had the dark comedy of a nefarious drug deal. Considerably more pleasant was the prospect that Heli Harri might be working behind the pharmacy counter. That fond image finally transported him to the warm, lush sleep he craved.

Seventeen

When Byron Bohley swiped his card through the electronic reader, he noticed that the reinforced steel door to the hospital's rooftop had been wedged open by a pen with Averill Pharmaceutical's advertising on the barrel. By God, he'd yank the Buildings and Grounds manager into his office for a come-to-Jesus-meeting on this breach of security. Write up the infraction and put it in his personnel file.

The CEO leaned his weight against the door and stepped out onto the snow-covered asphalt. Alayne followed closely behind. With six inches of snow, he wished he'd worn his Gore-Tex boots. Then he saw the footprints.

"Bohley! Miss Ludemann!" The voice came from the southern corner of the penthouse roof, beyond the air-handling HVAC units and the electrical switch gear. Dr. John Dahl, the hospital's chief of pathology, peered through a 35 mm Leica M rangefinder camera positioned on a tripod. "What a pleasant surprise to see the two of you in my viewfinder. It should be a stunning photograph, although it would be better if I'd used a graduated filter to color the background. The sky's a bit dull today."

Bohley glanced sideways in Alayne's direction and willed her to say something trite. Weren't nurses good at this sort of thing? She returned his look but said nothing.

"I should have been here earlier for better sun. Sharper contrast for the hoarfrost on the trees." Dahl nodded as he looked toward the east. "You're not from around here, are you, Byron?"

"Uh, no."

"Have you ever seen a more stunning landscape? This horizon is the best kept secret in America."

Bohley remembered Dahl's award-winning black and white photographs gracing the corridors of Swedish Hospital. Did every Tom, Dick and Harry have access to the penthouse? He hadn't realized just how porous security was. Suppose some nutty pathologist emptied a vial of germs into the air-handling system up here on the roof? No wonder he was paranoid.

"Sorry to have interrupted your creative process, Dr. Dahl. Miss Ludemann and I are here to check out the air-handling system. Best to do it on a Saturday morning, we thought."

Alayne nodded with a well-practiced smile.

Dahl looked in the distance where the newly fallen snow frosted the cottonwood trees along the river. "I see." He removed the Leica from its tripod. "I certainly can't speak for other departments, Byron, but I don't believe we'll need air-conditioning in the lab quite this early in the year. June, maybe." The pathologist gathered up his camera equipment and proceeded toward the door. He glanced at his watch. "Better return to the lab. Always a diagnostic mystery waiting under the lens of my microscope." He looked back with a prying smile. "My photograph of the two of you: would you like a copy made?"

Bohley understood the innuendo and smothered a response. When the door closed behind Dahl, the CEO exhaled slowly. Should he be worried about being seen with a foxy female manager in this ridiculous circumstance, or simply flattered? He settled on worry.

"Well, now that he's gone," Alayne said after an uncomfortable pause. She rubbed her mittened hands together.

How can she seem so unflappable, Bohley wondered, while he entertained the possibility of jumping off the roof? At two times his salary, the death benefit from his life insurance would keep Betsy comfortable for awhile. What if Betsy *and* Alayne had conspired to murder him?

"Let's go," he said, motioning to the door.

She touched his arm. "About Lavelle. What do you want me to do?"

He imagined what the hands under those mittens might be capable of. "Tighten the noose around the bastard's neck. I've lost my patience with him."

"And in return for my efforts?"

Her voice was soft but direct. He recalled a book he'd seen in an airport kiosk that described Alayne to a T. *Lions Don't Need to Roar*. So he'd been right after all. This was business to her, simply another transaction. "The year-end bonus wasn't good enough?"

"You were generous, Mr. Bohley, but now you're asking me to take some additional risk and I think it deserves an appropriate reward."

Hands down, women were better wheeler-dealers than men. Something about the way they can slide the knife right up under your spleen with a pretty pink smile on their face. The question incubating in his mind leapt from his tongue prematurely. "What drives you, Alayne?" This woman had more balls than any man on his staff.

"Someday when I'm not freezing to death," she shivered, "I'll be happy to share. It's your typical hard-luck story."

Bohley couldn't imagine what was coming next. Little house on the prairie?

"I want to be in the Board room with the big boys, Mr. Bohley. At the table where decisions are made, asking tough questions about the bottom line."

"That's it? No husband? Kids?" Not even a golden lab to come home to?

"I've had my fill of unfaithful men and snotty-nosed children." Her shivering stopped and her face turned serious. "After my mother ran off with a Methodist minister, my father crawled into a bottle of gin and I ended up raising two baby brothers. They were a handful." Her shutterfly smile beamed success. "One is a product liability attorney in Boise and the other, a financial planner, somewhere in Thailand."

Then she moved closer to the CEO and he knew what was coming next. The tips of his ears were freezing.

"My brothers and I know how to survive. That's why I agreed to do your dirty tricks, Mr. Bohley. In return, I want to be Swedish Hospital's first chief nursing officer."

Bohley reflected on the many times in his career when one bad decision had led to another. Here he was on another slippery slope. He'd have to create the position, justify it and find a reason to ignore other contenders who were more qualified. The medical staff would go berserk with another nursing bureaucrat. On the other hand, an ambitious nurse who might be his eyes and ears on the hospital wards could be useful to his administration. Correction: his *team*. *T*ogether *E*veryone *A*chieves *M*ore, like the consultant preached for a hideous fee. What the hell. It would be worth it if Alayne Ludemann was able to serve Lavelle's ass up on a silver platter.

"Get it done and we'll talk later."

Without another word, Bohley approached the door and started down the internal stairwell. Alayne followed. As the heavy door slammed shut, his timeworn ears did not pick up the slight click, perfectly timed with the door's closure, from the cassette recorder hidden in her jacket pocket.

Eighteen

Was it road rage, or was it because the snow crew hadn't bothered to clear the streets in the poor part of Fargo? From the window of the Runyan apartment, Brigid watched as Trevor's red Ford fish-tailed along Second Avenue, skidding over icy streets through piles of fresh snow. They should have given Chrissy the medicine by now. Chrissy will be all right, just like before. Soon Trev would bring home the news. He'd not bothered to call even though Anya was worried sick.

She'd been tending to his daughter most of the day, just like every other time Chrissy ended up in the hospital. Picking up the pieces seemed to be her calling in life. Good 'ol BG: always there for the rescue like a St. Bernard crossing mountains to drag a lost child home. That breed was becoming extinct; at least that's what she'd heard Peter Jennings say on the evening news. No use for dogs like that anymore.

He was carrying grocery bags from Stop-n-Shop. So he hadn't come straight home. Anya, who'd been building a fort in the front yard out of the moist snow, ran to him. Did he set the bags down to give her a hug? No. Just kept walking with the kiddo tagging behind, reaching in the grocery bags for a surprise. S'pose that meant no hugs for BG either. He used to though. Put his arms around me, gentle-like.

"Daddee's home!" Anya's squeal echoed down the stairway of the four-plex.

Brigid heard something about a Klondike sandwich as she opened the apartment door. "Just fed her an hour ago, Trev. Honest to God, I did. How's Chrissy?"

"Resting."

He was a man of few words. This, too, drove her crazy. Couldn't he let go with her once in awhile?

"Will Mommy come home soon? Can I call her? Can I send her an email? Donna said I could."

"Who's Donna?"

Brigid grunted quietly. Home health nurses come and go so fast he doesn't even recognize their names. She bit a hanging cuticle from her little finger. Just as well with this nurse. A nosy type.

"Donna's my new friend. But she didn't play with me like she said she would." Anya sighed. "Nobody does."

"Give your Daddy some space, kiddo. He's tired. We're all tired. We've been through this routine before."

which are usually unobserved."

Lavelle felt as though he had just been accused of being an interloper in an office whose rent he, not she, paid monthly. Perhaps Phyllis needed a reminder of that fact.

"I plan to spend the entire day here," she announced on her way to the office refrigerator where she placed her lunch bag next to a tray of vaccines. The room now smelled faintly of tuna fish.

"Despite the extra hours," she continued, reaching for his coat from the back of her chair, "it's becoming impossible to stay ahead of the insurance companies and their senseless requirements. My goodness, one wonders at the necessity of it all."

Lavelle had never really understood what she did all day. Hours of bickering on the phone, greeting cranky patients and poring over the blistering detail of the health care business. Some life. Hers must be the dreariest job in world.

Phyllis opened a locked file drawer and pulled out a stack of rejected insurance claims. With reading glasses propped on her nose, she spread a computer generated payment listing across her work space. Its minute rows and columns blackened the page.

"Devil's in the details, eh?"

"No," she said, "the devils are in the Board rooms and the executive suites and the Halls of Congress. Too many devils making greedy financial decisions that affect our patients. Despite all the talk about reform, the situation is getting worse instead of better. More complicated, more costly, more bizarre. It's all about money, isn't it, Doctor?"

"My sentiments, exactly." Lavelle nodded. "Speaking of insurance companies, what about this letter from Eastern Shore." He waved the letter in the air.

"The name was completely unfamiliar to me, except, of course, until it appeared in our mail this week."

"I don't understand," he said. "You must have prepared the original letter. They enclosed a copy." He shoved the letter her way.

She scanned the letter carefully with an intensity typically reserved for end-of-life matters. "No, Doctor, this is not my letter. I'm unfamiliar with either the company or this correspondence. I'll check my computer, but I'm certain the letter will not be there." She scrolled rapidly through a series of electronic folders. "No, just as I thought. Nothing here for this company." She looked up over her glasses. "I did not prepare this letter."

"No need to get defensive, Phyllis. I'm simply curious."

"Then what's this about?"

"Come here, little girl." Trevor lifted Anya and set her on the kitchen countertop. "Mommy's sick, but people at the hospital are taking good care of her. She sleeps a lot." His voice warmed when he talked to his daughter. "She asked about you. Wanted me to come home to make sure you were ok." He turned to Brigid. "And to give your auntie a break."

Can't he even say my name? Nope, not unless it's linked to a favor. 'Brigid, do this, Brigid do that. Brigid, can you help out? Brigid, take care of. . . .'"

He moved to the archway between the kitchen and living room, making a full-circle inspection of the space. "Wow! You've been busy cleaning up the place. The apartment hasn't looked this good since Christmas," he said, giving her a quick squeeze.

"No problem, Trev." She felt his touch long after it ended. "Helps to stay busy." To tell the truth, she was dog-tired, keeping the same late hours he was, but since when was her trouble worth asking about? Should she tell him now? No. Not yet. No way. "Chrissy's gonna be ok?"

"I think so. Seems to be another infection." Trevor opened the refrigerator door and placed a carton of milk on the empty shelf. "Suppose I should call your mother."

"I'll handle it." Brigid hesitated. Maybe now was the time. Anya was digging through the grocery bags like she'd been starved all day. Give her a bag of corn curls, and she'd be quiet for awhile. It might be the only chance she'd have to talk with Trev about the past forty-eight hours.

Someone knocked at the apartment door. Trevor peered through the peephole and opened the door. "Hey, Buddy" he said, "what's up?"

"Brigid. . . . here?"

"Yup. In the kitchen. Come on in."

Brigid felt Buddy's wild stare like a pair of rodent eyes in a ditch.

"Need my pills. No sleep." He rocked steadily. "Up all night. Heard somethun' 'n the basement."

Back and forth, back and forth, worse than she'd ever seen him move. Thought he might actually fall over. Hit his head against something.

"I heard something too, Buddy." Anya slid off the counter to the floor below and rushed to her father. "I really did, Daddy." She pushed the last corn curl into her mouth, leaving an orange mustache above her lips. "Not bats, though. In the hallway.

Funny, slippery noises."

Trevor knelt down, eye-level with his daughter.

He loves her, Brigid thought. No denying that. He's trying to be a good dad but what this kiddo needs is a mom. Someone who gets out of bed and plays Crazy Eights with her. Makes popcorn in the winter and S'Mores in the summer. Knows how to take a crappie off the hook. How come some people have kids and don't take care of them and me, wanting one so bad it hurts, ends up with nothing. No kids, nothing. It's not fair. How come?

"What you guys heard last night was me coming home to check on you and Mommy. You were sound asleep, Anya. A mighty brave girl with a bad storm outside." He walked to the far end of the kitchen where Buddy rocked near the refrigerator. "You've got to take your medicine, man. Every single night. If you miss even one dose, well, things go bad for you, Buddy. No good if you don't follow the directions. Got to do exactly what it says on the label. Understand me?"

"You heard what Trev said. He made the noise last night." Brigid tugged at a strand of hair falling in front of her eye. Did Trev care that she'd quit taking her medicine? No way. Chrissy gets all the attention in this house.

"Need . . . pills. Noises." Buddy looked at Brigid with eyes fixed and frightening. "You get my pills?"

She fidgeted for a moment. "Plumb forgot, Buddy. I'll pick up your refills soon as I can. Promise I will. I have to go to drugstore anyway. Quit worrying, will you?"

"You can count on BG. She takes care of all of us." Trevor almost smiled.

It was the closest thing to a compliment Brigid had ever heard from her brother-in-law. It just about made up for all the times she'd been taken for granted. Just about, that is. Ever since high school, she'd covered for Trev and Chrissy, lying to her parents about their whereabouts. Taking care of everybody, keeping everybody happy.

"Look, Buddy," Trevor continued, "Christine is in the hospital and we've got plenty to do, so go back home now. BG will get your pills like she always does. But you got to take them, hear?"

Buddy dropped his chin, turned and shuffled out of the apartment without saying another word.

When the door closed, Trevor shook his head. "He's sure a mess. You ever see him doing anything strange around here?" He placed a six-pack of Budweiser in the refrigerator.

So he'd stopped at the liquor store, too.

"He's spooky, all right," Brigid said. "Hulking around the basement, trailing Anya at every turn. You bet I'm worried with him around. Off his medicine, he sees things. Hears noises. What do you call that—hallucinating?"

It had to be now. No better time coming. Anya sat cross-legged in front of the television watching the Rugrats.

"Trev," BG asked, "you got a minute?" When her brother-in-law turned to listen, she let go. "I've got some problems. Job problems at the Jade." She heard his long sigh and wondered what it meant.

"They cut your hours, didn't they?" Trevor snorted mean-like. "I told you it was coming. That's what they do to avoid paying benefits."

Brigid felt like a fool for crying, yet tears poured from her tired eyes. How had Trevor known? His arms might have reached out to comfort her, but they didn't this time. "He cut my hours last week from forty to twenty-four. Right after my shift was over. Says he'll put me on an hourly wage so I can keep the job and the tips, but no health insurance. That little bastard! How can he do that? Cut my hours just so he doesn't have to pay insurance."

Trevor started to speak but Brigid cut him off. "I'm sorry, Trev. You don't need any more problems. I've been thinking. I figure I'll quit tonight, then talk to Mom and see if I can take over the Bait Shop in Muskee. She doesn't know a thing about night crawlers and fathead minnows, and we've got to get ready for the fishing opener in May. Since Pop died, she's let things go."

"I don't know, Brigid. You need some kind of real job with a decent salary and benefits. How can you make a living in Muskee?"

"I got some money coming in, maybe enough to buy Mom out."

"Not another part-time job. You know we need you here when Christine comes home."

"Yeah." Brigid looked down.

"Buying the family business is going to take more money than you have."

"Maybe, but I could get my old job back cleaning the funeral home at night."

Trevor clenched his fist. "Listen to me. Haven't I always said—you've got to find a job with health insurance? How much are you spending on your medicine?"

Brigid had to use both hands to count the number of

prescription bottles in her medicine cabinet. One, the allergy pills that had gone over-the-counter and were no longer covered by insurance. Two, the heartburn medicine they advertised on the six o'clock news. Three, the high-priced salve for psoriasis that covered her body. Four, pain pills for the awful itch. Five, her antidepressant and six, a new pill her shrink at County Social Services had just added this week for her spells. "Somewhere in the neighborhood of four hundred dollars a month."

"That's exactly my point! Jesus, how can you afford that without some kind of insurance?" Trevor paced back and forth in the small kitchen. "Why do you think I stay where I am? You think I don't have thoughts of busting loose, doing what I want to do, but I'm locked in a job because of the benefits. We could never pay Christine's bills without it, and I can't risk changing jobs because she might not get coverage with a pre-existing condition. That's their trick to avoid insuring you." He clenched his fists again, and cracked the knuckles of his fingers. "Like it or not, BG, you have to go where the benefits are."

"I'll figure it out, Trev." Why had she brought this up to him now? "That's why I don't want you to call Mom. No point in telling her everything right now. Bad luck's easier to take when you spread it out."

Trevor returned to the refrigerator and opened a Bud. If he'd just say something nice to me, BG thought, I wouldn't feel as awful as I do right this minute.

"Anya," BG continued, quietly, "I'd miss taking care of her. You know how close we are." After a long pause, she asked, "Could Anya come live with me in Muskee? I'd be good for her, Trev. Take real good care of her. Protect her. Be like a mother to her."

"Are you out of your mind?" Trevor shoved a kitchen chair against the table. "Don't ever say that to me again." He went for his jacket. "I've got things to do."

Their conversation was over. She watched him leave the kitchen and head for the bedroom that he shared with Chrissy. Moments later, she heard the closet door slam shut. Out he came carrying two cardboard boxes, heading for the apartment door.

"What you doing, Trev? Where you going? You mad at me?"

"Stop it. Get off my back. I can't take it anymore." He turned to his sister-in-law. "I'm going out for awhile. Can you stay with Anya?"

"Where you going?" Would he tell her if he was going to *her* house? That little love-nest he thinks I don't know about? I hear the hospital crowd at the Jade talking about him and what's-her-name with the plastic fingernails. I know about the fancy perfume you gave her on Valentine's Day. What about me? Well, I have my own now. Fancier bottle than hers. So there. She watched him chew the inside of his mouth like he always did when he got a case of the nerves.

"I'm taking these GEM boxes out to my truck. Got to get rid of them."

"Why you doing that, Trev? Trev? That stuff's expensive."

Anya jumped up, loosening herself from the Rugrat's grip. She edged toward the commotion in the hall. "Daddy?" BG grabbed her, clasping a pair of hands around the child's neck to stop her. "Daddy? What are you doing with Mommy's medicine?"

He turned around, his dark eyes peering over the boxes. "Mommy won't be needing this anymore. No more questions, honey. Trust Daddy on this one."

And then he was gone. Brigid wondered what she should do next.

Nineteen

His choices were few. Either a Royal Checker cab with a gnarly male driver or Lucky Lady Transport whose pensioners wore tuxedos over bulging bellies. Lavelle glanced at the clock in the hospital lobby: 2:30PM. After a bizarre night and a tense morning, he was ready to be home alone for what remained of the weekend. And he deserved to be chauffeured in style.

"I'll need a Town car," he said to a white haired, pink-smocked member of the hospital's volunteer brigade. "Can you arrange that?"

"Certainly, Doctor. And where will you be going?"

The request threw him into a metaphysical tailspin. Where *was* he headed on this particular Saturday? Toward professional Armageddon with Bohley and the hospital's Medical staff committee over the Exvantium silliness? To Federal prison on kickback violations for his involvement in the shady GEM Pharmacy business? Or to bed, wrapped in Egyptian cotton in his bedroom suite for a luxurious nap, alone and unavailable?

"27 Blenheim Heights," he answered with a tinge of embarrassment. Since Fargo lacked much altitude or the baroque architecture defining Churchill's grand estate, he considered the address to be another ridiculous example of prairie aspiration. Insinuating grandeur might have worked during the railroad days of Dakota territory when promoters, desperate to attract homesteaders, had overly romanticized the northern plains but now it seemed laughable. Claudette mightily disagreed, convinced the savvy positioning strategy still worked in the local real estate market.

The pink lady repeated the address into the phone. "Lucky Lady will be here in less than five minutes, Dr. Lavelle. I mentioned this was a priority. You look so weary. A long night?"

"Very."

"I can imagine the baffling cases that come your way. Mabel Gelling is a friend of mine. She credits you for being alive today."

"How very kind of you, and of course, Mrs. Gelling." He scrolled his memory for someone by that name. Ah, yes, the hypochondriac with nasty halitosis. "Mabel is an inspiring patient," he answered with the unctuous tone of a fundraiser. "But don't tell her. I'm not supposed to have favorites." Flattery warmed him. Yes, everything will be all right, he thought. Everything will be just fine for Mark Raymond Lavelle, MD. He glanced at his watch. "Thanks so much, Mrs. . . . ."

"Tronsgaard. Ruth Tronsgaard. My pleasure, Doctor."

"If I can ever be of service, please call my office and tell Phyllis to put you through directly. Don't put up with her protestations. No waiting for you."

"My goodness, Doctor. Thank you."

As the black Lincoln maneuvered through snow-crusted streets toward Pill Hill, Lavelle turned on his cell phone and punched Eddy's number.

"Eddington here. Is that you, Fargo?"

"I can't decide if I worry more, or less, when I don't hear from you." Lavelle did nothing to hide the smugness from his voice. "It's been hours. Can I assume you've managed your GEM crisis?"

"You can assume anything you damn well like," the voice hissed back. "The truth is that the Federal government doesn't work on Saturdays so we know nothing more than what I've already told you."

Eddy was a workaholic. The concept of a relaxing weekend completely eclipsed the imagination of his closest friend.

"Did you destroy the paper trail? Trash the TPN bags?"

"Drop the authoritative tone, Eddy. You hold nothing over me, and I am not obliged to take orders from you." Lavelle looked out the window as the Town Car veered around a tow truck disengaging a yellow Volkswagen bug from a confection of snow. The scene released a memory of lemon curd in a nest of meringue from Chez Marbella in Philadelphia. "Nevertheless, I've put the matter to rest." If only he were in Philly now, tasting the sweet life. "However, there may be a related problem."

"What kind of problem?"

Lavelle noted the faded luxury of the Lincoln's interior. Cracks in the leather, coffee stains on the carpet, a missing cap on the lock. No sliding panel of glass partitioned the back seat from the driver so he turned aside and lowered his voice. "I have a Crohn's patient, a young woman with a history of multiple bowel resections and short bowel syndrome who requires TPN."

"And . . .?"

"She's been on TPN for some time. Improving, actually, until rather recently."

"And. . ."

"She was admitted to our hospital this morning with fever and chills." Lavelle drew in a deep breath. "There's been a pattern of recurring infections in her case, but in light of the GEM recall, . . and *your* contamination problems, . . . and since she has been using *your* solutions, I. . . ."

"Sweet Jesus, why didn't you tell me sooner?" It was the reaction Lavelle expected. "Good god, Fargo, this is exactly what we don't need now."

"I'll be sure to tell her that, Eddy, although in her semi-comatose state, I doubt she'll care very much that she's ruined your day."

"What are you doing for her? Did you. . ."

"I'm not asking for an Oncology consult. I'm quite capable in my own right to care for this patient. It's likely another line infection, but I've broadened the spectrum of antibiotic coverage. She's being treated with big guns, not without some risk, I might add, to her eighty-five pound constitution. My chief resident is utterly discombobulated." He imagined by now that Venkata had thoroughly searched the Center for Disease Control's on-line library for documented case studies. "Relax, Eddy. Unlike your specialty, *my* patients tend to survive their hospital stay."

"Dammit! Do you have any idea how serious this is? There's been no other report of a GEM patient getting sick anywhere in the South, much less hospitalized, from our pharmacy products. This could mean the shit is rising around us. For once in your life, Mark, listen to me. Do not let anything happen to this patient! Understand? We need a damn quick recovery. Do what you have to do to make this issue go away. Spare no risk; accept no blame." He stopped and Lavelle knew it was for heightened effect. "This is bad, Partner. We didn't come this far together to be brought down by an incidental death in, of all goddamn fly-over places, Fargo, South Dakota."

The cabbie looked over his right shoulder, his toupee inching forward on his scalp, as he approached Lavelle's residence. "No way I'm pulling in there." He pointed to a sizeable snowdrift in Lavelle's driveway.

There goes your tip, Lavelle muttered silently. "I'll get out here." If some pharmacist had the derring-do to ski her way through a storm, he ought to muster the resources to scale a few snowdrifts to his back door.

To Eddy he replied, "I'll be in touch." The cell phone snapped shut.

Once inside the mudroom, Lavelle kicked off his boots and threw his jacket toward a wall hook. It missed and slumped to the floor. He noticed that the computerized security system panel by the door read, *zone faulted.* Somebody was in the house. Odd, he thought. His illusion of solitude was fading fast.

"Mark, is that you?"

Claudette's soap opera voice, florid and outré. He hadn't expected her back from Minneapolis until evening.

"Look at you, darling! Where *have* you been? The Caddy was in the garage. You, nowhere in sight. Our bed, still made. The phone ringing." She opened her arms to him. "You've been working, haven't you?" Claudette exuded the freshness of spring in a lettuce green sweater set and matinee pearls.

He kissed her on the forehead. "Working long hours to pay for everything you require to be comfortably nested."

"Why did a cab bring you home?"

"The subway was crowded."

"Silly you." Claudette moved into the kitchen and ran the cold water tap.

"Call someone about the driveway," Lavelle ordered. "We're the only home in the cul-de-sac with an impassable snow drift."

"Later," she replied over the sound of rushing water. "First, a word."

"Claudette," he sighed, "I am exhausted. I'm going to bed."

She followed him up the spiral staircase to their bedroom suite. "You *were* at the hospital last night, weren't you, Mark?"

Lavelle recognized the change in her tone. *Sotto voce.*

"Do you have some reason to doubt me?" The second time within an hour he'd endured unwanted interrogation.

"Of course not. It's just that . . . well. . . the phone was ringing incessantly when I returned this morning. Your accountant, what's-his-name? He said he'd been calling steadily since Friday afternoon."

"My accountant called me at home?" Lavelle flared. "I specifically instructed him not to disturb me here. Tell him to call my office and get in the queue with the rest of the masses."

"Yes, but that's exactly the point. He said it wouldn't be *wise* to call you at the office because it's a very delicate matter. Some accounting issue. I can't remember everything, but he used the word 'irregularities,' and he wanted to speak to you privately."

"Bean counters! Patients pour out sensitive health matters in my office, and he can't discuss accounting 'irregularities?'" Lavelle turned abruptly.

"I'm merely the messenger, darling." She reached for him. "Come." When he moved to her embrace, her finger stroked a tender patch of skin inside his sweater neckband. "So shoot me," she whispered.

He pulled away from the cloying Chanel scent. "Not now.

I'll be downstairs at 5 PM. Have a cocktail ready."

Twenty

Leap from the bed; no dallying. Hoist the Murphy bed up, out of sight. Peek between blinds to check the weather. Stretch: hamstrings, quads, crunches for the abs, kick-ups for the butt. Lunges and spine twists according to the *Prevention* article taped to her wall. Then the payoff: a rejuvenating shower as long as the antiquated boiler in the basement delivers enough hot water. Heli turned the porcelain handles, listening to the rusty pipes gasp and choke like air moving through the tarred lungs of a smoker. She rotated the shower head until its jets pummeled her body. Steam filled the room, creating the aura of the Finnish sauna in the woods of her parents' northern Minnesota home. On Memorial Day, she would plant rosemary, *Rosmarinus officinalis*, pungent and warming, on each of their graves. Her botanist mother often quoted Gerard who'd said the herb "comforteth the harte and maketh it merie."

Toweled and dried, she tottered from the bathroom to the closet, suspending the usual argument with her strong-willed hair. Hangers slid across the rod until she came to the aubergine sweater, its tags still attached. She pulled the turtleneck over her head. In the mirror that hung on the closet door, she studied her image. Passable. With last year's grey flannel trousers, the new and the old were happily paired. Gloss to her lips and a dab of powder to her shiny nose were the limits of make-up artistry. She'd mist perfume on her pulse points from a tester at the cosmetic counter downstairs. Out the door with a granola bar and her white smock and down the squeaky wooden steps to Corner Drug by 4PM.

"Jayson," Heli said as she approached the dispensing counter, "I just dreamt that I lived deep in the forest in a house made of birch-bark, surrounded by lupine and comfrey, and where there was no such thing as debt. Bring me back to reality. What's happened during my nap?"

"Refills pouring in from our usual stress puppies." Jayson answered without turning around. "Phone hasn't stopped ringing since you left." He shook his hands vigorously. "Will someone pul-leaze push the pause button?"

Heli looked beyond the pharmacy counter and watched two teenage girls forage the magazine stacks. Murlene would have to straighten the mess once the store closed at 6 PM. An elderly

Venkata left the library, satisfied that this nugget of information would redeem his standing with Dr. Lavelle. He located a hallway phone near Medical Records and requested the hospital operator's assistance to reach nurse Donna Wadeson at her home number.

As the telephone rang, Venkata crafted a strategy to filch extra blankets from the supply room if #5 was still occupied. The prospect of sleep obsessed him.

"This is Donna Wadeson at 701-692-5920. I can't take your call just now. Leave me a message and I'll. . . Hello? Hello? How do you shut this thing off? Hello? I'm here. Are you there?"

"I'm calling for nurse Donna Wadeson. This is Dr.Venkata at Swedish Hospital."

"That's me, all right," the friendly voice affirmed. "Is this about the Runyan woman? I've been calling the ER all morning and nobody will talk to me."

"I am one of Mrs. Runyan's doctors. I hope you can provide some information."

"How *is* the poor dear? I just completed my chart notes on her, but first I had to shovel snow because the city's plow came by and blocked the driveway where I park my car, and the snow is compacted real hard, and my husband used to do this sort of thing for me, but he died and now . . . ."

"Please." The endless chatter robbed Venkata, minute by minute, of life-extending sleep. "I have been waiting for the chart notes."

"Oh, my," Donna gasped, "I had no idea. Goodness."

"Mrs. Wadeson, I need to know if . . . ."

"Anything, Doctor. I'm so sorry. It was the storm, and all the snow, and the pitiful girl in that abysmal apartment, and the terrible scare in the laundry room . . . ."

Venkata picked up immediately on her reference to his patient's living conditions. "Please tell me more about the home."

"A god-awful mess. Terribly neglected. Filthy by my standards, although I realize they're dealing with a lot at the moment. But there is a child living there."

Not an optimal environment for a patient with an indwelling catheter. Had this contributed to Mrs. Runyan's history of multiple infections? "About the infusion bag. Your note said you removed it."

"Yes. The bag was nearly empty and the infusion pump had stopped." After a slight pause, she asked, "Is there something wrong?"

couple compared vitamin products from a stand-up promotional display of natural products. A speckled adolescent studied the fine print of an acne product. Corner Drug's commotion cheered her. Robust activity on the first day of a new month was a good sign for the store's bottom line.

"Darvon. Percodan. Ultram. Codeine." Jayson read from the list of refill requests. "When did painkillers become a food group?"

"When doctors started prescribing them like candy." Heli glanced at the spindle by the phone where several handwritten notes waited. "Any messages?"

"Uh-huh." Jayson grinned, fingering the gold ring that pierced his eyebrow. "Either you're in really big trouble, or your social barometer is spiking."

She looked up at the mention of trouble. Why was Jayson smiling?

He read from the message. "a San-deep Ven-ka- tah called. Bee-u-tee-ful Indy accent. Said he'd stop by later this afternoon." On the far side of the counter, a printer spewed out a prescription label. "Not that it's any of my business, but who's the guy with the Dove Bar voice?"

"He's the chief resident at Swedish." Her ribbed collar seemed to be tightening around her neck, and she twisted uncomfortably. "We talked at the hospital last night."

"Awesome." Jayson waved an envelope receipt in the air. "And this news will kick it up another notch," he said, before reaching for an in-coming call.

The green neon sign above the entrance to Corner Drug flashed on at 4 PM as if to signal the final shopping countdown. Last-minute purchases—oral contraceptives, anniversary cards, stool softeners and condoms—were big sellers during the two hours before weekend closing. Heli made a mental note to check the OTC shelves for Nicorette patches, pregnancy test kits and Depends.

Near the greeting card rack, she heard a voice behind her, soft and loamy like rich soil. She hardly recognized him in something other than green scrubs. He clutched a Stop-and-Shop bag close to his chest as though it were a trophy.

"Am I disturbing you? You seem quite busy."

She stepped back against the rack, upsetting a row of Easter cards. "Welcome to Corner Drug, Dr. Venkata. My other life, so to speak."

"Please, call me Sandy. It is an acceptable abbreviation, yes?"

"Sandy it is." She nodded, drawn in by his plum-brown eyes, dark like the center of a sunflower. "About my call last night. I might have come on a bit strong , . . but I had to. . . ."

"Hospital bureaucracy. You were diplomatic. Patient safety is very important."

"Thank you." Then a pause. Where was this conversation going?

"I hope we might continue our conversation over a coffee, perhaps at Latte Da. You were going to explain the meaning of your license plates. That is, of course, if you have any interest." He looked around. "My timing is disastrous, yes?"

So he's nervous, too. She glanced at her watch. "I work again tonight at Swedish. A twelve hour shift beginning at 7PM." For once her heart was outpacing her head. "I usually go across the street for a quick dinner at the Jade Garden." Jayson would surely close up tonight. "Care to join me, Sandy?" *Hyvä!* an inner voice cheered.

"It would be my pleasure." His smile broadened naturally over perfectly formed teeth. "And your timing is excellent. I have," he looked down at the Stop and Shop bag, "a few errands and a lab result to check. Shall I. . . ."

"Meet me at the Jade at 6." Her sweater was damp with perspiration.

"Excellent."

On her way back to the pharmacy Jayson, with the playful Moomin face, met her with a bottle of spring water.

"Can you lock up tonight?" she hedged, unaware that she was biting her lower lip. "I know it's Saturday night and you might have plans."

"Hey, my night of pub-crawling doesn't launch until nine or ten-ish. Sure, I'll lock up. Do a little web work here. By the way, did I just detect a heat-generating chemical fusion over in aisle 3?"

"By the way, yourself." Arms crossed over her chest screamed *enough, Jayson*. "What about the other message. The really important one."

Jayson slapped his forehead. "Sit down for this." He pulled an envelope from a locked drawer under the counter. "Mondo money. Cold cash."

Heli glanced discreetly at her watch. In less than an hour she was due at the Jade. Was everything in life ultimately reduced to time and money? Plopping herself on a stool, she said, "how *much* money?"

"Thirty-five hundred dollars. Want me to say that again?"

He waved the envelope in an airy figure eight. "Crisp and green: thirty-five Ben Franklins smiling at us. Gotta admit that counting cash sure beats counting pills."

News like this concentrated her attention. Heli set the half empty water bottle on the counter near a stone mortar and pestle. Thirty-five hundred dollars could take her to the moon and back, giving her the financial oxygen she needed to make payroll and to claim the discount for paying invoices by the tenth. This might be enough to wheedle a smile out of her dour accountant and to regain his confidence. Patients before profits, she'd once argued in a blistering exchange with Erickson. "No money, no mission," he'd countered, zoning into her fear of failure. Since that conversation, it seemed that money had taken on uber-importance in the daily realities of running a small business.

Her brow furrowed, taking on a life-is-tragic look.

"If this is some kind of April Fool's prank, Jayson, it's cruel. Finns aren't wired for humor."

"No mickey, Boss. Payment in full on Runyan's account. Trevor dropped it off this afternoon while you were playing hide-and-sleep."

He handed the envelope to Heli and she thumb-rolled through the wad of hundred dollar bills.

"I never expected to see this." Her eyes met Jayson's. "His wife's still on TPN. I made an infusion for her last night after a home health nurse phoned the hospital pharmacy." Heli reached for her water bottle, tendering the realization that her own coffers had now been restored at Trevor's expense. He must have plenty of debt. "Did he say anything to explain?"

"Said he was sorry it took so long to pay up." For once, Jayson looked pensive. "Kind of a sad trombone, that dude. Said the mail-order pharmacy didn't work out after all.

"Told you so."

"Seems Trevor no longer buys the deal that Lavelle was pushing with the mail-order pharmacy." Jayson reached for a stock bottle of nicotinic acid and poured the tablets onto the counting tray. "Says he wants to come back here if we'll have him." With a spatula, the pills skimmed across the tray, five at a time. "And one more fascinoma."

Too much good news made her wonder if St. Urho was acting on her behalf, driving debt, along with the frogs and grasshoppers, out of Corner Drug.

"Runyan leaked the name of the mail-order house. Ever heard of GEM Pharmacy?"

Heli paused, shook her head. "Not a pharmacy in this state. If it were, I'd recognize it." She tossed the water bottle into the recycling bin and moved closer to the computer. The boundaries of her competitive marketplace had obviously stretched beyond Fargo. "We need to check this out. If I'm at risk of losing other infusion clients, I have to understand the competition."

Jayson squared up to the computer and peered into the screen. "I will definitely google my way to GEM's front door."

"I want to know everything: registration, ownership, services, pricing."

"No problem, Boss. You can't hide in cyberspace."

Another benefit for having Jayson on the payroll. In his cyber-world, they agreed that she was a digital immigrant.

She returned the cash-stuffed envelope to the locked drawer for safekeeping until Monday's deposit. In a moment of indulgence, she leaned against the pharmacy's exposed brick wall, eyes closed. Jayson's fingers tapped at the keyboard while the printer coughed out a prescription label. Moments later, she heard the screech of cellophane and knew Jayson must be attaching the label to a vial. The phone was quiet, and she could have easily fallen asleep on the spot. Jaysons's voice broke her reverie.

"Earth to Hell—i."

Her eyes opened abruptly; she checked her watch. Forty minutes until her first date in Fargo. The rank sweater had to go. What else might be hanging in her closet? How she looked now mattered. A few choices came to mind. Black was always safe.

"Thanks, Jayson. I owe you on this one."

"Double-true." His lips curled into a mischievous grin. "And you thought I was just another twenty-something slacker."

"Be sure to lock the back door when you leave."

She hung her smock on a hook and reached for her ski jacket. A quick look in the mirror found her smiling. Everything seemed to be working out amazingly well in an untypically Finnish way. It wasn't necessary to remind Jayson of lock-up procedures; he'd closed hundreds of times. But feeling this good was reason to inject some caution.

"And check the door twice."

Twenty-One

Always one foot in the future. Venkata thought often about the phrase that appeared in a letter of reference for his residency application. The Dean of his medical college in Mumbai described his "familiar reflective pose" and his "quiet musings." Like the teenage chess champion he was, Venkata had been merely organizing information in his mind, analyzing patterns, comparing alternatives and making reasoned choices. In Fargo, this quiet behavior was often misinterpreted as cultural conceit or quirky intelligence. It was neither. The chief resident was simply calculating his next move.

His decision to pursue a Fellowship in Infectious Disease at Duke after his year as chief resident did not follow the advice he'd been given. Cardiology, gastroenterology and oncology were the favored pathways for internal medicine residents. Those specialties attracted the brightest physicians and, as Dr. Lavelle had pointed out, the truly avaricious. He'd warned Venkata that an ID doctor could never afford a home on Pill Hill unless he married an ophthalmologist with a laser.

"It's as simple as this, Sandy. You've got to find a gimmick that pays well. Scope every bodily orifice you can find, feed a balloon or a stent through an artery, stick a needle in an organ or push toxins into a vein, and you'll be financially rewarded for the rest of your professional life. No questions asked. That's how the system works. It's insane, but nobody pays a doctor to think anymore. Surgeons have known that for years."

For a brief moment, Venkata imagined the future into which he was stepping as he waited at a red light on his way back to Swedish Hospital. For now, the present demanded his full attention. The empty infusion bag rested beside him in the passenger seat of his Audi A6. Considering how important the shriveled bag seemed to Dr. Lavelle, he thought of buckling the seat belt around it for added security. The dashboard clock read 4:35 PM—just over an hour before his dinner date with Heli—and adequate time to drop off the infusion bag at his apartment near the hospital before checking on the young Crohn's on Six Main.

At 5:15 PM, the chief resident reached the ward on the sixth floor. He meandered around a dietary cart reeking of baked potatoes, and passed by two patients strolling through the halls in ill-fitting blue cotton robes. IV poles clattered at their sides. Otherwise, the ward was unusually quiet. A gaggle of nurses conferred near the desk where the medical charts were located.

"You looking for 604? I've got the chart right here. Just finishing up."

"You are Mrs. Runyan's nurse?"

"All day and all night, unless someone comes in to relieve me. Roxy's the name."

Venkata accepted the chart and reviewed the notes. Christine Runyan's blood pressure and temperature had been charted every thirty minutes as he'd ordered. His patient was still febrile and her blood pressure had fallen periodically throughout the afternoon, always resolving after a bolus of fluid.

Christine was sleeping when he entered her room. The subtle pulsing of the IV infusion pump assured him that antibiotics were streaming into her central line, fighting an unspecified infection. Once again he mulled over the details of the Runyan case. Her history strongly suggested another catheter-related infection, but Venkata had not contented himself with the obvious. He'd ordered the radiology work this morning to rule out other potential sources of infection. The flat plate of her abdomen came back with good news. No free air on the x-ray from any perforations of the stomach or intestine. This he knew substantially minimized the possibility that the infection came from an abdominal source. Still, he'd ordered a CT scan to be sure. He'd accompanied Mrs. Runyan to the Imaging department and watched the computed tomography scan with the radiologist as her midsection was sliced horizontally, one painless centimeter at a time, on the computer screen. The power of technology amazed him. No abscesses were found, and her pancreas and gall bladder appeared normal.

As other sources of infection were ruled out in the differential diagnosis, Venkata felt that the probability of a central line infection intensified. Although his initial hunch was supported by the radiology information, he craved certainty. Confirmation from a definitive lab result would not be available until Sunday morning, a full twenty-four hours from the time of sampling. This anticipated delay had not stopped the chief resident from calling the Microbiology staff several times in the early afternoon for preliminary results.

"We'll call you, Venkata," Dr. Dahl answered tersely. "Our automated systems monitor the cultures every ten minutes, twenty-four hours a day. You don't need to call us that often. We'll call you."

As he watched Christine take one labored breath after another, her weakened body struggling to ward off the infecting agent, Venkata reaffirmed the decision of his heart to pursue an Infectious

Disease fellowship. He wanted to be both a healer at the bedside, and a warrior in the constant maelstrom of man-versus-nature. The battle against infectious agents had never been completely won, never completely lost, and the sway of death persevered. Hadn't Black Death wiped out a quarter of Europe's population? Another plague pandemic spreading along the Hong Kong trade routes four centuries later? A grim chapter in North Dakota history detailed a devastating small pox outbreak in 1837, killing more than seventeen thousand Mandan, Hidatsa and Arikara people. Now, an AIDS epidemic in Africa and talk of biological warfare with anthrax and smallpox. There was so much work to be done, and Venkata wanted to be a foot soldier in the battle. Politicians may worry about nuclear war, but he feared the human species was far more susceptible to mass annihilation by an elusive infectious agent.

Roxy lumbered into the room and interrupted the stream of Venkata's consciousness.

"She's been pretty wifty all day. I talk to her for awhile when she's awake. Minutes later, she's gone. Seems real scared."

"Her family? Has she been alone all afternoon?"

"Pretty much. Husband was here this morning—a real sourpuss. The little girl called. I held the phone for Christine— couldn't help but hear the conversation. Really bizarre. She talked about waking up in the middle of the night. Hearing things. Bad dreams."

Delirium, Venkata concluded. It was still too early to expect the antibiotics to be working. Her lips, although pale, were not cyanotic and there were no petechiae on her skin.

"Has Dr. Lavelle been here?" The chief resident flipped through the chart to check for urine output. "I do not see his note."

"You kidding me? It must be cocktail hour now. I doubt. . . ."

"Please," Venkata interrupted, "do not disparage Dr. Lavelle in front of the patient or me. It serves no purpose." He retrieved a pen from the pocket of his white coat and wrote orders in the chart. "We must repeat the CBC, platelets, electrolytes, glucose and creatinine. Please watch her urine output closely. I am not on call tonight, but I want to be notified immediately if her condition changes." Venkata turned to leave. "Thank you, Roxy. You have been very attentive to Mrs. Runyan."

"Dr. V, Christine's lucky to have a couple of pros like you and me taking care of her."

The chief resident was not depending on luck. He was on his way to the lab.

***

Heli dodged puddles of melting snow as she crossed the avenue to the Jade. The last sound she heard before escaping from the back door of Corner Drug was an older woman approaching the pharmacy counter, calling "*yoo-hoo, yoo-hoo*." Jayson had stepped forward with his leave-this-high-maintenance-one-to-me look and Heli obliged. After all, she needed time to settle down and catch her breath before Sandy arrived at the restaurant.

The Jade's happy hour crowd had already gathered in post-storm revelry. Heli circumvented a boisterous troupe of women in purple and red garb who were toasting someone's birthday with Kir Royales. She followed the green carpet with gold medallions along a meandering path to the dining room. It took several minutes for her eyes to adjust to the low-level light emerging from the red dragon lamps on the walls. Mr. Wang waited by a busing station to greet her.

"One this evening, Heli?" Mr. Wang pulled a single menu from behind the counter.

"Two, actually."

"Ah. " Mr. Wang raised his trimmed eyebrows and bowed slightly. "Certainly." He brought out a second menu. "May I seat you near small pagoda under Chinese longevity knot?"

Everyone seemed to be a matchmaker.

"A bit premature, Mr. Wang, but thanks anyway." She smiled at her older friend, a diabetic with a peripheral neuropathy that made standing for long periods of time extremely difficult. He led her over a small wooden bridge that spanned an ornamental pond stocked with angelfish leading to a row of booths at the back of the restaurant. He gestured to one side; she chose the other, and slid along the seat into the booth. The scar over her left eye would be less visible from this angle.

Mr. Wang placed the menu before her. "Mongolian beef. Very good tonight. Extra spicy."

Heli fidgeted in the booth. She was twenty minutes ahead of schedule, an unsettling habit she couldn't seem to break. A young waiter in Gap jeans filled her water glass. Other diners streamed in. An elderly couple, patients of Corner Drug, acknowledged her and she returned their greeting with a nod. Heli scanned the menu for new additions; there were none. She played with the salt and pepper shakers and remembered her mother's rule of etiquette: *salt and pepper, like a bride and groom, never leave each other's side. They are always passed together.* The sound system had abruptly changed from a tinny Cantonese opera to the torture of a country western balladeer. She turned in the direction of the speakers, hardly noticing how he'd noiselessly slid into the other side of the booth.

"I am late, Heli." His sparkling eyes signaled an apology. "The roads, the snow plows, the trains. . . ."

"Rush hour in Fargo."

"And a very sick young woman." Venkata seemed preoccupied. He cupped a hand to his ear. "Country music in a Chinese restaurant?"

"I'm afraid so. Sounds like he needs a painkiller."

"Do you listen to this music?"

"Only at gunpoint."

"Then we have something in common." Venkata smiled and reached for the menu. "The maitre'd informed me how pleased he was that I am dining with his special friend."

The candlelight flickered between them.

"Mr. Wang and I are good friends. We launched our businesses about the same time." She wanted to explain that he'd become like a father to her, but she repressed the instinct. Something about the ambience had kindled within her an optimism that they might share another time together. And another. Not everything needed to be disclosed now.

"We're co-dependent," she finally said. "The Jade meets my need for a kitchen, and Mr. Wang uses my drugstore as his personal medicine chest, although he doesn't think much of Western medicine. He's teaching me Chinese herbal remedies that would have startled my pharmacy professors."

Brigid Olander stopped at their table, ready to take their order. Heli nodded a hello that went unacknowledged.

Venkata scanned the menu again. "Have you made a choice, Heli? We must be sure you are at hospital on time. Seven, is it?"

Brigid scribbled their order onto a small green pad. Mongolian beef for her, Bean curd-Szechuan style with vegetable fried rice for him. Green tea for both.

"When I first arrived in Fargo three years ago," Venkata explained, "I had to learn to cook if I wanted to eat as I did in Mumbai. So I shopped at Whole Foods for fenugreek and cardamom pods."

"In my world, fenugreek is the answer for menstrual pain and abdominal cramping." She relaxed against the booth's cushioned back.

"I expect it will be easier to find authentic Indian food in

Raleigh-Durham. Perhaps then I can avoid obsessing about my next meal and concentrate on medicine."

"You're traveling to North Carolina? Soon?"

"Yes, in June I will be moving there. A fellowship at Duke."

"I see." The news nipped a growing bud of hopefulness deep within her. "A fellowship *and* better weather too. Congratulations. And then what?"

"My plan is to return in three years to Swedish Hospital as an Infectious Disease specialist."

"Not a typical story of people who leave Fargo."

"What do you mean, Heli?"

"Fargo is a springboard to bigger, better places. We're like a farm team feeding the minor leagues. It's not exactly a place to come back to."

"Yet you chose Fargo."

"For complicated reasons." With her finger she made rings around the rim of her glass. "I like the life I've carved out here in the drug trade. Meaning the *legitimate* drug trade, of course."

"Much less dangerous."

"Less profitable too," she added, "but it has other rewards."

His gentle smile was evidence to her that the evening was going well.

"I, too, have been happy here," Venkata said. "My training has been exceptional. Excellent physicians, interesting patients and very good technology. The weather? I once overheard Dr. Lavelle on the telephone with a colleague discussing the weather. He said, 'it's sixty-eight degrees in my office whether I'm in Fargo or Philadelphia. Medicine is an indoor job. What's the issue?'"

Heli shifted in the booth. "Lavelle does have a way of getting the last word, doesn't he?"

***

Venkata felt his pager quiver and worried that its interruption might portend a change in the evening with Heli that had so far unfolded nicely. He hadn't yet learned much about her with all his pointless talk of food and cooking and weather. Hers was a story he wanted to learn and to savor. But the moment demanded that he reach for his beeper where he saw the number for the laboratory at Swedish Hospital.

"Excuse me, Heli. I've been paged." Only then he realized that his cell phone remained in its charging unit by the bed in his apartment. "Do you have a cell phone with you?"

"I don't own one. Sorry. I'm sure Mr. Wang will be happy to let you use his phone. It's behind the aquarium near the lounge."

Venkata excused himself again and proceeded toward the raucous lounge where the screeching sounds called to mind Sita's myna birds squawking in his parents' back yard. Mr. Wang handed him the cordless phone, motioning him to use the relatively quieter staging area in the kitchen. The chief resident punched in the lab's number.

"Dahl here."

"Dr. Venkata returning your page. I assume you are calling me about the lab result of the Runyan woman in 604?"

"Yes, I am, Sandy. Sorry to bother you on a Saturday night but you seemed quite anxious about the report. Not out on the town, are you?"

"No. I mean, yes, but I am eager for news."

"Did you know that we have the newest generation of automated blood culture instruments in our laboratory? Speeds up the diagnosis of bacteremia significantly." Dr. Dahl explained at a leisurely pace. "The system uses a colorimetric photosensor . . ."

"I'm familiar with the instrumentation, Sir." Venkata mildly resented the time this lengthy explanation was stealing from his evening with Heli.

"The amazing thing about the system is that it can detect faint color changes well before the human eye can. A man of science like you can appreciate this, right?"

"About the Runyan report, Dr. Dahl. Did your instrument detect bacterial growth on the culture?"

"Yes, it did, young man. That's why I called you."

"And you followed up with a gram stain?" Venkata tried to hurry along the chief pathologist's message.

"We did exactly that, with a very curious result."

Venkata's attention sharpened.

"We're seeing both gram positive and gram negative organisms on the stain, and something is growing on the anaerobic culture as well. I'm afraid this preliminary report doesn't exactly identify the bugs, but it suggests something more complicated is occurring than the gram positive cocci you were expecting. We'll have to wait until tomorrow for more definitive answers."

The news unsettled Venkata. "I mean no disrespect, Dr. Dahl, but are you certain? Did all three blood cultures stain similarly?"

"Three out of three, Sandy. This isn't an artifact."

Venkata sat on small stool in the corner of the food prep area and tried to assimilate the pathology findings. "Thank you. I will have to think about what this means for Mrs. Runyan's management. Good evening."

He retraced his steps out of the kitchen, through the lounge, when he heard his name called behind him.

"'Yo! Doc! Over here." Reuben gave him the American thumbs-up salute from the table he shared with five female nurses from the ER.

Venkata turned around, nodded to the table of hospital employees, and continued along his way to the dining room where Heli sipped tea. Two plates of steaming food waited.

"Please excuse the interruption." He sat down on the seat and replaced a red napkin on his lap. "It was a lab result that I had not anticipated." He couldn't remember the direction their prior conversation had taken. A hirsute waitress came by and slapped a ticket on the table. He drank water from a red tumbler and watched Heli remove the wrapping from a pair of chopsticks.

"Can you ever really get away from it?" The question hung between them while she brought a thin slice of beef to her mouth, something that had never crossed his Hindu lips.

Before he could answer, the pager vibrated again. This time he grabbed it quickly and blanched when he saw the number that appeared on the read-out. "I will be back soon." He slid across the seat in short order and made the trip back to the kitchen in half the time of his earlier run.

"Dr. Venkata, it's Roxy from Six Main. Christine Runyan is tanking. First I gave her five hundred ccs of normal saline, and twenty minutes later, I gave her another liter. Nothing happened. Blood pressure's not coming back."

"How does she look?"

"Not good. Bad, I mean. Sometimes her pulse races up to 120 beats, other times I can barely feel it."

"Her blood pressure now?"

"80 over 50."

Septic shock. He reviewed the protocols in his mind. Survival was at best a fifty-fifty matter. Dr. Lavelle must be notified. Perhaps the family as well. "Start a dopamine drip, thirty micrograms per kilogram per minute, and have her transferred to the ICU. I will be there promptly— ten minutes away." Venkata knew his night of romancing was coming to an end. "Roxy?"

"Yeah, Dr. V?"

"Stay with her, please."

Venkata raced back to the booth and reached for his jacket. "I've been called back to hospital. Rude of me to leave, I know, but my patient is very ill." He picked up the check. "We will talk later tonight if not tomorrow. Perhaps you will allow me to prepare a special Indian dinner for you."

Her smile, tender and forgiving, was all the assurance he needed at the moment to lift his leaden heart.

Sunday, April 2, 2002

Twenty-Two

Early Sunday morning, Donna Wadeson entered Bethany Lutheran church through its modest double doors. Since moving to the city and after visiting fourteen Protestant churches, she preferred this intimate congregation where small town friendliness still abounded. Snow frosted the lawns of Fargo, but she dressed in a coral polyester suit, thinking maybe one had to coax spring along.

Weekly happenings at Bethany were featured in the church bulletin: fellowship coffee in the basement after worship, choir on Wednesday evening, Bible Study on Thursday noon, Altar guild on Saturday. Maybe she'd sign the visitor's form and express an interest in membership. Become a part of the church family, as the young charismatic pastor had urged.

The organist launched into a booming prelude to the opening hymn while the words, keyed in Power Point, projected overhead on a floating screen. The switch from hymnals to computer-generated slides was not to her liking, but Donna loved to sing so dearly that she would not be dissuaded by the church's shifting preferences. Her alto voice, strong and clear, harmonized with the congregation's, and she sang so heartily that a small child in the next pew turned around and covered his ears.

Hark! The voice of Jesus crying
Who will go and work today?
Fields are white and harvest waiting,
Who will bear the sheaves away?

Inspired singers in this church, she noted, proud to be among other Lutherans who knew how to sing in four-part harmony. Not bland like the Methodists, snooty like the Episcopalians or show-offs, those Presbyterians. The words stirred her soul.

Loud and long the Master calleth,
Rich reward he offers free;
Who will answer gladly saying,
Here am I; send me, send me.

It seemed to Donna that if there were any truth in the old hymn, the Lord might approve of her humble efforts with the homebound patients of Swedish Hospital. Not a high-powered doctor, not even a *baccalaureate* registered nurse. Yet she'd helped babies come into this world and held the frail hand of those leaving it. Care offered charitably at both ends of life made transitions a lot easier. *Here am I; send me, send me.*

Pastor Bob led the Introit, followed by the Collect, during which Donna wondered if she'd remembered to peel off those stubborn TJ Maxx stickers from the bottom of her shoes. It would be embarrassing to kneel at the Lord's table with discount tags in full view.

Next came her favorite part, Joys and Concerns—gossip made holy—where Pastor invited the congregation to pray for ailing congregants. A Somalian new to the community needed winter clothing and wool blankets. Premature triplets in the Neonatal Intensive Care unit at Swedish Hospital, each no bigger than a loaf of bread, needed prayers for their survival, as did Stella Magnusson, who Pastor Bob described as "full of cancer." A goner; Donna sighed along with the congregation.

"Finally, the Runyan family needs our love and support as they mourn the loss of Christine Runyan who died at Swedish Hospital last evening," Pastor Bob announced. "Her funeral service is pending."

Donna gasped aloud. The little boy in the pew in front of her turned around again and put a finger to his lips. "Sh. . .Sh."

Christine Runyan—*dead*? Why, only yesterday. . . . Donna's armpits dampened, and a band of sweat ringed her temples. She fanned herself with the bulletin, hoping no one would notice the hot flash. What happened? That poor family, that sweet child, now all-alone without her mother. What on earth happened at the hospital? Dear God, she prayed, forgive this faltering believer, but didn't we do everything we possibly could for her? How can calling Christine Runyan home factor into Your Big Plan?

When the rest of the congregation sang "Lord, Speak to Me, that I May Speak," Donna was mute, her jaw set and brow creased.

Pastor Bob's sermon had something to do with Christ's suffering on Golgotha, but Donna was absorbed in pain a little closer to home. Her mind bounced from the sad husband to the little girl, into the empty refrigerator and back to the troubled schizophrenic hiding in the laundry room. Something about the Runyan case had always troubled her. Christine, wax-white and looking like a skeleton, was one thing, but it wasn't just her physical appearance but something about the apartment—how it felt to be inside its walls—suffocating and bleak. No one seemed to really *live* there. Cluttered, unkempt and empty of the usual come-and-go of life—say, a geranium in the window, a grocery list under a refrigerator magnet, a wall calendar marked with special events. Any sense of a future seemed gone as though hopefulness turned out the lights months ago. What was life, if not to hope? It didn't make sense to her, especially after learning the Runyans were people of faith.

Perhaps she'd pay a visit to the family, bring over some food, say, her glorified rice. Everybody raved about the salad when she'd brought it to potluck suppers in Prosper.

Holy Communion time now. The usher gestured her pew to rise and to approach the altar. Others moved forward but Donna turned about-face and walked out of the church, full throttle, into a bright, sun-drenched morning. She was too upset to sit idly in church at a time like this. There was rice to boil, calls to make, questions to ask.

***

For a rare moment in his week, Byron Bohley was a happy man. Perched on a stool in the kitchen of Swedish Hospital, he knifed and forked his way through a warm caramel roll the size of a dinner plate. Probably enough calories here to feed a third world country but he doubted they would enjoy it more. The buttery glaze coated his fingers which he licked clean, one at a time.

It was his habit to visit Maynard, the hospital's head chef, in the Dietary department's stainless steel kitchen while Betsy attended the Unitarian service on Sunday morning. "Go and save the world with the rest of the Limousine liberals," he'd said to his wife. "Be sure to send your uninsured members to the public health clinic, not our ER."

Bohley wiped his hands on a paper napkin. "Mmmmm. You quit making these cholesterol cakes, and I'll fire you on the spot, Maynard. Understand?"

"You're the boss, Bohley. Management and labor represented here. Some give orders; some take 'em."

"Reminds me, can you put a little something together for a party we're having at the house next Wednesday night? Betsy can't pull off a meal for twelve to save her soul, and since we're hosting bridge club, I'd like people to leave without food poisoning. Can you make that work, Maynard? Maybe have your staff come over in the afternoon, stay and help us serve in the evening?"

"You're the boss. What time?"

His cell phone rang. With a shoulder raised, he reached under his spare tire and pulled the phone from its holster. "Bohley here."

"Oh, hi, Mr. Bohley. It's Alayne Ludemann. Am I disturbing you?"

The CEO wiped the corners of his mouth with a fresh napkin and slid off the stool. "Where are you?"

"In the ER; my office, specifically."

"What's on your mind?"

"We should talk, Mr. Bohley. There was a death in the hospital last evening. Christine Runyan. Does the name mean anything to you?"

"Not a damn thing. Should it?"

"Is there someplace we could talk privately?"

He was running out of discreet places to meet with this hot potato. No more rooftop soirées. His office was out of the question; Bohley assumed it was bugged.

"The private dining room off the cafeteria. Ten minutes." He ended the call and wedged the phone back onto his belt.

"Pasta, Maynard. Do something with pasta. Lots of cream and bacon. What do you call that: carbonara? By the way, are you still saving bones for Stueben?"

"Sure am, Boss. Good meaty beef bones. Stueben's a funny name for a golden retriever."

"Pedigreed and priceless. Best friend I've ever had. Slobbers all over my face when I come home at night. Obeys me like no one ever has in this hospital."

***

Sandeep Venkata seated himself on a rolling stool before one of the microscopes in the Microbiology lab. Sunday morning, and the first report on blood set #1 of Christine Runyan's sample had been issued. It confirmed Dr. Dahl's oral report last evening.

The chief resident asked the technologist for the plated cultures to verify what he'd already been told. He peered into the eyepiece, rotating the fine adjustment knob for better resolution. He blinked several times. Squinted. A profusion of purple, bluish gram-positive organisms of various sizes clustered on the slide and splashes of red rod-like gram-negative shapes, some large, some small, came into focus. There is no doubt, he conceded. The slide revealed a confusing array of mixed organisms, not the *staphylococcus* infection that would have appeared like a cluster of grapes under the lens as it had in her previous infections.

Venkata was confused, and his patient was dead. It was difficult to talk of the young woman in the past tense. Perhaps her autopsy held the answer.

***

Bohley waited in the wood-paneled dining room at the far end of the hospital cafeteria. The stuffy room with its boardroom-style teak table was usually reserved for special meetings and private luncheons. Portraits of distinguished physicians once on staff at Swedish Hospital barely smiled from the walls. The images of past hospital administrators appeared dour. Bohley contemplated the day his mug-face would hang on this wall of shame. When the time came, he'd probably have even less to smile about than these old buzzards.

"Sorry to keep you waiting, Mr. Bohley."

"Shut the door. Now, about some death, you say? Don't tell me we're getting sued again."

"Possibly, but not with much damage if we act quickly. And wisely. We've got Lavelle this time. He'd have to chew his leg off to get out of this trap."

Bohley listened as Alayne Ludemann reported the chronology of Christine Runyan's hospitalization and subsequent death. Her energy seemed to spike with the part about the husband's intention (she called him Trevor) to sue Dr. Lavelle.

"You think he's got a good case against Lavelle? I can't stand that S.O.B., but he's supposed to be a pretty good physician. Did he screw up this time?" Bohley hated lawsuits, hated lawyers, hated courtrooms as a general principle. Lavelle, he hated specifically.

"She died, didn't she? It will be a tremendous burden of sympathy for the jury to overcome. Rich East Coast doctor against a poor, pathetic thirty-year old school teacher with a husband and a five year-old kid?"

She's as cynical as I am, Bohley thought. What is happening to this industry?

"Seems to me there are still facts of the case that need to be proven before a malpractice judgment is awarded." The CEO loosened the clasp on his gold watch. "Besides, the hospital with its deep pockets will be dragged into the suit, and I sure as hell have no appetite for that." He thought about the Board's reaction to a potential suit and felt the prospect of his year-end bonus quaver.

"That's why we have to act decisively *now*." Alayne pulled her chair closer to the table. "Last evening, Lavelle scattered blame far and wide for the Runyan death. I saw through his diversion strategy immediately. 'Focus on Swedish,' " she waved scarlet nails wildly in the air as though imitating the ranting physician, " 'and cloud the death in the hysteria over hospital errors and patient safety.' "

Bohley flinched and reached into his pocket for a Rolaid. Damn it! None there.

"Lavelle says he's making a full report to the Joint Commission. . . ."

"Holy shit . . . ."

"And to Medicare, Medicaid, and the rest of the insurers."

"Hell's bells, he will!"

"And to the *Freedom Press*."

Bohley jumped to his feet. "Over my dead body, he'll do a goddamn thing like that!"

"In that case, Mr. Bohley, I repeat. We'll have to be smart and quick."

For a moment, the CEO was distracted by the dish across the table. If any of Alayne Ludemann's body parts had once held his interest—the sweepstake smile, the Marilyn Monroe legs, the slight cleft of her chin, nothing compared this minute to her big, whirling brain.

"What do you have in mind?"

"We go on the offensive. As CEO, you come on strong, deem the death to be a sentinel hospital event and launch a thorough internal review process. Put a risk management nurse on the details of the case immediately. Instruct the Patient Safety committee to investigate the matter. Have them conduct a root cause analysis of the situation. Raise questions about Lavelle's competency. Bring in the Chair of the Credentials Committee. And delegate . . . ."

"There's more?" Bohley had forgotten that several of the committees still existed. He'd never heard of others. The abstract lines of delegated power renewed his fondness of bureaucracy.

"And," Alayne continued, "we move up the meeting of the Medical Staff Executive committee to this Monday morning instead of. . . ."

"April 15, 9 AM." Bohley remembered the detail only because it was income tax day, and he liked to start getting a buzz on early in the afternoon. "By the way, how come you know about the meeting?"

"I read my email, Mr. Bohley. Every attachment, even the fine print. You can learn a lot about this place in the minutia others disregard."

He'd be damned if he'd start reading emails. It would add another two hours to his day. Notes of grumbling doctors, whining nurses and nervous accountants held no interest for him. He continued to read messages from Board members. The secret to career longevity involved pleasing the people in high places; the little people couldn't hurt him.

"We move up the meeting. Catch Lavelle off-guard. Expose his dealings with pharmaceutical companies: the kickbacks, the thinly disguised weekly dinners at drug company expense, all of his subsidized travel to bogus international meetings. Then, slam him with a mismanaged preventable death."

Bohley leaned back in his chair and crossed one stubby leg over the other. He rubbed his chin, weighing the risks against the benefits of a meeting he couldn't control.

Alayne's eyes were wide open. "We've got him on the Exvantium issue, Byron. Lock, stock and barrel. Half of the medical staff will be morally outraged by this infraction of hospital bylaws. The other half will be jealous of the profitable deal he pulled off with the drug manufacturers, and they'll hate him for it. Either way, we'll have the medical staff unified against Lavelle, the common enemy. Add to that, a malpractice judgment, and he's dead meat, just as I assured you."

And Alayne Ludemann is promoted. The CEO remembered his Faustian bargain yesterday on the hospital roof.

How sweetly the morning had begun, Bohley mused, and how it had suddenly soured into another set of bad alternatives. "I can't go changing the date of a standing meeting on a whim. Those docs have OR schedules to consider, office patients to see, other claims to their time. I can't ask them to drop their plans at a moment's notice."

With pursed lips and crossed arms, Alayne remained silent. The CEO felt the searing scorn of the old dead warriors staring from their walnut picture frames. He knew he was about to be skewered by a subordinate.

"I assumed *you* were in *charge* of this place, Mr. Bohley. If the inmates are indeed running the prison, well, of course, that's altogether a different strategy."

Twenty-Three

When the phone rang, Dr. Yolanda Kampela was seated at her dining room table in Fargo revisiting photographs from last year's medical mission to Zimbabwe. She'd joined the team of surgeons and nurses from her alma mater, Howard University, in response to the grave need for an infectious disease specialist in the sub-Saharan where AIDS was taking a devastating toll on children.

"This is Dr. Venkata calling from Swedish Hospital. Am I disturbing you, Dr. Kampela?"

"Quite all right. Merely enjoying the Sunday morning sunshine over coffee and several hundred photographs that beg to be cataloged. Are you consulting me on a patient?"

Venkata shifted his weight to the other foot. "Yes, but perhaps, too late. I fear we, that is, Dr. Lavelle and I, should have brought you in sooner. A patient has died, but the questions of her case persist." He listened to the sounds of paper shuffling and a chair slide across a floor.

The chief resident relayed the details of Christine Runyan's history of Crohn's, her repeated central line infections and the preliminary pathology findings. "She is dead, and as yet, I lack a source for the infection."

"Has a post been performed?"

"Yes, minutes ago, and that is equally puzzling. Dr. Dahl performed the autopsy and found essentially a quiescent bowel. No evidence of active disease. No perforations, no fistulas, no free air in the abdomen to suggest a source for the infection there."

"From her history, I expected bacteria might have entered the blood stream from a tear in the gut." Dr. Kampela paused while paper shuffled in the background. "In one such case I can recall, the liver looked like a sponge full of gas—an unforgettable sight."

"But this liver was normal," Venkata interrupted. "Aside from some intestinal adhesions from past surgeries, everything looked normal."

"Hmm. Dr. Dahl is quite certain?"

"Unequivocal. And, the findings of the autopsy are consistent with yesterday's CT scan. No free air in the abdomen. So I am puzzled. A 'real head scratcher,' according to Dr. Dahl."

"You may never know the source," she answered calmly after a considered pause, "and that is very difficult to live with. Our patients expect definitive answers and so we search with every technological tool at our disposal. Physicians might be wiser if we'd emerge from the shelter of charts and machines and simply talk to patients. And with each other."

"But she is dead!" Venkata blurted out like an undisciplined schoolboy. "Although I've persisted, the laboratory is reluctant to release the identity of the pathogens at this time. Dr. Dahl said the bugs appear to be so strange that he will repeat the testing. The retesting will take *another* twenty four hours."

"I don't understand how the delay will matter to your patient. You've acknowledged that she's expired."

"But my curiosity has not, Dr. Kampela." Venkata wondered if his irritability was showing. He hoped not. Yolanda Kampela was a respected ID specialist nationally known for her work with Legionnaire's Disease. Thirty years of practice with over two hundred publications to her credit, it was not his place to be impatient with her. "If I have missed something in her work-up, I must know as soon as possible," he explained in a confessional tone. "If others have been negligent in her care, we must correct the situation."

"Where are you going with this?"

Dr. Venkata paused. He longed to study the expression on her elegant face, for what he was about to say might be outrageous, libelous or prescient. "The patient was on TPN home therapy. Dr. Lavelle seemed very concerned that we locate the infusion bag used in the home. I located the bag and it is in my possession." He paused again, but she did not interrupt. "If we cultured the contents of the infusion bag, we might determine if it is the source of infection." Venkata waited for her response but the line remained silent so he continued. "I conducted a literature search on the subject of parenteral solutions that have been inadvertently contaminated during the manufacturing process. In such instances, clinical sepsis has been reported." Again, he waited for a response before sealing her attention. "This could be a public health issue, and if so, we must report it immediately."

"Not out of the question, Dr. Venkata, but rather unlikely. Have there been other unexplained cases of sepsis in the hospital? In other hospitals? An FDA recall?"

"No, not to my knowledge."

"I know the statistics on catheter-related infections, as do you, Sandy. Poor hygiene by family caregivers, substandard nursing practices or a break in the catheter insertion protocol account for the majority of problems."

"Yes, of course, you are right."

"Then why are you chasing this zebra? Wouldn't it be more prudent to consider the obvious?"

"Because," Venkata replied, his confidence wavering, "Dr. Lavelle was so focused on the infusion bag. I have learned to pay attention to his instincts because he usually has his reasons, even if he doesn't disclose them . . . ."

"Ah, Dr. Lavelle." She chuckled. "The presumptuous Dr. Lavelle who never requires my consultation. And what does he have to say about your theory?"

"He will not take my calls. Very grieved over Mrs. Runyan's death, I fear. Terribly angry over the care his patient received at Swedish. I hope he will come to some peace over this and restrain his intention for legal action against the hospital."

"My goodness, legal action?" The sound of finger-tapping drummed over the line for a time that seemed interminable to the chief resident. "Your sample may be too old for a useful culture."

Venkata said nothing.

"All right, Sandy. I'll write the order for the bag to be cultured. The lab will protest the unnecessary expense. We can hardly bill a dead patient for a lab test, can we? Dr. Dahl is on a tight budget like everyone else in the hospital, but I have a hunch he'll do it for me. I have a spectacular photo of a sunset over Gweru that he'll want to critique." This time she chuckled louder. "You bring the sample to Pathology; I'll manage the rest."

"Thank you. Thank you. I am very grateful."

"By the way, Dr.Venkata, I hear you're off to Duke this summer—an excellent choice for an ID fellowship. You seem to have everything required for the specialty. You're intelligent. Inquisitive. Persistent. And," she clucked her tongue three times, "terribly suspicious."

***

It was not sleep that he craved so much as a dark, blank space where he could step inside to take cover. Draw the shutters and batten down the cracks of his foundation to keep the storm at bay. The bourbon didn't help. Neither did the benzodiazepines—made him dopey and paranoid. Doubly hung over. Claudette's psychobabble added to his despair.

"Look, Darling, people die. I'm sure it's hard to lose a patient. I know how awful I feel when I lose a commission. In time, you'll forget all about this, Sweetie."

Time was exactly what he didn't have. The unavoidable calls he had to make. He stared at the phone, turned away, clenched his fists, turned back. It must be now.

"Eddison here. Is that you, Fargo?" An empty silence filled the line. "Hello? Hello? Mark, is that you?"

"Eddy," Lavelle hesitated, "she's dead. The Crohn's I spoke of yesterday."

"Sweet Jesus! What in the hell happened?"

Facts of the Runyan case blew over the line to Louisiana. Lavelle spared no detail and assigned no blame. He spoke without emotion at a languid pace. Eddy interrupted him only once to ask if he'd been drinking.

"Not nearly enough," Lavelle answered. It was 10 AM on Sunday. He swirled tomato juice spiked with two aspirin in a tumbler.

Neither physician spoke for what seemed like a long commercial break during a rerun of "The Sopranos."

"How come she died?"

"An overwhelming polymicrobial sepsis." Lavelle wondered if the typically keen mind of his best friend was also pickled. "It had to be from the TPN solution."

"I absolutely, categorically, refuse to believe that, Mark."

"Of course you don't. You're incentivized to think that way, my friend. Personal risk and financial ruin are clouding your logic. The rest of the world doesn't have your disadvantaged perspective. Quite the opposite, actually." His head was pounding. The faint humming of background noise roared in his ear. "What did Sherlock Holmes teach us long ago? 'Nothing is more deceptive than an obvious fact.'"

"Then we'll find another fact, a goddamn better fact, to hang this death on. Hear what I'm saying?"

Lavelle could feel fear building on the line.

"It won't matter, Eddy." Lavelle's speech slurred slightly. "I'll be sued by the husband. He knew about the TPN problem. I explained the recall as some governmental triviality, but the facts will come out in time. He lost his wife. He's angry. He's not stupid and he needs money."

"Then we'll pay him off." Eddy's voice seemed to brighten. "If he's money-hungry, hell, we'll dish up some green gumbo, and he'll drop the suit and go away. That's how we're handling the GEM problem. Get to the guys in the regulatory agency and press their palms with whatever it takes. Money talks. We'll be fine, Mark. You've got to trust me."

Lavelle swirled the glass too aggressively and tomato juice spilled over its side. "You don't feel the slightest responsibility to other patients who might have swamp water running through their veins?" Lavelle wiped red pulp from the front of his velour sweater. "What's happened to you, Eddy?"

"I got rich, pal. Money: the best mood-elevating, pain-killing, life-altering drug on the shelf. Definitely, my drug-of-choice. When it comes to the almighty dollar, enough is a place I never get to. Lucky there's so much easy money in the system. All you got to do is bend over and scoop it up."

Eddy snorted like an anteater.

"Here's the deal, Cowboy. Do nothing. Say nothing. Speak to no one until this little storm blows over. If you get some pushback, I'll send a bobsled your way with an attorney strapped on. Be cool. Should be no problem with your weather. Still snowing on the 47th parallel?"

Lavelle glanced out the leaded glass window of his study. Weather jokes had come to irritate him. The winter landscape of the early morning was beginning to disappear. Snow dissolved on the sidewalks, leaving muddy edges and open patches of exposed lawn. The earth was losing its coat of white, and so it seemed, was he.

Twenty-Four

Sunday mornings belonged to Mr. Wang. Heli perched on a stool in the Jade Garden's kitchen with the obit section of the *Freedom Press* sprawled across the stainless counter. News of Christine Runyan's passing appeared in the death notices but no obituary followed. Barely twelve hours had passed since Venkata's pronouncement. Heli's brow creased with sorrow.

"Whatever trouble you," Mr. Wang announced, "Goji berry tea sure to help." He shuffled toward her with a teapot balanced on a teak tray. "Tea: one of seven daily necessities."

The cranberry scent rose up to greet her. Between sips, she improvised her own list of necessities. Uninterrupted sleep. Warm bath. Long run by the river. Barley bread with Cheese Whiz. Dry boots. Sun to my face. Venkata's voice. Stop! Fingertips pressed against her temples as if to halt the fantasy from spilling onto the counter. Exhaustion was weakening her usual guard. She swiveled, facing Mr. Wang.

"Besides good tea, must be rice." He held up a bulk container of soy sauce. "This too plus good oil." He nodded. "And salt." He pointed to a shelf of cooking ingredients over the imposing gas range. "Vinegar."

"That's six," Heli answered, warding off a yawn.

"And fire." He nodded. "Must be fire to heat things up."

Mr. Wang was obviously fishing for a tell-all about Venkata but she didn't bite. Of course she wanted to—intended to—tell him that her otherwise tepid life had inexplicably heated up, but the words weren't quite there. Only the feelings. Warm. After a long cold winter, warm now, like the palms of her hands cupping the tea bowl.

"Fabulous tea, Mr. Wang." She folded the newspaper and stacked the sections together with the April 2 headline on top: *Spring Storm Disrupts Life in Fargo*

"Old Tibetan proverb," Mr. Wang replied as he filled a rack with clean glasses from the dishwasher, "Goji berries in morning make you happy entire day." He reached for the plates. "Boosts energy, reduce cholesterol, improve blood."

Heli refilled the cup with tea. Watched the rosy liquid curl around the bowl. Breathed in the sweet fumes. Remembered the code. Thought about Venkata. Relieved that Mr. Wang's talents stopped short of mind reading.

"Read yourself." He handed to her what appeared to be a package insert from the tea tin. "'21 Claims for Goji.' Enhance beauty. Good for sleep disturbances."

"Now you've got my attention." Heli muffled a cavernous yawn. "Will Goji burn fat? Restore my youth?"

"That too!"

With glasses and dishes racked, Mr. Wang continued his Sunday morning routine by degreasing the grill. Heli knew the gas wok burner was next. Then he'd clean the meat slicer, the steamers and the pressure cooker. Before mopping the floor, he'd sharpen his prize collection of Asian knives: cleavers, the bird's beak peeler, boning knives, the seven-inch Santoku and the stripping knives. During each of the tasks, he'd talk almost as though he were alone in the kitchen, floating proverbs, dispensing advice, dropping bits of news like spices in the wok. This time she decided to interrupt.

"Christine Runyan died last night."

"I know."

"You know? You've already read the newspaper?"

"No," he shook his head slowly in a gesture of compassion. "Brigid called away from work last night. She telephone with bad news early this morning." Mr. Wang looked at the clock on the wall over the busing station. "She coming soon to clear out locker. Get last payroll check."

"She quit her job?"

"I cut her hours. Insurance too. She get very angry. I feel bad, but what to do?"

Heli slumped on the stool. Her premium rates hiked up another 14% this year. What business can afford this? She rubbed her forehead at the premonition of a headache. "My mortgage or my medicine?—that's the decision for patients. They take their medicine, not as prescribed, but when they can afford to."

Mr. Wang rubbed the boning knife's blade against carbon steel.

"What will Brigid do?"

"I tell her to take some time, whatever she needs, but she want to quit now."

The banging on the heavy back door of the restaurant needed no explanation. Mr. Wang removed his plastic gloves and left the kitchen, leaving Heli alone with a stillness that was unnerving. The prospect of seeing Brigid Olander brought another round of dread and pulled her back to last night at Swedish. Brigid, barging down the hallway with Anya close behind. In her memory, the scenes were spliced together like old film. Black became white, ghoulish and unnatural. She heard the exchange of voices beyond the kitchen: one, growling, the other, consoling. A locker door slammed.

The rear door into the kitchen opened.

"Heli," Mr. Wang called, "someone to see you."

But Heli saw no one except an occasional sighting of Mr. Wang's head popping beyond open shelves of pots and pans. When he turned the corner by the humming Cold Tech, a pink and purple parka followed him.

"Please," he said, "watch little girl. Give her orange juice. Show her Koi." Mr. Wang waved his arms helplessly. "I deal with Brigid alone." He left without another word.

The moment turned awkward as though a yellow biohazard tape had suddenly been strung across the kitchen aisle. Heli squatted, eye-level with the child. "Anya, about your mother. I'm so sorry." Hugging seemed like a natural thing to do, but the invisible tape stopped her.

Anya retreated like a cat bow-backs away.

The same age my own child would have been, thought Heli. Years of longing had driven her to search for her unborn infant in the face of every child she encountered.

"Are you hungry, Anya? Maybe thirsty? How about a can of pop?"

No response.

"Orange juice?"

Anya slid down against the wall, hugging her knees.

Heli offered a hand but Anya turned a shoulder in protest.

"Maybe an Egg McMuffin at McDonalds?" For once Heli was willing to overlook corporate profiteering at the expense of society's health if Anya showed any interest in the Golden Arches.

Still no response.

Heli drummed the countertop for inspiration. Sensed the child's despair. Groped for some common denominator to bridge the gap of silence.

"I see Dr. Anya has her medical bag along. Is it filled with surprises?"

The hint of a smile on the child's face was encouraging.

"Have you used the Little Mermaid band-aids yet?"

Anya nodded slowly, pulling up a red corduroy pant leg to reveal an adhesive mermaid tattoo above her anklet.

"Very cool," Heli said. "What else do you have in there?"

"Nothing."

"Nothing? You must have something in there."

"Nothing."

"Well, then." Heli glanced at her watch, wondering how much time she had. The conversation beyond the kitchen walls had subdued. She heard the old hand lever of a Burroughs adding machine. A box slide across the floor.

"Maybe we should go across the street to Corner Drug and find something. Would you like that, Anya?"

A head of matted hair nodded a slow yes. Heli scribbled a note on the corner of a Jade menu: *Back in 10 minutes. HH.* She zippered Anya's parka, slipped into her Polar fleece and led the little girl out of the Jade's front door.

Church bells tolled in the background as Heli and Anya, hand in hand, jaywalked across the deserted Devine Street. A warm sun melted the snow that two days ago had stalled downtown traffic. The air was brisk and fresh in a way that the Jade's kitchen was not. Standing in front of Corner Drug, Heli pulled keys from her pocket and opened the door to a darkened store. With sixty seconds to disarm the security system, she sprinted back to the pharmacy where the keypad was located. Anya scampered behind.

"Kinda dark in here," Anya said timidly.

"Watch this!" A single bay of overhead lights came on with one flick of a switch. "Follow me, Anya." Heli headed toward the wound care section. "For someone who has nothing in her doctor bag, how about more band-aids?"

The little girl looked around quizzically. "You got anything else?"

"Like what?"

"I dunno." With small dexterous fingers that reminded Heli of her own at that age, Anya opened the plastic snaps of the Fisher Price clutch. "This is what I've got."

"A cotton arm band with a Red Cross identifier," noted Heli as she wrapped the cuff around Anya's arm. "Very important in a disaster."

"And this. A heart thing."

"A stethoscope," Heli clarified. "Every doctor needs one."

"Daddy showed me where the heart is." Anya placed her hand over her chest. "Here, right?"

"Exactly. I'm impressed."

"What's this thing? I forgot."

"An otoscope. Good for finding elephants in ears."

"And this, for fevers." Anya spun the dial on an oversized

thermometer. "It's just make-believe, though."

She knows more about the tools of the trade than most five year olds. More than a child of her age should have to know.

"And this thing." In her palm, Anya held out a syringe with its needle still attached. The needle guard was missing.

Heli winced. This was real. "Where did you find this, Anya?"

"Just found it, that's all. Finders, keepers. . . ."

"Losers, weepers." Someone had to be a loser with a capital L to be this careless with needle safety. Surely Trevor Runyan knew better, or home health, if they were to blame. The endless possibilities for viral transmission from dirty needles made her shudder. "Finders, keepers; losers, weepers. I know that rhyme too." Heli's instinct was to come on strong. Wrest away the syringe from Anya and explain the danger of an eighteen-gauge needle lying at the bottom of a toy bag. She'd mention the incident to Trevor. Extract a promise from him to be more careful around children. Self-righteousness flamed in her cheeks. Then, the reality of what Trevor was probably dealing with at the moment tempered her zeal, calling forth a kind of wisdom from an untapped maternal reservoir. There was a better way.

"How about a trade, Anya? If I had something you really, really wanted, would you trade that syringe?"

"Like what?"

Good question. Near the cash register by the pharmacy, Murlene kept rolls of pediatric stickers for kids. Round fuchsia labels that read "Purrrfect Patient." Lime green Mr. Yuk stickers for household poisons. Smiling balloons, happy whales and dancing dinosaurs.

"How about some stickers?"

"Nah. Don't need stickers. Mommy gives me lots of stickers." She wrinkled her freckled nose. "They're kinda' boring."

Heli scanned the aisles of Corner Drug. Not exactly Toys-R-Us. If stickers were boring, what would Anya think of a pediatric dosing spoon, surgical paper tape, a hippopotamus-shaped toothbrush or an icy-cold pack? Something from Burt's Bees line? She raised her eyes to the tinned ceiling for ideas.

Anya put away her toys into the medical bag as Heli's searching paused at the front window.

"Wait! Come with me." She took Anya's hand and led her to the St. Urho display where in the midst of rubber grasshoppers, a shoal of stuffed green frogs were immobilized in apparent flight.

Heli grabbed one pliable toy.

"See this green frog?"

Anya leaned in for a closer look.

"*Goonk! gunk! gunk*! That's how green frogs sound."

"Do that again." Anya giggled.

"*Goonk! gunk! gunk*! This particular species of green frogs sounds like plucking a loose banjo string. *Goonk! gunk! gunk*! I hear them when I fly fish along the river flats."

"I know how to fish. BG helps me."

"What do you catch?"

"Sunnies."

"Right off the dock, I'll bet." Heli moved closer. "May I see your stethoscope, Doctor?"

Anya complied with a shy smile.

Heli curled a frog leg around the stethoscope's tubing, and smiled. "Now you look like a real kids' doctor."

"Let me see."

They moved to the cosmetic counter for a look in the mirror. Anya adjusted the spindly frog legs around the tubing. Put the plastic earpiece in her ears. Fingered the drum. Seemed pleased by the look.

"How about trading a green frog for the syringe?"

Her eyes brightened, yet she paused momentarily. "Okay, I'll trade this thing," she held up the syringe again, "for *two* frogs. One for each side."

"You drive a hard bargain, Doctor Anya." Typical physician—demanding advantage—thought the pharmacist. "It's a deal." Heli fetched another green frog from the display, offering silent gratitude to St. Urho. She wasted no time getting the syringe and needle from Anya's bag, slipping both into a #10 white envelope from a rack in the window display. The envelope addressed to the Fargo Finnish Society settled in the pocket of her fleece jacket.

"But I won't trade you this. Not for all the froggies in the world." Anya brought out something more from the bottom of her medical bag. She held up a small ornamental bottle with a stoppered top. "Found it, too, and it's mine now."

Heli bent forward for a closer look. "May I see?" She held the small glass globe against the bright eastern light streaming in through the store's front window. "Wow!" She slowly rotated the object, noting the tiny oriental landscape with orange Koi and water lilies painted in reverse style inside the vessel's chamber. "Very cool." Memory transported her back to a college course in pharmaceutical history. In Asian culture, snuff was believed to cure migraines, relieve tooth pain. This was a snuff jar. If authentic, the bottle might be very collectible, although it was probably a repro. She was no judge of art. What was Anya doing with it?

"Do you suppose somebody might be looking for this, Anya?" Heli bit her lip at the gaffe. Clearly Christine Runyan no longer had much use for pretty objects. She thought about Mr. Wang's Chinese proverb of seven necessities. Thought about her own impromptu list. Realized how quickly needs change when the earth shifts from under us. Anya needed something of her mother's to hang on to, to relieve the profound sadness of loss. Didn't we all? Heli thought of her mother's botany textbooks and her father's fishing gear stored safely in her apartment—how she fingered the fragile pages, felt the steel jaws of the vice for some connection. More than Goji tea, more than sleep, more than sun on our face, we need our memories, our hopes and our delusions to get us through our day.

"There's BG!" Anya grabbed the glass bottle from Heli's hands and buried it in the bottom of the medical bag. She snapped the lid shut and scuttled to the front door where the face of Brigid Olander, framed by open palms, pressed flat against the window.

Heli heard Brigid's gruff voice as she unlocked the door.

"Come along, kiddo. Grandma's waiting for us."

"O. . . . kay." Anya moved toward her aunt, looking back over her shoulder as though she had something to say. She craned her head around a second time in Heli's direction. A faint smile lit up her otherwise vacant face. *"Goonk! gunk! gunk!"*

Heli smiled back. The eerie rumble of ice cracking on a frozen lake, the quiet rush of summer rain, a throaty *gunk* of *Rana clamitans*. The power of ancient sounds to connect and soothe the living went well beyond anything she could dispense in the pharmacy.

Twenty-Five

Venkata exchanged his earlier grip on the microscope for the handle of a vacuum cleaner. From the Serapi rug in his apartment, he hoovered up dust that gathered, undisturbed, during his rigorous week at the hospital. He enjoyed the mindless cleaning. The monotonous motion freed him from the usual vicissitudes of his day. He straightened a Kilm textile stretched above a black leather couch and dusted the low coffee table that looked more like a desk with its pile of textbooks and papers. A stack of medical journals was consigned to a bureau drawer and Nikes, kicked under his bed. He stuffed grey running shorts and a Swedish Hospital sweatshirt into a laundry bag which he hid in the bathtub behind the drawn shower curtain.

Two o'clock in the afternoon on Sunday translated to approximately midnight in Mumbai. With so much to do, the email to his parents could wait. A chicken marinated in a smooth paste of yogurt, garlic, ginger, lime, cloves and cardamom in a clay baker in his kitchen. Were his mother near, she would advise, "remember to use a whole pound of butter. Don't skimp, Sandu!" Smiling, he removed four sticks of unsalted butter from the refrigerator. The Chicken Makhani must be perfect tonight.

The phone rang feebly under a damp towel on the floor of his bedroom. He sat on the edge of his unmade bed, admiring the stark black-and-white poster that hung on the opposite wall. *North Dakota: Life in the Vast Lane.*

"Donna Wadeson from home health would like to speak to you," the hospital operator announced. "I realize you're not on call, but she won't take no for an answer."

"Put her through, please." Venkata glanced at his watch, wondering how long the chatty old nurse would divert him from his evening preparations.

"Dr. Venkata, this is Donna. You know, the nurse with the TPN bag in Corner Drug yesterday."

"Yes, I remember you."

"Is it true?"

There was little doubt to what *it* referred.

"Yes, Mrs. Runyan has died."

The nurse launched into an explosion of questions. When? Where? How high? How long? Did she suffer? Then the question Venkata dreaded most. "Why, Doctor? What killed her?"

"She became septic. That is all we know at the moment. A definitive lab report will be issued tomorrow."

From her sounds, Venkata knew Donna must be blowing her nose. "Well, thank you for the information. I wish someone would have notified me." She sniffed. "Wouldn't really change anything, but I liked her. This news . . . there's something strange . . ."

The nurse's observations of Christine Runyan's prior status had been accurate and astute. Perhaps she had something to add about the home environment that might be instructive. "What, exactly, do you mean by 'strange'?"

"Nothing I haven't already told you."

"Please try," Venkata urged. Early in his training, he'd learned that people could always remember more than they thought if gently prodded.

"Well, then, . . ." The nurse seemed inclined to talk. "The family lived in a way that seems strange to the likes of me. I shouldn't be talking about the dead at a time like this, but the place was a god-awful mess."

Venkata looked about his bedroom and winced.

"Do you have any reason to believe that the family, the husband, in particular, might have been neglectful in sterile procedures when he administered the TPN or dressed the wound? I ask because I can find no endogenous source for the infection."

"He's a paramedic, for goodness sakes. If he doesn't know proper technique, who does? Besides, Christine was taught to hook up the TPN herself. Simple enough for a child to do."

"I see." Venkata thought about the new information momentarily, and redirected his questioning. "How about other home health nurses? Have all of you followed strict aseptic processes?" As soon as the words left his tongue, he regretted it.

"Pardon my bluntness, but I've dressed more wounds than you've probably *seen* in your lifetime. You're barking up the wrong tree if you think nurses slipped up on the wound care protocols, Doctor. The gauze dressing around the insertion site was changed as ordered. Period. Bacterial filters, too. What are you getting at?"

"We are both sad over Mrs. Runyan's death. Please, think again. Did you see anything else that seemed irregular?"

"I've already told you—very little seemed regular. If I have any regrets, it's that I didn't bring in Social Services for an evaluation. I worry about the child. She's pretty much left to her own devices during the day and night." The nurse paused, and

Venkata waited. "It wasn't what I saw as much as what I didn't see. Bare cupboards, empty refrigerator, stale air." Her voice quieted. "It seemed Christine lived in a small world, almost as though she had to shrink herself to find a place to fit in. Sometimes I wonder if she sensed it—that she wasn't going to get better. She was terribly afraid of going back to the hospital."

Venkata listened carefully, visualizing the stark environment she described. He saw his patient spiraling down a lonely vortex. Her suggestion of Social Services surprised him. In India, this was a family's duty.

"Goodness, I've gone on and on."

Venkata glanced at his watch. Time was evaporating.

"Ever tasted glorified rice, Doctor?" Without giving him time to answer, she prattled on. "I'm making a nice salad for the family so there'll be something in that Runyan refrigerator. Adding some red candy hearts to pink it up for the little girl. Make her feel better. Well, good bye, then, and thanks."

Venkata replaced the cordless phone on its base, wondering how rice could be glorified. Only then did he realize he'd completely forgotten about tonight's dessert.

***

"Well, well, well. You're the very last person I expected to interrupt my Sunday morning tennis match. Mark, why are you calling after all these years?" His voice, normally groomed and gentrified like every other medical school Dean in the country, turned irritable. "I believe we settled our differences years ago with money and your promise to go away. Far away."

In a sea of change, Lavelle knew his ex-father-in-law's regular Sunday morning tennis match at Pennsylvania's Wynnewood Country Club would remain inviolate. At seventy-two, Dr. Clifton L. Magers had recently retired as Dean of Jefferson Medical College and still enjoyed emeritus status in the medical community. For the latter reason, Mark made the difficult phone call.

"How is Maxine? And Katherine? Your health, Clifton?"

"Cut through the butter, Mark. You never paid much attention to your mother-in-law when you were a part of our family. Spare me your feigned concern now. As for Katherine, she's done very well for herself after you walked out on her six years ago. In May, she'll receive a Master's degree in Counseling from U Penn. Married a football coach with two young sons. They're poor as church mice, but she's happy. Joy she never experienced with you," he added cryptically. 'Katherine is in her second trimester." He sighed. "My first real grandchild."

"Congratulations. Give her my best."

"I will do nothing of the sort. She will never know of this conversation. Now, kindly explain your audacity to re-emerge in my life, and the presumption that I have any interest in making small talk with you."

Lavelle steadied himself. "I may be in a bit of trouble."

A malevolent laughter blasted across the telephone line. "Why is that not difficult to believe? Oh, Mark, what is it this time?"

The din of clubby conversation with occasional bouts of hilarity echoed in the background. Once a member of the "Club," as it was abridged by the privileged, Lavelle could picture the sunlit green room with the marble bar and a view of the sprawling golf course. A feeling of isolation and longing swept over him. His entitled past life seemed remote, inaccessible.

"I need a lawyer. A good one."

"Serious trouble, eh? Exactly what type of attorney? Divorce? Tax problems? Bankruptcy? Malpractice?"

His father-in-law's interrogation sounded like the multiple-choice questions he'd despised during his student days. There was never one single answer to a problem—in this case, all of the above—and more. Product liability and Medicare fraud were also possible. The current mess required an essay to explain.

"I'm asking you to make a call to Ed Mancino on my behalf. As the managing partner of his law firm, he can't be taking many cases anymore, but I need someone with a national reputation. Someone with an extensive network he can call upon if necessary. Someone who can handle the press. Someone powerful and terrifying."

Dr. Magers paused on the other end of the line. "You must be in *very* serious trouble if you need Ed's help. He's reached celebrity status along the eastern seaboard and his hourly fees are obscene. Aren't there lawyers in Dakota?"

"Yes, there are lawyers in *North* Dakota, but most are associated in one way or another with Swedish Hospital where I admit, and they're unlikely to take my case. 'Conflicted' is the term they use." Scared would be a better word, Mark thought. "Besides, a big name beyond the Midwest is useful in sending the message that I'll have a sterling defense against their empty charges."

"What, exactly, are the charges?"

"Nothing yet, but a Crohn's case went south, and I'll probably be sued for malpractice."

"Can you afford Mancino?"

Lavelle hesitated.

"You need money from me as well? You have incredible nerve."

"Money is no issue." Lavelle lied convincingly. "I have a burgeoning medical practice here and I've invested wisely." He had no idea where the money for legal fees would come from. The house on Pill Hill might have to go.

"Surely our score has been settled, Mark. I don't owe you anything. Why would I intercede on your behalf?"

Lavelle floated an answer that he believed still bound the two physicians to a common ideal. "Because you care about the profession of medicine, that is, what's left of it. Because you are not passive in the face of medical injustice. Because when one physician is dishonored, the entire profession is sullied. Because you and I have always agreed that physicians need to reclaim the profession from the government, from insurance companies, from Hillary Clinton and her political ideologues, before medical care becomes completely socialized. Because you care about patients, Clifton, and the careers of young medical students. You care about the truth."

The buzz of a blender in the background suggested that his father-in-law must be near the health bar where the bartender was preparing a fruit smoothie. "I suspect I'm being set up as the outsider that must be brought down. I'll admit to some mistakes, but this matter could destroy me."

"You've destroyed others, Mark. My dreams, in particular, for Katherine and for the family life I expected to enjoy as I grow older."

Lavelle said nothing.

"I'll never forget when you were a resident in the late eighties—the time you made that rare diagnosis of *hereditary angioneurotic edema* on a patient that had confounded all of the attending physicians. You wrote it up and submitted the case to the *Annals of Internal Medicine*. Remember? As far as I know, you're one of a handful of students ever to be published in a peer-reviewed journal during residency. I was terribly proud to have you dating Katherine. Your future together seemed so prosperous. What happened, Mark? At what point did your life begin to unravel?"

Lavelle overlooked the slur, heartened by the trace of fondness that still lingered inside the old codger. "I can't change the past, Clifton, but you can influence my future. And, the future of medicine that has completely derailed. I'm asking for your help now. You've always been a moral compass for me."

If lying was easy, begging was not.

"I'll see Ed at a museum fundraiser in Philly in a few weeks. I'll mention it to him. No promises." Lavelle listened as Dr. Magers slurped his beverage through a straw. "Although I can't think of a reason why Ed should have any interest in helping *you*." The glass clinked on a marble counter. "On the other hand, he may have an interest in humoring me."

Lavelle's breathing quickened.

"Ed's mediocre grandson from Toledo has applied to Jefferson Medical College and stands little chance for admission without some intervention. Dismal MCAT scores in the low twenties. He's been turned down by every other medical school of any status."

Exasperated, Lavelle interrupted the slow promise of help that seemed to be brewing in his father-in-law's mind. "Clifton, I need Ed Manicino in Fargo, maybe as early as this week."

"You always had a flare for drama." Another long slurp. The glass had to be nearly empty. "I'll do what I can, but if your problems are that acute, you'll need more than Ed Mancino and the entire firm of Mancino, Barner, Gaynor and Nigrelli on your side."

"Thank you, Clifton. That's all I can possibly say at a time like this."

"Odd, isn't it? Ed and I are of an age where trading favors is the only real currency we have left. Two ageing men, leveraging friendships to reconcile family disappointments."

The blender droned in the background.

Twenty-Six

The penetrating scent of cilantro from Chicken Makhani diffused throughout the room. Candles flickered in the dim light over the small dining table in Venkata's apartment. With a madras napkin, Heli dabbed the corners of her mouth, leaving only a trace of saffron rice on the plate.

"There's good food, even great food, but this dinner," she drew a long, indulgent breath, "goes straight to memory." She smiled, placing silence around the thought to give it full bloom. Venkaka, she noticed, had rarely taken his eyes off her. The feverish warmth rising from her neck could not be explained by spicy food. "Everything was lovely. And you make it look so easy. Me?" She canted her head. "Emulsions and tinctures I can do, but anything in the kitchen poses a great risk for company. I know my limits." She slid her chair back across the parquet floor. "But I can help you clean up."

"Please, this can wait." Venkata guided her from the table into the living room. He cast aside two red silk pillows, each with a pair of embroidered royal elephants, to clear a space on the leather couch.

"An aperitif, yes?"

Heli plunged into the soft cushion and closed her eyes. Smooth jazz streamed from a black television screen. The reverberating notes of a string bass in the background were hypnotic. The evening had unfolded beautifully, defying every possibility her anxious mind had contrived. She opened her eyes and panned the apartment's comfortable chaos. A *Harrison's Textbook of Medicine* had been repurposed as a doorstop against a heaving closet door. Miles of computer cable snaked out from behind Sandy's desk. Every slot of a tall CD rack was filled. Curious, Heli rose from the sofa for a closer look. The plastic covers of Sting, Norah Jones and U2 were free of dust. A jeweled picture frame on his desk showcased the photograph of a young woman in a rich turquoise costume. Her waving arms, heavy with gold bangle bracelets, appeared frozen in rhythmic stance. The photo was of studio quality, and Heli imagined the gigantic electric fans used in the photo-shoot to have caused her dark hair to flow so breezily.

"My sister, Deepthi," Venkata commented as he returned with two glasses of Lillet Blanc.

"She's beautiful." The sibling similarity, alert brown eyes and killer smile, was obvious.

"Very talented, Deepthi. She will be dancing in *Bombay Dreams* when it opens in London's West End in June."

London. Mumbai. Fargo. Dots on a map lit up in Heli's mind.

"Perhaps someday you will meet her. She is like you: spirited, self-reliant and," Venkata hesitated, "courageous when others are not."

Heli swirled vermouth in the bowl, past a water spot near the lip, and sipped amber liquid from the chilled glass. A bittersweet burst of honey, orange and mint coated her tongue. His compliment, she avoided entirely.

"This was to have been served a half hour before our meal. It is supposed to stoke the appetite," Venkata apologized, "but I completely forgot. So many things need attention at the last minute." He shook his head as if he were addled. "There would have been no dessert without your contribution, Heli. A new taste for me: Finnish cloudberries."

"*Rubus chamaemorum*. Good for gout and scurvy; not bad on Haagen Daz."

"You have an amazing grasp of taxonomic detail."

Her chin dropped. "But not such a firm grasp on a bicarb ampoule."

Until now, there had been no reference to the code at Swedish the prior evening. Like the pair of floor pillows, the subject of Christine Runyan was the third elephant in the room, set aside and unacknowledged.

"It made no difference to her outcome, Heli. None whatsoever. Mrs. Runyan died of polymicrobial sepsis. Do not take Dr. Lavelle's harsh words personally. In time, he will realize the team performed admirably. The patient went beyond our reach."

"Meanwhile, are we to simply put up with his verbal abuse?"

"It is not my position to question authority."

"Hmm. I think we should stand up to intimidation, to injustice, to the abuse of power." Sandy's utter deference to Lavelle stood out in her mind like a slight smudge on his otherwise flawless character. No bigger than a water spot on a wine glass, this was difficult to overlook. An argument formed in her mind, but she suppressed it.

"I suppose I'm wired differently. Finns stand up to bullies. Consider our history." Heli studied the medallion in the center of the Serapi rug. "I've paid dearly for my outspokenness in the past. I suspect I'll pay again."

She lifted her head, waiting for his reaction. Venkata simply smiled which was impossible for her to interpret. She stared into her glass and sipped more Lillet. The music stopped and the potential for the evening seemed to be sliding toward a finale.

"I knew her. That's what makes it so difficult. She was a patient at Corner Drug. Stopped by the store on Friday with her sister and daughter to drop off a roll of film."

Venkata set his glass on the coffee table. "Perhaps it will help to talk about it."

Heli hesitated. "Until recently, I've dispensed all of the family's meds for years. One prescription after another: sulfasalazine, steroids, B-12 injections, iron supplements, antibiotics, pain medication. I even prepared her home TPN solution until a few months ago." She observed Venkata shift on the cushion, his attention sharpening. "I'm sorry, Sandy. This has been so lovely and I've just laid black crepe over the evening."

"Do not apologize. The death troubles me as well. All day I tried to distract myself by cooking, and with the thought of seeing you. Yet, my mind will not settle until I understand the cause of her infection."

He explained the atypical laboratory findings of the blood sample. Heli listened intently, assimilating the clinical findings with her own impressions.

"Do you know Mr. Runyan as well?" Venkata asked.

"Only as a customer. Trevor is a man of few words," she reflected, staring across the dimly lit room, "but I've had a glimpse into his life." She turned to Sandy. "A patient's medication history reveals a story that doesn't always require words to explain."

"Mr. Runyan abused drugs?"

"No, no." Heli replied. "What I meant was that over time, a person's health, or lack of health, can be interpreted to some degree by the medicine dispensed. It's all there on the medication profile. Every entry means something."

Whatever spark of romance there might have been for the evening now seemed to have been doused by shoptalk. The words of her mother rose in her mind: *every dinner invitation obligates a guest to be interesting.* And I have become tedious, Heli concluded.

"Tell me more, please. I want to understand your perceptions."

"Well," she continued, buoyed by his interest, "as Christine's drug regimen intensified, I knew her condition was worsening. It had to have been very difficult for Trevor, for Anya and their family life." She recalled the syringe in the toy medical bag and reconsidered her decision to spare Trevor the riot act for his carelessness. "I saw him leave the family room last night after getting the news of his wife's death." Heli lowered her head. "Even though I've had . .. . issues with him, I felt such genuine sympathy for the family, and the difficult road before him."

"Issues with Mr. Runyan?"

Despite her renewed intention to be light-hearted, even charming, the Runyan story poured from her lips like spilt wine. "Early this year, we stopped dispensing the TPN infusions for Christine. Trevor switched to a specialty mail-order pharmacy, leaving a hefty outstanding balance at Corner Drug." Heli's finger circled the rim of the glass. "What terrible irony! Yesterday, the very afternoon he pays up her pharmacy bill, Christine dies six hours later."

The phone rang in Venkata's apartment. Heli glanced at her watch: 10:30 PM. She should be leaving. Had no interest in doing so.

"I am expecting the lab to call," Venkata explained. "Perhaps you can find some music to play," motioning to the rack of CDs with one hand, holding the cordless phone in the other. "This will take only a moment."

***

The chief resident was not surprised to hear a voice from the Microbiology lab on the other end of the line. He thought of moving into his bedroom to take the call privately, but he stayed to watch Heli instead. What CD might she choose, and what meaning might it portend for the rest of the evening?

"Hey, Dr. Venkata, Jenny here in the lab. You asked us to call if there was any growth on the culture from the TPN bag."

"And?"

"There is." Her voice was young, sweet and rapid. "I did a gram stain, and it shows mixed organisms, both gram-positive and gram-negative, and something is growing on the anaerobic culture too. Really, really strange."

Venkata sat up on the couch and leaned forward.

"Repeat the report slowly, please."

He'd heard correctly the first time. The news both startled

and excited him. The preliminary path report matched the findings of Christine Runyan's blood culture. This implied that the infusion bag might be the source of his patient's infection. It was not a definite conclusion, but at the very least, a step forward. He checked his watch; too late on a Sunday evening to call either Dr. Lavelle or Dr. Kampela with the news. They would no doubt require validation before acceding to his theory. Dr. Kampela was quick to point out yesterday that the sample may have been too old for reliable results. In the morning, he would visit the lab for the final report before starting rounds at 7 AM.

Heli selected a Branford Marsalis performance recorded at Carnegie Hall, and the quiet room filled with the bluesy, beckoning rhythm from an alto saxophone.

Venkata thanked the lab tech and hung up the phone. Progress, he thought happily, some progress in the steady march toward an answer. Perhaps Dr. Lavelle's confidence in him might return. And Heli's choice of music was also encouraging.

She was examining a row of textbooks on his bookshelf, her head cocked to read the vertical titles. Venkata studied her. There were a thousand ways to describe a female body with all its splendid details, but it was her crisp voice and her curious mind that first captured his affection. She turned to him and smiled gently, as much with her Arctic blue eyes as her drawn lips. He felt the traction of her words pull him back into a state of reflection. The hint of tension in her voice, the edgy friction of her phrases intrigued him. So unlike Rashmi who waited for him in Mumbai according to the arrangement of their families.

If a patient's medication profile told a story as Heli had suggested, perhaps books on a shelf might also reveal a life. A tinge of embarrassment clouded his confidence. Too much medicine at the expense of other joys. It was time to redirect the course of the evening, and he would do exactly that after asking one more question that still gripped him.

Rising from the couch, Venkata approached the shelves and wrapped an arm around Heli's shoulder. Her accommodating, lean-in, response felt reassuring. "Come." He guided her back to the sofa, "I was in Carnegie Hall the night of this recording. I will tell you about it, but first, something you mentioned about the Runyan case perplexes me. It seems she will not leave us alone tonight."

"She brought us together."

"Indeed." He pulled her in closer and detected sandalwood, like the woody scent from the carved chest where his mother stored precious silk shawls.

"What is it, Sandy?"

Venkata drew a breath, seriously questioning his timing, but there was little choice but to go forward now. "Mail-order pharmacies: is this common, sending away for IV medication by mail?"

He felt her shrink ever slightly from his embrace.

"I'm afraid so. Growing by leaps and bounds." Heli nodded as if annoyed by the trend. "It seems every attempt by the government to rein in costs does nothing more than nurture a new business ready to profit from the demise of others." Her face was determined. "Greed meets need. It's become big business in oncology."

"Ordering tablets and capsules by mail, yes, but accepting sterile infusions prepared by strangers—is it not without some risk?"

"I'd say so. 'Let the buyer beware.' Patients are much too willing to trust a system with essentially no federal oversight. We're all alike in their eyes."

Venkata pieced together in his mind what he'd just heard. "Dr. Lavelle directed me to find the IV bag. I could tell it was important to him. I believe he suspected the infusion bag all along."

"Yes, of course he would." Heli's voice became icy. "Dr. Lavelle seems inclined to believe that every problem can be somehow tied to the failure of a pharmacist." She set her empty wine glass firmly on the table and turned on the cushion to face him. The silence lasted a long time. Gradually, Venkata saw her face begin to soften. He was relieved.

"Carnegie Hall; what's it like, Sandy? Tell me everything."

"The concert hall is intimate, enormously tall, 105 steps to the top balcony. Acoustically, near perfect." Venkata read her cues and tightened his arm around her. "And dark, much darker than this room." He reached across the couch for the lamp switch, his body stretched over hers, and turned off the single remaining light in the apartment.

***

Sheltered within his arms, she found the peacefulness of a river at predawn, quietly pulsating with life, waiting to be discovered. Her father had taught her the importance of reading a Minnesota stream, its current and seams.

"Look down," he'd said to his young daughter years ago. "What do you see, Heli?"

"Nothing."

"Look harder. Ignore what is pulling your attention away from the water."

"Still nothing."

"You must learn to see what is before you. Like a puzzle, you must unfocus your eyes until you see the pattern. We're not leaving until you can spot a hundred fish."

She watched herself in memory, hunched knee-deep in the Hay Meadow Creek, studying the irregular currents of the stream. A good river—gravel bottom, deep holes, broken limestone beneath the gin-clear water. But still she could not see beyond the shimmer and shadow of the creek.

A sand hill crane patrolled overhead. The reeds shivered, swayed in the wind and a caddis hatch swarmed around her. A squirrel nosed at the lunch box near her creel while water licked the rocks along the shoreline. Yet, the spell was unbroken. She waited, watched, waited, watched. Nothing.

Suddenly, an explosion of brook trout pooled near her waders. Hundreds, maybe thousands. Memory exaggerates, cannot always be trusted.

"Daddy," she'd screamed. "I see them! I see at least a hundred fish."

"Well done, little girl. Well done. Now you've become an angler."

She rubbed her eyes to clear away the dream. It was nearly midnight. "Sandy, I should go."

"Must you?"

She heard the disappointment in his voice. He is a gentleman, a gentle man. "It's late. I've had a wonderful evening."

"In that case, I will see you home."

"Thanks, but the Saab will deliver me."

"May I call you tomorrow, yes?"

"I'd like that."

"Good night, then."

His slow kiss on her forehead felt as light as a gossamer tippet. She looked up at him, craving this man who could flood her senses, tame her fears and rouse the tenderness of childhood back into the moment. His second kiss tasted pleasantly of Neroli Oil, distilled from the fresh flowers of *Citrus Aurantium*. Calming and rare.

The full moon was her companion as she coursed through the

streets of Fargo. Neither traffic nor slushy roads delayed the short trip from Sandy's apartment to her own. She turned into the dark alley off Main Avenue to park the car when she noticed another vehicle approach from behind. A car door slammed and she reached for the flip-top canister inside her bag.

Advancing footsteps sluiced through the melting snow. He knocked on the passenger window, and Heli turned in her car seat to see the commanding image of Officer Tim LaDuke beyond the glass pane.

"Out pretty late on a Sunday evening, Heli."

"Not exactly a criminal offense, Officer. Is there a 10 PM curfew in Fargo?"

"Not curfews exactly," he replied authoritatively, "but definitely a DLR."

She didn't indulge the acronym. Why did every profession succumb to its own undecipherable codes?

"Doesn't Look Right, a young lady coming home by herself after midnight, without a cell phone, through an unlit alley into a pitch black apartment that sits over the biggest drug stash in town."

"It must be a slow night in Fargo for me to receive such personal attention. Thanks anyway."

"I'm waiting in the squad car until I see lights upstairs. Be careful, Heli."

Minutes later, she switched the light in her apartment on, off, on, off, on, off. She pulled the Murphy bed down, shed her clothes and snuggled beneath the duvet in the darkened room. Already her mind had preserved the evening like an exotic insect in a drop of amber. She fell asleep quickly without noticing the orange blinking light on her answering machine.

Monday, April 3, 2002

Twenty-Seven

Sandeep Venkata arrived at PerkMeUp at 5:50 AM, ten minutes before the hospital's coffee bar opened. The barista yawned as she prepared her station for the early stream of Monday business, mostly physicians who began their day here trading weekend stories and conferring about patients.

"Hey, Doc. Your coffee bells go off early too?" Reuben Norbutas fell in line behind the chief resident. "Too bad about your weekend."

After an hour's workout in the gym, the chief resident felt anything but bad. Last evening with Heli had filled him with such gusto that he ran an extra mile on the treadmill and boosted the Nautilus weights another twenty pounds.

"No comment, huh? According to the email, looks like we've got another law suit on our plate."

"Email?" After leaving the gym, Venkata had gone straight to the lab to consult Dr. Dahl but found his darkened office empty. That he'd been too early for the pathologist provided the luxury of time for a latte before checking messages in the residents' lounge.

"You *haven't* read Bohley's latest?" Reuben reached for his wallet inside the deep pocket of his white cargo pants. "Bohley blasted an email early this morning to everybody involved with the Runyan case. I mean, *everybody!* You, Lavelle, the code team, the entire ER staff, Six Main, ICU, some home health nurse—everybody that had anything to do with her care. Even the billing office." Reuben lowered his voice. "According to the attorney, this is a 'vulnerable' case—meaning the hospital will probably be sued. No one is supposed to talk about the case." He pointed a finger like a drawn pistol. "Jobs could be on the line."

The espresso machine knocked and hissed, calling Venkata's attention to the barista who waited to take his order.

"A twelve-ounce latte with whipped cream, please." After his inspired run, such an indulgence was deserved. To Reuben, he said, "I have not read this email but surely it is an overreaction by the administration. The patient's care was excellent. A very sad outcome, but a review committee will find little to challenge in our work-up."

Over and over, the chief resident struggled to understand the American response to death. Perhaps the availability of vast medical technology implied a promise to patients that in every case, death could be kept at bay. Physicians knew better. The ancient Greeks accepted fate. So did Shakespeareans. But

Americans seemed to view medical tragedy through the prism of fault. Death was no longer an acceptable outcome. Someone must be blamed, held accountable, sued for malpractice. Unflattering for such an otherwise evolved society. Indian physicians still enjoyed exalted status; few mean-spirited patients challenged their medical decisions. The poor were grateful for any medical attention at all.

"A double-espresso for me." Reuben teetered back and forth on the cushioned heels of his loafers.

A line was forming at the coffee bar. Venkata counted at least ten surgical employees in green scrubs waiting to be perked up before their day in the OR.

"Let's duck in here." Reuben pointed to an empty vending room across the hall.

The chief resident followed him into the narrow space between rows of coin-operated machines offering candy bars and soda. Venkata remembered he'd skipped breakfast.

"Here's what the rumor mill is saying, Doc. Her care at Swedish was fine, just like you said. From the ER to the wards, we all did our job. No one's blaming you for the death. We know better. This time, *he* went too far."

"He?" Venkata braced for another assault on Dr. Lavelle. A growing number of employees at Swedish seemed to loathe the man for whom the chief resident held great admiration.

"Trevor; that's who." Reuben's voice dropped to a whisper. "Like I've been telling you, everyone is saying that Trevor's behind all of these infections. Trust me; he gets her just sick enough to be hospitalized. That way, insurance covers everything. Then she's discharged with a boatload of free medicine, and Trevor has a couple of days to cat around. Trust me on that, too. A nurse in the ER has a brother who works at Lake Agassiz EMS. Says Trevor takes off in the middle of his shift and is gone, sometimes for an hour at a time. Think about it—the way he lurks around the ER. It's disgusting. But this time, he went too far, way too far. And his wife didn't recover." Reuben leaned forward. "I'm not saying he intended to kill her, but he was playing a dangerous game with the insurance. Now she's dead."

Venkata was shaken by the conjecture, but maintained a perfectly refined composure. "I cannot believe this."

"Look, I'm just repeating the talk that's going around. Fingers are pointing at Trevor. With his wife out of the way, he's a free man."

"Please, say no more."

"Fine." Reuben protested with outstretched palms. "But if you think I'm kidding, watch Ludemann in action."

"Who?"

"My boss. You've seen her: bee-stung lips. Ice running through her veins. She and Trevor are . . . canoodling on the side. Oh man, you didn't know that either? Geez, Doc, close the books and look up once in awhile."

Venkata remembered this woman, Alayne Ludemann, with her improper smile on Saturday evening when Dr. Lavelle had decompensated so badly in the family room.

"Ludemann is on a witch hunt to pin the Runyan death on someone. Anything to direct attention away from Trevor. For some reason, she's set her sights on Lavelle. He's an easy enough target and she seems to want to bring him down along with the pharmacist, the ham-fisted one at the code—you know, what's-her-name from Corner Drug. Ludemann thinks they're in cahoots. Said the pharmacist wouldn't deny having an affair with Lavelle."

Reuben's words stung like venom. Heli, an affair with Dr. Lavelle? For a split second Venkata felt such nausea that he might not be able to conduct morning report. "This is not true." The latte curdled in the back of his throat. "It cannot be true. There are other explanations . . . for such empty rumors."

"Whoa! Did I strike a nerve, Doc?"

The chief resident tossed the latte cup into a trash bin.

"Sorry if I stepped on some toes." Reuben shifted, scratched the back of his neck. "You're a decent guy, Venkata. Here's my advice: keep your head down and stay low. It's gonna get bloody."

"No. We are here for our patients. They must come. . ."

"Listen to me." Reuben edged in closer. "At Swedish, you got your friends and your enemies." He glanced down the hallway. "You gotta know upfront who's on your side. Who isn't. Gotta find that out early, the first day you walk into this hospital. Trust me. This is no time to be naive. Take the blinders off, Venkata. See how the system really works."

***

Parliamentary elections in the Ukraine. Maryland defeats Indiana in the NCAA Men's Basketball championship. An earthquake in Taiwan. Monday's *Today* show projected from the screen in the kitchen, but even the empty-headed Katie Couric was incapable of engaging Lavelle's interest. Between spoonfuls of Grape Nuts, he stared at the puzzle in the New York Times. Nearly all of the white squares were filled in, but Will Shortz had stumped him with a teaser like 18-down. An eight letter word for 'deep-six cargo.' In the midst of his turmoil over the Christine Runyan matter, the puzzle had been a gratifying distraction.

"Why is your ex-father-in-law calling you, Mark?"

He shoved the Times across the granite counter. Time to float a story to Claudette about the weekend events. Call it the truth, tempered. Lavelle cleared his throat before finishing his tomato juice.

"The death of a young woman on Saturday evening could result in a malpractice case against me." He rocked the glass between his fingers. "Totally unfounded, of course, but I need to be prepared. Clifton is opening a few legal doors so we can out-lawyer the plaintiff's attorney. Nothing more."

"Malpractice?" His wife gasped. "Mark, promise me this won't be in the newspaper!" She hurled a kitchen towel into the sink. "It's not fair. Why doesn't this ever happen to a chiropractor?"

Lavelle slid his stool back across the Brazilian cherry wood floor. Ever since a chiropractor occupied the Southern colonial across the street, the wives of Pill Hill had shouldered the shame of a pseudo-scientist in their midst. There goes the neighborhood.

"A lawsuit," she repeated. "Is that why the phone is ringing so early this morning? Phyllis called around 7 AM when you were showering, and Dr. Venkata, soon after."

Deep-six cargo. An eight-letter word. Double 't' in the middle. Lavelle sighed at the multiple conundrums facing him. The chief resident deserved something close to an apology. Eddy's advice: do nothing, say nothing, admit nothing. Yet, Venkata was pivotal to his defense strategy; a conversation was necessary. If he could persuade the chief resident to accept that the hospital had indeed failed in enough instances to raise serious doubt about Christine Runyan's care, he might be able to ride the current media wave exposing hospital errors. On the other hand, if Venkata was as thorough as Lavelle feared, persisting with an exhaustive pathology investigation, it could mean trouble, especially if the chief resident detected a link to the TPN solution. In that case, Lavelle would have no other choice than to explain he was merely trying to assist Trevor by keeping pharmaceutical expenses down. In the meantime, creating some distance from Eddy and GEM would be necessary. After all, how could he, an innocent investor in a pharmacy business fifteen hundred miles away, possibly know it was a sham?

Runyan was another matter. Eddy was right. Money would easily bend Trevor's will. A few days after the funeral, he'd call Trevor. Console him. Offer to help work through his financial alternatives. There ought to be some life insurance and Social Security death benefits to mitigate his loss. Wring the benefit out of years of premiums. And he'd suggest that Trevor levy a malpractice suit against the hospital—without naming Lavelle, of course—that would be the deal for putting together the medical basis for his case. If Trevor brought up the TPN problem, he'd explain that a lawsuit against GEM could be very expensive. Product liability cases go on forever. Forget about a second lawsuit and settle for whatever GEM Pharmacy will pay. Eddy could surely find enough money to quell Runyan's modest appetite.

"Darling, have I lost you?"

"Sorry." Deep-six cargo; eight letters beginning with a j. "Yes, I suppose I'm preoccupied." He motioned her over to the stool. "You look very dressed-for-success today. Another open house?"

"I'm showing a high-end historic property by the river." She moved toward him. "If I close on this one, I'll pocket a huge commission and be on my way to the Million Dollar Club."

"You always get what you're after, Claudette."

Deep-six cargo. Was this a cryptic, a double-clue, a homophone? Sometimes Shortz was coy, turning nouns into verbs.

"Not this morning," she drummed her fingers on the counter. "I've been looking forever for that glass thingy I brought home from Hong Kong to give MacKenzie for being our 'sales rookie of the year.'" She looked off in the distance. "I'm sure I left it on the sideboard by the front door but it isn't there. Have you seen it?"

Exasperated, Lavelle stared over his glasses with a look he usually reserved for trembling residents. "I haven't a clue what you're talking about."

Aha! Deep-six cargo. He grabbed the crossword puzzle and scribbled eight letters into the remaining squares. Imagine having a problem no bigger than some cheap *j-e-t-t-i-s-o-n*-end junk from Asia.

Twenty-Eight

Heli intended to phone Venkata with the news, but patients bombarded Corner Drug on Monday morning with empty prescription vials and pent-up questions from the weekend. Answers came easily.

Always start with prune juice.

You could be. Remember my caution? Antibiotics can decrease the effectiveness of birth control pills.

There is no medical evidence that rubbing Vicks on the bottom of your feet will stop a cough.

There are better alternatives than butter on a burn.

They Always Take Their Secrets to a Druggist. Harry Zane's book authored in the sixties still rang true. Being a family pharmacist was like having a skeleton key to every medicine cabinet in Fargo.

"Hello, are you a druggist?"

Pause.

"I'm calling for a friend who has a problem."

Heard that before, Heli smiled.

"He can't get it up anymore. Is it those damn pills?"

Today's pharmacist had more to do than worry about kids stealing licorice from the candy counter.

When the calls slowed to a reasonable pace, her mind diverted to Jayson's voice mail of last evening. Venkata would be interested to know this.

Hey, Boss, pick this up if you're there. I'll wait. Where are you on a Sunday night? You're missing 'The X-Files.' Ok, so you're gone.

I goggled GEM Pharmacy. Just like we thought, a specialty mail-order house. From their web site: "supplying personal infusion pharmaceutical services in the homecare setting." Mail order, personal? Erghrm . . . postman answers Rx questions? I. Don't. Think. So. "Chemotherapy, hydration therapy, Total Parenteral Nutrition, Ionotropic Therapy. Blah, blah, blah. Oops, hold on; tape is running out. I'll call back. Bye-O.

Me again. GEM is privately held—no filings or public information available. Home office in Baton Rouge. Are you ready for this? I called the telephone number late Saturday night and got into voice jail with some public radio voice: "The office of GEM Pharmacy and its satellite outlets are closed until further notice."

Do I stop here? No way. Tomorrow I'll be mining business databases at the U. Checking the archives of the Louisiana newspapers. Hey, the FDA and the LA Board of Pharmacy, too. Love this gumshoe stuff! Oops, time's up again. More later. Bye-O.

***

A gaggle of wide-eyed residents and curious medical students filed into the hospital conference room at 7:30 AM for Monday's morning report. Word that Dr. Venkata would be presenting the case study had traveled throughout the service, and the white coats were eager to test their clinical reasoning skills on a case that had so far stumped the venerable chief resident. The mystery of atypical cases exhilarated them.

Venkata provided a review and analysis of case MRN 996784-2 with limited pathology information available. Although he'd studied every facet of the Runyan case with a jeweler's precision, he maintained an open mind to the possibility that the close watch he'd kept might have prevented him from perceiving something better detected at a distance. The energizing curiosity of his audience was useful. He fielded their questions and patiently considered their cobbled theories. As the session ended, the discussion had added little to the elusive case.

Luke Holman, a third-year resident from western North Dakota, clapped Venkata on the back as the two walked toward the residents' lounge after the meeting.

"What a damn stroke of luck to be able to sink your teeth into a case like that! And right before starting an ID fellowship. Someday, I'll read about this case in the *Annals,* Sandy."

"For now, we must identify the pathogen and discover its portal into the body," the chief resident answered modestly, "and also care for eleven new patients added to our service." Venkata turned his attention to the list of admissions. His duty was to assign cases—congestive heart failure, urinary tract infections, diabetic ketoacidosis, strokes and pneumonia—to the first and second year residents.

"Do you want to manage the upper GI bleed on 3 Main?"

"Sure. Good diversion from the frequent flier in Psychiatry. Third time my barking mad patient up there is threatening to jump out the window and fly home." Luke ran a hand over his buzz cut. "Takes a better mental mechanic than me to figure out what makes some people tick."

Venkata's beeper murmured. He moved to the nurse's station to take the call, feeling the flush of praise after morning report tempered by the unrelenting weight of Reuben's speculation. Why, if he did not believe such rumors about Heli and Dr. Lavelle, did they continue to press upon him?

"Dr. Kampela calling. Are you able to meet me in the lab in a few minutes?"

"You have seen the final lab results of our patient?"

"Get up here ASAP. We'll talk face to face."

The chief resident brightened momentarily. A good decision to have Dr. Kampela involved, since Dr. Lavelle seemed to be avoiding his calls. Perhaps this would be another forward step in understanding the pathogenesis of the Runyan case. He consulted his watch: 9:10 AM. The discussion of microbial theory at morning report had delayed his work rounds by almost an hour. The rest of the day unfolded in his mind: work rounds, attending rounds, a noon conference, new patient work-ups with afternoon rounds resuming at 4 PM. When would he have time in the hospital library for additional research? Once again, his pager vibrated. This time, the operator asked if he would take a call from Corner Drug.

He hesitated, desperately wanting to hear Heli's voice, but still wary that he might have been duped by his own desire.

"I am unavailable."

"I'll relay the message," the operator replied.

The chief resident cantered up the back stairwell and found Drs. Dahl and Kampela admiring the artwork in the pathology chief's office. Framed black-and-white photographs covered every available inch of the vinyl-covered walls. Rock formations in New Mexico, the craggy coastline of Nova Scotia, grassy buttes of western North Dakota. Visually strong, solitary geography that aroused Venkata's desire for travel.

"I have what you're both looking for." Dahl waved a computer-generated lab report. "But I'm not releasing it. I don't believe the screwball results."

The chief resident's shoulders dropped.

"Can we at least know what's on the report, John?" Dr. Kampela persisted. "We're not asking that you stake your reputation on it."

"Not this time. Results like this frustrate the hell out of me." He shook his head and bifocals slid down his nose. "Frankly, these results look like they might have come from the bottom of a dirty sink. *Pseudomonas. Mycobacterium marinum.* And some weird organism I've never seen in my thirty-five years in this lab. There's nothing about this report that I will stand behind. We'll have to retest the blood sample."

Dr. Kampela approached the chief resident. "The *Pseudomonas* most likely killed her, Sandy. In her weakened, immuno-compromised state, she couldn't possibly have rallied against such a nasty infection notoriously resistant to antibiotics."

"Yes, yes." Venkata's mind was spinning. Dr. Kampela was no doubt correct about *Pseudomonas*. The gram-negative rod with minimal nutritional needs was everywhere and a common inhabitant of soil and water. An opportunistic pathogen, always ready to exploit a vulnerable host with poor defense mechanisms.

"This is not good news for the hospital." Dr. Kampela crossed her arms and stared at the framed Polynesian sunset behind Dr. Dahl's desk. "My friends at the CDC tell me that *Pseudomonas* now accounts for nearly ten percent of all hospital-acquired infections. If Mrs. Runyan's problems resulted from a lack of aseptic technique or improper cleaning of catheters, Mr. Bohley will have some explaining to do with the Joint Commission."

"And the sample taken from the TPN bag?" Venkata persisted.

"Still growing." Dahl wagged his finger. "We'll read those plates this afternoon."

The pathologist read the report once more. "I'm sending this out to a reference laboratory for confirmation. Speaking of Bohley, I got a note from him about a potential lawsuit on the Runyan case. Trembling on a witness stand is not how I intend to celebrate my retirement."

"A lawsuit?" Dr. Kampela appeared stunned. "In that case, how much time are we talking about? If, by chance, we're dealing with a bad product lot, there could be risks to other patients. I'd like to get the infection team involved as soon as possible. Cover our bases."

Venkata was as tense as a coiled spring. Unreliable lab results, strange pathogens, suspicious products, cruel rumors, threatened lawsuits. And Dr. Lavelle, nowhere in sight.

Like a gravitational force, Dr. Kampela seemed to draw the uncertainty spinning around the room into a single focus. "For the record," she added soberly, "this case has my unqualified attention."

***

179

As she drove away from the Agency's parking lot, Donna gunned the motor of her Blazer and six cylinders pounded in response. Jerry had always spun his tires like this on the gravel road by their farmstead whenever he got mad about some crazy farm bill or a broken down tractor. Now she was mad, and the little act of rebellion felt good.

During case reviews at the early Monday morning staff meeting, her manager stifled discussion of the Runyan case.

"A lawsuit is likely. Therefore, no contact with the family or their representatives," she'd specified. "Mr. Bohley has spoken. Do I make myself clear?"

Donna had first met Bohley, that Buddha-bellied stuffed shirt, on videotape during her orientation. Quality this, quality that. His speech was so peppered with the word that she wrinkled her nose at the mention of his name.

"The Runyans would never sue the hospital," Donna had blurted out during the meeting, prompting nervous sideway glances among the agency nurses. Only then did she realize that her role in the case might explain the troubled look on the manager's face.

"The husband has issues with the care Mrs. Runyan received at Swedish Hospital. Since you were involved in the case, Donna, you can expect to be called in. I hope your documentation is in order."

"So this means we stop caring about what happens to the rest of the family?"

The manager moved on to the next agenda item. Donna said nothing more for the remainder of the meeting, thinking instead about the glorified rice chilling in her refrigerator. It would be a shame for it to go to waste.

Twenty-Nine

Although the door to the Boardroom was closed, Dr. Lavelle barged in at 12:14 PM on Monday as though knocking implied weakness. Bohley and the chief of staff, Dr. Andy Thorson, rose from their leather chairs as he entered. Two other men pushed their chairs from the boardroom table to stand at attention. The younger of the two was middle-aged with thinning red hair and a flesh-colored scaly patch below his left ear. A basal cell carcinoma, Lavelle suspected. Very common in the fair skinned population of the northern plains.

"Mark," Dr. Thorson said amiably, "thanks for attending on such short notice. I assume you know everyone here: Mr. Bohley, A. Spenser Perrault, the hospital's attorney, and Kevin McCaffery, Vice President of Human Resources."

"What is it this time, Andy? Am I tardy on my charts, or have I crossed a yellow line in the parking lot? Eaten too many donuts in the physicians' lounge? Ordered too many enemas?" He looked squarely at Bohley.

"This is serious." Dr. Thorson's good humor seemed to dissolve in the rarefied air of the Boardroom. Perrault reached for a legal pad. McCaffery pulled a series of files from his leather briefcase. Bohley returned to his chair, sat down and laced his fingers over a protuberant stomach.

"Of course, everything is grave within these walls." Lavelle glanced about the windowless surroundings. "In stark contrast to our medical wards where silliness prevails." Framed posters promoting the organizational virtues of *Leadership, Teamwork, Excellence*, and *Quality* adorned the walls. He'd often noticed the popular art advertised in cheesy airline magazines.

"I'm sorry, Mark." The chief of staff cleared his throat. "I'm invoking disciplinary action in light of your unprofessional conduct as a member of the medical staff. Your privileges at Swedish Hospital have been suspended until the results of an internal investigation have been reviewed by the medical staff Executive Committee."

Lavelle sucked in a breath. He felt dizzy breathing such thin air. One could suffocate in this near vacuum.

"The hospital bylaws specify in Article 3, Sections 1.3-1 through 1.3-9," Perrault read from a page in a black three-ring binder, "that an investigation will commence, and that the appointee. . . ."

"Appointee?" Lavelle gasped. "I am a *physician*, not an appointee."

"That the appointee," the lawyer continued, "shall be entitled to a hearing according to the procedures outlined in the Fair Hearing and Appellate Review Procedure."

"Andy, what is this parasite talking about?"

Perrault stopped reading and made an additional note on his yellow legal pad. McCaffery perspired as he scratched his ear and ruffled through reams of paper. Dr. Thorson nodded to the CEO as if to tip the ball in his direction.

Bohley unfolded his hands and rolled his chair closer to the table. "A claim of harassment has been levied against you, Dr. Lavelle. Your behavior on Saturday evening following the code of Mrs. Christine Runyan was unprofessional, disruptive, and constituted a hostile environment for certain employees of Swedish Hospital."

Anger displaced Lavelle's initial shock. He seethed inwardly but steadied himself into a silence that he hoped might pass for strength. His mind called up the list of possible names who might have filed the complaint. Venkata? Never! The resident knew the unwritten rules about residents beholden to attending physicians. Moreover, the caste system was duly inculcated into the Hindi experience. Alayne Ludemann? Unlikely. Calling Security was just a cover. Her provocative behavior toward him in the past signaled an unmistakable sexual message. Clearly, she'd been charmed by a physician of his status. The piggish nurse with the bad teeth? She certainly lacked the temerity to challenge a physician. She needed her job, and rubbing doctors the wrong way wasn't good for career longevity. Lavelle continued his mental rounds of the family room on Saturday evening until the image of the sanctimonious pharmacist solidified into focus. So it was that radical Finn! He tasted revenge.

"Your privileges may be reinstated if you comply with the following orders." Bohley pulled bifocals from the pocket of his suit coat and referred to his prepared notes. "One, you will apologize to the code team. Two, you will attend a sensitivity training course on appropriate workplace behavior developed by our Employee Assistance personnel."

Stoic and restrained, Lavelle did not take his eyes off Bohley.

"And, three, you will attend a twelve-week course on Anger Management directed by the hospital psychologist."

"Guilty until proven innocent." Lavelle's mind twisted

around the double helix of his new defense. "Such is the democratic process in this hospital. I should have expected no less." He glared at his accusers. "I will fight this capricious and discriminatory action with the full force of my considerable resources."

"If you disagree with the charges, the bylaws specify your right to appeal the complaint." Dr. Thorson seemed relieved to be able to offer an alternative. "You have thirty days to make your case. Meanwhile, please make arrangements for your hospitalized patients, as you will not be permitted on the wards until your privileges have been reinstated."

Banished from the hospital? The besieged physician dropped his head. Suppressed an instinctive urge to accelerate verbal combat. Realized that anger was a dull weapon in the war being waged against him. He turned to the chief of staff.

"Andy, how can you permit this to happen? Swear to me that you haven't sold out to this shameless administration by turning on your medical colleagues."

Dr. Thorson was tight-lipped and appeared visibly shaken.

Lavelle perceived a fracture in Thorson's resolve. "Since when has justifiable frustration with hospital errors and substandard patient care become fodder for a false claim of harassment?"

"It's a new world, Mark." Dr. Thorson squared his shoulders and straightened his stance. "I promise to oversee a fair process. You are entitled to representation and to offer any testimony that sheds light on the investigation. But if you fail to comply with Mr. Bohley's stipulations, your privileges will not be reinstated. In that case, the National Practitioner Data Bank will be notified." Dr. Thorson adopted a more collegial tone. "Think about it, Mark. Do you really want a blemish on your otherwise impressive record?"

"Meanwhile," Bohley piped in, "your appearance at the April 15 meeting of the Executive committee will proceed on a parallel track. Consider the Exvantium issue unresolved. And," the CEO continued, "your role in the death of Mrs. Christine Runyan will be reviewed by a committee of your peers."

Lavelle walked toward the door. He turned around momentarily to fully absorb the welter of the last fifteen minutes. Could this be happening to him? Here in the long dark winter of the northern latitudes where he'd come to start over? He closed his eyes briefly and recalled the Styrofoam coffee cup that Thorson had minced into confetti-size pieces. Bohley, elevating the pneumatic lift on his ergonomic chair to its highest position.

Perrault's crisp white cuff with its monogram, ASP, advancing from the sleeve of the attorney's silk suit.

Shaken, Mark Raymond Lavelle, MD, left the room feeling the tenterhooks of a long, drawn-out public humiliation whose countdown had only begun.

***

As the Blazer braked for a stoplight, Donna mentally defended her plan one last time. If President Clinton could parse certain words and get away with it, she could deliver a bowl of glorified rice to the Runyan family and not exactly *talk* to them about matters pertaining to the lawsuit.

Tupperware bowl in hand, she rapped on the Runyan's door. No answer. She rapped again. Still no answer. She remembered the key; had it been returned? She placed the Tupperware bowl on the bottom step and dropped to her hands and knees, crouching dog-like, to check under the doormat. Then, from behind, she felt something nudge the sole of her boot.

"My stars!" she shrieked.

"Not home." The man behind her rocked back and forth. "Not home."

When her sensibilities returned, she remembered his name. Buddy. She pulled herself up from the floor, an aching effort made even more unpleasant by the gaping man who tracked every movement. "Hello. . . Buddy. You scared the daylights out of me. I. . . stopped by to bring a little something," she reached for the Tupperware bowl, "for the family. So awfully sad about Christine, isn't it?"

Buddy kicked the baseboard repeatedly with the toe of a tennis shoe. He looked down at the carpet while pulling the drawstring of his navy sweat pants. Donna wondered if he'd changed his clothes in the two days since they'd first met.

"Not home."

"So you've said, Buddy." Saying his name several times eased her insecurity. He's harmless. It's the drugs that make him drool. He can't help it, probably isn't even aware of his tics, his grunts. Donna parked her hands on her hips. "There used to be a key under the mat. If it were here now, I'd let myself in, put the bowl in the refrigerator and little Anya would have something tasty when she returns."

"Went to Muskee. All of 'em. Trevor, Brigid, Anya."

"Well, isn't that nice. The family, all together at a time like this."

"Key's in the suitcase." Buddy pointed to the rear of the apartment complex.

"Suitcase? What suitcase? The key is supposed to be under the rubber mat. At least that's what Christine told me." Donna paused.

"W. . . w . . . wait." Buddy turned and shuffled along the hallway to his apartment. He turned his head back and repeated, "wait."

So Donna waited outside #3 as Buddy disappeared into #4. Her watch read 12:20 PM and she was due at her next visit at 1 PM. Was it really so important to leave the salad with the Runyans? Yes, food was comfort. That the family was coping together made her feel better. *Blessed be the tie that binds*, she hummed. Life goes on. She lifted the cover of the salad bowl. The rosy pink rice grains against the green container reminded her of spring. Blossoming crab trees and fertilized grass. She snapped the lid back on the bowl and burped the cover. 12:27 PM. Where was Buddy?

He returned, dragging a dilapidated suitcase, struggling with its weight.

"Found this downstairs." Buddy set the suitcase at her feet. "Keys r'n there."

"Goodness, I don't think we should be . . . ."

Buddy stopped his pill-rolling movements long enough to unlatch the closure. He rummaged through the contents—lacy girl's anklets, flannel nightgown, jeans, several cotton turtlenecks—until he reached an elastic pouch secured to the back of suitcase. The key was tucked in the corner by the lining seam.

Donna smelled trouble. "I'll just slip in," she said uneasily, "put this salad in their refrigerator and be off. Buddy," she warned, "you have to put this suitcase back exactly where you found it."

Buddy nodded.

"Everything. Do you understand? It belongs to the Runyans. We shouldn't have . . . rummaged through someone's . . . but, oh dear, our intentions were good."

Buddy reached into his pocket and produced a prescription vial from Corner Drug with his name on the label. "Wrong."

The nurse cocked her head. "What do you mean, wrong?"

He shoved the prescription vial into her hand and she read its label: *fluphenazine 2.5mg, two tablets every six hours*. Donna wrestled off the child-resistant cap and poured a line of two-toned green capsules across her palm.

"Not right. Different. Wrong pills."

Donna studied the capsules cupped in her hand. "I don't know what to say, Buddy," she admitted, spotting the discrepancy immediately. "The label says 'tablets' but these are capsules, aren't they? Could be a generic, or a different brand, I suppose. Or, it could be the drugstore's mistake. Have you taken any of the capsules?"

He shook his head vigorously. "No. Wrong."

Donna checked her watch again: 12:46 PM. Being late for a house call was not her style, nor was leaving a vulnerable adult alone to deal with a questionable medication. "Would you like me to check this out with the druggist?"

Buddy nodded—yes, yes, yes.

"That's exactly what I'll do." Call Corner Drug and straighten this out. "I'm off now. You tell the Runyans I stopped by. They can send the salad bowl back after the funeral. I taped my name and address on the bottom."

She doubted the Tupperware would find its way back to her galley kitchen. If a father couldn't remember to take his little girl's suitcase with him when they left town, how would he ever have the common sense to return a salad bowl?

Thirty

Venkata reached the hospital theatre at 12:20 PM just as the lights dimmed for Dr. Hardy's noon conference on *Avian influenza in Italy from 1997-2001*. The auditorium was packed. Whether this was due to the timely topic or the hot buffet, the chief resident could not say. He saw Dr. Dahl pecking at a stuffed cabbage roll from a tray balanced on his lap. Dr. Kampela was in the front row. Dr. Lavelle was nowhere in sight. Recognizing an opportunity, he grabbed an apple, shoved it into the pocket of his white coat and left the auditorium.

"I would like to speak with Jenny," he explained to an assistant when he reached the Microbiology lab.

Overcrowded and warm, the lab reeked of bacterial emanations—wet wool, rotten eggs and caramel corn. He wrinkled his nose and felt nauseous, glad he'd avoided the noon conference lunch.

"Hey, Dr. Venkata. You looking for me?"

According to her nametag, the perky young woman in a white lab coat was Jenny. He recognized the singsong voice from her call on Sunday evening.

"Yes. We spoke last night about the gram stain results on the infusion bag you cultured for Dr. Kampela."

"Right, right." Her ponytail swayed as she tossed her head.

"The final report; has it been issued?"

"Not yet." Jenny smiled, exposing a row of perfectly aligned teeth. "Dr. Dahl said you'd be hounding us."

"Another question. The infusion bag from which you drew the sample—may I have it back? We are suspicious it may be a contaminated product in which case, we must notify the manufacturer with its lot number."

"Sure," Jenny shrugged her shoulders, "except we usually toss the container once we get the sample. I mean, look around here." She swept the air with a gloved hand. "Do you see any room for storage? We always lose space wars in this hospital."

The chief resident silently reprimanded himself. Now he would have to track down the name of the mail-order pharmacy and trust the quality of its record keeping. Heli's help would be valuable, but he resisted the idea of calling her until he found time to settle the warring emotions he'd so far kept at bay. He longed to call her, ask her about an alleged affair with Dr. Lavelle. Reuben's stories had thrown him off center, his affections spinning at the possibility of a double betrayal. If it were true, he would have to confront his own naiveté. If not, he would have to acknowledge how easily he'd slid from fact to fiction, a dangerous habit for a physician.

"Hey, don't worry!" Another flash of ivory brightened her face. "We froze the sample. Just the bag is gone."

"I see." Venkata rubbed his chin. "One last question. This morning Dr. Kampela and I met with Dr. Dahl about the final report of Christine Runyan's blood sample. Are you able to retrieve it for me?"

Jenny threw him a skeptical look. "If the report on her blood sample has been released, it should be in the chart."

"It has not exactly been released," Venkata clarified, "but he did share with us the name of two organisms. *Pseudomonas and Mycobacterium marinum.*"

"Yup." Jenny leaned against the lab counter. "Water bugs. *Pseudomonas* could be a really big nightmare for this hospital. Hope this isn't the start of some kind of outbreak on the wards. That would really rock the administration, huh?" Her face expressed a faint delight. "The bug is everywhere—inside respiratory tubing, clinging to plants and fruits, in sink drains and floor mops. The blue pus is *so* disgusting!"

"Yes." The chief resident recalled how the ubiquitous bacteria actually grew in distilled water during one of his medical school labs. "There was one additional organism that I have forgotten—something very unusual. Perhaps you recall the name?"

"Right. A really strange one," she answered without hesitation. "We had to look it up since none of us girls had ever seen it before. Really, really strange."

"And its name was . . .?"

"Nice try, Dr. Venkata." Her roguish smile told him what he didn't want to hear. "You'll just have to come back and find out."

"I see." So much for his political maneuvering. "Thank you." The chief resident was already plotting his escape to the library where he could surround himself with Microbiology textbooks when her voice interrupted his thoughts.

"Dr. Venkata?" Jenny moved uncomfortably close to him. "Would you ever, like, want to go out for a beer or something? You know, hang out together?"

The chief resident clutched the apple in his pocket that he imagined might be covered with the fruity alginate slime of

Pseudomonas. He needed little reminding that a living virulent world thrived invisibly around him.

"No time, I'm afraid," he replied as an inner voice taunted him that in spite of his constant busyness, he was getting nowhere fast.

Thirty-one

Four prescriptions waited on the compounding bench. Mazur's wart paint for the Hendrickson teenager. Nomland's lotion for Noreen Power's flaking skin. Morphine lollypops for Hospice. Methimazole gel for Cricket's ear—the fractious Siamese who refused to swallow bitter tablets. Heli glanced at the clock on the far wall: 2:40 PM. She reached for the stone mortar and pestle and wiped the ointment slab with disinfectant. *Secundum artem,* she uttered like an incantation. The Latin phrase always united her with kindred spirits—priests, monks, shamans, medicine men—who'd once labored in the chemist shops of history. *Secundum artem.* Maybe *Väinämöinen's* magical powers were first imagined by Elias Lönnrot in a Finnish apothecary before he wrote the legends of *Kalevala.*

She gathered the ingredients to prepare Nomland's, the old dermatological standby for itchy skin. Where was Jayson? The 3 PM rush at Corner Drug would soon begin and prescriptions were piling up. Jayson was due fifteen minutes ago; it was unlike him to be late.

With the tip of her spatula, Heli weighed the sodium borate and dissolved the powder in isopropyl alcohol. She triturated resorcinol crystals and cornstarch with glycerin into a smooth paste in the bottom of the mortar. The phone rang. She rested the pestle against the mortar's lip. Might it be Sandy this time? All morning, she'd waited with a subliminal hope that the voice on the other line might be his. Such schoolgirl pining was embarrassing.

"Web Detective reporting in."

"You're late, Jayson."

"Here's the deal, Boss. I can stay on the cyber trail of GEM Pharmacy or come by the store. Your call."

Heli's curiosity spiked. Sandy had seemed interested in the mail-order pharmacy. Being useful might draw him closer.

"What have you found so far?"

"Errgm. That you were valedictorian of the Prestegaard class of 1984. Science Fair Winner. Lettered in track. Tenor sax in the marching band. Big hair. Bad glasses. Ouch!"

"About GEM. I'm not paying you to snoop into my past." She reread the formula for Nomland's and reached for the pink calamine powder. "What have you learned?"

"I know how old you are. Every address where you've lived since pharmacy school. No DUI's, no criminal record, no liens, no registered trademarks. . . ."

"About GEM!" Heli cradled the phone against her shoulder as she reached for a six-ounce oval.

"Not exactly a slam dunk. Private companies don't have to file with the SEC so I had to dive deep. Skimmed the Baton Rouge Advocate for news of GEM's closing—zippo. Then, searched the business journal database for hits. Bingo. FAST magazine pushed a lead article last year called 'Profitable Players in Health Care.' Can you guess who made the top ten?"

Heli put the bottle down and reached for a pen.

"I quote, 'GEM Pharmacy Services, a company formed in 1998 by three Louisiana oncologists: Michael Marthaller, Alexander Grossman and J. Pierce Eddington . . .Started with mail-order chemotherapy infusions for cancer patients, then expanded the product line to IVs for bleeding disorders, nutrition' . . . Basically anything insurance covers."

"Very enterprising." Heli doodled on a note pad, circling the first letter of each name she'd written. "G for Grossman, E for Eddington, M for. . . ."

"Marthaller. Names mean anything to you, Boss?"

"Absolutely nothing."

"These docs were definitely raking in big bucks." Jayson's attention seemed to be back on the article. "Fast, too. Launched a Midwest expansion last year. That's the subject of this article. Hang on, I'm chasing another link."

During the silence, Heli shook the Nomland's solution vigorously and attached an 'External Use Only' to the bottle.

"Here's a quote from Grossman: 'Our business model is scalable, our service, excellent, and we're profitable. Hence, our motivation . . . to expand quickly . . . targeting physicians whose homebound patients require infusion services.'"

Murlene tapped on the pharmacy counter to draw Heli's attention to five new prescriptions. An anxious mother with a screaming child paced back and forth in the aisle. The second line on the phone lit up. Could this be Sandy?

"We still don't know why GEM has been shut down." Heli could disguise the frustration in her voice. "I'll call the Louisiana Board of Pharmacy and talk with their investigator. If disciplinary action has been taken, it's public record."

"You sound swamped, Boss. I'll be right in."

"Not so fast." Heli mentally scrolled ahead through the next five hours. Invoices waited, payments needed posting and phones, answered. Warts and a hyperthyroid cat demanded her compounding expertise. She'd get to it, everything in its own time, without Jayson's help. "Follow the bread crumbs, Hansel. I want to know where this leads."

***

Cloistered in a remote carrel within the hospital library, Venkata considered his options. He had fifteen minutes before afternoon rounds began. That he had not retained the infusion bag, not even removed its white computer generated label which would have specified the necessary information, bruised his confidence. For all of his lofty theorizing about the infusion bag as the potential source of Mrs. Runyan's infection, he'd overlooked a simple but essential fact: the name of the mail-order pharmacy.

Who could help him? Heli would be his most expedient source, but he resisted the idea of calling her, his mind, still unsettled by doubt and innuendo. Could desire so blind one's judgment?

Nurse Wadeson might also be helpful since she must have handled the infusions directly. At the moment, he had little time for her lengthy prattle, but her documentation should be available in the home health agency's electronic medical record. He moved to a computing station and attempted to log on but his access was denied. An error message explained that the entire system was down. *Unavailable; try again later.*

The chief resident returned to the carrel and slumped into the chair to consider other options. He phoned Dr. Lavelle's office again on the chance that his receptionist had run out of excuses for putting him off.

"I don't see how Doctor can possibly be disturbed so late in the afternoon," she explained. "He has a very busy practice . . . and . . . what's that? Just a moment, please."

As he was holding, Venkata wondered what Heli was doing at this very moment. Had their evening together meant anything to her?

"I will put you through to Doctor," the office receptionist answered curtly.

Venkata sat upright in his chair. Nearly forty-eight hours had passed since the two had exchanged words.

"Sandy, what is it?"

His voice sounded guarded, the customary bravado, subdued.

"Sir, I had hoped we might discuss new findings in the Runyan case."

"I don't have much time. Someone is holding on the other line. Make your point."

The chief resident distilled the facts into a succinct summary. "*Psueudomonas, Mycobacterium marinum* and a third bacterium, yet to be identified. Also, the path report of Mrs. Runyan's blood sample matches the culture we obtained from the TPN solution." He waited for an affirming reaction but heard only silence. "I believe you were right about the bag all along. Brilliant on your part, Sir."

"The lab report probably means nothing," Lavelle growled. "If you've concluded that a contaminated bag was the source of the infection, your assessment is premature. More likely, it's the opposite—the patient's blood probably infected the infusion. Did you consider the possibility of a backflow of blood into the bag?"

Venkata swallowed his protest. How did Mrs. Runyan become infected in the first place? This was not like Dr. Lavelle.

"Or suppose her infection was simply a case of translocation. Bowel bugs have been known to move through the intestinal mucosa into the blood stream without any perforations at all. In the end, the answer you are desperately chasing will no doubt come down to someone's error. A *misadventure*, as Bohley euphemizes such blunders. And like every other time, the mistake will go undetected or covered up. Move on to the living, Sandy. This case is closed."

What was the greater puzzle—Dr. Lavelle's unreceptive response to the lab results or his curious diagnostic theories? The chief resident could not be certain.

Dr. Lavelle hung up before Venkata had time to ask about the mail-order pharmacy. Confused, he dialed the ward clerk on Six Main. No, he decided, this case is not closed.

"May I speak with a nurse named Roxy?"

"No one here by that name."

"Please, check again. I am sure of her name."

"Nope, no luck. I'll transfer you to Human Resources. Maybe they can help."

Venkata checked his watch and waited restlessly through the annoying ballads of Celine Dion.

"I understand you're looking for Roxanne Vetter, LPN?" The female voice was courteous but firm. "She no longer works for Swedish Hospital."

"How can this be? She cared for my patient over the past

weekend. Now she is gone?"

"She no longer works for Swedish Hospital. That's all I'm allowed to say."

Addled, Venkata muttered a thank you, and hung up.

On his diminished list of options, Reuben was at the very bottom. The chief resident braced at the thought of another interaction. He checked his watch. Time was fleeting. The male nurse had tended to Mrs. Runyan when she presented to the ER on Saturday morning. It was worth a chance. He dialed the hospital operator and asked to be put through to Reuben Norbutas.

"Not here, Dr. Venkata," the unit clerk answered. "Do you wish to speak to his Manager, Ms. Ludemann? I'm supposed to direct any calls for Reuben to her."

"No, thank you," he replied.

Five minutes remained before he was due on Three Main. He dialed Medical Records and requested that the chart of Mrs. Christine Runyan, MRN 996784-2, be couriered to his desk in the residents' office.

"Impossible," a terse voice explained. "Her chart is embargoed pending litigation. If necessary, you may access the record here in the department but only under the direct observation by a member of our staff."

Venkata's marble composure began to crack. "I do not understand. I am, was, her physician."

"Doctor," he heard her sigh, "ever heard of tampering with a medical record? Our observation rules preclude such a possibility. You got a problem with the rules, call administration. In the meantime if you change your mind, Med Rec closes at 8 PM."

Defeated at every turn, the chief resident shuffled up three flights of stairs, ready to exchange the incongruities of hospital bureaucracy for the rational protocols of clinical medicine.

***

Heli studied the label on the prescription vial and, incredulous, tried to reconcile the error. She could not. The hard gelatin capsules, double-aught in size, two shades of green, rolled onto the counting tray. A silent alarm went off as the childhood rhyme, once taped inside her grade school chemistry set, rose in her mind:

> Little Matti was a chemist
> Little Matti is no more.

If the vial were properly labeled, small yellow triangular tablets should have poured from the bottle.

What he thought was H_2O
Was H_2SO_4

"Goodness, I thought it didn't look right, and Buddy kept saying, 'wrong, wrong, wrong,' so lickety-split, I brought the pills back to you." The animated head and shoulders were all the pharmacist could see of Donna Wadeson beyond the prescription counter. "Don't look so frightened, Heli. Buddy assured me he didn't take any of the capsules. Not a one. He knew he'd been given the wrong pills. No harm done."

"Thank you for intervening, Mrs. Wadeson. I'm at a loss to. . . ."

"Now, now. Call me Donna. We've met before, at the hospital. Remember?"

"If you have a minute, Donna, I'd like to confer with Jayson, my assistant pharmacist. Would you excuse us?"

"Long as I get home by the 6 o'clock news. I never miss the weather report on channel five. Some storm we had this weekend, wasn't it? But my knees are telling me that spring's in the air."

Heli nodded appreciatively. She signaled Jayson back to her small office in the rear of the pharmacy. The space was hardly larger than a phone booth, but this matter required privacy. She placed the two prescription vials on the blotter of her desk. Their labels incriminated "JJ," the dispensing pharmacist.

"What? No way! Can't be!" His rapid-fire defense sounded like the stutter of a jackhammer.

"Mistakes happen, Jayson. Let's try to figure out why. Do you remember dispensing this refill on Saturday afternoon?'

"Like it was five minutes ago. You'd just gone upstairs to pretty-up when this wait-staff person Brigid from the Jade brings me two refills. Her antidepressant and Buddy Nustad's antipsychotic. So I pull up her profile first. A few days too early to refill the nortriptyline, I noted. Insurance won't pay until the 5th. Then she gives me the I-dropped-the-pills-in-the-toilet story. Lame try, like it's the first time I've heard that excuse. I refilled it, not because I believed her, but she's been compliant and she definitely needs to be on medicine." He pointed to the screen on Heli's desk. "The documentation is all there."

"And Buddy's meds?'

"Pulled up his profile next. Same antipsychotic for years.

When he takes his meds, both oars stay in the water."

"Maybe you switched the labels. It would be easy to do."

"This was no brain-fade, Heli." Jayson's face blanched. "I swear I didn't make that mistake."

Her attention diverted to the empty twelve-dram vial and the scattering of green capsules on the tray. She counted twenty-two caps. Had Buddy taken the capsules as directed on the label, two every six hours, he might have approached toxic levels of nortriptyline. But, according to Donna, he hadn't taken any of the capsules. In that case, there should have been thirty capsules in the bottle. Thirty capsules tumbling across the tray.

From the bins under the pharmacy counter where empty plastic vials were stored, Heli pulled out a sixteen-dram and a twelve-dram vial. Her jaw clenched. "I believe you, Jayson. No way could you have squeezed thirty capsules into this twelve-dram vial. Thirty capsules of nortriptyline would require at least a sixteen-dram."

Their eyes met, and without a word, the two pharmacists appeared to reach the same unfathomable conclusion.

Heli spoke first. "We have no control over the contents of what we dispense once the vials leave the pharmacy."

"Exactly, Boss." The color was slowly returning to Jayson's face. "You think someone's been down mischief alley?"

"Put a note on his profile," Heli directed. "Nobody but Buddy Nustad picks up his medication from this point on."

***

When Donna Wadeson reached her apartment at 7:45 PM, she'd not only missed the weather report but also the start of *Antiques Roadshow*. Finding an old musket worth several thousand dollars in the attic was just the kind of luck she wished for most people. Helping out and spreading cheer: the world needed more of both. Buddy now had the correct medication, the Runyans, their glorified rice and she, a heating pad over her knees.

The phone rang an hour later, and she was pleased to hear the pleasant foreign doctor on the line.

"My goodness, another call about the infusion bag?"

"Mrs. Wadeson, do you recall the name of the mail-order pharmacy that supplied the IV infusions to Mrs. Runyan?"

"Why, yes I do, Doctor. That would be GEM Pharmacy Services of Baton Rouge, Louisiana. A week's worth of bags came every Wednesday." For a moment, Donna worried that she might have been responsible for canceling this week's standing order. If so, she'd been negligent.

"Excellent. I will contact them promptly."

"Why?"

He didn't answer right away, and Donna feared she might have put him on the spot because of Mr. Bohley's warning about keeping mum on the Runyan case.

"The preliminary pathology findings lead me to suspect the infusion might have been contaminated. For safety's sake, we should notify the mail-order pharmacy immediately."

"Mercy! Are you talking about the same bag I brought over to you at Corner Drug on Saturday?"

"Yes, exactly. Its contents have been cultured and the growth matches Mrs. Runyan's blood sample."

Donna turned the volume down on the remote to be certain she'd heard correctly. "In that case, there's no need to make a long distance call to Louisiana. That TPN bag was prepared in the pharmacy at Swedish Hospital. Picked it up there around 7:30 Friday night, brought it over to Christine's apartment and hung the bag myself."

The words of her manager earlier this morning surfaced in Donna's mind, and the deep ache in her knees spread all the way up to her throat. *Since you were involved in the case, Donna, you can expect to be called in. I hope your documentation is in order.*

The chief resident's voice broke the long silence. "Sorry, I am taken aback by your new information. I fear it is not good news for the hospital."

Nor for the pharmacist either, Donna reckoned, recalling the initials 'HH' on the infusion bag's label. That's another mistake on her watch. They say trouble comes in threes. Goodness, what's next for that poor girl?

Thirty-Two

A giraffe neck lamp shot a concentrated beam of light over the kitchen table where Heli organized her fly-tying equipment. Thoughts of springtime, of the surreal clarity of Gracey River, of the trout that always eluded her streaming nymph, calmed her. She secured her father's sturdy vise and slipped a shiny bead over the point. In her mind's eye, the shimmering trout still swam in a slow lazy circle just below the stream's surface. Last summer, the fish had come easily at first, rising to her caddis fly from the shallows. Double-haul casts of unfurling line with the wind at her back, waiting for the strike. She'd been foolish enough to wade upstream alone over the slippery rocks for the romance of hooking the fish. But each time she'd tried to bring the trout back, it turned and moved out into the river. This year she'd be ready with a beaded Prince nymph. Its peacock herl would tease the fish to bite—bite hard—against its will. She'd strip the line until she felt the full weight of the fish. No lifting of the rod prematurely, as her father had always cautioned. Net the trout while Sandy admired her from the riverbank. The image made her glow with pride. Maybe later, walk with him along the trails among tall white birch and trembling aspens. Fairy slipper orchids, fiddlehead ferns and nodding trillium. A picnic in a field of wildflowers, a reciprocal gesture for his supreme dinner last evening. And a sauna, cleansing and medicinal, in old Tapio's cedar bathhouse in the woods. Every life has at least one fairy tale, her father once promised. A smile broadened as she wrapped copper wire over the peacock herl.

The telephone startled her. All day she'd tethered herself to it in hopes that Sandy would call as he'd promised. He hadn't. It was 11:15 PM.

"Heli, we must talk. I know it is late."

Sandy's lush voice had an urgency that aroused her.

"I'm glad you called."

"Please, there is something I must say to you. I know it is late, but I saw light in your window, so I assumed you are still awake."

"Where exactly are you?"

"In my car, across the street from your drugstore."

A curious shiver rippled up her spine. In felt clogs, she padded across the worn carpet to the window that overlooked

Devine Street. Discreetly, she separated two slats of the wooden blinds. The engine of an Audi A6 was running in front of the Jade with its parking lights on.

"I'll need five minutes, Sandy. Pull around behind the store. I'll meet you by the back door."

Heli glanced at the alarm clock by her bed and considered how much she could accomplish in sheer minutes. Shed her sweat pants and t-shirt for jeans and a sweater. Apply concealing make-up over her scar. Release the partially assembled beaded Prince from its vise. Vacuum the rug and remove other evidence of her solitary life.

Instead, she hoisted the Murphy bed back into the wall and grabbed a tin of breath mint pastilles from the bedside table. Licorice, *Glycyrrhiza glabra*, and eucalyptus oil, *Eucalyptus globulus*. She flew down the steps with a light heart, trusting the label's promise of 'long lasting pleasure anytime, anywhere.'

***

If pacing were an Olympic category, Lavelle was well on his way to a gold medal. All Monday evening, he'd waited for the call from Philadelphia. Because he was too frenzied for his usual diversions, he roamed about the five thousand square feet of his Pill Hill home, thinking and plotting.

"Mark, sorry about the lateness of the hour." The deep patrician voice of J. Edward Mancino III finally broke the long silence of Lavelle's night. "The board meeting at Boat House Row went longer than expected—another tedious argument over the fine points of next month's sculling races."

Lavelle remembered the joy of crew on the Schuylkill during early misty mornings in Wynnewood. Gone. Replaced now by different circumstances where he was still rowing upstream, this time for his professional life, without direction and alone, lacking the coxswain's cadence and the stroke of oarsmen.

The mantel clock in his study finally chimed at midnight. At Mancino's $800 hourly rate, Lavelle calculated that simply telling the attorney the full extent of his troubles had cost him over a thousand dollars. He supposed the long silences on the other end of the phone were billable minutes too.

"Have you told me everything?"

"Absolutely." Lavelle had been unusually candid about the threat of malpractice over the Runyan death, the harassment allegations at Swedish Hospital and the ongoing dispute with the

Medical Staff Executive Committee concerning his questionable research association with Averill Pharmaceutical. But he'd withheld specifics of his financial involvement with GEM mail-order pharmacy. Time enough for that later if Eddy failed to get the messy situation under control.

"I will ask one more time. Do I know everything that I need to know? Forewarned is forearmed, Doctor."

"Yes." Lavelle instinctively reached for a glass of bourbon that wasn't there. Earlier in the evening he'd committed to be sober for this conversation.

"Your problems are mounting at an alarming pace. In my experience," Mancino declared after a deep sigh, "a man who racks up a string of problems this quickly usually has other problems as well. Financial difficulties, substance abuse, sexual dysfunction, a gambling addiction, a psychiatric disorder. I must ask, Mark. Are you falling apart, or is somebody out to get you?"

"*Compos mentis*, I assure you." Since when have lawyers become mental health experts? "I am of exquisitely sound mind, and I have maintained my performance as an excellent physician here in North Dakota. But I am an outsider, and according to the prevailing social norms, somehow this has come to mean that I cannot be trusted." He had more to say about the cultural quirks of this uptight, laborious community, but at Mancino's hourly rate, he decided to forego an oral documentary on the lymphatic temperaments and the mute, staid faces that populated his medical practice. Instead, he returned to the second half of the attorney's question. "There is a self-righteous pharmacist who may be behind the harassment allegation." The image of Heli Harri made him bristle. "Like spores of the plague, she never quite goes away. An annoying vector for trouble."

"Hmmmm. I'll require more information about her. Anyone else?"

"Not that I can think of."

"Will anyone come to your defense?"

"Unlikely." The attorney's question sharpened Lavelle's sense of isolation. This was not the first time he'd felt alone with nowhere to hide on this impossibly flat land that unfolded like a great sea, interrupted only by an occasional water tower or decaying farmhouse. Friendless, too, except for the steadfast loyalties of Phyllis and Sandeep Venkata.

"As I see it, the most pressing issue you have is your credentialing problem. We'll address other problems in time if and when a malpractice suit is filed. You must do whatever is required to regain your privileges at the hospital. Enroll in the anger management class and show up enthusiastically. Be the star pupil. Prepare a written apology and deliver the letters personally to those employees you've insulted at a special meeting with the hospital's Human Resources staff present. If you can't be sincere, give an Academy Award performance. Meanwhile, I'll contact the hospital's attorney for a copy of the bylaws to insure that due process is carefully followed. Do you understand?"

"Yes," Lavelle replied, "but I'll need you out here. I'm not paying merely for advice, but for the actual presence of J. Edward Mancino III standing at my side before the Executive committee."

"Certainly." The scratching of a pen on paper traveled over the line. "How exactly do I get to Dakota?"

The pacing stopped and Lavelle collapsed into the leather chair behind his desk. "Board a 757 heading west. If you see the Rocky Mountains, you've gone too far."

***

He heard the deadbolt lock slam back, and the heavy steel door opened to her lean silhouette. In the warm glow of the security light over the back entrance to the brick building, she appeared softer, more vulnerable than he'd remembered. Her tousled hair invited stroking.

"Hi Sandy." Heli bolted the door shut and motioned him upstairs. "Follow me."

Venkata hesitated and looked about the small entry at the base of the staircase. Another steel door must open into the drugstore. "May we talk in your pharmacy? This will not take long, I assure you."

He watched her face cloud over with apprehension. She seemed to waver, then sorted through keys on a ring, and opened the second door into the rear of the pharmacy. A bank of harsh fluorescent lights illuminated a room where tall vertical bays formed a narrow canyon through which she guided him. Her hand was warm to his touch. Along the way, he noticed a small office overcome with paper. Nearby, a secured wall cabinet displayed pharmacy antiquities—blue Delft apothecary jars and glass bottles bearing Latin names: *sp. Juniper and Lycopodium*. A glass shelf with patent medicines, Lydia Pinkham vegetable compound and Wampole's Tonic and Stimulant, intrigued him, but he dared not slow down to indulge this distraction.

After meandering around shipping boxes, they reached the

dispensing area. Free-standing shelves in three U-shaped configurations displayed row after row of medicine bottles, standing side by side like a regiment of soldiers, waiting to be deployed for battle. Venkata was struck, if not slightly intimidated, by the sheer volume of drugs. The orderly, immaculate environment in which Heli practiced her profession was a surprising contrast to his own chaotic experience in the hospital. His nose wrinkled at the ether-like scent.

"Flexible collodion," she explained, as though she could read his senses. "Seems to be an epidemic of warts in Fargo. Blame the frogs of St. Urho."

"Oh?" What did frogs have to do with an infection of the human papillomavirus? He was too embarrassed to ask.

"Never mind." Heli smiled and walked around the center work island. "Elixirs, extracts, tinctures and syrups," she explained, pointing like a docent in a museum. "Plasters, liniments and ointments to my right. Orals in the bays, injectables near the laminar hood, nasals and ophthalmics above the counter." Her hands assumed the orans position of a priest. "My very own pharmacopeia."

He would always remember how she looked at that moment: proud, optimistic, trusting. Now he had some physical context to understand her daily life, and scenery for his idle musings.

She slid a tall stool away from the prescription counter over the rubber mat to where he stood. Once on the padded seat, he curled the toes of his Rockports behind the stool's lower rail. Heli sat directly across from him, bistro-style, without a table between them. No place to hide nervous hands or fidgety legs.

"Last night was lovely, Sandy."

Venkata looked into her eyes, convinced that in matters of the heart, a first impression is rarely wrong. He felt a strong desire about to derail his evening's mission. Her framed pharmacy license hung on the far wall, its fine print barely discernible from where he sat. *Heli Harri, R.Ph., issued, 1990.* He did the math in his head: thirty-six. Three years older than he. This would be another problem for his Hindi parents who believed wives should be younger than husbands. Fantasy was overtaking his sensibilities. He resumed a proper posture and redirected the conversation.

"The Runyan case preoccupied a great deal of my attention today. There is something I . . ."

"I've some interesting news for you on the mail-order pharmacy," Heli interrupted, looking intently across the invisible table. "GEM Pharmacy has been shut down as of Saturday, April 1."

"Heli . . ." Rather than being put off by his awkwardness, she seemed eager to talk.

"The pharmacy's license has been revoked under a provision of the Louisiana Penal Code. All five mail-order outlets operating in the state. That's all I know at this point, but . . ."

"Heli. . . ." This news confused him but he could not permit disruption.

"Disciplinary action is a matter of public record, so I've requested minutes of the hearing, but there's red tape involved and it may take at least three or four days to . . ."

"Heli . . ."

"And, Jayson, bless his cyber-wired heart, has identified the owners of the pharmacy. Three oncologists . . ."

"Please, Heli, it does not matter now."

"Of course it matters!" Heli slid off the stool. "Connect the dots, Sandy." The impatience in her voice stung him. "Blood infection-contaminated bag-sanctioned pharmacy-septic shock-death. Of course, Dr. Lavelle is obsessed with the infusion bag. I didn't mention this on Sunday night, but I have an idea that might explain his interest. If true, it's very seedy."

The rarely befuddled chief resident looked beyond her to a framed photograph hanging next to the pharmacy license. A younger Heli with mounds of hair next to a shaggy male, each garbed in maroon graduation gowns. She, with a double gold Honors rope, he, looking down furtively to avoid the camera's eye. Who is he, Venkata wondered? That Heli might have a past had never occurred to him.

"Heli . . ."

"Trevor explained that Dr. Lavelle had actually encouraged him to leave Corner Drug and to use the mail-order pharmacy for Christine's TPN infusions. I'm very suspicious that Lavelle might be financially benefiting from this type of referral to GEM Pharmacy. If you ask me, it all adds up to something very unprofessional."

"No, I'm afraid it doesn't."

"Oh, yes it does. Lavelle could face criminal charges for violating the federal kickback laws. The Stark physician self-referral rules were specifically legislated to prohibit this kind of greed."

"And this would please you? To see Dr. Lavelle in more trouble?" Was it possible she could feign such antipathy if they were romantically involved? No, he decided, Reuben Norbutas had been terribly wrong. His heart lightened, if only slightly.

"If he's abused the law and jeopardized Christine Runyan's care, then he must stand up to the consequences. I know you admire him, Sandy, but yes, justice must be served."

"Heli, please do not interrupt me again." Venkata rolled off the stool and put his hands on her shoulders. "I, too, have information, and I cannot permit my feelings for you to stand in the way of the hospital's investigation."

"Investigation? What are you talking about?" Her eyes narrowed.

"I no longer believe that GEM Pharmacy has anything to do with Mrs. Runyan's case."

"But the bag . . ." Her face was now wreathed in apprehension.

"Mrs. Runyan's TPN bag, the solution that infused through her veins the morning of her death, was prepared at Swedish Hospital." Venkata watched the uneasiness of her expression transform to anxiety. "You prepared her last infusion, Heli." He paused. "Your initials were on the label with the date of Friday, March 31. I have verified this fact with the Director of Pharmacy."

"Of course, I prepared the TPN solution. I don't deny it, Sandy. But she's been on GEM's product for months."

The fear in her eyes overwhelmed him like a sudden attack of vertigo.

"It never occurred to me that our hospital bag was hung. The home health nurse picked it up rather late Friday evening, well after Christine usually started her PM infusion." She bit her lip. "I'm under an internal investigation?" Her voice was barely audible.

"The entire case is being reviewed." He watched her fighting back tears. "The mystery of how Mrs. Runyan acquired the infection still eludes me. But GEM Pharmacy is beyond my suspicion."

"What exactly are you saying, Sandy. That you now suspect me?" Bitterness coated her voice like resin. "Is that it, Sandy? You believe I've made some fatal compounding error that ultimately killed Christine Runyan?"

Venkata drew her close. "No, Heli, there are other possible explanations." He felt her heart hammer against his chest. "We will find answers. Mrs. Runyan was in a state of compromised health and vulnerable to many pathogens. Any lapse in aseptic technique by those who cared for her, perhaps improper cleaning and monitoring of catheters, may be responsible for the contamination." He hesitated. "Or the dextrose solution, or any of the additives—insulin, potassium chloride, vitamins or trace elements—you introduced into the bag might have been contaminated."

"I prepared at least ten infusions on Friday evening. In that case," Heli argued, "every bag would have also been infected. Have there been other cases?"

"Not to my knowledge. For that, we can be grateful."

She wrestled loose from his embrace as though she were suddenly very frightened. Or was it her sudden distrust of him? He could not be certain. Perhaps he should leave, although he didn't want her to be alone. The news was certain to be painful for her—this ritualized self-chastisement that every health professional succumbed to after the discovery of a medical error. It was late. He was so weary he no longer trusted his judgment to decipher the facts of the case or to understand his powerful feelings for this woman.

A loud rapping on the windowpane at the front of the drugstore startled him. Heli left him alone in the pharmacy as she hurried down the aisle.

"Everything ok in there?" The long beam of a flashlight patrolled the darkened store.

"Yes, Officer LaDuke. I'm all right. Thank you."

Venkata heard a door unlock and the male voice was now inside the building. He moved quickly to the front of the store where Heli stood by a vitamin display.

"Who's that with you?"

"This is Dr. Sandeep Venkata, Officer. He and I were," she swallowed, "consulting on the details of a hospital case."

Officer LaDuke threw a contemptuous look at the chief resident. "I believe you. Thousands wouldn't buy that story, Heli, but I believe you." He turned the flashlight off and the room blackened. "Next time, find a better place than a drugstore for your monkey business." He turned around to leave. "Lock the door behind me."

"He's right," Heli turned to Venkata. "You shouldn't be here. I want you to leave."

"Please." Venkata felt he'd been terribly misunderstood. "I only wanted to share with you the new information as I have learned it. Do not be overly concerned. The hospital's investigation will uncover additional facts that will exonerate you. The contents of the vials used in the TPN preparation are being tested for bacterial growth." By the look on her face, his words held little comfort.

She moved with deliberation down the dark center aisle back to the dispensing area. He followed closely. The gap of silence between them was painful as though he'd lost her forever. When they reached the pharmacy, she opened a drawer under the counter—paused—then handed the chief resident a slightly bulging white envelope addressed to the Fargo Finnish Society.

"Open it carefully, Sandy."

Confused, Venkata picked up a spatula from the pharmacy counter and slid it under the envelope's long sealed flap. He looked inside, then at her, said nothing, hoping for an explanation.

Her fixed stare and stoic posture sent a message to him before words left her lips.

"The syringe came from the Runyan home. My fingerprints are all over it. Before you rush to judgment, culture its contents too."

Tuesday, April 4, 2002

Thirty-Three

Tuesday's *Frontier Press* no longer hallowed the weekend storm in its headlines. With April temperatures in the fifties, the local meteorologist had reclaimed his popularity, and Corner Drug regulars, their good humor.

Heli buttoned her white jacket as she watched customers queue up at the check-out counter. Delores Rude was first in line followed by Sophia from Latte Da who cradled a spring bouquet of red tulips in her arms. Behind them, a stranger in an ill-fitting trench coat waited with a folded newspaper under his arm. When he reached the counter, coins tumbled from his hand into Murlene's. Why he laughed so spontaneously, his head thrust back like a whinnying horse, was anyone's guess, and of little interest to Heli after a sleepless night that not even valerian could subdue.

The phone lines in the pharmacy were unusually quiet this early in the morning, so she relapsed in her desk chair, deciding what she could accomplish in the next fifteen minutes. Attack the mail piling up on her desk? Pay the Pfizer invoice? Catch up on some professional reading? Or empty the wastebaskets—a mindless task that offered instant gratification? The glossy leaves of her ZZ plant were beginning to droop. Its botanical name? Z something. Heli yawned so widely her jaw cracked. Z. . .Z. . .Z. . *Zamioculcas. . . zamiifolia:* the plant able to withstand months of abuse in low-light.

That Venkata had failed to call her in the middle of the night, saying he'd made a terrible mistake, that there would be no investigation, had not happened. Instead, she'd battled those feelings of unfairness that had been pushing her mood down since Sandy's news had taken root. *You prepared her TPN infusion, Heli. Could you have made a mistake?* Suspected of an error that might have killed someone? Disbelief progressed to stomach-cramping fear as the facts morphed into cunning what-ifs. What if stubborn pride blinded her to her own fallibility? Twice in the past twenty-four hours, she'd been confronted with evidence she'd had to explain. Maybe this schedule was unsustainable, the demands too heavy and the consequences, too great. Heli imagined the worst—a charge of professional negligence, losing her license, her job, her store, even Sandy. Was this Finnish fate at work?

Above the desk Sean, preppie and charismatic, looked down at her from their wedding photograph, smiling through his low back pain before OxyContin addiction had enslaved him. She reached for the picture frame and her mind wrapped itself around a

December evening in St. Paul, 1995.

Her husband, Sean Hennessey, unemployed but clean for two years. Let's celebrate, he'd said. Early reservation at Chez Francaise. Hurry! Roads are icy and we can't be late. Okay, I said. Wait for me in the dispensing area. How could I know the patient at People's Drug would have a thousand questions about anticholinergic side effects? Hurry, he shouts! Finally, we leave. Sean, now irritable, drives like a madman. Slow down, I say. He accelerates. First, an icy patch, then guardrails coming at me, one after another, like painted horses on a crazed carousel. Raining glass. The rest, a blur. White coats and hazy images of an ICU. I'm sorry. . . Mrs. Hennessey. . . . . . .your husband. . . dead. My baby? Oh, no . . . no . . .

Heli drew palms down slowly over her face. Color stained her cheeks.

The story, retold with additional facts. Sean's blood sample: positive for OxyContin. Hillbilly heroin, pain drug-of-the-year, popular with addicts. With five minutes alone near the narcotic cabinet, Sean made his fatal choice. Their future is lost. His father-the-politician is obsessed with keeping a drug scandal out of the newspapers. Money buys favor, and the full facts of the accident are never reported. Perhaps you should start a new life somewhere else, his parents urge. We'll help anyway we can. Thanks, but I like my job here.

She watched the nightmare of seven years ago unfold with the distance of a cinematographer. She is a younger version of herself, tentative and naïve.

The missing OxyContin—my Boss says a month later after I return to work—we assume you conspired in the theft. Your fingerprints were all over the cabinet lock. Of course, my fingerprints are there. I'm a pharmacist; I dispense narcotics. Only then do I comprehend the world of politics. Someone must be responsible for the missing OxyContin, and with his father's political future at stake, it wasn't to be Sean. The matter will be dropped with no further investigation and no reporting to the State Board of Pharmacy if you leave quietly. But I had nothing to do with the theft. It would be best if you left immediately, Heli. Get a new start. Am I being fired? Call it anything you like. Just leave. All aboard for the getaway train to Fargo.

Heli closed her eyes. Past and present: the similarities were there. Yet in the retelling of her life so far, she knew that if she were to live the life she was meant to, something more was required of her now. After all, this was not her first time in the sauna. Heat not only sharpened the senses and cleansed the mind; it also built endurance and nurtured new strengths. Getting to the bottom of Christine Runyan's death was her only chance for exoneration. If that required determination and some pushback, Finn-style, so be it.

"Miss Heli?" Murlene tapped on the pharmacy counter three times. "Miss Heli, someone to see you."

With eyes wide open, Heli shoved the rolling chair back from her desk, drew a restoring breath and left her office to find the stranger with the newspaper resting his elbows on the high pharmacy counter. Another pharmaceutical rep? This one lacked the groomed presence and smarmy artificiality of the industry's typical marketing troupe. And he was male—no match for the growing female sales force who more easily maneuvered their way into physicians' offices.

The man pulled a business card from an inside pocket of his trench coat and slapped it down before her. "Name's Roger Kenney. A few minutes of your time should be all I'll need."

According to the card, he was a private investigator from Minneapolis, a taller, older Columbo look-alike with the same disarming style. His slow eyes combed the historic building as though every nook and cranny might harbor the clue he was chasing.

"Ever have a soda fountain here?"

"Afraid not," Heli answered. "Not enough room." And no margin, her accountant echoed. Leave nostalgia where it belongs: in a museum.

"Story goes that Lana Turner was discovered in a Hollywood drug store."

"Schwab's Drug Store." Heli wished she could bankroll the number of times she'd heard this fact.

"What a doll she was." Kenney wrestled out of his overcoat and tugged at his shirt collar as though it were choking him. "A real shame drug stores got rid of soda fountains. Beautiful marble countertops and stainless back bars. You could buy a cherry coke or a Lime Rickey for a quarter back then. Myself, I can't get into this fancy coffee fad. Nope," he concluded, "nothing beats the old time soda fountain, the real backbone of Main Street."

"How can I help you, Mr. Kenney?"

"Is there somewhere we can talk?" He looked beyond her to the consultation area.

"About what?"

"You come right to the point, don't you, Ms . . . Harri?" He wrinkled his nose as though it itched. "Used to be "Hennessey,' right? Well," he dropped his chin, "I'll get right to the point too. Is Trevor Runyan a customer of your drugstore?"

"Who wants to know?"

Kenney loosened the knot of his tie. "That would be the MidAmerica Life Insurance Company out of the Twin Cities. I've been retained to investigate a death claim on the deceased, a Christine Maleah Runyan, DOB, 1/31/1974." He rolled his shoulders and rotated his head in a slow arc. "We're cooperating with the Insurance Department from the state of Maryland."

The stark abstraction of Christine's life—wife, mother, teacher, patient, reduced to a mere policy number on an insurance claim—was chilling. Heli tried to set her naiveté aside. Every profession required some emotional detachment, yet this stranger's wistful memories of bygone soda fountains and dead movie stars was difficult to reconcile with his indifference to present human loss. It was at that moment her wariness spiked.

"Mr. Kenney, surely someone in your line of work understands that I'm not going to disclose anything about Christine Runyan or her family that you don't already know."

"Sure, sure. Wouldn't ask you to do anything improper. Midwest sent me up to Fargo to make sure everything's on the up and up. The policy was flagged in the computer twice: once, when the policy was sold and again, when she died. The company got a claim, but no death certificate." He shook his head, "Nobody's getting a dime without signed paper to back it up."

Heli maintained her silence. Just then, Jayson made an unexpected entrance through the back door. She turned around, grateful for a second set of ears.

"Hey, Boss. Big news on GEM." He unzipped his jacket and hung it on a hook by the door. "Oops, sorry. Didn't realize you were with someone."

"Was there anything more, Mr. Kenney?"

"How come the woman died?"

"Sorry, no comment."

Roger Kenney threw his head back and laughed in the same horsey manner. "I gotta tell you," Kenney chuckled, "before I retired, I worked in the Reagan administration. State Department—protected royal Saudi families for the American Embassy." He looked beyond Heli to the shelves of medicine behind her. "Take it from me, the Saudis have nothing over Swedish Hospital when it comes to keeping secrets. Nobody's talking. Except, of course, the disenfranchised," he smirked, "and they sing like birds." He craned his neck in Jayson's direction. "Let's change the game. I'll throw out some names. You tell me if you recognize any of them. Whether you know someone or not can't be a matter of confidentiality, right?"

"No games, please." Heli crossed her arms. "I have real work to do."

His cajoling personality and simple questions were like a trap buried under new snow. Reading from a small spiral note pad, he persisted. "Trevor Runyan."

Heli stared at him impassively.

"We always start with the most obvious in surveillance cases, and nine times out of ten, we're right. Who stands to gain from the death? I've got quite a profile on Runyan already. You have any financial problems with the guy? He sold the insurance policy on his wife and she dies two months later. Any idea what makes a guy that desperate?"

"You've asked me a series of questions."

"And you don't intend to answer any of them, do you?"

"Right, again."

"How about Reuben Norbutas? Now there's a guy with a lot to say."

Not a muscle of her face twitched.

"Roxanne Vetter."

Stony silence from the pharmacist.

"Jack Slama."

Heli sighed and shifted her weight to the other foot.

"Mark Raymond Lavelle?"

She pursed her lips. Stayed mum.

"A reaction to that name." Kenney smiled and made a note on his tablet. "I got a copy of letter dated February 28, 2002, signed by a Dr. Mark R. Lavelle asserting that Christine Runyan would be dead within twenty-four months."

Dead in two years? Did Sandy know this?

"Of course, Dr. Lavelle is too busy to talk to me. I hear he got himself in some kind of trouble at the hospital. Wouldn't happen to know anything about that, would you?"

Heli looked at her watch: 9 AM. Doctors' offices would be emptying and the patients' march to the drugstore would soon begin.

"How about the Eastern Shore Life Settlement Company? It's a viatical company. Name mean anything to you?"

Mercifully, the phone rang and Heli picked it up. "Game's over, Mr. Kenney. This player has to go to work."

"You got a great business here, Ms. Harri. I like to see women running businesses. Adds some style to Main street. I'll be back to see you. In the meantime, give me a call if your tongue loosens up."

Heli returned to the dispensing area where Jayson waited. "Did you . . ."

"Every last name. Like you taught me, Boss: listen with pen in hand." On the back of a prescription blank, he'd written the names: Runyan, Norbutas, Vetter, Slama, Lavelle, Eastern Shore. "Nice work, Boss. He got squat out of you."

Heli studied the list. "Besides Trevor and Dr. Lavelle, the only name I recognize is Roxanne Vetter. She was a nurse at the code."

"I saw that dude, Reuben, at the Jade last night. Cranberry-eyed and chemically inconvenienced. Been fired at Swedish."

"How about the other man, Jack. . .?"

"Jack Slama, an insurance broker. He's our patient. A smoker, trying to kick the habit. Nervous guy. Let's pull up his profile." Jayson clicked his way until a medication profile screen flooded the page. "Right here. Nicotine replacement therapy. He's tried everything: patches, gum, inhalers. Now he's on bupropion 150mg every morning. Complains of cotton mouth." He tabbed to another screen. "Good health insurance. Makes his co-pays without any pushback."

"The other names have some association with Christine Runyan. What's his?"

Jayson shrugged his shoulders in a how-should-I-know response. "And what's a v-i-a-t-i-c-a-l?"

Heli checked her watch. "No clue, Sherlock, but we've got five minutes to find out before the morning rush begins."

Thirty-Four

Since he no longer had hospital rounds, Dr. Mark Lavelle headed directly to his office building early Tuesday morning to begin the vexing tasks associated with reinstatement at Swedish Hospital. In his mind, he'd crafted a skeletal letter of apology but hadn't mustered the resolve to put his thoughts on paper. His concentration always unraveled. Why hadn't Eddy returned his calls yesterday? What new findings might Venkata uncover today? Should he place a call to Trevor in order to gauge the threat of law suit?

He booted up his computer, opened a new document and keyed "April 4, 2002: to whom it may concern." Who did it really concern, he wondered? The name of his accuser hadn't been provided, although he had little doubt that it was the cheeky pharmacist with the lopsided smile. How was he to write a convincing letter if he couldn't be certain to whom the apology was addressed? One more example of this hospital administration's surreptitious dealings with physicians. *They,* the powerful band of conspirators, simply could not be trusted. Lavelle reached inside his desk drawer for a note pad. At the top of the page, he wrote, "to be discussed with Mancino:"

1. due process—the name of accuser(s)??

Since last evening's phone call with his lawyer, Lavelle had rebuked himself for not calling attention to other issues that had escaped him during their conversation. For example, Andy Thorson had assured a fair process, yet access to his patients' hospital charts had been denied. How could a physician reasonably maintain an office practice without inpatient medical information?

2. undue restrictions—possible restraint of trade??

"Due process" now seemed to be nothing more than a ruse. The hospital administration had him jumping through hoops with no perceived end in sight, like the internal case review regarding his management of Christine Runyan's care.

3. insist on an EXTERNAL case review by a qualified internist.

He searched for other examples of half-truths and chicanery, but couldn't put a finger on one until Phyllis walked through the door with a stack of insurance papers.

"Do you recall the conversation we had Saturday morning about my signature being copied on hospital stationery?"

"Forged was the word I used, Doctor."

"Retrieve the letter. I want another look." Mancino's question—*are you falling apart, or is someone trying to get you?*—roused him. He added another item to his list:

4. <u>hospital using my signature without authorization???</u>

"Certainly. Will you be taking calls from Dr. Venkata this morning? He's been quite persistent."

Anything to avoid this letter of apology. "Put him through, Phyllis, and close the door."

While he waited for the chief resident's call, Lavelle reconsidered the calculated risk he'd taken by withholding news from Mancino of his financial involvement with GEM Pharmacy. If someone was indeed out to get him, this information could be combustible. Mancino would be furious to learn it second-hand. Reluctantly, he reached for the note pad and added a fifth point as the Bollywood voice came on the line:

5. <u>the GEM Pharmacy detail</u>

"Good morning, Sir. I am calling with an update on the Runyan case."

Lavelle sighed dramatically. So, Venkata had not dropped the case.

"Although you do not give much credence to the causation between the match of Mrs. Runyan's TPN bag and her blood sample, this fact is interesting to Dr. Kampela, the Infection Committee and the hospital administration."

The office chair squeaked as Lavelle rocked back and forth. He massaged his temples in advance of the tension headache that was building.

"Especially," the chief resident hesitated, "since the TPN was prepared in the hospital pharmacy."

Lavelle fell forward in his chair. "What . . . did . . . you . . . say?"

"Not the mail-order pharmacy as I had assumed. My mistake, Sir."

"Are you absolutely certain, Sandy?"

"Quite. I have confirmation from the hospital pharmacy. I assume that is why I've been called by Mr. Bohley to an urgent meeting later this afternoon."

Lavelle leaned back in his chair and looked out the window beyond his desk. Snow on the asphalt surface of the parking lot had completely melted. He longed to run out of his office. Indulge the first sweet breath of spring.

"May I say, Dr. Venkata, your news merely confirms my distress over the safety of patients at Swedish Hospital. It's no surprise to me that the source of the trouble lies in the pharmacy. In light of this new evidence, my long-standing unease with this administration and its feeble attempts to assure quality has, at last, been validated."

Venkata did not respond immediately. "Sir, I know of your credentialing problems. I hope the matter will be resolved promptly."

"It certainly will be." Lavelle removed a vintage fountain pen encased in a gold velvet box from the center drawer of his desk. The writing instrument had once belonged to his grandfather, a Federal Appeals court judge in New Jersey, notable for his oft-cited opinions on First Amendment liberties. Slowly, the pen's nib expelled a thin ribbon of ink over the last entry on the note to Mancino:

5) the GEM Pharmacy detail.

"After Mrs. Runyan's tragic death, it is our obligation—yours and mine—to redirect this hospital on a fresh path toward excellence. The mantle of leadership is heavy, Sandy. Are you ready for this challenge?"

When the chief resident didn't answer, Lavelle hung up the phone and promptly shut down his computer. His need for letter writing was over.

Thirty-Five

Alayne Ludemann arrived in the Executive conference room shortly before noon on Tuesday, well before the impromptu 4 PM meeting called by the CEO. Styrofoam coffee cups littered the table and stapled handouts were strewn across the surface. She cleared the mess of others with the resentment of one accustomed to cleaning up after careless younger brothers.

Being early meant she could arrange the seating to her advantage. Mr. Bohley at the head of the table in the tallest chair with an agenda to guide him. His favorite stone coffee mug and strong brew to keep the idiot alert. She, to his immediate right, in order to feed him notes unobtrusively if it came to that, and to keep an eye on the clock. Armed with files and legal pads, Mr. Perrault required adequate space to Mr. Bohley's left. With Dr. Kampela and the chief resident directly across the table, their body language could be easily monitored when Bohley dropped the bomb. Dr. Dahl, too, where she could watch him squirm after the rooftop fiasco. The others—members of the Infection Control committee and the chief of pharmacy—mattered less. She turned the temperature control in the room down to sixty-two degrees. The meeting was bound to generate its own heat.

***

Heli reached for *Cassell's Dictionary of Foreign Words and Phrases* from the pharmacy's reference shelf. Between spoonsful of peach yogurt, she thumbed her way through the table of contents to the Latin section. Prescriptions were still written with phrases like *quantum sufficiat, pro re nata* and *bis in die*. A beautiful language, so full of mythical allusions. It was Tuesday noon, the first spare minute she'd had to check the meaning of the word tossing about in her mind since early morning. Jayson's announcement added one more delay.

"Dr. V on line one for you, Boss."

"I'll pick it up in my office." She closed the textbook and balanced her working girl's lunch on the book's cover, carrying the improvised tray to her desk.

"Hello, Heli. Am I disturbing you?"

Midday, and already his voice sounded weary, but she was unable to read anything more into his tone. Yet, he called, hadn't he? Earlier this morning she believed that Sandy Venkata had evaporated from her life with the shower's steam.

"I've wondered how you are today," he paused, "and whether we have more to talk about."

"Do you actually care to know more?"

"I care very much, Heli."

This micro-dose of encouragement was enough for Heli to explain how she'd come to possess the mysterious syringe from Anya Runyan's toy medical bag. Venkata's clarifying questions convinced her that he was listening objectively. When he asked for specifics, she delivered one detail after another. As the conversation progressed, her defenses relaxed. The tide of his suspicion seemed to be receding.

"All night long I have tried to understand the significance of that syringe. Mrs. Runyan's home health nurse once intimated that there might be social problems in the home. You know the husband, Heli. Do you agree?"

"I thought I knew him. Now I'm not sure." A misplaced syringe. A cash windfall. An insurance investigation. "Trevor should have known better than to toss a used syringe with an exposed needle into a waste basket. Surely he's been trained in proper needle disposal. That's why red sharps containers exist. What was he thinking?"

"Who can say? He may have been too exhausted to give proper attention to such matters."

"Unless," she hesitated, realizing that her suspicion had slipped into overdrive. "I've wondered, especially after this morning." Another drawn-out pause. "Whether Trevor might have . . . I know it sounds crazy. . .but. . . what I'm thinking is unspeakable." She drew a breath. "Something smells fishy to me."

"Perhaps I can guess. A hospital nurse suggested as much. Reuben was convinced that some financial advantage existed for the husband by having his wife in hospital. An insurance benefit, I believe. I dismissed the idea as mere speculation."

The prescription blank on which Jayson had scribbled the names used by the investigator lay on her desk. "This nurse—did you say his name was Reuben?"

"Do you know him?"

"No." Heli maintained her silence in hopes that Venkata might elaborate on his line of thinking.

"There is a psychiatric condition called Munchausen's by proxy," Venkata said, as though he were thinking out loud. "Do you know it?"

"Only because I read an occasional mystery. The syndrome where mothers poison their children just enough to get medical attention, right?"

"Yes, very hard to believe, but it has been reported in the medical literature. However, the cases I have reviewed always involved children."

"Here is it!" Heli interrupted, shrugging away from the sordid details of Munchausen's to fully absorb the Latin word on the page. "I've been trying to locate the derivation of a Latin term I heard this morning."

"Another taxonomic detail? I marvel how your mind works."

"The word has nothing to do with botany." She debated temporarily before plunging into the news. "A private investigator from Minneapolis called me this morning with questions about Trevor Runyan. Mentioned that a death claim on Christine had been filed. Cast a web of suspicion around Trevor. He used an unfamiliar word in the context of insurance that I was certain had a Latin derivation. I have an ear for that sort of thing."

"Indeed you do. And this word is ?"

"'Viatical.' According to my dictionary, it comes from the Latin 'viaticum.'"

"Meaning?"

An apparition of the withered young woman whose life had ended prematurely in the ICU three days ago rose in Heli's memory. "It means," she paused, swallowing to mask the eeriness she felt, "'provisions for a journey.'"

"Ah." Venkata's eloquent silence was a signal that he grasped the sober undertone. "In Mrs. Runyan's case, a final journey. Yes."

"Sandy, did you know Christine had only a short time to live?"

"No, quite the opposite. According to the medical record, she had been doing well. This is why I am so perplexed."

"Then why did Dr. Lavelle attest in a letter to an insurance company that he anticipated her death within two years?"

"This cannot be true! There was no evidence for such a prognosis. Heli, you must stop believing the worst about Dr. Lavelle. He is a good physician and very conscientious with his patients."

Brick wall again. Link Lavelle to a dram of suspicion, and the conversation skids to a halt. Heli sighed. Pushing too hard only results in a headache. She ran a hand over her brow, tapping into the calm reasoning of her mother and the generous spirit of her father. Patience and goodwill must triumph over stubbornness and wild suspicions. Only then could a future with Sandy be possible.

Viaticum. Heli whispered the word prayer-like. As for Christine Runyan's final journey, whatever God was on call the night she died was benevolent to have placed the compassionate Sandeep Venkata at her side.

***

Byron Bohley strutted into the conference room and filled the empty chair at the head of the table. "I assume all of you understand why I called this meeting."

The chief resident barely heard the words of the sweaty man in a blue silk suit. Afternoon rounds were to begin shortly. Since he was on call, he was duty bound to be present. Heli's suspicions still shrouded his mind. Now he found himself summoned to a meeting where he least wanted to be.

"To the contrary, Mr. Bohley." Dr. Kampela answered. "We presume the agenda has to do with the hospital's interest in the death of Christine Runyan." She paused, shifting gracefully in the chair. "Why the administration has taken such an interest in the case is still a curiosity, at least to some of us."

"This hospital faces potential litigation, and I, as its chief executive officer, need to get my arms around the risks we're facing. If the Board gets wind of this before we get our facts straight, there'll be hell to pay."

Venkata listened as the man's voice grew tense. Alayne Ludemann nodded in what seemed to be a conditioned Pavlovian response.

"If I may, Byron," Mr. Perrault interrupted. "I should explain that today, under attorney-client privilege, we are in a position to talk freely about the details of the case. Our discussion will not be 'discoverable' should the matter go to court."

"In that case, shouldn't Dr. Lavelle be present?" Dr. Kampela leaned forward in her chair. "After all, he was the physician of record. Certainly his contribution might enlighten the hospital's defense."

"Lavelle doesn't enlighten anything," Bohley snarled. "I consider him to be a separate but related problem. At the moment, he's facing disciplinary action from the Executive committee. In his place, we have Dr. Venkata who oversaw most of the Runyan woman's care."

At the mention of his name, the chief resident stirred, feeling the weight of the world on his shoulders. He was about to speak, but Dr. Kampela nudged his foot under the table: keep quiet.

"Ms. Ludemann informs me," Bohley continued, "that we have an oddball lab report."

"I sent the sample to a reference laboratory for confirmation, just in case we get sued," Dr. Dahl answered. "Their report should be issued tomorrow. If the results validate our findings, we're dealing with *psuedomonas, Mycobacterium marinum* and another, as yet, unidentified bacterium. The identified pathogens are intrinsically resistant to antibiotics and associated with nosocomial infections. Of course, this is a great concern for our other hospitalized patients."

"Which is why," Dr. Kampela interrupted, "we've initiated an internal micro-surveillance process. The immediate caregivers from home health have been interviewed and their sterile technique, observed. We've examined the clean room in the pharmacy, cultured every water-based additive used to prepare the TPN solution and cross-checked the manufacturer's lot numbers with FDA recalls."

"And?" Bohley peered over his bifocals.

"Nothing extraordinary has come to light. No other cases reported. No recalls of any products under suspicion."

Alayne Ludemann lurched forward. "Certainly the GEM Pharmacy bag must be considered a source of contamination."

"I repeat, Ms. Ludemann. There have been no recalls of any products under our suspicion."

Venkata noticed the tension in the room had risen several degrees with Dr. Kampela's unequivocal response.

"I've personally notified the local Public Health officials." Dr. Kampela crossed her arms and stared at Bohley. "They have their own processes, heightened significantly since 9/11. The state epidemiologist is very interested in the case. He'll be contacting the CDC once our lab work is completed. Even raised the possibility of bioterrorism."

"Good god, are you saying we've got a terrorist on the loose?"

The attorney furiously turned the page of his legal pad and continued writing.

"Very unlikely. Instead, we have an infusion bag and a blood sample whose cultures match, and no way to explain it. With enough time and money, we could subject the samples to PFG—pulsed field gel electrophoresis. For the layperson, this means DNA fingerprinting. The banding patterns could prove that these are genetically identical organisms."

"So what? This *layperson* isn't tracking your fancy theory." Bohley slurped his coffee.

"So what, indeed." Dr. Kampela shook her head. "Without additional leads, our pursuits could easily reach a negative evaluation on the Runyan case. We may never learn the source of her infection."

"What does that mean for the hospital?"

"It means we have to wait for the final lab report," Dr. Dahl insisted.

"I agree." Dr. Kampela said calmly. "We have explained Christine Runyan's death as an overwhelming polymicrobial sepsis. While we cannot explain *how* she became infected, it is not unusual for a chronically ill, immuno-compromised patient with an indwelling catheter to succumb to this kind of infection. In that regard, hers is not a reportable death."

"The first good news I've heard today." Bohley pushed his cup in Alayne's direction. She filled his mug from a coffee urn on the table.

"And," the infectious disease specialist continued, "if our micro-surveillance finds no substandard care or detectable contamination of hospital products used when Mrs. Runyan was in our direct care, we will have exhausted our reasons to be concerned about the safety of other patients."

"Which is exactly what we are held to: a standard of reasonable care." The lawyer seemed energized by the legalese he could wrap around Dr. Kampela's assessment.

Bohley perked up. "I like the sound of that. Does this mean the case could be closed?"

"As long as we have no reason to suspect anything untoward," Dr. Kampela cautioned.

"If we suspect some kind of foul play, it's a matter for law enforcement, not the hospital." The lawyer squinted. "Are you putting such a notion on the table?"

"No," Dr. Kampela turned her head. "I'm merely giving you the facts that you've asked for."

"Then, absent other findings, the Runyan case can be remanded to the annals of oblivion." Perrault laid down his pen.

Bohley swallowed more coffee and looked at the physicians across the table. "So Lavelle had nothing to do with this?"

"To the contrary, he and Dr. Venkata have managed her case in a manner beyond reproach." Dr. Kampela smiled at the chief resident. "An external review will likely affirm this conclusion."

Venkata sucked in his breath. As long as the envelope remained in his pocket, he could not be completely at peace.

"The family will demand that someone be at fault." Alayne Ludemann blurted. "How will we explain the contaminated infusion bag? As a matter of strategy, why not let pharmacy take the hit?" She spoke directly to the pharmacist. "Don't you have some itinerant pharmacist, Heli Harri, who works weekends?" Before he had time to respond, she continued. "This had to be an error by an unqualified part-timer. She should be terminated immediately, Mr. Bohley."

"Precipitous action like that is counterproductive to the hospital's interests." Perrault glared first at Alayne Ludemann, then the CEO.

"For God's sakes, Alayne, if we can shimmy through this without any blame," Bohley argued, "why would we want to finger the major revenue-producing department of this hospital?"

Like a Ping-Pong match, Venkata thought, wondering where the little white ball of blame would be served next.

"Tomorrow, our knowledge will grow with the identification of the third organism. It's an important piece in this puzzle, and all we have to go on at the moment." Dr. Kampela leaned back in her chair, adopting a regal posture.

"Not entirely." Venkata disliked the diffident tone of his voice. He cleared his throat. "Excuse me, please. I wish to add something."

The CEO left his chair and returned with a glass of ice water. A nod to the chief resident implied permission to speak.

"This case will not be closed in my mind until I understand how Mrs. Runyan acquired her infection. I concur with Dr. Kampela. Our surveillance so far points nowhere." Venkata cautiously reached into his pocket for the envelope. "Perhaps if we culture the contents of this syringe," he said without any specific knowledge of where his suggestion might lead, "we will be drawn in a new direction."

The stunning silence lasted no more than a minute before the clamor of voices broke free.

"Now I've heard everything! The mighty brotherhood of physicians looking out for each other!" Alayne Lundemann scribbled angrily on a note that she passed to Bohley. "This is nothing but a last minute stunt to divert attention away from Lavelle."

"Sandy," Dr. Kampela turned in her chair to examine the syringe. "Are you suggesting this syringe is relevant to the

Runyan death?"

"I don't know exactly."

Alayne ejected from her seat and with hands splayed across the boardroom table, leaned forward. "Then what's the point of pulling a syringe out of a hat?"

"Quiet! Let him answer." Perrault reclaimed his pen. "This is exactly the kind of thing we have to know."

Dr. Kampela asked, "where did you find this, Sandy?"

"In the home, near the bedside of Mrs. Runyan, the morning she became ill."

"Why haven't you told us that you'd been to the Runyan home?"

The chief resident realized there was no going back to blissful anonymity. "I have not, exactly, been, as you say, to the Runyan home."

From across the boardroom table, he felt the searing heat of Alayne Ludemann's anger. Surely such rage must now be melting the reputed ice in her veins.

"Then explain to us how you came to possess it."

"I'll tell you what this is all about," Alayne hissed. "He's trying to protect Lavelle and to implicate Trevor. Why else would he bring this up at the last minute?"

"That's enough out of you!" The CEO's face was chili-pepper red.

The chief resident thought once again about the case in its entirety. It was like a block of Swiss cheese with more holes than cheese. Had his romantic infatuation with Heli caused him to misperceive the facts, to exaggerate the importance of certain clues, to imply significance to the absence of others? He dismissed the notion that being so completely happy could make him a poor physician. Somewhere in the empty, unexamined spaces, an explanation resided for how and why Christine Runyan died.

"We're waiting, Dr. Venkata."

"Yes. The syringe was placed in my hands by someone who is very courageous." Venkata answered slowly, permitting clarity and conviction to carry his message. "Someone who has absolutely nothing to fear from the truth revealed."

Thirty-Six

"Have you forgotten who signs your paycheck?" Byron Bohley slammed the door to his office so violently that a United Way plaque trembled on the wall behind Alayne Ludemann.

"Absolutely no," she said. "The meeting was so out of control that I tried to be useful by getting us back on agenda."

"*Your* agenda?" The CEO blustered past her to his desk in search of a Tums.

"I assumed we were playing good-cop-bad-cop in front of the physicians like before. I was simply being *very bad*, trying to stick it to Lavelle and his girlfriend, the pharmacist."

"From what I just heard in the boardroom, Lavelle did everything right. Dammit! I told you to dig something up on him. You told me you had him under control." Bohley collapsed in his leather chair.

"I don't exactly know what happened with the infusion bag mix-up, but I'll get to the bottom of it. No more surprises, Mr. Bohley, I assure you."

"Do you mind explaining what was *supposed* to have happened to that prick?"

Alayne sat down and rested her elbows on the edge of the desk. "Dr. Lavelle has some deal going with an out-of-state pharmaceutical infusion business. He prescribed one of their products for Christine Runyan. I figured it was simply a matter of time before she presented in the ER with the TPN bag, and we'd have the proof we needed to nail Lavelle on an ethics violation."

The CEO chuckled. Chalky powder clung to the corners of his mouth. "Pillow talk with Trevor Runyan, eh?"

Alayne stiffened, squared her shoulders. "I resent your lewd suggestion."

Byron Bohley realized that if there was any shred of satisfaction in the moment, it was seeing this damn fine-looking woman squirm. He'd never completely trusted her. Long ago he'd learned that if he were to survive as an administrator, he must harbor a shrewd mistrust of everyone around him. Conventional wisdom held that once you made the corner office, nobody ever again tells you the truth. Yet, he'd convinced himself that Alayne Ludemann's ambition was so boundless that she could be manipulated into doing whatever was required for her next promotion. Such raw ambition he no longer understood. In his own career, every promotion had torn him farther away from the yelping dogs and mewing cats in the pet store of his dreams.

"No point denying it. It's hardly news around Swedish. Personally, I don't know what you see in Runyan, but that's your business." The CEO began to separate the pile of memos accumulated on his desk. He glanced at *Modern Healthcare* headline: "Patient Safety: Any real progress on the fight to reduce medical errors?"

He looked up. "Or is it the insurance money you're after?" The CEO brought his palms together, fingers pushing up one of his chins. He rocked in the chair. "Of course. A malpractice judgment requires someone to be negligent. That's why you were so eager to finger pharmacy for the fall. Your idea, wasn't it?" He rocked faster. "You disappoint me, Alayne. I never believed you'd betray the hospital. I've worked the ropes to make you a vice president, but in light of your performance today, it will never happen."

The room became so silent that the CEO could hear the secretarial chatter beyond his closed door. Something about whose job it was to clean out the dregs drawer from the Italian coffee machine. We've always done it this way, someone argued; why change?

Finally, Alayne's laser-sharp voice: "You really are a dull little man."

Her composure was impressive. For a brief moment, Bohley reconsidered his decision. A piss-and-vinegar attitude like hers might be handy if some S.O.B. doctor needed dressing down in the future.

"And," she continued, "you're actually quite wrong about my future. You see, I *will* be the chief nursing officer at Swedish Hospital." From the pocket of her white jacket, she exposed a mini-cassette player. Her red tapered nail engaged the play button.

Bohley listened to the tinny garbled voice on the recorder and was shocked, then embarrassed, to realize it was his own. He laughed. Closed his eyelids and rubbed them with stubby fingers. Shook his head. Laughed again, louder this time. Took the time he needed to figure out exactly how to explain to Alayne Ludemann what it meant to hold the seat on the power side of the desk. How many asses he had to kiss to get here. Where the power came from. Who could take it away. He looked around his office. There were few books on his shelf. He had no use for the management theories of Peter Drucker or Tom Peters, or the righteous trends of Deming, Covey or Senge. Running a hospital full of doctors, nurses and bean-counters required a strategy borrowed from Eastern bloc dictatorships. Control the information, reward the informants, punish the saboteurs, and pit one citizen against another. Like Betsy's refrigerator magnet: *Old age and treachery overcome youth and skill.*

The CEO sat upright and stilled the rocking chair. "I need people around me who are loyal and who do not make mistakes. You've given me no reason to believe that you fit this bill."

The tape stopped and the words *tighten the noose around the bastard's neck. I've lost my patience with him* hung like icy buildup on power lines. He looked out his corner window that had, hands-down, the best view in the hospital. River to the left, the Fargo skyline, such as it was, straight ahead. Five in the afternoon, and it was still light outside. He wondered if Tuesday night television was full of reruns.

"I'm leaving now, Mr. Bohley, to give you some time to rethink your decision." Alayne rose from her chair with the grace of a loon taking flight. "Neither Dr. Lavelle nor the Chair of the Board needs to hear this tape quite yet."

He watched her walk confidently to the door and waited until her slim hand reached for the door knob.

"Hold on one minute."

She turned around and leaned back against the closed door, a faint smile drawn on her ceramic face. He couldn't help but notice how well she used those bedroom eyes.

"Your brother, Dan. He's the lawyer in Boise; right?" Bohley studied her for a reaction. "Both of you must stay pretty busy keeping track of baby brother Bryan. I think you told me that snowy day on the rooftop that he's the financial planner in Texas."

Her smile began to unravel, and he was a tad ashamed of the buzz he felt brandishing the stun gun before watching her mouth drop in disbelief.

"Bryan Ludemann: nice, clean sounding name. How's he doing in drug rehab? Was it heroin or cocaine? Must have taken a heap of money to feed a habit like that."

She maintained a pretty good poker face, Bohley thought. Time to force her hand.

"Tell me. Is Bryan still bilking Midwestern snowbirds in the Rio Grande valley out of their life savings?"

No cracks yet. A cool character. Time to turn up the heat.

"From what I hear, he promises the retirees a 100% rate of return on some bogus insurance investment. Doesn't tell them that he pockets a double-digit commission up-front." Bohley chuckled again, waving a file in the air. "Is everybody an ambulance chaser in your family?"

"You have no right to . . . you've violated my rights."

The CEO shook his head. "He keeps bad company too. Friends arraigned for money laundering, insurance fraud, mail fraud, interstate transportation of money obtained by fraud. If Bryan doesn't join a better social club, you'll have a jailbird in the family tree."

"Cut to the chase, Bohley. What else do you know?"

Over the course of his career, the CEO had come up with a line for exactly this moment. Polished it for clarity, rehearsed it for impact.

"More than enough to stay on *this* side of the desk, Alayne."

Sliding down in the chair, he crossed his legs at the ankles and propped them up on the rim of the wastebasket. He might look ridiculous but he didn't care. After all, he was the man at the top of this hospital with his own pissing toilet. Rarely had he enjoyed the executive experience as much as he did this minute. A ridiculous player in a ridiculous healthcare system. And every two weeks a ridiculous amount of money, to which he had become addicted, was deposited into his checking account. It was a system he'd helped to advance, and now he was forced to live or die with the product of his fabrication. The massive flow of money would continue for a ridiculously long time as long as he kept his Board stroked and stupid, kept his political knives sharpened, and did absolutely nothing to disturb the status quo.

Thirty-Seven

Venkata waited in the ER for his patient to arrive. A seventy-four year old hypertensive male in atrial fib with left sided hemiparesis was being airlifted from a rural North Dakota hospital. With stroke, time was everything. While he waited, he asked the lead nurse where he might find Reuben Norbutas.

"You won't. He's gone." She rolled her eyes. "That's all I can say officially." Leaning in closer, she added, "try the Jade Garden. Between you and me, Dr. Venkata, we never had this conversation. People who get on the wrong side of this administration have a way of disappearing."

The chief resident received an updated ETA from the flight crew. Twenty-one minutes until touchdown. He'd be paged ten minutes before the helicopter landed on the hospital's million-dollar helipad. Time enough to compose a long overdue email. He found a vacant computer terminal and organized his thoughts.

Dear Mum & Dad, another busy night of call. Soon a stroke patient from western ND will arrive by air transport. I will thrombolyze with a clot buster drug costing $3,000 before damage occurs. This convinces me that American healthcare system is the finest in the world. No one questions the cost.

Residents' Awards banquet is June 20. I have marked my calendar for June 15 when you arrive, with Deepthi flying in on the 17th. There is much to celebrate. In addition to graduation, I have been notified by NIH that my grant to study nosocomial infections in patients with hematologic malignancies has been approved. Duke will be sending out an announcement later this month. The other surprise must wait for your arrival in US. Good fortune has followed me to Fargo.

If you have room, please bring cardamoms (both green and black) and amchoor powder. Very bland food here in the middle of America.

Your son, Sandeep

Wednesday, April 5, 2002

Thirty-Eight

Not so much as a gibbous moon hung in the 5 AM sky beyond her window. Shrouded by dense cottonwoods and towering elms, the running path along the Red River of the North would be deserted this time of day. Nevertheless, Heli laced her Rykas, stretched her hamstrings and quads, and hurried out the door to face brisk April temperatures. After all, this was Fargo, seventh among the hundred safest places to live in America.

She sprinted along Devine Street toward the Red, past the darkened storefronts of Latte Da, the Jade Garden and Second Time Around. At Seventh Avenue, she veered left through a residential neighborhood of 1940 bungalows, past the American Legion baseball diamond, until she reached a parking lot near the entrance to Riverside Park. She paused under a street lamp to re-tie the laces of one shoe, then dashed across the empty lot until she reached the jogging trail that terraced the river. The long empty path with a rolling view of the river at dawn was exactly the distraction she needed to escape her Runyan obsession.

A bracing headwind numbed her cheeks as she reached the first turn of the trail. Running too fast made her calves sing so she stopped near the second mile-marker to stretch. The dark sky was barely visible through the long fingers of the elms' canopy. Her eyes swept the side of the trail for movement, but only a nervous brown squirrel broke the stillness as it darted up a tree with amphetamine-like speed.

Wednesday, she puffed, resuming her run. Peak-of-the-week. Her one day off took shape in her mind. Behind the prescription counter all morning. Relieved by Jayson at 2 PM. Hardly a free afternoon though. She'd cocoon in her office to attack the mounting paperwork. Do battle with gum-snapping clerks at the Pharmacy Benefits Management call center over rejected claims or "approved" lists. PBMs were toxifying the profession of pharmacy. How the shady business model of unregulated PBMs had eluded government scrutiny was beyond her grasp. Profits and market share had positioned drug companies and their PBMs at the very top of the health care food chain. Independent pharmacies without political clout sank to the bottom. She drew a deep, diaphragmatic breath. The entire mess felt like twenty-pound weights around her ankles and the hills she had to climb, much steeper.

An American elm, its trunk painted with a red "X," marked

the end of the third mile. *Ophiostoma ulmi.* Heli panted the words out loud as she passed the condemned tree. Repeated the words twice to bring her attention back to the moment. The infecting Dutch elm fungus had caused entire urban forests in the Midwest to wilt and die. *Ophiostoma ulmi.* What's in a name? Order and distinction among all living organisms. Wasn't that Adam's first task in the garden? Naming had always been her tool to make sense of the world.

Wednesday, she chugged. Hump Day. Today Sandy will learn the name of the third organism. Their late night phone call last evening replayed in her mind. She'd been in bed for an hour, distracting herself with *American Angler.*

"Did I wake you?"

"Not a chance."

He'd recapped his day on call.

"In ER most of the night . . . acetaminophen overdose . . . then, a very bad GI bleed . . . we lost her. Male schizophrenic . . . head trauma . . . in critical condition. Such violence is difficult to comprehend in Fargo. In the afternoon I was summoned to a meeting with Mr. Bohley about the Runyan case."

The magazine fell to the floor when she sat upright in bed.

"Dr. Dahl expects the final lab report on Mrs. Runyan's blood sample sometime Wednesday. This may shed some new light on the case."

In her mind's eye, Heli saw a complex tree diagram with the name of the organism cascading through the branches in progressively greater detail until it found its final taxonomic slot. Her breathing intensified as she sped along the trail. A name might add some clue, point in a new direction. A track in the snow, a marker along the path. A way to make sense of this case. Resolution for Sandy. Exoneration for her.

"I sensed," Sandy continued, *"that if the pending blood sample adds no further clues, Mr. Bohley and the hospital lawyer will deem the case to be closed, marked 'unexplained death; human error without attribution.'"*

His words had tripped a siren in her head, and she'd kicked back the bedcovers in disbelief.

"This is supposed to be good news, Sandy? If this case is closed without getting to the truth, I'll be forever associated with a fatal mistake that I didn't commit. I'm not at fault, and I won't live under this kind of suspicion. Never again!"

"What do you mean, never again?"

"It's a story that needs explaining, but not now."

"As you wish."

His abiding composure was such a contrast to her own short fuse.

"Someone must be very afraid of the truth. Lavelle, probably. He's got to be involved in some underhanded way. I haven't given up the notion that GEM Pharmacy is somehow involved."

"Heli, please. Do not. . . ."

"Or Bohley. Of course! He'd rather blame a death on an employee's error than to admit some management failure. As long as the hospital appears to run smoothly and he stays out of the headlines or the courtroom, he keeps his job. Swedish can't endure any more negative publicity, let alone another malpractice suit. So he buries a mistake."

Heli grimaced at her unintended pun.

"We're all so busy protecting ourselves, Sandy." Another long pause. *"Christine trusted us. Every patient trusts us. If they had any idea what goes on within the bowels of a hospital . . ."*

Near the four mile-marker, she passed three more Dutch elms branded for removal. Without immediate intervention—trenching the root system, pruning dead branches and girdling cuts to the trunks--every other elm along the path would be vulnerable to the fungus and its beetle vector. There were consequences for doing nothing. Someone had acted. This recognition fueled her energies.

Wednesday, she wheezed, resuming her run with determination on the last mile of the trail. After her outburst on the phone last night, Sandy had remained silent until her diatribe on hospital politics expired.

"Heli, I believe you had nothing to do with Mrs. Runyan's death. Absolutely nothing. How she died, I cannot explain. Let us wait for more information."

His voice possessed the calming qualities of medicinal tea.

Then, another surprise.

"May we have dinner Wednesday evening? I want to talk with you about matters that have nothing to do with Mrs. Runyan's death. Is this possible?"

Oh, yes. No need to check her social calendar. It was disconcerting how this man could so easily make himself at home in her heart.

"Excellent. I will call for you promptly at 6. We will go somewhere special. No beeper tonight."

When the parking lot came into view marking the end of her five-mile run, Heli accelerated for the home stretch. Still dark, another two hours before sunrise. Enough time for a long hot bath in her claw-footed tub, soaking in water softened with her special concoction of Epsom salts, glycerin and lavender blossoms. Recompense to well-worked muscles and new resolve.

As she ran up a small slope near the parking lot, the headlamps of a distant car idling in the far corner caught her off-guard. The lot was otherwise empty. Fear jumped up on hind legs. Let it be a policeman on patrol. LaDuke—working undercover. Wind-chill penetrated the layers of her fleece hoodie and she shivered. Let it be LaDuke—accept a ride home in his warm squad car. She invented the conversation. Pharmacy folklore— how a pinch of coca leaves once found its way into the soda fountain of Jacob's Pharmacy in Georgia. Drug stores and the cocaine trade. LaDuke would like that.

A light-colored Ford panel van crawled forward in her direction. This wasn't LaDuke in the panda colors of the Fargo PD. Fear reared its head again. Had she roused a sleeping drunk? Interrupted lovers coiled on a mattress in the back of a van? Suddenly, the vehicle gunned across the lot toward her. Was this some speed freak in a rolling meth lab tweaking in her direction?

Instinct prevailed. Go right. Cut through a tangle of trees bordering backyards of the neighborhood. Bob and weave over fences, across frozen gardens, between houses and garages. Become invisible. She bolted toward the darkened houses where families slept unaware. Speed and focus came easily. Another wake-up call for action.

Thirty-Nine

The amber light of her unpublished line lit up at 11:55 AM on Wednesday. Heli narrowly avoided overturning the Robitussin syrup as she reached for the phone. A handful of people had access to this private number and Sandy was among the few.

"Clyde Erickson here. Have a minute to talk?"

She hedged. Agree to talk with the nervous accountant, and he might conclude she had too much time on her hands. Put him off, and the rest of her day would be clouded with the inevitability of bad news.

"Your timing is as precise as your numbers, Clyde. It's the lull before the afternoon storm."

"This may come as a surprise," the droll voice continued, "but I've some good news."

Good news had been an infrequent visitor this week, and good news from Clyde Erickson required a near lottery mentality. Heli pulled a stool next to the dispensing counter. For good news, she'd need to be sitting down.

"Someone wants to buy Corner Drug. Everything: the business, inventory, accounts receivable, even the building."

Her breakfast of fresh pineapple turned somersaults in her stomach. She gripped the pharmacy counter. "Who is this 'someone' and how did 'someone' know you were my accountant?"

"I don't know. The proposal from Bullis, James and Hawthorne out of Omaha arrived in my mailbox over the weekend. I've been sitting on it until we'd have some time to discuss the terms. Today's your day off, right?"

"What's a day off, and who's the buyer?"

"The identity wasn't disclosed in the cover letter. However, the firm represents that he, or she," the accountant qualified, "is financially equipped to consummate the deal."

"Why haven't they approached me directly?" Heli's cheeks flushed. Another round of deal-making behind her back.

"I can't explain that either. Fargo is a small town. Could be that the buyer prefers to deal with a man. And it's certainly not uncommon to involve a private investment firm in business acquisitions."

Her gaze shifted to the front door where noon hour traffic was increasing. A loyal crowd of readers ruffled through the weeklies in the magazine stand. Murlene was restocking the Natural Products shelves with Gingko Balboa and Saw Palmetto. Two mothers carrying babies in pouches slung around their necks were applying testers from the lip color spring display. Downtown employees strolled the aisles during their lunch breaks for aspirin, antacids and 35 mm film; their purchases would leave in white bags imprinted with *Corner Drug, Heli Harri, R.Ph., Proprietor.* This wasn't just her livelihood; it was her life, and she cherished all of it.

"My business is not for sale, Clyde." Heli slid off the stool. "I've worked too hard to walk away and start over."

"You should at least consider the offer. It's a good price." Erickson's tone turned pencil-sharp. "The buyer is willing to pay a market multiple of eight times EBITDA with no strings attached. Pharmacies like yours rarely go over a multiple of five."

She scribbled the financial terms on a message pad. Eight times earnings before interest, taxes, depreciation and amortization. She underlined 'eight' twice.

The sound of rustling paper traveled over the line.

"An offer like this doesn't come along every day. We've got thirty days to respond." Erickson softened his voice. "You ought to take some time to think it through."

"I don't see what will change in a month."

"That's exactly the point. Nothing in the world of pharmacy will change for the better in thirty days, maybe thirty years, unless the whole damn system collapses." He cleared his throat. "It's my duty to advise you that Corner Drug's numbers concern me, and I see no relief in sight. Fee schedules are bottoming out. Cuts to the Medicaid budget are disastrous. Medicare, the growing part of your business, is your weakest margin. You have little negotiating clout with payers and absolutely no leverage with the government programs. Face it, Heli; you're in a no-win game." Erickson took a breath. "Frankly, I'm surprised at your reaction. You could get out before the second Walmart opens, and dump the business risk while you still can. Take a pharmacy job at some hospital where you'd be working half as hard, or find a desk to hide behind in some big corporation where you'd be guaranteed a paycheck just for showing up. Think about the future, Heli. You could be debt-free with some extra change in your pocket."

She sat back down and slumped in silence for what seemed like a painfully long time.

"I'll think it over, Clyde. Sorry to maul the messenger when you're looking out for my interests."

Financial uncertainty. Accusation and blame. A flicker of romance. Might as well throw a buyout into the hopper. Heli hung up the phone and drummed her fingers on the prescription counter. Corner Drug was now crazy busy. Time to get back to work.

***

The chief resident walked down the long corridor that opened to the ER after Wednesday's noon conference. He noticed the frayed carpet and wondered how many of his own steps had contributed to the wear.

"Hey, Doc. How's it hanging?"

Venkata turned around and gave the familiar male nurse an inquiring glance.

"Reuben, is that you?"

"Sure is. Dress me up in a suit and tie like this and I could pass for a VIP, that's very important prick."

"I'm surprised to see you," said Venkata. "I called for you in ER earlier this week but the admitting clerk told me you no longer worked at Swedish."

"Easy come, easy go." Reuben shrugged his shoulders jauntily. "Fired on Monday by Ludemann; rehired by Bohley on Wednesday. You might say I had a busy Tuesday circling back."

"Fired? For what reason?"

"Knew some things I wasn't supposed to know. Saw some things not meant to be seen. The information seemed to interest Bohley." Reuben's eyes rolled. "I talked; he listened. He talked; I listened. Put out a few feelers for the little guy with the big job. This morning we traded favors, and here I am, employed once again in the ER with the shift of my choice." The nurse puckered his lips as if to whistle. "The CEO told me I have real administrative potential."

The chief resident was annoyed with himself for being taken in by such bravado, yet he did nothing to interrupt the flow of curious information.

Reuben grinned. "Ludemann will go berserk over this. Bohley sure put a hitch in her giddy-up."

Venkata's brow furled. "I do not understand."

"What comes up, comes out; that's what I'm saying, Doc. Brains and claws—a bad combination in a woman. Alayne got a little sloppy climbing her way to the top, like using the hospital's email as though nobody was reading it. How stupid is that?"

Reuben shot a pointed finger in Venkata's direction. "I told you once before, you gotta know who your enemies are at Swedish. This place has its own way of doing things." He nodded as though agreeing with himself. "By the way, what did you want when you called?"

"I have more questions about the Runyan case."

"Still dogging that one? Sounds like Swedish will get its ass waxed over this fuck-up. I heard the weekend pharmacist screwed up royally."

"That is not my conclusion." Venkata hesitated. "You mentioned that Mrs. Runyan frequented the ER. What history do you recall of these visits?"

"What are you talking about?"

"For example, who cared for her in the home? Who usually brought her in for admission? How did she answer the standard admitting questions about personal safety or hazardous situations in the home? Any concerns of patient neglect?"

"Why not review the medical record? The information should be there."

"Her chart is not available." Venkata studied Reuben's reaction. "I'd hoped to correlate Mrs. Runyan's infections with some common variable, perhaps the source of her TPN infusions, the source of her supplies, her home health caregivers, her medication regimen and the time of day, the day of the week, the day of the month during which she presented in ER over the past year."

"You looking for some kind of pattern to the infections?"

"Precisely. Epidemiologic studies examine the same illness in many people. I had hoped to use a similar approach by examining many illnesses in the same person." The chief resident paused to assess Reuben's understanding. "But I have not been able to proceed because the hospital's medical record has been sealed due to pending litigation."

"Did you try the home health agency records?"

"Also sealed."

The nurse rocked on the heels of his loafers. "S'pose I could talk to a few people in my network, but Bohley was pretty clear about this case. 'Keep your bowels open and your mouth shut,' were his exact words." Reuben hesitated. "Nope, can't help you on this one, Doc. I'd say give it up. We tried; she died. You keep digging; you'll get dirty."

***

Jayson breezed into the pharmacy at 1:30 PM and waved a brown expandable file in the air. "Juicy reading material for your afternoon delight. The *True Secrets* of GEM Pharmacy with a few tidbits about Dr. Mark Lavelle in the margins." He slapped the file down on the counter and checked the computer screen for prescriptions waiting. "Looks like we're swamped. I'll dive in."

"Not so fast," Heli interrupted. "Humor me with a quick overview, and I'll read the details later this afternoon while I'm on hold with insurance claims."

Jayson grinned. "I've been on the web-trail for the past three days. Spent a few bucks too." He slid a stack of stapled receipts across the counter. "You owe me $179. Criminal background checks and people searches aren't freebies."

Heli put the receipts in her pocket and wondered how she'd explain this accounting entry to Clyde Erickson. Finnish curiosity was becoming expensive. "Give me the sixty-second elevator version."

"Too complicated for sound-bytes." Jayson took in a deep breath. "The FDA totally shut GEM Pharmacy down last Saturday. Seized their products, files, and business records too."

"But why?" Heli tapped her empty water bottle on the counter.

"Got to frontload with the Food and Drug Modernization Act of 1997 to really understand." Jayson shoved a thick stack of paper her way.

"What does the FDMA have to do with GEM?"

"In a nutshell, the Feds draw a line between 'compounding' which any pharmacy is licensed to do, and 'manufacturing' which requires FDA approval. Once a pharmacy begins interstate distribution of heavy-duty amounts of compounded drugs, the Feds think such a practice looks more like drug manufacturing and wholesaling than traditional retail pharmacy business. You know, Boss, if it looks like a duck, walks like a duck . . ."

"Move it along, Jayson." Heli nodded impatiently. "I've got a stack of rejected claims to argue."

"The Feds spin it like this: compounding pharmacies should be subjected to the same adulteration, misbranding provisions and new drug application processes that manufacturers are held to. Are you with me? Some kind of MOU, that's . . . . "

"A memorandum of understanding."

"Yup, a MOU with the Feds would have permitted GEM to sell up to 20% of their total compounded orders across state lines, but GEM's owners apparently blew off the MOU process.

Arrogance like that belongs in the bad-idea file. Turns out that close to 80% of GEM's compounded products were actually mailed out-of-state. I guess the Feds didn't like GEM's one finger salute so they closed them down."

Heli rubbed her temples. "So the recall of infusion products was simply a paper problem and not an issue of patient safety?"

"Could be bad product, but that's up to the Louisiana State Board of Pharmacy. I downloaded their state regs and brighted the section on sterile compounding." Jayson handed her the document.

She thumbed through the document, reading aloud a highlighted section. "'The pharmacist . . . is responsible for . . . proper preparation, labeling, storage, dispensing and distribution of sterile products.'" The word 'proper' had been circled.

"Keep reading," Jayson interrupted. "If GEM isn't following the letter of the law with a written quality assurance document, they're in a world of hurt. For now, the Board has temporarily suspended GEM's license and is cooperating with the Feds. There'll be a hearing sometime. At least that's the buzz from my new friends at the Lousiana Pharmaceutical Association."

"That's it?"

"That's it for the dull stuff. Now the story spices up."

One of Heli's eyebrows rose skeptically. "Mark Lavelle is somehow involved?" Lavelle, the one minefield in her relationship with Sandy.

"Lavelle: later. More on GEM." Jayson twisted the earring that pierced his brow. "Three physicians own the company under a privately held corporation. Dr. Alexander Grossman seems to be the mastermind of the outfit. Baton Rouge native from an old money family, graduated from some offshore medical school in the Caribbean, and practices oncology without ever passing his Boards."

"To desperate, unsuspecting patients," Heli interjected, "with good insurance."

Jayson gave his thumbs-up agreement. "Dr. J. Pierce Eddington, also a southerner, graduated from Jefferson Medical College in Philadelphia, opened a private practice along Florida's coast, moved around quite a bit, and worked as a medical director for a small pharmaceutical manufacturer before joining up with Grossman. His name pops up on the bad-boy list of the Florida Board of Medical Examiners."

"Just how bad was he?"

"For a copy of the disciplinary proceedings, we need a request in writing. The b'crats make it pretty difficult to get anything that

to the tundra of Fargo in 1997. He's squeaky clean. No disciplinary action in New Jersey, Pennsylvania or North Dakota by the states' Board of Medical Examiners. His name doesn't show up on the EPLS or the OIG sanction list." Jayson paused. "When I google him, he pops up hundreds of times, mostly with pharmaceutical firms where he's either speaking at some conference or part of ongoing Phase Four clinical research."

"In other words, a bottom feeder with Pharma," Heli said.

"Totally. The Averill rep says his expense account is drained on dining favors for Lavelle's 'exquisite palate.'"

"That's it, Jayson?"

"Not exactly." Jayson produced a single page from the back of the file and placed the sheet in Heli's hand. "Seems Dr. Lavelle keeps some bad company."

She studied the wedding photograph on the photocopied page from the Princeton Alumni News, dated October, 1991. A younger Mark Lavelle, preppy in pinstripes and a cutaway jacket with tails, stood with his demure bride who seemed lost in clouds of tulle, and surrounded by a bridal party in what must have been an elegant summer garden wedding. The caption under the photo read *Mark Lavelle (class of 85) marries Katherine Magers in Bryn Mawr, Pa.*

"Clearly not his current wife," Heli observed, "nor anything like the one that flutters around our aisles looking for spray tan. I wonder if Katherine Magers was too intellectually challenging for Lavelle's ego?"

"Put your eye to the fine print, Boss."

Squinting, Heli moved from left to right across the page, matching the names with the corresponding members of the bridal party. Bridesmaids: Bunny Landphere, Callie Bryant-Armstrong, Brooke Alexander. Groomsmen; Jonathan William Rafferty, J. Pierce Eddington, ...

"J. Pierce Eddington?" she gasped. "*The* Eddington of GEM Pharmacy?" Heli slapped the page down on the counter. "I knew it! I absolutely knew he had to be involved with GEM! Jayson, don't you see the importance of this?"

"Like cream on your latte, Boss. And there's more."

"More?" Heli's eyes opened wide. "I'm turning inside out over this whole Runyan situation, and you've been withholding . . ."

"Whoa!" There was an uncharacteristic pause in Jayson's chatter. "Something's definitely come over you in the past few days, Heli. Understand, we'd do anything to help you, even cross a line, so to speak. So Murlene and I sort of put a plan into action."

"What are you talking about?"

"Here goes." Jayson blew out a breath. "It's a nano-world. You've heard about 'six degrees of separation'—connect to anyone on the planet through a chain of five acquaintances?" Jayson rubbed his hands together. "In Murlene's case, six shrinks to three. She's still a node in the South. Big network; strong web." He contorted his hand into an imaginary phone. "Jabber, jabber. She bridged some lines, one-two-three . . . finally landed a payroll clerk who once worked in GEM's accounting department."

Heli sucked in a quick breath.

"The clerk, who was just pink-slipped by GEM, remembered sending monthly checks to one of the company's medical directors. A Dr. Mark Lavelle in *Fargo*, North Dakota. Said she'd never forget the mailing address. Absolutely loved that movie."

Forty

Venkata felt his beeper groan as he wrote orders at the nursing station on Five Main. Throughout Wednesday, he'd managed his hospital workload with customary efficiency hoping to flee the building by five to meet Heli. The page could mean a new patient work-up, the last thing he needed at three in the afternoon.

Only seventy days remained before the chief resident could sever the nagging electronic leash that tied him 24/7 to Swedish Hospital. With his residency completed in June, Venkata pledged to join other third-year residents on the hospital rooftop for the liberating ritual of pitching beepers down to the parking lot below. It would be worth every dime of the fifty dollars he'd be assessed for damages.

Pathology's number appeared on the screen. Venkata brightened. This might be the news he'd been waiting for all afternoon.

"Micro, Jenny speaking."

The chief resident recognized the saccharine voice and hoped the call was not more silly flirtation. Reuben Norbutas had once described Swedish Hospital as the hottest social club in Fargo. It was not an outrageous observation.

"Do you have final results on the third organism?" Venkata asked. Given all of his calls to Microbiology this week, it seemed no longer necessary to add the name of Christine Runyan to his question.

"Not yet, although I expect the fax machine will spit out something from the reference lab any time. I promise you'll be the first to know."

"Thank you." Venkata was about to hang up before Jenny oozed with new information.

"That syringe you brought us last night . . ."

"Yes?" Venkata had not forgotten about the questionable syringe he'd carried to the lab last evening, nor how difficult it was to convince Micro to culture the few drops that remained in its barrel. He simply thought it was too early to expect results.

"It's growing something."

Jenny's brevity could only mean that she too comprehended its significance. His mind raced in search of the next question, but this time, Jenny was a step ahead of him.

"Did a gram stain and plated it out." She paused as if she

were expecting a grateful acknowledgement. "I knew you'd be asking."

"Excellent!"

"Looks exactly like the blood sample from your patient. And exactly like the sample from the infusion bag. A carpet of mixed organisms: gram positive, gram negative, and something is growing on the anaerobic culture. Definitely weird."

The chief resident's heart was pounding. "I will come to the lab immediately and look at the culture myself." Regretting the implication that he might be second-guessing her findings, he added, "I must be certain. Dr. Lavelle will certainly ask whether I've viewed the slide personally."

"Totally fine with me."

Venkata vaulted up the back stairwell turning Jenny's news over and over in his mind. Although it was true that Dr. Lavelle would question him thoroughly, his thoughts were about Heli. According to her, the syringe had been found by the child in the Runyan home. With all his heart, he'd tried to believe the story unconditionally. Why else would Heli bring forth a suspicious syringe? But he'd required something more. Now he was certain beyond all doubt that she had been unfairly accused. That he so wanted to believe her, yet required definitive proof, was a matter to ponder at a later time. For now, the chief resident's attention redirected from a contaminated infusion bag to an incriminating syringe. The most recent lab finding raised many questions about the domestic environment. Had the source of Mrs. Runyan's infection been factitious? The question chilled him.

Anticipating the unpleasant mix of odors that might assault him, Venkata took a deep breath before entering the Microbiology lab. The bacteria did not disappoint him. Today's emanations in the warm, cramped room were sulphuric and grape-like. The chief resident felt slightly nauseous. Showering was a must before his evening with Heli.

"Over here, Dr. Venkata. I've got the microscope set up for you. Have a look while I check the fax machine." Jenny drew her long coppery hair into a ponytail and secured it with a neoprene band. "I hear it whirring. Could be the reference lab."

A rolling stool waited by the microscope. The chief resident sat down and adjusted the eyepiece as he had a thousand times before. He knew what he was about to view had consequences that went beyond the medical uncertainty of Christine Runyan's death. Tension built in his mind like a slow drum roll as he dialed the specimen into focus.

Dense bluish purple and red stained shapes filled the field. Venkata moved the slide around on the stage for a comprehensive look. After a few minutes, he retreated from the microscope and maintained a thoughtful silence. There is no doubt. The specimen on the slide matched the Runyan blood sample and the culture grown from the infusion bag.

Jenny returned with a faxed lab report. "Just what the doctor is looking for. Guess what? We were right all along. The reference lab confirmed the same totally weird bug we grew here at Swedish. I can't wait to shove these results in Dr. Dahl's face. Maybe then he'll have some confidence in us."

Venkata sprang from the stool. "Jenny, I must see the report."

When he read the single faxed sheet of paper, his face became flushed and his throat tightened.

"I told you it was weird. We've never seen the bug before in this lab." Jenny cupped her chin in her hands in the classic Garbo pose and leaned across the countertop. "What do you know about *Edwardsiella tarda?*"

Very little, an insecure voice sounded inside Venkata's head. Perhaps he had read about the organism in some bacteriology textbook during his medical school training, but not so much as a hint of recognition surfaced in his mind now. The chief resident grew agitated. How could he *not* know the answer? With his superior memory, Dr. Lavelle would certainly have recognized *E. tarda*. For the first time this week Venkata was relieved that his mentor was nowhere in sight to witness this personal humiliation.

The chief resident pivoted to leave. Nothing about the Runyan case had been typical, and this troubled his ordered mind. Every answer posed new questions. The identity of the third organism pointed him in a single direction: the hospital library.

***

Sandy's call with news of the lab report, however brief in the middle of Wednesday afternoon, had been like a mustard plaster to her bruised confidence, drawing out bad humors deep inside of her. Now he believes me, Heli sighed. *I will call for you at six as we planned*, he'd said minutes ago, *but now I must hurry off to the library.*

She closed her eyes and slid deeply into her office chair to indulge the sweet aftertaste of absolution. The path report seemed to have acquitted her of error, and with such pardon, her breathing relaxed and the anxieties of the day lifted. She might have been seduced into sleep right there despite the persistent telephone and a noisy printer spewing out prescription labels, but a grain of reality chafed at her peace. If she was not to blame for the contaminated infusion bag, then whom? The syringe was nothing more than a transmitting vector, like a bark beetle feeding in the crotch of elm branches, inconspicuously inoculating fungus into the trunk.

Heli sat upright in the chair with a sense of purpose. Time was tight, but she could hurry. Nothing about the visit would be easy. She grabbed a textbook from her shelf and raced out the back door, leaving Jayson to deal with a parade of new prescriptions during a spectacular 4 PM rush at Corner Drug.

*****

Venkata opted for the remote carrel in the library. Afternoon rounds had already begun, and he was sorely pressed for time to accomplish everything and still be punctual for Heli.

With impatient fingers, he logged on to the computer, and found his way to the homepage of WebMD, keying *"Edwardsiella tarda"* on the search line.

"We're sorry, your search for "Edwardsiella tarda" did not match any documents. WebMD suggests that you browse our medical library." The absence of hits puzzled the chief resident, but he followed the suggested link.

After reaching the WebMD medical library page, Venkata rekeyed the name of the bacteria next to the blinking cursor. He declined the free weight loss assessment offered him while he waited for the search engine's results.

"We're sorry, your search for "Edwardsiella tarda" did not match any documents."

The chief resident glanced at his watch: 4:20 PM. He keyed his way to the PubMed home page. If the National Library of Medicine which boasted sixteen million citations from biomedical articles back to the 1950s had never heard of *Edwardsiella tarda*, maybe he needn't feel so inadequate after all. He hit the "go" button forcefully. Nine seconds later, two hundred nineteen hits appeared on the screen. Venkata's appetite quickened. So much information; so little time. He quickly scrolled through the titles and printed out the entire search results. Twenty-nine pages spewed from the printer. The librarian shot him a cross look.

On his way to the hospital ward, Venkata recapped in his mind what he'd learned about the unusual organism in the past fifteen minutes. A gram negative enteric bacillus usually cultured from stool specimens associated with gastrointestinal illness. Majority of infections occur in immuno-compromised hosts. Wound infections—the most common manifestation. Bacterium is associated with freshwater ecosystems.

The chief resident reconsidered his evening as an urgent curiosity gripped him. Hundreds of articles begged for his attention. Could Heli possibly understand how driven he was to make sense of this new information? And he must remember to call Dr. Kampela now that he could feign some knowledge of the organism. Then he recalled the hospital's only infectious disease specialist was en route to Mexico City for the International Conference on Emerging Infectious Diseases.

One thing was certain: Dr. Lavelle must be given the news. When the chief resident called his mentor's office from a hallway phone, a cryptic voice answered.

"Doctor has someone with him at the moment. Call back in the morning."

With her brisk dismissal came the clarity Venkata needed. *E. tarda* must be addressed before dinner. The rest of the evening would not unfold exactly as he had planned. This time he would not seek Heli's agreement. Her protestations he would deal with later.

Forty-One

She rapped on the apartment door, estimating how much time had passed since first standing here, bearing the infusion pump, supplies and TPN bags for her patient, Christine Runyan. Six months, maybe seven? Around Thanksgiving, Heli recalled. Christine had been so optimistic, even joked about enjoying her holiday dinner from Corner Drug instead of roast turkey from her mother's oven in Muskee. Today, the pharmacist came bearing condolences and looking for answers.

The door opened and Heli expected to see Trevor. Instead a glassy-eyed older woman appeared in a dark print dress with a lace-edged handkerchief tucked under the cuff of one sleeve. Her face looked too bleary with heartache to be welcoming.

"I'm Ada Olander," she explained. "Christine's mother."

The mother-daughter resemblance was striking. The woman was Medicare-age with a slight dowager's hump.

"Grandma," a child's voice called from the distance. "Who's at the door?"

"If you're looking for Trevor," Mrs. Olander explained, "he's not here." She ignored the child's question. "I'm here with Anya. Trevor came home from the funeral and left right away. Seems he doesn't know what to do without anyone to care for, so he runs here, runs there, trying to stay busy." The woman began to sob in short staccato bursts. "Oh, my," she sighed, "this is all so difficult."

"*Grand* . . . ma, who's at the door?"

"I'm Heli Harri from Corner Drug, Mrs. Olander." The heavy shoulder bag slid down the length of her arm until she caught it with the other hand. "Actually, I came to see Anya."

"She's not come out of her room since the funeral. Won't have a thing to do with anybody. Not her daddy. Not even Brigid."

"Christine and Anya used to visit my drugstore at Main and Devine. I admired how your daughter coped with Crohn's."

"I thought those high-priced pills and the IVs were helping. Life seemed to be getting back to normal—at least that's what Trevor said." A pool of tears spilled down the mother's cheeks. "I suppose you never know when your time is up."

"Grandma! Grandma, *who's* at the door?" The insistent voice in the distance brought out a weary sigh from the older woman.

"But life goes on, doesn't it?" Ada Olander blew her nose. "You want to see Anya? Well, come in then. She's in the back bedroom. Follow me."

Heli found the child sitting on the floor with a bed pillow propped against her unmade bed. Sticky chocolate cupcake wrappers littered the carpet. A curled snapshot of Christine Runyan holding a baby rested against a dimly lit table lamp.

"Hi, Anya." Heli longed to draw back the heavy curtains to encourage whatever healing light the late afternoon sun could offer.

A phone rang somewhere in the apartment, and Mrs. Olander turned around in the doorway. "People have been so kind to call now," she paused, then scuttled out of the room.

"What's in your bag?"

Heli dropped down to the shag carpet near the child and reached into her shoulder bag. "My favorite book. I thought you might like it." She slid a worn medicinal textbook in Anya's direction. "It's about every plant on earth, and how we keep track of them."

Anya paged indifferently through the textbook before shoving it back to Heli. "It's a big people's book. I can't read big words yet."

"Oh, but you're a clever girl, and this book has amazing stories." Heli reopened the book and smoothed the fragile pages. "Have a look at this plant: *Angelica archangelica*."

Anya squinted and leaned over the book for a better look at the tall plant with balloon-like flowers.

"Long ago, people believed this was a magical plant brought down to earth by angels to cure a very bad disease spreading throughout Europe."

The child looked skeptical. "Do you believe in magic?"

"Hmm." Heli considered the question with a pang, remembering her own mother at whose knee she'd learned to appreciate the natural world. Stories from Norse mythology rose in her mind, like how the first woman had emerged from the bark of an ancient elm. She wondered what might be going through the mind of this child.

"I believe that some kind of magic causes plants to pop out of the ground to make us feel better. Do you know that people still come to my drugstore to buy angelica for their cough and sore throats?"

A faint smile emerged on the child's face. "Mommy said you

were smart."

"She trusted me, Anya. Your mother trusted me to make her medicine. That meant a lot to me."

Heli watched as the child closed the book and retreated into silence. Minutes passed. It was 5:20 PM.

Anya finally spoke. "I thought maybe you brought something for my doctor bag." She reached under the bed skirt and dragged out the plastic toy.

The sight of the same Fischer Price toy sent needle-like shivers through Heli. Her theory was a long shot, perhaps no more than an invention of her suspicious mind. Nevertheless, any evidence that could link a dirty syringe to a carrier source might explain how Christine Runyan's TPN infusion had been contaminated. Truth mattered. That had been her initial motivation for the visit, not condolences. And yet, in the little girl's bedroom, Heli wondered when in her mind curiosity had changed places with compassion.

"Well, what do you need?" Having come this far, Heli dared to proceed. "May I have a look inside?"

"No!" The child clutched the bag to her chest and turned away.

"Why not, Anya? Is there something in there you don't want me to see?"

The child's hesitancy was enough of an answer.

"The pretty glass bottle," Heli asked. "Did it belong to your mother?

Anya dropped her head and looked down.

"Whose, then?"

The little girl avoided eye contact.

"Your grandma? Brigid?"

A shrug of her shoulders was the only answer the child offered.

"Had you ever seen the bottle before?'

Another shrug.

"Tell me, Anya, where did you find it? It's important that I know."

Slowly, the child relaxed the grip she had on the toy bag. Her small finger unhooked the latch. She removed a bright orange magnifying otoscope, a prescription vial filled with M & Ms and the make-believe thermometer with its oversized red bulb. Finally she pulled out the round glass bottle with Oriental painting.

Both pair of eyes focused on the object.

"It was in the waste basket by Mommy's bed. I took it." The

child's voice crackled with fear. "Was that bad? Is that why Mommy died?"

Heli closed her eyes and tried to comprehend what death meant to a five year old. Of course Anya was frightened. Had she tried to make sense of the tension and the sadness in her home by filling in the gaps with her own imagined explanations and unrealistic guilt? Had Trevor neglected to respond to her childlike curiosity? *Where did mommy go? Who will take care of me? Who will die next?*

Instinctively, Heli slid across the shag carpet and draped an arm around Anya's shoulder. A moment passed before the child nudged closer. The two rocked back and forth quietly as Heli stroked her braided hair. Words were unnecessary, and silence, more consoling than clever euphemisms of death. Compassion, not laughter, was the best medicine.

In a voice no louder than a murmur, Anya asked. "If I get a fever, will I die?"

"No," Heli spoke gently into her ear. "A fever is the way our body tells us something is wrong."

"Then why did Mommy die? She had a fever."

"Your mommy was very sick, Anya. Nothing you did or didn't do could have made her well." Heli drew a deep breath. "The doctors are trying to understand why she died and I'd like to help them. Would you like to help?"

The little girl looked up pensively.

Heli held the painted snuff jar in the palm of her hand. She removed the red glass stopper and peered inside. A small amount of liquid remained in the chamber. "I think this bottle might be important. Will you trust me to keep it for a few days? It will be safe; I promise."

Anya's head nodded a slow yes. The rocking continued in silence for another five minutes until Heli gently released her hold to check the time and to shove the snuff jar inside her shoulder bag.

"Your mommy would be very proud of you, Anya." Heli gave her a tender squeeze. "You'll be an awesome doctor some day."

Forty-Two

Heli ran a finger along the plunging V neckline of her nearly new sweater. Black cashmere was the perfect choice for a dinner date with Sandy. At least that's what the handwritten note had promised, tucked with the baby-soft sweater inside a shopping bag from The Second Time Around. Signed, sealed and delivered to her apartment door sometime during their afternoon coffee break. Murlene and Delores Rude must be in matchmaking heaven.

It was 6:12 PM and Sandy was late. A tidal wave of panic hit her. She walked to the window that opened to Devine to check for the dark blue Audi. No sign of it. She paced. Picked up scattered magazines—*US Pharmacist*, an Orvis fly-fishing catalog—and placed them on a footstool. Put out fresh bath towels and a new tube of herbal toothpaste. Unscrewed the cap and smelled the spearmint: *mentha viridis*. Removed coffee beans from her freezer and wiped the grime from her stainless percolator. Swallowed two horse-sized calcium tablets. Turned on NPR. Turned it off.

Only when she heard the gentle knocking on her apartment door did the emotional dust finally settle.

***

Venkata steered the Audi north toward Swedish Hospital. At 6:25 PM, a fierce sun colored the horizon golden, sending out rays like threads of saffron dissolving in the western sky. He wondered how to tell Heli, buckled in the passenger seat next to him, about the change in plans for their evening. The opening lines he'd rehearsed on his way to Corner Drug now seemed contrived. To break the silence, he punched a button on the radio dial and mellow jazz filled the gap in conversation.

"Sandy," she finally asked when the Audi passed the hospital without slowing, "where are we going?"

"Yes," he answered too quickly, "I was about to explain." He swerved the car into the turning lane and veered right onto a winding street that hugged the Red River. "A brief stop to make before dinner. I hope you will understand."

The chief resident was so intent on verifying the address he'd scribbled on the back of a prescription blank that he barely noticed the rolling view of treeless boulevards that fronted new homes of increasing dimension.

"We are almost there, Heli."

He checked the slip of paper once again and turned right into Blenheim Heights. The sprawling development of mammoth homes with sloping lawns and acquired charm rested on a broad knoll overlooking Fargo. Sapling trees in the front yards looked like match sticks to Venkata, and seemed oddly incongruent with the overbuilt dwellings. Did Americans really need this much space to live? For a brief moment, he missed the crowded streets of his home in India, frenzied with screaming sirens, noisy food vendors and millions of Mumbaikars fighting for a rare bit of space to call their own.

Heli turned sideways in the leather seat. "Where exactly are we going, Sandy? And don't ask me to believe you're making a house call on Pill Hill."

The doubtful tone of her voice matched Venkata's reservations about the next hour. He braked the Audi as he approached an imposing brick colonial with a brass house number "37" catching the glint of the western sun. It was 6:40 PM. He parked the car in front of the house, leaving the engine running. Twenty minutes early. He turned to face Heli. She was unusually quiet. Words could not explain what he was about to ignite.

Was there another way to make all the lines of the Runyan case intersect at a point of common understanding, if not to bring those he trusted most together? If so, a determined Venkata could not see one. He'd felt a duty to take command of the situation this evening, even if doing so defied the propriety that had thus far guided his life.

"We are at the home of Dr. Lavelle. He is expecting me." Venkata summoned a deep breath. "I need your help. You must set aside your mistrust of him long enough to join me in presenting what we have learned today about Mrs. Runyan's death."

After a long, strained silence, she answered. "You. Me. Dr. Lavelle. This cannot possibly go well. I've learned something about Mark Lavelle this afternoon."

"Not now, Heli." Venkata reached for her hand. "Whatever moral lapse might be in Dr. Lavelle's past, I need him to make sense of this case." Her hands, so soft and creamy white, stirred him. "And I think you need him, too." He felt the muscles of her hand tense.

"No. What I need is to hit the pause button. Time to think. Time to process what all of this means," she looked away from him, "and I thought that might happen tonight by talking over dinner with you." Her hand withdrew from his. "Frankly, I'm disappointed."

Venkata dropped his head and took in another controlled breath. "We both need to understand why Christine Runyan died. You were wrongly accused, Heli. Surely you must want the truth as much as I do. You have said as much."

"My truth has come from other sources."

"Indeed. You found the incriminating syringe in the home. Extremely helpful, yes. Not only has it absolved you and the hospital pharmacy, it has raised new questions in my mind about the home environment. Dr. Lavelle must be told."

"There's a reason he's off the case."

"Please do not object. Regardless of the allegations against him, Dr. Lavelle will not permit a misdiagnosis or Mrs. Runyan's death to be simply labeled 'unexplained.' When it comes to patients, his intellectual integrity always prevails. He must be told about the syringe and the similarity of the pathology reports. A physician has a right to know what killed his patient."

"On the other hand, maybe Dr. Lavelle knows more than he's revealing to you."

"How could he? He has been barred from hospital premises. Administration will not give him the benefit of the doubt despite that the investigation into his alleged misconduct has not yet been completed." The chief resident paused. "A physician of his status deserves better. I ask that you trust him as I do."

Heli's deeply set lapis eyes narrowed, and Venkata readily understood that her resolve matched his.

"I have more to add, Sandy, but talking to Dr. Lavelle seems terribly important to you." She reached down for her shoulder bag. "Let's get going." Her right hand searched blindly for the door handle. The faint smile under a drape of flaxen hair sent a promising message. "Just know that it's you, not Lavelle, in whom I place my confidence.

***

A slim woman with an energetic voice answered the door.

"Mrs. Lavelle, I am Sandeep Venkata. This is my friend, Heli Harri. Dr. Lavelle is expecting us. I should say he is expecting me."

"How perfectly wonderful! Mark didn't tell me, or I might have dressed for company." Claudette Lavelle removed the sweatband from her forehead and wrapped it around her wrist.

255

"Do come in."

Venkata nodded politely and guided Heli into a handsome foyer where he caught their reflected image in a mirrored rosewood étagère. He liked what he saw. For a moment, his mind projected forward, beyond the immediate tension to the evening that was to follow, alone with Heli without call obligations or humming pagers.

"Have a seat in the living room, and I'll drag Mark out of the theatre." Claudette shrugged her small shoulders extravagantly. "Another cowboy flick."

The chief resident chose a winged armchair opposite Heli who sat on a divan of shiny damask. He studied the crimson patterned Bokhara rug on the hardwood floor. The heavy knotting of Pakistani origin must be of museum quality. There were knots in his stomach, too. He noticed that Heli's eyes darted around the room, taking in the reproduced splendor of the Far East.

"Dr. Venkata," a patrician voice called from the hallway, "early as usual. You must set your clock back at least twenty minutes to be in step with the rest of America." He wore a Polo tracksuit and looked inebriated. Claudette scampered into the room behind him.

The chief resident sprang from his chair as though it were spring-loaded. "Dr. Lavelle, very good to see you, Sir."

"I didn't realize you were bringing along an acolyte."

"You know Heli, of course."

"Our paths have crossed."

Heli nodded. "Good evening."

Venkata felt it must be his turn to speak but the stiff recitation he'd prepared regarding progress on the Runyan case felt entirely wrong. For someone who revered the orderly progression of thoughts, he was grasping for a way to proceed.

"Sandy, was there something you wished to discuss?" Lavelle approached the chief resident. "Perhaps we should leave the girls to chat here in the living room while you and I excuse ourselves for some privacy in my office."

"With your permission, Sir," Venkata answered, "I'd like Heli involved in our conversation. Her observations have been very keen. She has uncovered something I believe to be important in the Runyan case."

Lavelle swirled amber liquid in the glass tumbler he carried. "Very well." He set his glass on a side table. "Claudette, this is a hospital matter that should take no more than ten minutes. Leave us to our devices, would you?"

"Not until I've offered our guests something to drink." She spun around in Heli's direction. "Mark makes a *perfect* Manhattan. The secret is cherry juice," she whispered. "Or maybe you'd rather have sherry." She put a finger to her lip. "I could uncork a perfectly wonderful Syrah from our Napa collection."

"Ice water will be fine, thank you."

"For me, as well." Venkata noticed how every phrase that left Mrs. Lavelle's lips seemed to end in an exclamation point. "I hope we are not interrupting your evening."

"Not at all." Claudette snuggled under her husband's arm. "We rarely have company. Right, darling?" She looked up at her husband as the idea must have turned in her head. "We could have a party! Why don't I order take-out from the Jade?"

Lavelle cleared his throat with the same authority Venkata had heard him use to silence a roomful of jostling residents. "I'm sure that Dr. Venkata and Ms. Harri have more indulgent plans for the evening than eating out of cardboard boxes with us. Besides, the Jade doesn't deliver."

"Why, Mark, of course they do."

"No, Claudette, they do *not*."

"Do too!"

Venkata looked down at his Rockports which he noticed needed buffing. He heard Heli cough.

"Don't you remember?" Claudette persisted. "Last week we ordered in. I had Kung Pao chicken; you ordered Szechuan. Of course the Jade delivers, darling. You simply have to leave an outrageous tip!"

Mark Lavelle rubbed the back of his neck with obvious irritation. "Now that you have established that I am wrong about everything, and niggardly as well, will you please allow us some privacy?"

"Of course, darling. Get on with your dreary business." She turned to leave. "I'll be back with something to cheer you up."

Her departure created uncomfortable static that charged the room.

"So, Miss Harri," Mark Lavelle spoke from the leathery embrace of his wing chair, "you have made another 'keen observation,' have you? Should I assume this one is as baseless as the claim of harassment you've filed against me?"

Venkata leaned forward in the chair.

"Tell me," Lavelle asked, "is this something more than a professional rift? What exactly have I done that causes you to want to ruin me?"

table but only melted ice water remained. He leaned forward in the chair. "*E. tarda*? I've never seen a case in my entire career." With hand to chin, he stared beyond his guests as if deep in thought. "It's been reported, however. *Journal of Clinical Infection*, I recall. Are you certain the lab has correctly ID'd the bug?"

"Yes, yes." Venkata felt redeemed. "The identification has been confirmed by Mayo's reference laboratory."

"So you're telling me this isn't just another hospital mistake?"

"Hardly, Sir." The chief resident's breathing quickened. "I cannot explain the finding. Surely the *Pseudomonas* infection killed Mrs. Runyan but the *E. tarda* remains like a marker demanding our attention. Where did the bacteria come from?"

Although Lavelle remained in the wing chair, he seemed to have vacated the living room and taken up residence in a private sanctum off limits to his guests. Nothing was so disconcerting as his silence. When he finally spoke, Venkata was at full attention.

"Only recently has *E. tarda* been recognized in humans," Lavelle mused. "Another waterborne pathogen. How did Christine Runyan pick up a bug like that?"

Neither the chief resident nor Heli interrupted his train of thought.

"The infection has been associated with people who eat raw fish. Or those who handle reptiles or tend aquariums with exotic fish."

Venkata nodded in agreement. That much he'd already learned by scanning the articles near the top of his search. He marveled once again at his mentor's remarkable command of the medical literature.

"Brackish water too. People with open wounds who have been exposed to polluted water. I recall a journal article about a crab fisherman in Thailand who lacerated his forearm on a submerged brick and became infected." Lavelle drummed his fingers on the tabletop. "There was a report out of Kentucky of neonatal sepsis caused by *E. tarda*. Mother swam in contaminated water during pregnancy and had vaginal colonization of the bug at the time of delivery."

Heli was the first to interrupt his monologue. "Hardly sounds like Christine Runyan. She couldn't eat solid food or raw fish. Not a snake handler as far as I know, and I doubt she was doing much swimming during a North Dakota winter."

"Another of your keen observations?" Lavelle shot back. "What else do you have for me, Sandy? Anything that incriminates Swedish?"

The chief resident exchanged glances with Heli. "To the contrary, Sir, we have something that directs our attention away from the hospital to the home environment."

Lavelle scowled. "Get to the point."

"Heli has recovered a syringe from the Runyan home that may turn out to be very important." Venkata motioned to Heli to supply the details.

"Anya Runyan, the five-year old daughter, found a BD syringe with its needle still attached in the waste basket by her mother's bed the morning Christine was admitted," Heli explained. "The little girl retrieved it and hid it in her room."

"We have cultured the residue remaining in the syringe." Venkata joined in. "Just this afternoon I have learned that the preliminary growth matches both the blood sample and the infusion bag." He tried to read Lavelle's reaction; he could not be certain what the senior physician was thinking. "I am now very suspicious that the source of Mrs. Runyan's infection might be factitious."

Lavelle jumped to his feet. "How very convenient!" His face, suddenly crimson, matched the color of the carpet where he now stood. "Sandy, are you so besotted with this woman that you can't see through her devious ploy?"

Venkata flinched. "Sir?"

"First, she seduces you and then inveigles her way into the Runyan case where a pill pusher has no business to be." Lavelle's voice grew harsh. "She manufactures some evidence to exonerate her mistake, and tricks you into believing a preposterous story about a dirty syringe she just *happens* to find in the Runyan apartment. Not only are you beguiled by this improbable explanation, you permit your attention to be deflected from a history of egregious errors at Swedish Hospital that might very well explain a bizarre lab report to which you so desperately cling. A shrewd physician would see through this in a New York minute." Lavelle paced around the room shaking his head in disgust. "Next thing you know, she'll have you believing that Christine Runyan was murdered. How could you be so completely gullible, Sandy?"

Venkata heard a clock on the mantle chime seven times. He was perspiring heavily now. No one spoke while Lavelle's question hung in the air. As the final gong reverberated throughout the great room, Heli bent down to reach into her shoulder bag.

For a Kleenex or a weapon, Venkata wondered? A

spontaneous doubt gripped him. Was it possible that his trust had been so abused? His parents had warned him about cunning American women. The hateful words of Reuben Norbutas echoed in his mind. *You gotta know who your enemies are at Swedish. . . . This is no time to be naïve . . . . Take the blinders off, Doc.* Venkata felt nauseated for the second time today. Surely a house this big must have at least one bathroom nearby

"Does *this* look like it came from Swedish Hospital?"

From her shoulder bag, Heli produced a small glass vessel painted with an colorful Asian motif. Confused, Venkata leaned forward for a better look as Heli placed the snuff jar on the elmwood tea table. "Anya found this next to the syringe in the same waste basket by her mother's bed. According to the child, the snuff jar didn't belong to her mother, nor had she ever seen it in the apartment. She loaned it to me because she wants to know why her mother died."

"How far is this going? Taking advantage of a child's trust for your own self-interest? Outrageous! This proves nothing more than a little bit of knowledge in an untrained mind can be a dangerous interference."

Heli ignored the slur. "There's a small amount of liquid remaining in the chamber. If it's cultured and also found to be contaminated with the same organism, we might assume the snuff jar was used as a carrier for tainted water."

The kernel of doubt evaporated as Venkata suddenly grasped the significance of her theory. "Are you suggesting that someone might have actually injected a contaminated substance into Mrs. Runyan's central line?"

"Or directly into the TPN bag."

Their eyes met, and Venkata could not deny the plausibility of her hypothesis.

"By tracking down the owner of the snuff jar, we can start asking the obvious questions. Who? When? Why?" Heli looked directly at Lavelle. "You see, I *do* believe Christine Runyan was murdered. I just don't know where to point the finger."

"Here I come!" Claudette entered the living room, balancing a teak tray with two iced tea glasses, a crystal hock brimming with wine and a cut glass tumbler of bourbon. "Clear some space for me on the tea table, darling. You all must be perfectly parched by now."

Instinctively, Venkata rose to assist her. He was the first to see the shock in Mrs. Lavelle's eyes.

"Darling, you've found it! She slid the tray across the tea

table, spilling bourbon over the side of the glass and reached for the snuff jar. "I've been searching *everywhere* for this little glass bottle. . . trinket thing. . .whatever-you-call-it, that I brought home from China. I absolutely knew I'd left it on the étagère by the front door, and then it was gone! Vanished! Mark, how terribly clever of you." She pressed the recovered bottle to her bosom in animated Academy Award flair before pulling her husband into a tight embrace. "You're full of surprises, aren't you, darling?"

Stunned, Lavelle wrestled free, averted the startled looks of his guests and bolted out of the room without a word, leaving no uncertainty that the party at 37 Blenheim Heights was over.

Forty-Three

Without a doubt, it was the best hand he'd been dealt all night. Ace, king, queen, jack and two little diamonds. Strong hearts, the ace of spades. Twenty four points in all.

Byron Bohley twisted in his chair to conceal a rumbling burp. Maynard and the dietary staff had outdone themselves tonight with pasta carbonara for his Wednesday night bridge group. Cream and bacon floating over fettuccine may not be healthy but it was damn good advertising for Swedish. Made believers out of these fools who groused about the hospital's bad food.

"Pass," muttered Doug Reimer, a circumspect claims examiner who worked for the state insurance department.

When his bridge partner, Natalie Bjornson, pre-empted with three clubs, Bohley felt a pulsing confidence. Hell, she must have two face cards in clubs, and his nine gave him entrance to the board.

"Such terrible cards all night." Lilly Melhus tipped her head back and forth like a storybook doll. "I'll have to pass."

Bohley pounced in the game with a bid of seven no-trump. He'd played cards long enough to know this was his night.

"My goodness, Byron," Natalie twitched, "I hope you know what you're doing."

Bohley bristled. In his mind, he was Omar Sharif in a French casino with a grand slam in the offing.

A pair of wifely hands needled the back of his neck. "Phone call for you, Byron."

"Take a message, Bets." Bohley glanced at his watch: 8:45 PM. Lilly led a heart and he suppressed a smile. Either she was unknowingly finessing her partner or she was leading from a king. It didn't matter. He was going to get the two heart tricks he needed. Doug played low and Bohley took the trick with the ten. He was going to have tricks to burn. All he needed was that break in hearts.

Betsy leaned over his left shoulder and whispered into his good ear. "You have to take this call."

Bohley threw the ace of hearts in the center of the table and watched Lilly flinch as she sacrificed her king. He knew how much she hated to lose even one hand of bridge.

Forcing a whisper, he turned his head wifeward, fanning out the cards before her. "And walk away from a hand like this?" The king of diamonds glared at him. "Who is it?" The possibility made him cringe. "Don't tell me it's Hellenbolt." Why would the Chair of the

Board be rousing him at home on a Wednesday night unless all hell had broken loose?

"Worse than Hellenbolt." Betsy seemed agitated. "It's Mark Lavelle. He insists on talking to you."

"Tell him I'll call him back later."

"I already did. He said he'd hold."

The image of Mark Lavelle waiting irritably on the line gave his executive ego a satisfying rush. "Fine; his choice." Bohley threw out the ace of spades and swept the trick home. Diamonds, next. He was unstoppable.

Natalie shrieked. "Byron, I do believe you're going to pull off a grand slam."

The card slapping continued until thirteen tricks stacked neatly in front of him. Bohley glowed with pride. "Add 1500 points to our tally," he instructed Doug, the scorekeeper. Remembering the call waiting, the CEO somehow knew the hand would be his last win of the evening. Fleeting happiness morphed into tension.

He walked into the farm-style kitchen where a dietary staffer in a green Swedish Hospital uniform was scrubbing hardened ribbons of pasta from a serving bowl. Bohley grabbed a bread stick, hoisted himself onto a counter stool and picked up the phone. He motioned to the second worker, up to her elbows in dishwater, to fill his wine glass.

"Bohley here."

"Very important that I see you tonight."

Same damn uppity tone that needed no introduction.

"It'll have to wait until tomorrow, Doctor." What kind of spike does Lavelle have up his ass tonight? "I've got a houseful of company and . . ."

"Meet me at my office in the Medical Arts Building on 4th and McCormick. ASAP."

"Don't bait me, Lavelle. If this is about your Exvantium trouble, there's no way I'm going to get in the middle of the Exec . . ."

"Ten minutes. No attorneys. No press. No Chair of the Board. Just you and me."

Lavelle, the Drama Doctor. The CEO shook his head in bewilderment. Being bothered on bridge night was over the top, yet the eerie urgency signaled something more than a doctor's typical demand for attention. Bohley felt the hair on the back of his neck stiffen. He scratched but the anxiety didn't lessen.

A basic principle of politics scrolled through his mind. Ignore anyone who is annoying you unless he actually represents a threat and is capable of scoring points against you. The onions from Maynard's salad were doing battle inside his stomach.

Bohley reached for a toothpick and mined food between his teeth. Could Lavelle have something on him this time? The S.O.B. hadn't been on the wards since banned from Swedish on Monday noon. At least that's what his informers had reported. Maybe Thorson wasn't keeping tabs on Lavelle like a chief of staff was supposed to. The CEO could never really count on one doc squealing on another unless, of course, it involved a dollar bill. When it came to money, they fought like pigs at a trough.

Had Lavelle's hotshot lawyer from Philadelphia discovered some legal technicality in the Exvantium issue? The toothpick splintered in his mouth. He grabbed another with a fresh point. Or was Lavelle, so shamed by his woodshed treatment in the Boardroom on Monday, now seeking pardon? Prepared to swallow the bitter medicine and to stop undermining the hospital administration? The CEO snorted.

Or could it be something new on the Runyan case? Bohley felt the onions crawl up his throat. Maybe Lavelle's call implied he was in a bargaining mood. Agreeable to muzzle Trevor Runyan and his talk of a lawsuit in exchange for reinstatement on the medical staff. No dice! What that asshole didn't realize was that he, the CEO of Swedish Hospital, held a trump card or two to foil a malpractice suit if one materialized. He wouldn't hesitate one minute to throw Alayne Ludemann under a bus if he had to. Generally, he didn't give a damn who slept with whom as long as everyone kept quiet, and the bedroom antics didn't come back to haunt him. Did Ludemann really think she could get her hands on Runyan's malpractice award? In that case, he'd have to hang out her dirty laundry in a new breeze. What a family. One brother, scamming snowbirds out of their inheritance. Another, a lawyer hiding a shady past. With bloodlines like that, he should have suspected the woman was up to no good. She'll cave. Lavelle will be castrated by the Executive committee and the Runyan woman's death will blow over like last weekend's storm.

Bohley motioned for more wine as Steuben's happy bark announced his entry into the kitchen. Background noise on the other end of the line informed him that Lavelle was still holding.

"Come here, Steuben, you rascal."

The golden lab playfully rolled over on his back near his master's feet.

"Need a belly-rub, Steuben?" Bohley slid off the stool and crouched by the golden lab, still holding the phone. "Got some mighty fine bones for you, courtesy of Swedish Hospital," he said as he stroked the soft fur of the lab's underbelly. Getting the upper hand with a dog was so easy.

What maddened him most was Lavelle's reference to Hellenbolt.

Dropping the Board Chair's name alerted every button of executive suspicion. If Lavelle really did have something damaging, Bohley wanted to hear it first-hand, not filtered through the sugar beet brain of Wendell Hellenbolt. That was a risk he couldn't take. As long as Hellenbolt was happy, Bohley kept his job, his paycheck, his year-end bonus and enough pasta carbonara to carry him to retirement when his last shot at happiness might actually begin.

Bohley swirled a gulp of wine around in his mouth. With any luck, the crowd of cackling bridge players would be out of the house by ten. Scandinavian stragglers took their time with good-byes. Tonight, they'd be Betsy's problem.

"I'll be there by 10:30," he finally answered. The CEO imagined how the rest of the night might unfold. He still had work to do before the Finance committee meeting in the morning.

"Now!" Lavelle demanded.

"And what am I supposed to tell my company?"

"Call it an administrative Code Blue." Lavelle snapped, and slammed the phone down before Bohley had a chance to reply.

***

Dinner turned out to be deli-prepared pita sandwiches and mile-high coconut cream pie. In Heli's apartment. Her suggestion.

Although several hours had passed since they'd left Dr. Lavelle's home, Venkata remained as stunned as his pancreas now was with the bolus of sugar hitting his blood stream. So intent was he to comprehend the startling turn of events that hunger and the possibility of romance had vanished. There was so much to talk about, to understand. Once again, Heli had been right.

"I have never seen him like this," Venkata admitted as he pushed the paper plate across the small kitchen table. "Where did he go? He is not answering his cell phone or his page. I am very worried."

"Another disappearing act by Dr. Lavelle. No explanation. No apology." Heli leaned back in her chair and closed her eyes. "Just when I thought I was beginning to see through this maze, there's another twist." She paused. "Are you upset with me, Sandy?'

Her question was a balm to the simmering embarrassment he'd felt since leaving Dr. Lavelle's home. "Of course not." He leaned forward and reached for her hand. "You were remarkably composed. To the contrary, I am proud of you for standing up to Dr. Lavelle's contemptible remarks. The evening was entirely my mistake." Venkata shook his head. "From the first day of training, residents are taught to have full command of the facts before an encounter with the attending physician. Tonight I was unprepared in every way." He stopped short of telling her that the ultimate disgrace was being upstaged, not by an inexperienced medical student, but by a non-physician female who happened to be his girlfriend.

Heli fidgeted in her chair. "At the risk of salting the wound, Dr. Lavelle may not be who you think he is. I tried to explain . . ."

"And I did not listen. Another mistake. From the very beginning, I have sensed gaping holes in Mrs. Runyan's case. I am in charge, and yet others seem to know so much more than I do."

"About the snuff jar," Heli said, "I had no idea there was any association with Lavelle. Did you catch the look on his face when Claudette first recognized it?"

"Oh, yes." Venkata rubbed his forehead. "Genuinely shocked. And equally taken aback by the identification of *E. tarda*." He glanced at his watch: 9:03 PM. "When did we deliver the snuff jar to the lab? I have lost all track of time."

"Shortly after eight."

The chief resident calculated the hours in his mind. His rapport with Jenny had paid off. She'd agreed to culture the specimen immediately. "By four or five tomorrow morning, the lab should be in a position to report any growth." Restless, he gathered up the wrappings of their dinner and stuffed the debris back into the take-out bag. "Do you have any idea how the snuff jar landed in the Runyan home?"

"I've told you everything I know. Anya Runyan was the source of my information and I believe her." Heli paused. "Do you want me to speculate?"

"Indeed," Venkata smiled. "I am starting to believe this case will be more readily solved with my ears than my eyes."

"When I first saw the glass bottle, it triggered a memory of something my clerk said a few months ago, around Valentine's Day, when Trevor Runyan came in to buy perfume. After he left the store, Murlene grumbled that Trevor ought to be paying his pharmacy bill instead of splurging as he did. Never mind, I said; Christine Runyan needs cheering up more than I need money." She hesitated. "Murlene may have been on to something when she asked, 'Would the little lady be cheered up if she knew her tomcat husband bought *two* bottles of *Jean Nate?*'"

"You believe that Trevor Runyan was having an affair?"

"That's the thought I'd entertained earlier. Perfume, an imported collectible: nothing like a string of excessive gifts to make a wife suspicious. Maybe Christine had knowledge of Trevor's antics and, out of anger, tossed a gift with any romantic association into the waste basket." Heli shrugged. "But now that we've learned the snuff jar belonged to Claudette Lavelle, my theory goes down the drain." She sipped sparkling water from a tumbler. "Unless it somehow came into Trevor's possession. But how? Did Dr. Lavelle ever make house calls at the Runyans?"

"Very unlikely." The chief resident recalled a spirited argument in the Doctors' lounge last month when Dr. Lavelle had insisted that inadequate reimbursement from the insurance companies had caused house calls to become nothing more than a relic of medical history.

Venkata crumpled the take-out bag. "There has to be an explanation." He walked over to a waste receptacle and opened the lid, wishing it could be as easy to discard what he'd learned about Dr. Lavelle this week. No matter how much he tried to curb his growing suspicion, the revelation about Dr. Lavelle's lapse in judgment could not be ignored. If the facts bore Heli out (which the chief resident was sure they would), Dr. Lavelle should never have involved himself with GEM Pharmacy, nor referred Trevor there for infusion services. This was an explicit violation of professional ethics. And, certainly Dr. Lavelle, who first believed Mrs. Runyan was admitted with a GEM infusion running through her central line, must have known about the underlying quality problems at the mail-order pharmacy. Such information would have been pertinent to the diagnosis and treatment of his patient's unexplained infection. It was obvious that Dr. Lavelle had flagrantly subordinated his patient's care for self-interest. What else had he failed to disclose?

That he'd been so deceived by someone whom he'd trusted completely was a wound to Venkata's spirit. It defied not only what the chief resident believed about Dr. Lavelle personally, but jarred his confidence in the sanctity of the profession. What American word described the amalgam of confusion, bitterness and disappointment he now felt? In time, the abscess created by Dr. Lavelle's deceit might wall over, but the dull pain would be with him for a very long time.

Heli was sitting quietly with her head down, her butter-blonde hair falling softly over the black yarn of her sweater. She was unusually quiet this evening, as lost in thought as he. Leaning against the doorway, he watched her open a squeaky closet door. She disappeared from his sight momentarily, then emerged with long loops of string draped over one arm and a wooden contraption in the other. Venkata had no idea what it was. She placed the apparatus on her lap without a word of explanation. Thin green line pooled on the floor beside her. Some kind of knitting? Weaving? He pulled a chair closer for a better view, feeling a pang of irritation that he'd lost her attention. She seemed miles away.

"What are you doing, Heli?"

"Thinking," she muttered, "while I load my fly reel. My father passed this line winder—his own creation—on to me." She ran her finger over the initials carved in the maple platform: EJH. "Erkki John Harri," she explained in a soft, almost faltering voice. "He taught me the old Finish proverb, *God did not invent hurry. Why should you?*" She snapped the empty reel into the winder's seat. "So I load my fly reel whenever life moves too fast. It forces me to slow down and to focus on the line—the connection between me and the fish."

She spliced one end of the flyline to the reel's yellow backing string with a blood knot. "A practical angling habit, too. If you leave nylon line stored on the reel over the winter, it develops a kind of memory that will cause the line to crimp." Her head tilted slightly as she looked up at him. "When I cast into the Gracey this spring, I want the presentation to be perfect."

"I see." It was her look of quiet determination that Venkata found so mesmerizing. Lavelle's indignant words echoed in his mind: *are you so besotted with this woman. . . .?* The chief resident had to admit his attending had been right about that. All too quickly, spring would ease into summer. What would happen to their relationship in the passing?

She cranked the reel's handle slowly and the monofilament line moved evenly across the spool.

Like Gandhi, Venkata mused, quietly spinning before his *charka.* An act of conscious examination, a symbol of self-reliance. The sound of the rhythmic winding calmed him, encouraging him to ask the kind of question he might have otherwise suppressed.

"Heli, do you believe that . . . Dr. Lavelle might have intentionally caused Mrs. Runyan's death?"

She didn't take her eyes off the reel. "Well, he acts like an angry adolescent. Among the most arrogant physicians I have ever known. Power-obsessed and money-hungry—which is hardly unique in this industry." She sighed. "It's common knowledge that he shills for the pharmaceutical companies. He's devious and, if I'm right about the kickback laws, he could be convicted of a felony." She stopped winding and looked squarely at Venkata, "But he's not a murderer."

"How can you be sure?"

She rotated the wheel again and flyline snaked across the floor. "Even I believe that Dr. Lavelle has some redeeming qualities." Heli stopped the wheel to untangle a knot. "His vices don't lead to murder and he has nothing to gain by killing his patients, especially Christine Runyan. Think about it. His clinical reputation is at stake. And, if money motivates him—say, revenue from office visits and hospital stays—she was worth much more to him alive than dead." She adjusted the arm to correct the tension. "Frankly, the last thing Lavelle needed was Christine Runyan's death to focus attention on GEM's problems."

"Then who? By your theory, who might have benefited from her death?"

"That's the obvious question." Heli shifted in the chair. "According to the insurance investigator who visited me yesterday, statistics typically point to the spouse. The motivation: money."

"Would a husband really do such a thing for money?"

"I'm no authority on husbands." Heli's cheeks flushed. "In Trevor's case, I'm not sure it makes sense. He'd apparently come into some money *before* Christine died. At least enough to pay his overdue bill at Corner Drug. Money didn't seem to be his immediate problem."

"Perhaps there were other motivations beyond money. If he were having an affair. . ." Venkata stopped in mid-sentence, appalled that his suspicions had deteriorated to the level of Reuben Norbutas. "I have never been entirely sure that he was the attentive husband Mrs. Runyan deserved."

"Who benefits from her death?" Heli stopped turning the wheel and the pooled line came to a rest. "Maybe Christine believed everyone would be better off without her. By participating in her own death, she might have coordinated the benefits for everyone."

"Assisted suicide?" Venkata pinched the bridge of his nose. His mind deferred instantly to Hippocrates: *do no harm.* Could Dr. Lavelle have possibly wandered so far from the sacred oath?

"I don't know, Sandy. I need to think."

The whirring sound of the rotating wheel resumed. Venkata found relief in its rhythm. The humble Gandhi had once declared that communion with God was possible through the spinning wheel. He reached down to open his backpack and retrieved the stack of articles on *E. tarda.* "You have inspired me. Perhaps the answer lies in the scientific literature."

"That would be too easy. Real life doesn't come with footnotes."

They worked in companionable silence for the next hour. The slow hum of her revolving spool mingled with the turn of his pages. Solitude drew them into a soothing intimacy. The slow drone of traffic below her apartment window went unnoticed.

Now and again, he would stand up to stretch, or to massage a knot out of her trapezius muscles as she bent over the flyline apparatus.

She brought him wild strawberry leaf tea with a sprig of lemon balm.

"*Melissa officinalis*," she whispered, "alleviates dyspepsia after rich desserts."

JAMA, Journal of Infection, Clinical Microbiology, Clinical Infectious Diseases. Venkata peered over the pages of the CID article and interrupted the stillness with a question.

"Heli, do you recall if the Runyans had any pets in the home? Birds? Tropical fish? Anything cold-blooded? "

"Not to my knowledge. Anya admitted a fear of bats, but as for pets, no, I don't recall seeing any." Heli repositioned the loops of line remaining on the floor. "Donna Wadeson would know about pets. She's very observant."

"An excellent idea. Too late to call her tonight, but I will do so first thing in the morning."

Venkata walked around the perimeter of her apartment several times. He called Dr. Lavelle's cell phone again. No answer. He paused to study the large paneled cabinet that occupied most of the space along the south wall without realizing that Heli was watching him.

"It's a Murphy bed," she explained. With one pull of the spring-loaded mechanism, the bed frame unfolded onto the floor. "A great place to watch the 10 PM news," she added, checking her watch, "which begins in exactly three minutes." With one hand she reached for the remote, the other propping up pillows at the head of the double-bed.

"Breaking news tonight from Walmart," the somber news anchor announced as Venkata joined her on the mattress.

"Not another new store announcement," Heli groaned, increasing the volume.

"Fargo police are investigating the torching of a white 1991 Dodge Caravan that occurred earlier this evening in the south lot of Walmart. A spokesman for the police said the vehicle was totally destroyed."

The pulsating cherry tops of two police cars emerged on the screen as a dramatic backdrop for Officer Tim LaDuke who responded to a reporter. "The incident occurred within range of surveillance cameras. We believe the tape will reveal a suspect, or suspects, who set the van on fire and then ran away." LaDuke wore a wry smile. "This is not shaping up to be the perfect crime."

The news anchor shuffled papers and smiled. "Turning to the weather, the forecast for Thursday. . ."

Venkata noticed that Heli's eyes were still locked on the screen.

"That van. . . ." she said.

Venkata muted the volume. "What about the van, Heli?" Never again would he deny her the opportunity to speak when something was on her mind.

"It was dark this morning when I jogged in Riverside Park." She stared at the silent television which now projected a radar weather map with patchy clouds over Fargo. "I first thought. . . that. . . the vehicle might have been the police but no. . ."

"And?" He had come to recognize how her jaw jutted out when she was searching.

"Who torches a vehicle in broad daylight unless . . . and what does this have to do with me?" Heli reached for the phone.

"The snuff jar," Venkata asked uneasily, "where is it?"

"Downstairs in the pharmacy, locked inside a steel safe," she said with the phone cradled to her ear. "The entire building could explode in flames and the snuff jar would be safe." She bit her lip as she reached for the phone.

"Put me through to Officer LaDuke, please."

Listening to the one-sided conversation put Venkata's senses on higher alert. Fear seemed to harden the features of Heli's face. What remained of the evening took a different direction in his mind as desire joined hands with duty. He would not leave Heli alone tonight. Tomorrow he would notify Public Health about the identification of *E. tarda*. The journal articles had convinced him that higher authorities, possibly even the CDC, must be brought in to investigate the string of suspicious findings.

"So," she said quietly after the phone call ended, sighing as one who'd been collecting air all day and only now had time to exhale.

The bed frame creaked as he leaned over to dim the lamp.

"So," he echoed, pulling her into his arms. "A day can only hold so much trouble." In time, he would explain the power of Sita's promise.

Gradually, Heli softened in his embrace. Against his chest, he felt her breathing relax and her heartbeat slow. The last sound he heard before falling asleep was the spring rain beating against the window.

Forty-Four

When Mark Lavelle entered his office at 9:15 PM on Wednesday, the overhead lights were already on, sending a blue chill over the empty reception area. He looked around but saw no one.

"Who's there?" a voice called from the rear of the office.

Fear had so dulled the logical working of his mind that he'd forgotten Phyllis occasionally stayed late in the evening to catch up on paperwork. With a sigh of relief, Lavelle shook the rain water from his umbrella and hung it on a rack along with his soaking Burberry raincoat. He followed the droning sound of the photocopier to the back office where his receptionist was inundated with medical charts and reams of paper.

"I hardly expected to see you this time of night," he said, trusting that his controlled voice obscured an inner anxiety.

"Oh? I often tie up loose ends in the evening when there are no interruptions."

Under normal conditions, he might have launched into a diatribe on the sorry state of the medical profession today. Subordinated by insurance companies and managed care organizations. Second-guessed by nameless corporate henchmen armed with rule books and sequestered in Dilbert-like cubicles. Existing only to demean a physician's authority, reduce his income and erode his status. Tonight, all he could summon was silent acquiescence.

Phyllis stopped the groaning machine. "The phones don't usually ring after closing although tonight is an exception. Dr. Venkata has been looking for you. Asks that you call him."

"No doubt he has." Lavelle turned on his cellular device. "Finish up your work, Phyllis; then please leave. I'm holding an impromptu meeting here and we'll need privacy."

"A meeting? Will you be needing something from me before I leave, Doctor? Too late in the evening for coffee, I suppose. Perrier, perhaps? How many will there be?"

Lavelle left the work room in the middle of Phyllis's string of nosy questions. Time was running out, and he could not afford to be distracted by her myopic issues when less than two hours ago, his own simmering problems had turned into a boiling crisis. One by one, he believed he could transcend an individual issue like the GEM fiasco or the Averill Pharmaceutical debacle, but the steady shots fired at him tonight by Heli Harri came from the barrel of a more potent gun. Despite her self-righteousness about the Stark kickback laws, he worried less about a Justice Department inquiry (the Feds certainly had bigger fish to fry) than the Oriental jar she'd produced from her bag. Damned if he'd ever seen the snuff jar before tonight. The echo of Claudette's exuberance sent a shiver up his spine.

Christine Runyan, murdered? I just don't know where to point the finger, the pharmacist had said. Lavelle glanced at his Tag Heuer. By now, he assumed the meticulous Sandeep Venkata had already taken Claudette's recovered tchotchke to the lab for culturing. If *E. tarda* grew on this culture, and matched Christine Runyan's blood sample, the linkage would certainly arouse enough suspicion to merit further investigation. With grudging reluctance, he had to admit that Heli Harri might be onto something. An atypical waterborne pathogen collected from a polluted source, stored in a glass bottle, drawn up in a syringe, injected into a TPN bag, and infused into the blood stream of an immuno-compromised patient was a plausible theory for murder. This may not be a random death, nor the result of human error at Swedish Hospital as he'd once hypothesized.

Nothing is random. Nothing. Scientists had determined that even a dripping water faucet followed an explicit pattern. Same with the flow of blood through fractal vessels, the irregular beating of the human heart. Chaos theory proposed that some hidden, intricate order underlay every random act, even the bizarre North Dakota weather patterns.

Had Christine Runyan's death been so coldly premeditated and ingeniously executed as to set him up—Mark Raymond Lavelle, the physician everyone loathed? By whom, and for what purpose, he could not fathom. Another chill rippled up his spine. That the third sample had come from a glass container known to be from his home would be impossible to deny. In front of two witnesses, Claudette's identification was an indictment he could never refute. The headlines of the *Frontier Press* would read, *Physician Charged in Death of Patient,* and the unraveling of an esteemed career in medicine would unceremoniously begin.

Lavelle shook his head in disbelief. No, this would not happen. On the blue-blooded honor of Judge Francis Hopkinson, he vowed not to go down without a fight. The best defense is a good offense. Lavelle repeated the mantra as he opened the door to his office. Tonight, in the march to defend his reputation, he intended to convert Byron Bohley from adversary to ally.

The proof of his innocence would begin with the letter. Until this evening, Lavelle had regarded the insurance letter bearing his forged signature with mild curiosity, but of little importance since it had been sent to an obscure out-of-state insurance company. Now the physician

"As you wish, Doctor."

Lavelle went back to his office to collect his thoughts while he waited for Bohley's arrival. Rain pounded against the window pane. Might the weather actually foil his plan for survival? He disciplined his attention to matters that were under his control, like how to spin the facts of Christine Runyan's case to the hospital administrator. On a prescription pad, he bulleted a three-point strategy: 1) divert and obfuscate, 2) pander to CEO vanity and 3) blame someone, anyone.

Sitting behind his desk, Lavelle pushed himself up from the arms of his chair to fully expand his chest. He exhaled, dropping back down into the seat. Three more times, he rose and fell in the chair. The physical act quieted him. Strength, not cowering, must guide the meeting.

"Raining cats and dogs out there!"

The blustery voice of Byron Bohley traveled down the hallway and brought Lavelle back to the present. He straightened up in the chair and resumed his mien of confidence as Phyllis led the CEO into his office. She placed the recovered briefcase by the side of his desk, and tiptoed out of the room, closing the door behind her.

Neither spoke. No spontaneous exchange of pleasantries or talk of the abominable weather. No thanks-for-coming-out-on-such-a-miserable-night. No fussing with coffee, documents, files. The initial minutes had the familiarity of a high stakes stare-down.

Lavelle broke the silence. "My patient, Christine Runyan, died in your hospital."

"For this you drag me out on such a night?" The CEO uttered a shrill laugh. "I know all about this case. I've reviewed the medical record. Know the names of everyone involved. Know as much as you do on this one, Lavelle."

"She should not have died." The physician drew his lips back, intoning every word with tense vowels and stabbing consonants. "Her death may be explained as a result of poorly functioning systems under your control at Swedish, or . . . ."

"Dammit, Mark! I'm not going to let you bring me down, or Swedish Hospital for that matter, over some death that you physicians can't explain. If this thing turns into a lawsuit that you've somehow coached the husband to file, I'm warning you . . . ."

"Forget a lawsuit," Lavelle counseled, "you may have bigger problems than an avaricious husband craving economic revenge."

"What do you mean?"

"Your problems may involve a serious public health crisis." Lavelle leaned forward. "Worse yet, Christine Runyan may have been a victim of foul play within the hospital you manage."

"Jesus, that's a helluva accusation."

"Since you've banned me from the hospital premises, my chief resident, Dr. Sandeep Venkata, has studiously followed the Runyan case. Tonight he came to my home with startling information. Three different cultures have grown a rather obscure bacterium, *Edwardsiella tarda.*"

"Yeah, Dahl told me about the odd bug this afternoon."

"Did Dr. Dahl also explain to you that the pathogen is typically isolated from organically polluted water?"

"We didn't exactly talk. He left a voice mail."

"In that case, permit me to rouse your interest in *E. tarda.*" Lavelle pushed his chair away from the desk. In his mind, he debated the best way to dilute the scientific literature to a level the CEO might understand. "In layman's terms, we refer to *E. tarda* as a water bug which means it lives, even thrives in a variety of environments, from fetid ponds to hospital fluids. Endotoxins capable of producing fatal sepsis have been detected in unopened vials of parenteral medications. This is especially dangerous in immuno-compromised patients like Christine Runyan."

"If you're still trying to blame the hospital pharmacy, you can forget it. We're clean. The infection people tested pharmacy stock solutions and found nothing. Clean as a whistle."

"Errgmm." Lavelle cleared his throat in a way that commanded attention so much better than words. "Byron, have you every heard of Legionnaire's disease?"

"Sure. State convention of American Legion vets in a Pennsylvania hotel, some twenty, thirty years ago. According to Dr. Kampela, this isn't Legionnaire's."

"Yvonne is correct; this isn't *Legionella pneumophila.* By the way, where is Dr. Kampela?"

"Away. Somewhere in Mexico, I guess."

"Your *only* infectious disease specialist is *away* when the hospital might be facing a crisis of historic importance?" Lavelle shook his head incredulously. "I trained in Philadelphia where Legionnaire's was first named. Bellevue-Stratford Hotel, 1976. Thirty-four deaths, 221 sickened. Do you know where they found the bacteria lurking?"

"I'm an administrator, not a scientist. I make rules and track dollars, not disease."

"Which is why you need to pay attention to Legionnaire's," Lavelle countered. "The bug was traced to the water supply system at the Bellevue-Stratford. I presume you have some authority over the water systems at the hospital?"

"Of course I do! According to Dahl, the Runyan case is the first and only time we've seen this bug in the hospital. If the water systems were contaminated, we'd be seeing more of it."

"True, because your surveillance testing has been limited. Christine Runyan easily succumbed to the infection because she was severely ill. Her death should be a wake-up call for you, Byron. It may be only a matter of time before others die." Lavelle observed that his visitor shifted uneasily in his chair. A good sign; the *divert-and-obfuscate* strategy was working. "Legionnaire's was detected in Madrid in 1996 and in the Netherlands in 1999. Most recently in 2000, the Melbourne Aquarium was the source of an outbreak of 101 cases with four deaths." The physician cocked his head. "I presume it isn't good administrative process to wait until a patient dies before some sort of surveillance is activated."

"We're fully compliant with every regulation out there." Bohley reached in his back pocket for a crumpled handkerchief. "What are you suggesting?"

"Since my patient has succumbed to an unusual waterborne infection, I want every water source in the hospital tested for *E. tarda* along with other waterborne pathogens. The water supply system, autoclave, laundry, water fountains, whirlpools, showerheads and sprinklers. Every aerosolizing device, the drain of every shower and bathtub throughout the hospital."

The CEO mopped his brow.

"Where is the HVAC located?" Lavelle inquired. "And who has access to it?"

Bohley squirmed. "On the roof." He wadded up his handkerchief and shoved it into the back pocket of his trousers. "Card entry access is limited, subject to my approval."

"The air conditioning unit has to be checked," Lavelle warned. "The cooling tower, condensers, valves, lines, vents. Everything associated with water."

"Sounds to me like you're trying to stir up a problem." Bohley's face was blotchy. "Next thing you know, we'll have Public Health in here and the word will get around that we're testing for some biohazard like anthrax. Then watch *Sixty Minutes* show up." The CEO shuddered. "Nope. The Board will go berserk, and I'll be driving the nitroglycerin truck over rocky roads for the rest of my career. All for nothing." Bohley glared across the desk. "You're jerking my chain, Lavelle. This is just another one of your stunts."

"Is that your answer to the Joint Commission when the reviewers deem this infection to have been a sentinel event requiring immediate investigation and response? Is that your answer to OSHA when they ask if you, as CEO, have upheld your duty to assure an environment free of hazards for patients and employees? Is that your answer if the Board asks whether you have followed sound industry practices with respect to a properly maintained water supply system?" Lavelle wove his fingers together. "I imagine a CEO can lose his job over this kind of negligence."

"For god's sake, I'll listen to you about bugs, but don't tell me how to run my hospital!"

Lavelle ignored him and refined his approach. *Pander to CEO vanity.* "I have no special expertise in running a complex hospital system like Swedish, Byron, but I do see an opportunity here for your leadership."

"What are you talking about?" Bohley leaned forward in his chair.

"Only this. A CEO should be out in front of this parade, not lagging behind." Lavelle leaned forward, narrowing the space between them. "Lead boldly, Byron. Seize the spotlight by going beyond what is merely required, to what is lofty and exceptional. Extend the testing beyond the water supply system and the pharmacy's stock solution to the broader inventory of fluids that exist within every department and in the storage cabinets of every patient floor throughout the hospital. From dietary to the morgue, neonatology to the ER. *E. tarda* had to come from somewhere. Can we be certain the hospital is not to blame until we've tested every possible source?"

"Something about this doesn't make sense." Bohley scratched the back of his neck.

"As an added safety measure, the disinfectant supply, the IV tubing, respirators, filters, blood pressure cuffs, stethoscopes and rectal thermometers should be tested," Lavelle urged, hearing in his head the sophistic protestations of his colleagues. "Even the mouthwash. Surely your Infection Control people would agree."

"Overkill," Bohley growled, "Got to be overkill. Besides, that Runyan woman came into the hospital infected, didn't she? That's what I was told."

"True," Lavelle nodded. "Someone had to be the first to die. Do you need another corpse before you act? Think about it, Byron. What have you got to lose? If the surveillance testing comes up positive, your prudent action will make you a hero. You'll be credited with saving lives and safeguarding the hospital's reputation for demonstrating an uncommon level of patient safety. Remember the Tylenol poisoning in the eighties? Being proactive pays."

"A lot of time and money wasted if testing doesn't turn up anything," the CEO argued.

"With a negative finding, you'll be hailed as an exemplary

executive with stringent operational control when most hospitals are making headlines for their inexcusable medical errors."

Bohley scratched his chin. "I see your point."

"However," Lavelle cautioned, "a negative finding does not mean the hospital is off the hook."

"Say what?"

"It merely brings us to the next stage of discovery. Like a differential diagnosis, we must eliminate one problem at a time."

"Good god, what next?"

Lavelle drew a deep breath. *Blame someone-anyone* time. "In the absence of any inpatient surveillance findings, I must remind you that Christine Runyan was attended in her home by employees of Swedish Home Health. As you correctly pointed out, she came to the ER with an infection. We have to consider that there may have been foul play by a hospital employee in Christine Runyan's home."

"Foul play?" Bohley choked. "You mean she was murdered? Don't be glib, Lavelle. Show me your cards."

"A syringe. . ."

"I know about the syringe. I told you, Lavelle, I've done my homework."

"It is not in your best interest to interrupt me," Lavelle said impassively. "This is too important, and may I add that our interests to persevere in this matter are very much aligned."

The CEO sneered. "It's a cold day in hell when you and I are on the same side of an issue. Go ahead and try to explain."

"Tonight I've been presented with some startling and potentially incriminating information. In addition to the syringe that was found in the Runyan home, a snuff jar. . ."

"A what? Snuff jar? What are you talking about?" Bohley's short fuse sparked once again.

"It's a small glass-stoppered bottle that looks like a paperweight except a narrow chamber has been bored down its center, ostensibly for carrying snuff in ancient China. Today, used for perfume, or, I suppose," Lavelle hesitated, "holy water, for the religiously inclined."

"What in hell does this have to do with her death?"

"The snuff jar was found along with the syringe in a waste basket next to Christine Runyan's bed." Lavelle paused to let the full import of the news permeate Bohley's brain. "It could turn out to be another link in the chain of contamination." Lavelle uncurled one finger at a time as he articulated every link, "snuff jar, syringe, infusion bag, blood sample."

"Straight up, what are you saying?"

"That you may have within your employed ranks, a middle-aged mercy killer wearing orthopedic shoes and carrying a home health nursing bag bearing the Swedish Hospital logo."

"A home health employee?" The CEO gasped.

"Moreover," Lavelle continued, "she's attempting to set me up for the murder of Christine Runyan."

"Unbelievable! This whole damn night has been unbelievable! Everything spouting from your mouth is craziness. Other people in the home could have done this. What about that money-hungry husband? Convenient for him if his wife was out of the picture." The CEO wiggled out of his chair and walked away from the desk, muttering words that Lavelle couldn't hear. When he reached the office door, Bohley turned around, his face wrinkled up like a question mark. "Do you even *know* Donna Wadeson?"

"I know the type," Lavelle reflected. "Angels of mercy. People like her regularly slip through nursing boards and the porous hiring practices of many hospitals. They usually come with a particular axe to grind against the established medical system. So bereft are they being around desperately ill patients whose lives are unnecessarily prolonged that they take matters into their own hands. Quite often, they feel an unqualified hostility toward physicians which might explain why she has attempted to entrap me."

"Donna Wadeson, a murderer? I just can't get there." Bohley continued pacing. "Why? How?"

"While I can't explain precisely how she executed her plan, it has to have involved breaking and entering my home. This nurse must have somehow gained access to my residence in Blenheim Heights and pilfered a snuff bottle, *the* snuff bottle in question, that my wife brought back from a trip to Hong Kong last December. Only this evening did I learn of the theft. I assumed you would want to know immediately, Byron."

"Donna Wadeson. I'll be damned." Bohley reclaimed his seat and slumped in the chair. "I've got a lot rumbling around in my head right now. I've got to think this over." He scratched the back of his neck. "You know, Lavelle, sometimes you can get a little paranoid. Happens to all of us when we're stressed. What makes you so sure somebody's out to get you?" After a long pause, the CEO laid out a theory that Lavelle had been expecting. "How do I know that I'm not the one getting set up here? Maybe you killed Christine Runyan."

Lavelle had waited patiently for this moment. He reached into his brief case for the file and opened it slowly. Minutes passed before he shoved the photocopied letter across the desk to the CEO.

"This letter dated Feb 28, 2002, asserts my opinion that Christine Runyan will likely be dead in two years." Lavelle's eyes drilled into the CEO's frozen stare. "This was certainly not my prognosis for her at the time, nor is the signature at the bottom of the letter my own. It is a forgery."

"Come on, Doctor. You sign your name a hundred times a day. The gal out in the front office probably typed it up and signed it to spare you the effort. Secretaries do that all the time. I had to get after Gloria last week for scratching my name on someone's expense form. Nasty habit those girls have."

"Look at the stationery." Lavelle watched the CEO lean over the desk and look through spectacles he'd removed from his shirt pocket. "We have no access to Swedish Hospital stationery in this office. Whoever did this had knowledge of Christine Runyan's medical condition, access to the medical record, a supply of hospital stationery within reach, and a minimal aptitude for forgery."

"Let me see that letter again." Bohley craned his neck. "Who'd the letter go to?"

"Some insurance company, " Lavelle replied indifferently. "The Eastern Shore Life Settlement Company. I've never heard of it until I saw the letterhead."

Bohley sat up erect as if the news had startled him. In Lavelle's mind, the CEO's sobering reaction to the name of the insurance company was the single surprise of their meeting. Up to this point, the physician was confident he'd commanded the meeting, tilting windmills as necessary to bring Bohley along with the breeze.

The CEO scratched his chin like an academic. "Are you sure it's a forgery?"

"Absolutely, without a doubt, a forgery," Lavelle said calmly. "And my attorney who will arrive from Philadelphia on Friday will certainly take great interest in this additional abuse I've endured being associated with this hospital. I can't cite the criminal penalties for forgery, but I know the news will reverberate throughout the medical staff and add a new dimension to your troubles."

The room became eerily silent. Even the rain beyond the office window had quieted as if to observe the momentous next steps that were being considered on both sides of the desk.

"I have to think about this overnight. Make a few calls."

Lavelle pulled back the letter and locked it in a drawer. "Don't wait too long. If I haven't heard from you by noon tomorrow, this information goes public." Lavelle stood up. "It should be of great interest to Wendell Hellenbolt and the rest of your Board that you needed time to think, to stall, to cover your administrative ass, while a dangerous pathogen or a serial murderer is running loose in your hospital."

Bohley kicked the walnut desk with the toe of his loafer. "I knew any meeting with you had to end in some kind of deal. What does it take this time, Doctor?"

Lavelle's face broke into a pretentious Ivy League smile. "Wave your administrative wand, Byron, and make the charges against me go away. Drop the Exvantium investigation, reinstate my privileges and settle the harassment claim." He leaned over the desk with his palms flat on its surface. "In turn, I'll work *with* you, not *against* you, to determine what happened to Christine Runyan. If she was indeed murdered, we'll find her assassin. The investigation will make you a hero. You have my word that Swedish Hospital will rise above the circumstances of this death at the expense of one psychopathological employee motivated by low esteem or morbid compassion."

"Why should I believe you? Never once have I known you to look out for anyone except Dr. Mark Lavelle and his pocketbook."

Lavelle walked around the desk to his office door, opening it to signal the meeting was over. Bohley rose in response. The photocopier's whine and the bite of the electronic stapler across the hall meant Phyllis was still immersed in her labors.

"Noon," Lavelle repeated solemnly. Church bells pealed in his mind. "Noon, Thursday."

Thursday, April 6, 2002

Forty-Five

"Go back to sleep, Heli," Venkata whispered as he bent down in the darkness to kiss her forehead. "No running along the river this morning. I will call later."

She rolled over in the Murphy bed, breathing in the delight of coffee brewing in the background. "Nice," she muttered, then dropped back into a hypnotic sleep.

An hour passed before she reawakened Thursday morning to a pink-gold sun squeezing through the window slats. She squinted until her eyes adjusted to the bright eastern light. Gazed around the room for a lingering trace of Sandy. Touched the indentation that remained in his pillow and sniffed the bedcovers still bearing the salty scent of their lovemaking. A Lancet article on *E. tarda* had fallen to the floor. More evidence that their night together had not been merely a dream. The slanting sunlight seemed to cast a halo over the small room. What was the word the Swedes used? *Allrum.* Her *allrum*—the room where happiness reigned.

The woody aroma of brewed coffee drew her from the bed to the kitchen. *Coffea robusta,* strong and hot. She reached for a chair and sat by the table where the loaded fly- reel remained, coiled and ready for action. Was she? A sneaky breeze crept into the room like a special envoy reminding her that despite the tender night with Venkata, the rest of her world remained steeped in turmoil. She wrapped her fingers around the mug to ward off the chill. Christine Runyan should not have died. Heli closed her eyes, then opened them and saw dust motes fluttering in the stream of light across the *allrum.*

***

After Thursday's Finance committee meeting concluded at 8:15AM, Byron Bohley left the conference room without pandering to Board members. Perhaps he should have. For the third consecutive quarter of the hospital's fiscal year, the margin continued to erode, fueling the rumor mill that the CEO's cost-cutting initiatives had been simply another round of BBs from the same old air gun.

He stormed down the corridor, past the coffee drinkers in the secretarial pool and proceeded directly into his office, slamming the door behind him. He dropped into his leather chair under the weight of the hospital's bleak future. With the dim revenue forecast and the potential public relations disaster that Lavelle had warned him about last night, the future that Bohley had secured for himself suddenly felt tenuous. Damn that Lavelle—getting the upper hand again. Dragging me out in a thunderstorm, lecturing me across his desk, wearing bad news like a tart with smeared lipstick. Damn him! Damn every physician that ever walked these halls!

He punched the four digit number for Gloria's line. "I need you in here, now."

When she arrived a moment later, Bohley shuffled papers on his desk without looking up. Alayne Ludemann's personnel file seemed to be missing, but he'd be damned if he'd ask for help finding it.

"Cancel my meetings for the day."

Gloria tapped the tip of her pen on the CEO's daily calendar. "Seven appointments in total," she counted. "You really want me to cancel the Children's Hospital spring luncheon? You're to recognize the donors in the Angel category."

Bohley considered the consequences of stiffing those well-heeled contributors necessary for building his legacy at Swedish Hospital. One can never have too many Angels gracing the donor wall in the main lobby. If posterity took any interest in him, it would be about the buildings he'd erected over the course of his career—each, a giant piggy-bank waiting for more and more Medicare money to drop in. Nothing between Minneapolis and Seattle could rival the Jenny Lind Women's Pavilion. Within a year, the seven-story cancer tower would open and the expansion of the Children's Hospital, completed. He couldn't remember a time since he'd started this job that a building crane hadn't been part of the hospital landscape. Bricks and mortar would be his legacy, and it required money.

"Keep the luncheon. I've called a special meeting of the Infection Control committee at ten. The rest of the day I'll be tied up with the Public Health people." He sighed with exasperation. "Find Dr. Kampela and get her home from Mexico or wherever in hell she is."

"What's going on, Mr. Bohley?"

"Time to smoke the bugs out of the rug." His secretary was not on the need-to-know list. "If the media show up, I'm unavailable."

"The media doesn't give up that easily."

"I'll make a statement when I'm damn good and ready." He resumed the paper shuffle. "By the way, get me the personnel file on Donna Wadeson, ASAP. And I need to talk to what's-his-name, the goofy ER nurse with the baggy pants that came to see me earlier in the week."

"Reuben Norbutas."

"Dark hair, about thirty years old, prances around like a circus pony?"

Gloria nodded, furiously scribbling on a notepad.

"And I want to see Alayne Ludemann in my office before the Infection Control meeting. Get Doug Reimers from the State Insurance department on the line."

When she left the room, Bohley recalled that he'd locked the Ludemann file in his credenza. The drawer slid open and he found the folder exactly where he'd placed it after reading Information Service's private query of Alayne Ludemann's phone log and office email. Plenty there to arouse his attention, if not his anger. For now, he had to overlook cheap shots about his administrative abilities and endless hospital gossip in order to find the specific piece of information that had piqued his interest.

The CEO's phone rang, and Bohley was relieved to hear his card-playing buddy on the line.

"Suppose you want to talk about your grand slam last night," Doug chuckled. "What a hand! You played it well, Byron, but even I could be a shark with cards like that."

"Sour grapes," Bohley shot back. "Tell me everything you know about viatical insurance."

"Viaticals? It's the latest scam in the insurance market. You can't be thinking about using your IRA for a viatical investment, Byron. People are losing fortunes to this kind of ploy, and we can't do a thing about it without some regulatory authority until it's too late."

"Tell me how it works." Why the hell hadn't Gloria brought him his coffee? He reached into his drawer for a Tums.

"Very complicated." Doug took a deep breath. "That's really the point. Make something confusing enough and it's difficult to trace the mischief."

Another blinding-flash-of-the-obvious from a government employee. Bohley glanced at the *Federal Register* on his desk describing thirty-two pages of Medicare regs on the new medical privacy rules.

"A viatical settlement company," Doug explained, "purchases a life insurance policy, usually from a terminally ill patient, prior to his or her death. The sick person gets some money up front, usually 50 or 60% of the face value of the policy, to pay bills that have mounted up during the illness. You know: high priced medicine, doctors' charges, hospital bills."

"So," Bohley interrupted, "once again, hospitals are villains because we expect to get paid for what we do. You think we don't incur real costs treating these patients?" Inwardly, he could appreciate the intent of viaticals, and he hoped, by God, that his hospital would get paid first, at least before the doctors, if the scheme ever caught on in this area.

"Just reporting the facts, Byron." A well-drawn pause followed before Doug continued. "Lots of people end up with tremendous medical bills that exceed what their health insurance will pay. The life insurance money may be their only source of funds, and they need the money before death, not after." Doug cleared his throat. "Sometimes the viatical settlement companies actually hire, for a sizeable commission, social workers, nurses, even AIDS volunteers to recruit patients with bad diseases."

"Jesus, that's creepy." Bohley shuddered.

"When the insured dies, the full cash value of the policy goes to the viatical company. Of course, by then the viatical company has sold this newly acquired insurance policy to an investor who is promised a so-called 'low-risk, high return investment,' because presumably, the insured will die quickly. The investor continues to pay the premiums and waits for the insured to die. If it's a quick death, the investor makes lots of money. It the person lingers, or actually lives past the predicted life expectancy, the investor can lose money."

"So, when a policy has been sold to a viatical company, there's an incentive for a quick death?"

"Exactly. The quicker, the better for the investor. Fewer premiums paid by the new owner of the policy means a faster ROI."

"Are you telling me there's somebody out there in a business suit who can determine when someone's time is up?"

"Actually, they wear white coats instead of pinstripes. The key to an investor's rate of return on viaticals depends almost entirely on the accurate projection of life expectancy. Actuaries do a pretty fair job of estimating the life expectancy of healthy people, but this prediction changes when an individual patient is diagnosed with a terminal illness. See what I mean?"

"Sure. Actuarial tables mean diddley then."

"The new prediction is a judgment call by a physician. Viatical companies may find a crooked doctor who will say the patient has a short time to live, and in that case, the policy looks very attractive to an investor. One doctor I read about is spending 150 years in prison for exactly this kind of insurance fraud. Be glad you don't have any bums like that at Swedish. The dirty ones seem to be living on yachts off the Florida coast."

Bohley shifted his weight from one cheek to the other, wishing he'd asked for a copy of the damn letter that Lavelle had shoved at him last night.

"Everyone gets a piece of the action when it comes to viaticals," Doug continued. The scumbags who buy and sell the death benefit pocket big commissions with literally no regulation. Crooked attorneys, estate planners and insurance agents who advise the senior market to invest in this kind of so-called guaranteed high-yield return, profit too."

"And I thought the pharmaceutical companies were obscene." Bohley reached across his desk for the printout of an email from Alayne Lundemann, dated March 10, 2002, to ludebr@aol.com. In lower case letters, the message read: *letter sent. event to follow. stay low. send egg money to Mn.*

"Doug, you ever heard of the Eastern Shore Life Settlement Company?"

"Hmmm." Doug seemed temporarily lost in thought. "Sounds familiar, but once I turned fifty, my memory isn't what it used to be. Wish there were a drug for that." Another pause. "There've been quite a few headlines in our industry newsletter about the legal problems of some viatical companies. That's probably where I've heard of Eastern Shore."

"Think, Doug. It's important." He reached for another Tums.

"As your dutiful public servant, I'll run a search." With the tapping sounds of a keyboard as background, Doug rambled on, as though his memory had been recharged. "The latest twist in viatical fraud is syndication—selling a policy to multiple investors, hundreds of them, in drug havens like Thailand and the Philippines. Throws off the investigators when it gets that complex. It didn't help matters when our government made viatical settlements income tax-free for the chronically ill. Without regulation by either Insurance departments or the IRS, viaticals have become a clever place to launder cash within the drug trade."

Bohley slid down into his chair. The armpits of his white shirt were already damp and it wasn't yet 9 AM. A long, sticky day lay ahead.

***

Sleigh bells jingled on the front door of Corner Drug announcing the first customer on Thursday.

"Let's get to work." Heli slid off the stool, a red-light signal that her pre-opening chat with Murlene was over. "I've got a Hospice order to compound. Jayson should be here around noon."

"And I'll get on the film order that just came back from the photo lab." Murlene put a finger to her forehead to summon a thought. "Add glucosamine to the wholesale order. The shelves are completely bare."

"Another worthless drug with the medicinal value of Pop Tarts. Who buys this stuff?"

"I suppose our boomers who watch the six o'clock news," Murlene said matter-of-factly, "and want to be play tennis with pain-free joints."

"Starve a cold, feed a delusion," Heli grumbled as she reached for the phone. "No wonder placebos work so well." When she heard Sandy's mellow voice on line one, her mood softened. This was no day to embrace her inner gloom.

"The news is not good." Venkata paused. "As we expected, *E. tarda* has been confirmed in the sample taken from the snuff jar. I notified the local public health officials but they had already been informed by hospital administration."

"Have you spoken with Dr. Lavelle?"

"He ignores both his cell phone and pager. The Infection Control committee convenes at 10 AM. There is to be a broad scale surveillance of nosocomial infections at hospital. The state epidemiologist is flying in from Bismarck. Mr. Bohley insists that I attend." A half-sigh traveled over the line. "Any word from Officer LaDuke?"

"Nothing yet."

"But you are safe, yes?"

"Preparing morphine lollipops all morning," Heli replied in her most convincing voice.

Line two turned out to be a hesitant female seeking verification that Robitussin cough syrup might help her to conceive a child. Damn the Internet, Heli thought, as she replaced the phone in its cradle. Would the next owner of Corner Drug take time to correct such nonsense?

Thursday's Hospice order was due by noon. She unlocked the steel safe that housed the morphine. Inside the vault members of the *Papveraceae* family waited in rows like armed military with enough ammunition to depress every central nervous system along Devine. The snuff jar, evidence if Christine Runyan had indeed been murdered, rested securely behind the methadone tablets. Good. Very good. Despite the self-talk, she was sufficiently skittish to have moved the handgun from her nightstand into a drawer under the dispensing counter early this morning. Girl with a Glock. Credit LaDuke for that.

***

Rat ta ta Rat ta. Rat tum.

"Someone's knocking at my door, Doug—probably just another whiny-butt doctor." The CEO chuckled nervously. "Thanks for the information. Where are we playing bridge next month? The Reynolds?" Bohley hoped so. Glenda Reynolds was one helluva cook, and he had a deep hunger for something other than this chalky taste in his mouth.

"Hang on to your money. You may be a good card player, Byron, but you won't win with a viatical settlement."

The door opened as Bohley hung up the phone. Reuben Norbutas shuffled in.

"Hey," the nurse uttered, something between a grunt and a salutation.

Bohley immediately took note of the sorry etiquette of a generation he couldn't begin to understand. Unpolished shoes, loosened tie-knot, not to mention the absence of direct eye contact and the customary shoulders-back respect to power. The CEO was disgusted that this meeting was still necessary. Trading information for privilege was testing his limits.

"Have a chair, Reuben." The CEO watched the nurse take the hot seat. "Have you learned anything more about Bryan Ludemann and Daniel Ludemann?"

"Sure," Reuben nodded, taking his time for the rest of the answer while he tugged at a loose cuticle. "So. . .talked to a few more people, you know, read a few emails, dug up somebody from their home town in Minnesota who knows the family. Good stuff."

"I'm waiting," Bohley drummed his fingers on the desk.

"That's the thing," Reuben countered, "I'm waiting, too, you know," his fingers making virtual quotation marks in the air, "for some talk of the 'Big Promotion.'"

Bohley wondered when *you know* had become a comma in the English language. Reuben was a piece of work, all right. The CEO changed strategies. He pulled out his favorite question for all of the young, aspiring meatheads who landed in his office. "Where do you want to be in ten years, young man?"

"You know, sitting where you are. Top of the heap, king of the world, master of my own destiny."

Bohley gazed across the desk, permitting his mind to alter the image of Reuben Norbutas into someone aged by a decade. Start of a paunch, receding hairline, ruddy complexion sallowed with age. No longer drinking Mojitos, but Chivas, straight up, one after another. A drawer full of Tums. The wind knocked out of his sails by another generation of entitled doctors whose demands never ceased.

"I like ambition in a young man." The CEO feigned a paternalistic smile. "Now tell me about Alayne's brothers."

"Hey, why not?" Reuben leaned forward in his chair. "Bryan is a money-man with some investment firm in Austin. Forgot the name right now. I'm kinda nervous, you know, being here in this big office."

Bohley brightened. It seemed Reuben had come to realize in the last few minutes that playing along with the hospital's entrenched feudal system still held advantage for him.

The nurse fidgeted. "Like I told you before, Bryan's got a few drug problems. Up-the-nose type, if you get my drift." He snorted as though Bohley might not understand. "Busted twice, failed rehab and then started dealing on the side. But the guy's got nine lives and a good lawyer who happens to be big brother O-Danny-boy in Boise. God, who'd want to live in that dust-bowl? Does mostly malpractice work for plaintiffs. Alayne is tight with both. When her office door is closed, you know she's talking with one or the other."

"Anything more?"

"That's it for now." Reuben raised an eyebrow. "Any word on a possible promotion, Mr. Bohley?"

"I've got my eye on you, Reuben." Godamn gadfly! "That's a good place to be for now."

As Norbutas left the room, Gloria reappeared. Without coffee, Bohley noticed. She was chewing the inside of her cheek—a nervous habit that had always annoyed the CEO.

"I can't locate Ms. Ludemann. No one in the ER has seen her since yesterday afternoon. She doesn't answer her home phone, cell or her page."

The CEO waved her out of the room as he walked to his office window that opened over the front lawn of the hospital. Calm and tidy like most of Fargo. Unlike the bedeviling news swirling inside his head, and the god-awful position he might soon be facing with the Board. He glanced at his watch: 9:20 AM. He had until noon before Lavelle's tirade about some weird bug moving through the wards would go public. *Responsible for the death of one patient already,* the slick-tongued physician had said last night, as though rehearsing a sound bite for the six o'clock news.

The worst-case scenario took shape in his mind. If Lavelle was right, the CEO would have to explain the existence of a dangerous hospital-acquired infection that he didn't understand, relying totally on his staff for accurate information and in their ability to fix the problem before public hysteria set in. Bohley's confidence in the people around him plummeted. Alayne Ludemann and Dr. Kampela weren't even on hospital premises. Yet, he'd be the one in front of the television cameras when the lid blew.

Best-case scenario: Lavelle is blowing smoke up my ass one more incriminates a physician."

"Did you try the National Practitioner Data Bank?"

"Zippo. Consumers have *no* access to that info. The AMA must have spent a bizillion getting that restriction written into law. Anyway, back to Eddington. His name also shows up on the exclusion list of the Office of the Inspector General. Means he can't get paid by Medicare, Medicaid or any other Federal health care program." Jayson grinned. "He probably doesn't have the paperwork you do, Boss."

"Don't bait me, Jayson. Eddington must have done something criminal."

Jayson pulled another sheet from the file. "Says here he violated section 1128(a)(4) of the Social Security Act."

"A felony controlled substance conviction." Heli shut her eyes and thought of Sean. Yes, she knew that section of the law very well. "And to this outfit Lavelle refers Trevor Runyan?" Disgust drove her to the refrigerator for a fresh bottle of water.

"The third musketeer is Dr. Michael Marthaller. He did manage to pass his Oncology boards after med school and a residency in Queens, but it seems he couldn't keep his hands out of the cookie jar."

"He's dirty too?"

"Convicted of embezzlement at the Veronica St. Clair Cancer Center in Scottsdale where he was a medical director. Used company credit cards to obtain funds. Wrote checks to himself. He's got grand larceny, forgery and criminal possession of a forged instrument all over his record. His name lights up like a billboard with the OIG and on the Excluded Parties List System (EPLS). Means he's excluded from receiving Federal contracts or certain types of Federal assistance. It's all there on the web."

Heli plopped down on the stool. "So, dirty docs see an opportunity in pharmacy."

"More like a gold rush. GEM owns at least eleven pharmacies, maybe more. Looks to me like they've been scooping up pharmacies merely for their licenses, and then running an infusion business out of the back door."

Heli twisted the top off the water bottle and drank greedily. Her cheeks were flushed. "Tell me about Lavelle."

"He's ducking under the radar screen. I spent $35 on a criminal background check, and I know every address he's had since leaving the family home in New Jersey. Dogged the e-trail from his undergrad days at Princeton to medical school in Pennsylvania. From Philadelphia where he practiced for five years

"Sir, surely you do not believe . . . "

"Sandy, please," Heli interrupted, "let me answer."

The chief resident watched her turn slowly on the cushion to face Lavelle with the same steely composure that was part of her allure.

"I'm here at Sandy's request," Heli answered, "but since you've brought up the matter of our conflict, let me ask why *you* seem determined to humiliate *me*?"

When Lavelle was about to protest, she cut him off. "I've made no claim of harassment against you, although I can understand why someone has, given your behavior during Christine Runyan's code." She pulled in her chin and gave Lavelle a leaching stare. "Despite what you think, I made no mistake in preparing Christine Runyan's TPN solution. The facts will bear this out." She paused. "However, I didn't join Sandy tonight to defend myself, or frankly, to expose you."

"As though you could." Lavelle snarled and raised the tumbler to his lips.

Heli pitched Venkata a forewarning glance.

"Oh? What do you have to say about your financial involvement with GEM Pharmacy? Swedish Hospital would certainly be interested in your referrals to an entity in which you have a financial relationship. The Feds too, with their focus on anti-kickback rules."

The senior physician pursed his lips. The grip on his tumbler tightened.

"It seems to me that you're ruining a brilliant career without any help from me. I agreed to join Sandy tonight because we have more important matters to discuss than your professional future."

Venkata realized he'd slipped into standby mode in the nightmare unfolding between his most respected attending physician and the headstrong woman who had aroused his well-guarded Brahmin desire. It was time to change course. "She is right, Sir. We have new information on Mrs. Runyan's case."

Lavelle slouched in the armchair, hands together, his fingers steepled, bending them pensively like spider legs on a mirror. "Tell me," he said quietly.

The chief resident called the clinical facts forth in his mind. "The blood culture of the third organism has come back. Besides *Pseudomonas* and *Mycobacterium marinum,* another strange gram negative rod has been identified: *Edwardsiella tarda.*"

The news was met with another raspy laugh from Lavelle. "That's outlandish!" He reached for his glass on the lacquered believed the letter might have been one pivotal step in a larger plot to criminally implicate him. Finding the document was critical to his meeting with Bohley. The last time he'd seen the letter, it was enclosed in a blue file resting on his desk.

He switched on the fluorescent lights in his private office. The walnut desk was orderly without the usual clutter of files and medical charts. The daily calendar had already been turned to Thursday, April 6, 2002.

"Phyllis," he bellowed from his doorway. "What have you done with the blue file I left on my desk?"

She leaned past the workroom doorway with a tight, smug smile. "Why, Doctor, I placed the file in your briefcase as you asked me to do this afternoon."

His mind retraced the steps of the past fifteen minutes—opening the car door, sheeting rain drenching him, the effing umbrella that wouldn't engage. He remembered goddamning the storm as the wind had whipped the umbrella inside out. In between all the goddamning, he'd forgotten to grab his leather briefcase, now still locked in the backseat of his Escalade.

"A problem, Doctor?"

Inky, rainy night, shivering cold, desolate parking lot. Those were his options if he were to reclaim the file. Yes, he absolutely must have it for his meeting with Bohley. No time to take chances.

She followed at Lavelle's heels as he stormed from his private office to the coat rack in the reception area. His sodden trench coat was halfway on before she interrupted.

"Allow me, Doctor. I'm leaving just now. No sense in both of us going out in this downpour."

"Kind of you," he muttered sheepishly. He removed his coat and rehung it on the hall rack. "Byron Bohley from Swedish Hospital will be here any minute. When you return, will you stay at the reception desk until he arrives and show him to my office?"

"Certainly, Doctor."

In a world that seemed out to destroy him, Lavelle felt a rare moment of remorse for how badly he'd treated Phyllis now and every other time during the past five years while she'd returned a doting loyalty. Why not let her finish up the endless paperwork? Pushing more claims through the system might improve the revenue picture even if it cost him a few overtime dollars. Although he'd never admit fear, her presence would add a measure of personal security to the meeting he was about to hold with the combustible Byron Bohley.

"Stay and finish your work as you've planned, Phyllis. Perhaps the rain will abate by the time we both leave."

time. Bohley bristled at the antics he'd endured from the bow-tied bastard over the past five years. This so-called germ theory of his is probably nothing more than another attempt to rile things up. But the CEO's rumbling gut told him otherwise. Although his lips were chalky white, an acidic fear still seared his throat. Maybe there's a case scenario involving more hospital deaths where bad bugs and hospital wards are convenient means to a greedy end.

Murder and egg money. He thought of calling the police. Instead, he reached for another Tums and prepared for the next meeting.

Forty-Six

He manages to elude security and gain access to the Holland Tunnel from Jersey to Midtown. The entrance has been closed since 9/11. He is alone in the black lumen except for rats that scurry around his feet and bats sluicing overhead. He's frightened but determined to reach Canal Street. Clinging to the rough, sooty wall, he inches sideways along the narrow passage that rims the roadway. Suddenly he feels the wall tremble as though it's about to buckle. A chunk of concrete falls like a Zeppelin, narrowly missing his head. Fear grips him. Terrorists again? He remembers being warned. He knows this time he will perish in the tunnel if he doesn't get out immediately. Water pools around his ankles. Time is running out. Water now gushes through the twenty foot wide roadway, reaching his knees. Moving is more difficult as though he has sandbags strapped to his legs. If he could find a ventilator shaft, he might crawl to safety like Sylvester Stallone in *Daylight*. The water keeps rising. Waist-high, now. He wonders how much time he has left. Chest-high. This is not how he expected to die.

Awakened by his own terrifying howl, Mark Lavelle bolted upright in bed, heavy-chested and short-of-breath. A headache unfolded like butterfly wings across his forehead. The sheets were sour with sweat. He stared at the digital clock for a full three minutes, 9:27AM, 9:28AM, 9:29AM, before he realized he must not be dead after all. The phone was ringing. Did phones ring in hell?

He was alone. Claudette must be off to her open house. Alone on this Thursday morning with no medical rounds to make. Alone and under suspicion, in the eyes of the chief resident and his impudent girlfriend, for the death of Christine Runyan. Alone and entrapped with new incriminating evidence. He sat on the edge of the bed in his silk boxers, massaging his temples to palliate the pain. The only way to stop the phone's piercing ring was to answer.

"This is Dr. Venkata, Sir."

"You must have news for me." Lavelle rubbed his eyes like a sleepy child.

"The preliminary growth on the culture from the Asian bottle matches all of the others—the blood sample, the infusion bag, the syringe. I have read the slides myself. There has been no time for a final report, and of course, no DNA matching, yet I am convinced, now more than ever, that the infection was somehow intentionally introduced into Mrs. Runyan's blood stream."

Lavelle arose from the bed slowly as though any slight jar might set off another tsunami of frontal lobe pain. He walked barefoot across the plush champagne carpet of the master bedroom suite to the east window where he drew back the draperies. The sun needled his eyes and his temporal muscles winced in pain.

"There are other explanations for the path reports, Sandy. Colonization in the laboratory's tap water source. A sterile filter missing from the outflow tubing of the tap water-deionizing unit. Exposure of the clinical specimens to tap water by a careless tech at Swedish Hospital. The lab could grow *E. tarda* from the Holy Grail if its own processing techniques were contaminated."

"No, Sir. I do not accept such theories. Mayo's external reference laboratory has already confirmed the identification of *E. tarda*. This is not laboratory error."

"What else do you believe, Sandy?" Lavelle closed the draperies and braced for the answer.

"That you must come quickly to hospital and redirect the efforts Mr. Bohley has instituted. In less than thirty minutes, he will convene a meeting of the Infection Control committee and public health officials. I am certain that we agree on this point. *E. tarda* is not some hospital-acquired infection that should concern public safety."

Lavelle dropped his head. "No, it isn't." The bug had to have come from somewhere, and as long as that question went unanswered, less inquisitive minds would settle for an easy answer.

"And you must come to hospital to defend yourself, Sir. When the final lab report is issued and others learn the snuff jar originally came from your home, you must explain how this happened."

Lavelle stood before Claudette's triple mirror with the cordless phone in hand. Haggard, unforgiving faces stared back at him. "I can't explain it," he said, his voice bleached of bravado.

Fool, the three mirrored images cried in unison. You, who failed to subscribe to the local argot of the northern plains, should have anticipated the consequences. You have been careless, ignoring the warning signs. You have run out of luck. There is no light at the end of the Holland Tunnel.

"Sir?"

Fool! You've bought into the church-basement congeniality of this culture, never suspecting that anyone could get the better of you. Explain to us how your razor-sharp wit, your Ivy League education and your blue-blood connections will get you out of this trap. Admit it, Lavelle. You, a misplaced East Coast refugee on a cold barren prairie, has been set up for murder. And brilliantly.

"I cannot explain any of it," Lavelle repeated, humiliated at the weariness of his own voice.

"Then we must find answers, Sir. Of course you are innocent of causing any harm to Mrs. Runyan. It's time we look for a zebra."

***

"I'm what?" A shaken Donna Wadeson shrieked into the phone. She pushed her breakfast, a wedge of reheated apple kuchen, across the kitchen table.

"You have been placed on administrative leave," the manager at Swedish Home Health Services said evenly.

"For missing a staff meeting?" Donna slid her chair back from the table. "My goodness, I can explain. You see, my diabetic amputee returned home yesterday from the hospital and demanded help with his stump, and . . . ."

"Donna. . . . ."

"So I knew I couldn't do both—tend to Alvin Heidner *and* come to the staff meeting. 'Patients first,' my instincts told me, just like it says on page one of our customer service manual. Alvin was so grateful—wanted to talk more, but I said I have to . . . ."

"Donna, listen to me. . . .

"Did I miss something important? Is that why you've called me at home? Really, I was just having a bite to eat on my way out the door."

"Donna, listen very carefully. Mr. Bohley has instructed me to place you on administrative leave while the case of Christine Runyan is being investigated."

"Administrative leave?" Donna stood up and peered out of her apartment window to see if the rest of the sky was falling. "Isn't that the new word for 'fired'?"

"Not exactly. You'll be paid until the matter is settled, but for the time being, you're not to come to work."

"I don't understand. I did nothing wrong. Has Christine's family complained about me? My documentation is up to date."

"I don't know anything more than what I've already told you. Your patients are being transferred to another nurse. Your computer access into the Swedish system has been terminated."

Donna drew a fiery breath. "This isn't one bit fair! I did absolutely nothing wrong, and I've a mind to come in and tell that wimpy CEO myself."

"Listen to me, Donna." The manager's voice softened to a confidential tone. "Stay away from the hospital; consider yourself a leper now. And keep quiet. *Don't* discuss the Runyan case with anyone." She paused. "You should get an attorney. It never hurts to be well represented in this kind of situation."

The line went dead. Donna hung up the phone in a slow motion gesture, waiting for the news to make sense. In the living room, Martha Stewart purred from the television screen about *good things.* She grabbed the remote as though it were a handgun and shut down the fantasy that life resembled anything like piping hot blueberry scones on a Spode plate.

"Look what they're doing to me, Jerry." Donna removed her glasses to dry tears pooling in her eyes. "I'm so tired of it all—the struggle to start over at this age when I thought you and I'd be making plans for a trip to Branson to see Andy Williams at the Moon River Theater. Now look at me. Sorting out a new job with changes hitting me faster than a laxative." She blew her nose. "They've taken my job away from me, and that's all I have left on this earth."

There he was. Not exactly in the flesh and blood like Jesus appearing to doubting Thomas, but there, in the stillness of the room, she heard Jerry's voice like an ear worm. *So when did crying ever solve anything, Donna Mae? You're a good person who's seen more of life and death than most. Have a good cry, and then find someone to listen.*

She blew her nose into Mount Rushmore, the only dry corner of her souvenir handkerchief from their last trip to South Dakota. Calling someone made sense, but who? Her nursing friends at the home health agency were off-limits. Pastor Bob? That shiny-faced minister was too slick to understand real grief like hers. Tears welled up once again when she couldn't think of another name to call. Friendless in Fargo, she sniffed. Now there's a movie title for you.

The apartment seemed to close in around her with suffocating pity. The keys to the Blazer lay next to her purse on the kitchen table. "Enough of this," she said in a voice loud enough to fire up her engine. No one has a right to push Donna Wadeson around like a side of beef. Not some manager or that weasel, Bohley. Thoughts of that little runt could keep her out of heaven. Tell me this, Mr. CEO: who did Christine call the morning she felt sick? Who made the right call when Christine needed medical attention? Who stayed around to clean up that filthy apartment and take care of the frightened little girl? This Donna Wadeson doesn't need a lawyer as much as she needs a friend. Someone who's had her own tussle with the almighty powers-that-be at Swedish Hospital.

The nurse grabbed the keys and charged out of the door on her way to Corner Drug.

Forty-Seven

"**S**'cuse me. So sorry. Won't take a minute."

With the telephone trapped between her head and a raised shoulder, Heli watched the fashionista in pointy-toed boots nudge through the small crowd of patients waiting for prescriptions.

"You left my home last evening with the glass bottle." Claudette Lavelle's airy tone turned crisp with privilege. She tossed a carton of dental whitening strips on the counter. "I watched you put it back in your bag. I want it back."

"I'll be with you in a minute, Mrs. Lavelle." Heli attached a label to the medicine vial that held orange tablets to calm someone's restless legs. From the corner of her eye, she watched Claudette readjust the designer sunglasses worn like a headband to subdue wind-blown hair.

"I'm *really* pressed for time."

Heli reached for the next prescription in the queue as Claudette's cell phone rang with an irritating rendition of *Somewhere Over the Rainbow*.

"My West coast client can't wait."

"Not much longer." Heli nodded as she poured prenatal vitamins on the counting tray. "Why not take your phone call? I'll be with you as soon as I can."

"Can't you just hand it over to me?" Claudette interrupted as her cell phone rang again.

"It's not that simple, Mrs. Lavelle. I have no authority to release it to you."

Claudette snapped the cell phone shut. "Authority? I shouldn't have to plead like a common beggar for something that belongs to me." She leaned forward over the counter under the Prescription Pick-Up sign. "What *authority* are you referring to?"

Good question, thought Heli, teetering on the rim of some moral code. "A woman died at Swedish Hospital this week. Your snuff jar might help us understand why."

Claudette's generous lips formed a perfect trout-pout. "This woman: was she Mark's patient? Is he in some kind of trouble?"

"That's a question for your husband. You know—confidentiality issues."

"He's such a good doctor. So awfully smart." She twisted the marquis diamond on her left hand. "Mark is terribly misunderstood, especially by his colleagues at the hospital. Green with envy, most of them."

"Mrs. Lavelle, it's really none of my business, but honestly, I'm curious. When did you first notice your snuff jar was missing?"

"Let me think." Her gaze shifted upward to the ornate tinned ceiling. "I'm sure I stored it in the bottom drawer of my armoire until early last week. Yes, exactly. I remember bringing it downstairs Thursday morning. I set it on top of our sideboard in the foyer so I'd remember to give it to MacKenzie Knuttila. It looked so pretty sitting there, catching the sunlight through the transom over our front door that I thought of keeping it."

"And. . ."

"Never gave it another thought until MacKenzie stopped by over the weekend. By then, I'd decided it was meant for her." She pushed a gold bangle bracelet up her arm. "I hadn't wrapped it, so I left her in our living room while I went to the foyer to fetch it." Her perfectly arched eyebrows lifted. "But it was gone."

Heli glanced at the desk calendar on the pharmacy counter. Between Thursday, March 30 and Saturday, April 1, the snuff jar had moved from the Lavelle home to the Runyan apartment.

"I suppose it would be easy to misplace something in a grand home like yours. You must require quite a cleaning staff."

"Merry Maids come every Wednesday."

"Anyone else? Other company?"

"No one. Absolutely no one. Mark and I work odd hours so we're not the type to have drop-in company. Besides, I was at a real estate roundup in the Cities on Friday. Wasn't that the day of the freak storm? Yes, exactly." Claudette nodded, and her sunglasses flopped down on her face. "Mark said he was stranded alone in the house Friday night with practically nothing to eat. Poor baby!"

"Interesting." Heli hedged, throwing out a little more line. "If I may ask, who, besides you and your husband, has access to your residence?"

"The very same question Mark asked me last night. The two of you sound like walk-ons from *Law and Order*. Scads of people have access. This is Fargo; I should worry? Besides the Merry Maids, my designer has been in and out with his measuring tape during the past month." Claudette tilted her head. "We're freshening up the dining room for spring."

"Anyone else?"

Claudette hummed. "Service people. The plumber has his own key in case the sump pump fails." She shifted the oversized bag to her other shoulder. "And, of course, Phyllis Reski—the gal who runs Mark's practice—has her own set of keys to everything. The office suite, Mark's Escalade, even our home."

Phyllis Reski. Heli scoured her memory for the face associated with the name. There it was—the long-suffering woman who stopped by Corner Drug every thirty days for her statin refill. A diuretic for high blood pressure and a histamine blocker for gastric reflux, too. Add an antidepressant to this regimen, and Heli could imagine how Phyllis Reski might be able to endure a boss like Lavelle.

"A lifesaver, that Phyllis. She's always running errands for Mark. He can be so forgetful at times." Claudette lowered her voice. "For all Phyllis does for Mark, he should raise her salary. But, *no!*" She sighed. "He can be quite chintzy about money. And stubborn, too." She paused, as though she'd violated some nuptial trust. "Mark can be *very* stubborn."

Declaring that Mark Lavelle might be stubborn was like saying Bill Clinton had boundary issues. Heli let the epic understatement slide.

"Mark always has to be right. Like last night when he insisted that the Jade Garden doesn't make deliveries." Her eyebrows rose like an elevator on its way to the penthouse. "Men! Some things just aren't worth arguing about."

The Toreador song from *Carmen* blared from her cell phone.

"It's my office." She pivoted on a spiked heel and then turned back in one graceful but deliberate move. "Mark would never hurt a patient." Once again, her eyes scanned the ceiling and the exposed brick walls of Corner Drug. "I absolutely *love* the tinned ceiling. So no-faux! I could do something with this building. Imagine a shi-shi wine bar. A see-and-be-seen kind of place, exactly what downtown needs." Claudette's gold bangled arm fanned across Corner Drug. "Add some funky track lighting—metal to play off the brick. Trendy art on the walls. Tap into the urban renaissance thing." She slapped a business card displaying her spectacular face and a series of phone numbers. "Let me know if you're ever in a mood to sell. Twenty-four hours max, and I'd have a buyer for you. Then Heli Harri becomes . . . *nouveau riche.*"

Heli's eyes focused on the calendar. Something was swimming around in her mind, darting back and forth, moving close, circling. "The Jade Garden," she said quickly when she felt a tug on the mental line, "when did the Jade make a delivery to your home?"

"You haven't heard a single word I've said!" Claudette Lavellé looked as though she'd been newly rebuffed. "You'd be wise to pay attention to the value of this property, Heli. Never become emotionally attached to real estate. Business is business; buy-and-sell is the name of the game. You can open a drugstore anywhere. Frankly, your kind of business belongs in a high traffic strip mall, not in historic property with ambience like this."

"Please," Heli pressed, "the Jade. It's important."

Claudette rolled her eyes and reached into her satchel. She opened her wallet, retrieved the check register and ran a manicured finger down the recent entries. "Here it is. March 30: check payable to the Jade Garden in the amount of $47.46. I remember now. We had nothing at home to eat Thursday night, and we were desperate for Chinese. Kung Pao chicken for me, and Szechuan lamb for Mark. Yum-yum. Makes me hungry and it's almost lunch time."

"Do you remember who actually made the delivery?" Heli knew the kids that Mr. Wang hired to make occasional runs. "Was it a tattooed college student with a pierced rod in his earlobe?"

"No. A lumpish woman with bad skin. I didn't have enough cash on me so she waited in the foyer while I ran upstairs for my checkbook. Gave her an outrageous tip." Claudette turned to leave a second time, then added with a gummy smile. "Money opens many doors, Heli. Working in the drug business, you must already know that."

Forty-Eight

At 10:36 AM on Thursday, Dr. Lavelle slipped unnoticed into the Boardroom of Swedish Hospital. The meeting was already in progress. Byron Bohley sat at the head of the table, his back to the door, with the usual palace eunuchs to his left. Drs. Dahl, Thorson and Gudmundsen were scattered among the dilettantes of the Infection Control committee. Three strangers with visitor tags (two males and a token female) huddled near the overhead screen at the front of the room. Lavelle surmised they must be Public Health officials trying to walk in the real world of medicine. The only bright light in the room was Dr. Venkata who bowed his head modestly when their eyes met.

"In conclusion, during my career as a public health physician, I've seen and heard it all. Fly-infested ORs. Urine and feces found in a patient's room. Dirty gloves lying on the floor near a patient with a contagious disease. Physicians urinating in sinks. Surgical residents caught on tape without washing their hands before entering the OR." The portly gentleman with a sallow complexion leaned back in his chair, seeming to enjoy a new audience for an old speech. "Nurses administering shots without gloves. Ministers, nuns and the cleaning crew—all in violation of handwashing protocols. Reports of surgeons wearing scrubs home, then returning directly to the OR."

The stone-faced members in the room said nothing. Dr. Lavelle reined in his temper at the smug litany of physician offenses. Nothing griped him more than a turn-coat doctor betraying the profession of medicine.

"Infections were once hospital secrets," the health officer continued. "Now we're experiencing a hidden epidemic of life-threatening infections as byproducts of unsanitary instruments, unwashed hands and other lapses of inpatient care. These infections kill more humans each year than car accidents, fires and drowning combined. Moreover, patients have been kept completely in the dark, never knowing which hospitals are most dangerous because state laws enable hospitals like Swedish to conceal the number of patients who actually develop infections. We need to fix that problem." He rose to his feet and turned his attention to the CEO.

Where does he intend to go with this sensationalized tirade, Lavelle wondered?

"So I commend you, Mr. Bohley, for the good work of your infection control program, and for the proactive efforts of those gathered around this table. You have transcended the pervasive 'no-tell' taboo that characterizes the hospital industry. That you are sufficiently concerned about the recent finding of *E. tarda* demonstrates that you take atypical infections very seriously. As public health officials, we will take action immediately . . ."

"This is not a garden-variety hospital-acquired infection." The timbre of Lavelle's voice interrupted the speaker's Oscar-worthy performance.

Bohley was the first to turn in his swivel chair. "Dr. Lavelle, you must be in the wrong place. Come to think of it, since you are no longer a credentialed member of the medical staff, you have no business on the premises of Swedish Hospital."

"Christine Runyan was my patient and she died in this hospital." Lavelle took a composing breath. "To the contrary, why she died is very much my business."

"Mark, don't add to your troubles by making a scene here. Let the process on your reinstatement play out," Dr. Thorson interceded. "Meanwhile, we've got an *E.tarda* issue that has us concerned. It's only prudent to involve public health."

"Concerned, yes. But there is no immediate jeopardy to patient safety. One patient, one infection, one time, can hardly be characterized as an outbreak."

"But it could be," Thorson argued. "If the hospital water system is somehow involved, we've got to look into everything."

Ignoring the improbable argument, Lavelle turned to the CEO. "Adjourn the meeting, Mr. Bohley. I have new information on the case."

"I'm not in the mood for your grandstanding," Bohley hissed. "Last night you insisted on broad-scale surveillance as a precautionary measure. Today, you come up with a different story. I'm fed up with your bait-and-switch tactics. I'm in charge of this hospital, and if we have some bug lurking in our water pipes or air vents, my Board is going to want to know about it."

"My advice to you last night was predicated on the best information I had at the time. Based on what I've learned this morning, this infection has been made to appear like another hospital-acquired infection when, in fact, Swedish Hospital may have been used as a convenient backdrop for murder."

Murder. The word incited gasps and dumbfounded gapes around the table.

Lavelle walked from the back of the room to where the CEO was seated. "Byron, we must speak privately. Adjourn this meeting."

"I don't take orders," the CEO replied defiantly, "I *give* orders."

"And you do so exceedingly well as long as Swedish Hospital

thrives. An impressive tenure that will certainly end if patients have reason to question their safety within these walls."

No one said a word.

Nothing is deadlier than silence in a Boardroom.

Slowly, the CEO closed the folder in front of him. "This meeting will reconvene in thirty minutes. Once again, Dr. Lavelle has managed to disrupt our plans." Bohley glared at the physician. Then he turned to the committee. "I apologize to our guests for his interruption."

Dr. Venkata jumped to his feet, followed by the infection control nurse and the pharmacy director. Then Dr. Dahl rose from his chair. Soon everyone was standing except the guests who fumbled with their papers.

"In my office, now!" Bohley snarled, motioning Lavelle to follow him out of the room.

***

She glanced at the computer screen: 10:55 AM. Jayson should be arriving soon to help with the backlog of refills.

"Miss Heli, a minute, please?"

The pharmacist nodded as she counted pills tumbling across the blue Abbott counting tray.

"I really don't know what to do about this." Murlene laid a bulky photo-processing envelope on the counter. "Last Friday, Christine Runyan dropped off two rolls of 35 mm film. Did you know she's a scrapbooker?"

"Yes." *Was. . .was* a scrapbooker, Heli thought, autocorrecting the tense of Christine's life.

"Well, Christine's photos came back today with the photo lab delivery. Should I call the husband to pick it up?"

"Mmm . . . I'll handle it." Heli bit her lip and reached for the photos, silently defying any of her employees to do what she was now considering which was to have a quick look just in case there was some slight but important revelation into Christine's life and the how-and-why it ended in this shroud of mystery.

The clerk hesitated. "Just wonderin' what you plan to do."

"An urgent look-see," Heli replied with her finger already sliding under the adhesive flap. "I'm curious, I'm suspicious, I'm Finnish," she said, as if that explained everything.

A stack of colored photos slid out of the mailer. With Murlene peering over her shoulder, Heli slowly thumbed through the 4 x 6 inch matte photos. Anya standing before a Charlie Brown-like Christmas tree with a new bicycle in the background. Long streamers dangling from the handlebars. Trevor adjusting training wheels. Anya with Brigid Olander building a snowman. Trevor shoveling snow. Anya by the computer. Two blurred shots of someone's boot. Other overexposed images; some with heads cut off.

"There's nothing here." Heli said with a trace of disappointment. Not a clue that might have explained the final days of Christine's life. Just snapshots depicting the ordinary day-in, day-out family scenes recorded by a mother. A smiling Anya sitting next to Buddy Nustad on the front step of the apartment building.

The last photo in the stack was a close-up shot of Brigid in her black and white Jade serving uniform. She was holding Anya in front of Mr. Wang's aquarium that fluoresced with a cool moon-glow. The date, March 30, 2002, had been imprinted by the photo lab along the lower right hand corner. Heli pulled the snapshot close for a better look. Blinked several times, then reached into a drawer for her botanical magnifying glass. Moved the optical device over the photograph until small details came into focus—a synthetic coral reef, an ornamental driftwood grotto, Sword leaf lace plants . . . *Aponogeton natans* . . , a bed of aquamarine pebbles mimicking the ocean floor.

"What is it, Heli?"

"Look closely. Do you see anything unusual?"

The clerk lifted her head and gazed through her red Sally Jesse Raphael bifocals. "Not really. Nicely composed. The colors inside the tank are wonderful, especially those pretty little anemones. Reminds me of the Georgia coast. Do you suppose Christine took the picture? Lordy, hard to believe she and her sister were peas from the same pod. What I couldn't do for that Brigid! Henna rinse, a year of Weight Watchers and a consultation at my cosmetic counter could work wonders." Murlene shrugged her shoulders. "That's about all I see."

"Look again." Heli's heart was racing now. For a moment, she relapsed into a childhood memory, her father at her side, walking a riverbed, spotting trout. "What you don't see may be as important as what you do see."

The clerk returned an exasperated look.

"Like I said, I see pretty colors and the 'before' stage of a makeover."

"Murlene, there are no fish in the aquarium. What's happened to Mr. Wang's tropical fish?"

***

Once inside the oak-paneled executive suite, Lavelle asked,

"Have you met Dr. Venkata? I've asked him to join us."

"Of course, I know Dr. Venkata. I also know that our chief resident knows a helluva lot more about Christine Runyan's death than you do. He was with her the day she died; you were nowhere in sight. Dr. Venkata ran the code on Saturday night while the team waited for you to arrive. And," the CEO continued, "he's been scratching around in the case when others, Dr. Kampela specifically, were content to close the books on the Runyan death."

"True." Lavelle spoke calmly. "Dr. Venkata has demonstrated exemplary diligence in pursuing the origin of Christine Runyan's infection. For his perseverance, both of us owe him our gratitude. This morning, he has new information from Pathology that forces us to consider this death from a completely different perspective."

"Sit down." Bohley directed the two physicians to a round conference table. The CEO filled his coffee mug without an offer to his guests.

Lavelle accepted a seat. "Byron, for the next few minutes, I propose that we bury our hostilities to consider what this new information means for the family of Mrs. Runyan, for patients of Swedish Hospital, and for both of us who, in very different ways, were responsible for her care."

"A suggestion like that from you can only mean your gun is smoking."

"Would I be here at this moment, trying to convince you that my patient had been murdered, if I somehow felt personally threatened?" Lavelle turned to the chief resident. "Dr. Venkata, please share the new lab information with Mr. Bohley."

What followed, Lavelle would later remember, was the chief resident's concise clinical history of Christine Runyan's hospitalization, her subsequent death and the post mortem findings. Venkata answered the CEO's barrage of questions without the slightest provocation, effectively explaining the significance of the chain of *E. tarda* transmission to the nuts-and-bolts accountant.

"Mrs. Runyan died of an overwhelming septicemia with many organisms present in her blood stream, including *Pseudomonas* which most likely caused her death." The pitch of Venkata's voice rose. "Because *E. tarda* is a highly unusual waterborne bacterium not typically found in hospital, it is a conspicuous marker that directs our attention to the pivotal question: how could this particular organism find its way into a patient's bloodstream?" Venkata glanced at Dr. Lavelle and then at the CEO. "That we have cultured *E. tarda* from the snuff jar, the fourth link in a chain of transmission, most certainly suggests that the organism was intentionally introduced into Mrs.

Runyan's TPN bag."

"I'll be goddamned." The color in Bohley's face was salsa red.

"A nearly perfect crime," Lavelle intervened. "And very sophisticated. With Christine Runyan's history of repeated *staph* infections, one more that ultimately led to a fatal septicemia is a credible explanation for death in an immuno-compromised patient. And, in light of the current hysteria about hospital errors and the so-called 'hidden epidemic' of hospital-acquired infections, the murderer had a convenient white drape to hide behind."

"If you're right, and I'm not saying you are," Bohley argued, "then aren't we dancing around the obvious? The husband must have done it."

"In a homicide," Lavelle answered as if his knowledge now spanned forensic medicine too, "it's always the spouse unless otherwise ruled out. Trevor Runyan certainly had the medical means and a clear knowledge of the consequences for improper sterile technique. Perhaps a financial motive as well. And he had ample opportunity to commit murder. But others—home health nurses and pharmacists—were also in the home and had similar means and opportunities."

"Nurse Wadeson has been very helpful in providing information about the home environment," Venkata broke in. "Surely she is not under suspicion. What possible motive could she have?"

"Her nursing days are over at Swedish. I took care of that early this morning." The CEO sipped his coffee. "If this bug, *E. tarda*, is so uncommon, where does a deranged person find it?"

"Most likely in organically polluted water," Venkata explained. "The natural reservoir of the bacterium is the intestines of turtles, pelicans, alligators, toads, snakes, lizards, even tropical fish."

"Fish?" For a moment, the CEO seemed to be enjoying the clinical intrigue. "I'll remember that when I open my pet store."

"Thanks to Nurse Wadeson, we know that the Runyans had no pets in the home," Venkata added.

"Eating raw fish, swimming in polluted waters, even exposure to marine environments like aquariums can be sources," Lavelle added. "Does the hospital still have an aquarium in Pediatrics?"

Bohley nodded. "One in the ER, too. Raises patient satisfaction scores when people have something to stare at other than the clock." The CEO drummed his fingers on the table. "Maybe Christine Runyan tried to do herself in. Injected some swamp water into her IV bag, threw away the syringe in the waste basket and hoped to wake up dead. Husband becomes an insurance-rich widower."

"A plausible theory, but where would she find swamp water in

March in North Dakota? More importantly, how did she enter my home and steal my wife's snuff jar?" Lavelle drew a fortifying breath to mask his trepidation. "Clearly, I have been set up for murder in case foul play was detected. Another clever touch."

"The victim status doesn't become you, Doctor. Looks like you finally got your wit in a wringer." Bohley grunted. "Who, besides the twenty or thirty people I can think of off the top of my head, might want to set you up?"

Lavelle straightened in his chair, sensing a bitter metallic taste in his mouth. "Motivation has its own logic. Greed, vengeance, professional jealousy; who can say? A misguided colleague, some disgruntled nurse, an unrequited patient, an avaricious family member with a willing lawyer. Success is the invisible mantle I have always had to bear around those of lesser abilities. Your question is better placed before those who seek to injure me."

"Well," the CEO scratched his chin, "who found this snuff jar?"

"An inquiring pharmacist who knows the family," Lavelle answered. "Proprietor of Corner Drug. Actually, Ms. Harri is a part-time employee here at Swedish."

"Really," Bohley smirked. "Little birdie told me you had something going with her."

Inside his Rockports, Venkata's toes flexed.

"Preposterous!" Lavelle recoiled. "How very disappointing, Byron, that you, in addition to every other employee of Swedish, draw your conclusions from the hospital rumor mill. Factual information appears to be the exclusive province of medicine while hearsay and innuendo thrive in hospital lunch rooms." Lavelle regained his composure. "Not the first time, I should add, that you've been given bad information about me." He shook his head convincingly. "As for Heli Harri, she is vigilant, but much too obstreperous for my tastes. I find her sense of moral purpose irritating."

Venkata's eyebrows converged into a V over his nose.

"But her penchant for observation may be useful in solving this case," Lavelle added.

"This snuff jar belongs to your wife? Maybe she's got an explanation."

"Only the murderer can explain how he acquired it." Lavelle stared soberly at the CEO and asked the question he'd been withholding until the optimal moment. "Can you explain how my name was forged on the letter to the Eastern Shore Life Insurance Company?"

"Turning the tables on me again, aren't you?" The CEO smirked. "As a matter of fact, I've got a pretty good idea who might have forged your name, Lavelle, and I think I know why."

"I demand to know." Lavelle was more surprised than angry.

"You'll know when I'm ready to tell you," Bohley glared back. "You physicians like to believe that what you know is superior to what the rest of us know, but you're wrong. Dead wrong. I know what motivates people. What it takes for the rat to crawl through the maze to get the pellet. Management is about human behavior and the power of incentives." He popped a Tums into his mouth. "Find out what somebody wants and what they'll do to get it." The CEO leaned back in his chair and rocked. "Your signature on that particular letter might have meant a lot of money to someone. It's starting to add up in my mind, but I'm holding my cards until I'm sure."

"While a pathological killer strikes again before he's discovered? In your hospital, Byron? How sure do you have to be?"

"Don't provoke me!" Bohley's rocking stopped abruptly. "I don't need you reminding me that this woman's death could pull me down with her."

In that instant, Lavelle wondered if he'd underestimated both the man sitting across the table and his job in the corner office. How very strange to realize that a gram negative rod had already brought death to an unsuspecting young woman and now threatened two lofty careers. Fear clarified his purpose. Identifying the murderer in an expedient manner was the surest way to convince others of his innocence.

"Byron, you and I are in the business of treating patients in a safe environment. If we can no longer assure that safety, let us not stray from our collective expertise to matters better left for law enforcement."

Only the barely audible chirping of Venkata's beeper pierced the silence.

"It's Heli, Sir. The page is marked urgent."

Forty-Nine

"You must slow down, Heli."

"The aquarium at the Jade—Mr. Wang's tropical fish are dead. I just spoke with him. He found the last angelfish floating dead in the tank ten days ago. Scooped it out and never told anybody, not even me, because he thought it was a bad omen."

"I am in a meeting now." The chief resident glanced uneasily at Dr. Lavelle and Mr. Bohley who seemed impatient with the interruption. "I will call you back very soon."

"Sandy! You said *E. tarda* is found in aquariums. Don't you see the significance?"

"Excuse me, please." Venkata moved to the far side of the office near a window that overlooked the hospital entrance where he was out of earshot. "What I said," he whispered into the phone, "was that *E. tarda* can survive in the GI tracts of ornamental fish and be excreted into aquaria water. The organism is a part of the fish's commensal flora. Not a likely explanation for why the fish died, Heli."

"But tank water *could* be the source of the contamination, right?"

"Yes, possibly."

"Then stop thinking like a physician, and start thinking like a madman!"

Venkata hesitated. "That would be very difficult for me."

"Exactly." Heli shot back at an insistent pitch. "That's why we've stumbled. What you've seen under a microscope lens puts a name on the organism and identifies an environment like an aquarium where it can thrive. But if we reel back and imagine how someone, say, with murder on his mind, might look at the Jade's aquarium, the contaminated water seems like a means to an end."

"Yes, I can agree, but you are losing me with this train of thought."

"Water so contaminated that fish can't survive might be enough to kill a person too, especially if injected into the central line. Don't you see, Sandy? It's not merely about the facts, but how we interpret them through a different lens. A clever, virtually undetectable death attributed, as you have said repeatedly, to an 'overwhelming septicemia.'"

"A theory, I suppose, although I tend to agree with Mr. Wang. It is easier for me to believe in a bad omen than to conceive that someone so evil might harm a defenseless patient in this way. I would need more evidence."

"Dr. Venkata," Lavelle called out, "do you have some news pertinent to our discussion?"

The chief resident covered the mouthpiece of the phone. "Not exactly, Sir."

"Then please rejoin our conversation. The police will be here shortly."

"Sandy, there's more. The snuff jar. . . I know who. . . ."

"Later," Venkata interrupted her nervously, "I will return your call shortly."

***

Stunned by his rebuff, Heli slammed the phone into the headset. Nine new prescriptions waited on the ledge as Murlene added a handful of refill requests and phone messages to the queue. It was 12:10 PM. Jayson, due to arrive at noon, was late. Tension spread across her shoulder blades. In a funky chicken pose, she pulled bent elbows together behind her back and slowly inhaled, slowly exhaled. Time to get to work.

The first prescription called for BIP ointment. Amazingly, the old dermatological standby was still popular despite a throng of commercially available products riding on boundless advertising budgets. Heli creased a small glycine paper and placed it on the pan of the electric balance. With the tip of her spatula, she added bismuth salts until exactly 10.2 grams collected in the pan. She checked the wall clock: 12:14 PM. After weighing the purified iodoform, she ground the powders together in the stone mortar and wet the mixture with enough mineral oil to make a stiff paste.

The back door of the pharmacy opened as she reached for the white petrolatum. "It's about time, Jayson" Heli shouted irritably over her left shoulder. "Your shift begins at twelve noon sharp. You're late, and I'm swamped." Thirty grams of the white ointment rested on one side of the glass slab, the liver-colored paste on the other.

"Jayson," she snapped, "patients are waiting." She levigated the petrolatum into the paste until a smooth ointment resulted. "I'm expecting a phone call from Sandy any minute. I'll finish this compound; you start on the new prescriptions."

The telephone rang. Line one lit up like a flare.

"See what I mean? I'll pick up. Scripts for ketoprofen gel and coal tar solution are waiting."

"My first opportunity to call you back, Heli." Venkata's voice was brittle with tension. "Mr. Bohley agrees that the facts surrounding Mrs. Runyan's death merit further investigation. He has information that corroborates an attempt to frame Dr. Lavelle. Officer LaDuke is here taking statements in the Boardroom."

"LaDuke, at the hospital?" The news rolled around in her head. "Listen to me. I think I know who might have taken the snuff jar from the Lavelle home. Christine's sister, Brigid Olander . . . ."

"Heli, with Mr. Bohley's new information, we are following a completely different path. Very likely, a hospital employee has been involved in a sophisticated plot to harm Mrs. Runyan."

"No! Listen to me, Sandy. The Jade . . . last Thursday night, she. . . ."

From the corner of her left eye Heli glimpsed an empty weighing paper float faintly across the counter as though set in motion by some invisible force, like the subtle eddying of a current in an otherwise soundless stream.

"Hang on, Sandy." She turned fractionally. "Jayson?"

No answer. That was the clue that sent a radiating chill curling around her like shrinkwrap. Jayson never entered quietly. The banter always began the minute his key turned in the lock. A sense of danger concentrated her focus. With instinct guiding her, she reached for the stony pestle, a weapon-in-reserve, but not soon enough before a fierce arm intercepted, jerking the phone base from the wall. The line went dead.

Fifty

The cordless phone flew from Heli's hand, shattering a stock bottle of penicillin tablets that rebounded across the countertop.

"What are you doing in here?" She gasped as she regained her balance and canvassed the room. "Who let you in?" The back door into the pharmacy was ajar. Had she left it unlocked? Impossible. She remembered checking the lock. Always did. Besides the security company and the police, only she and Jayson had keys. She gulped, fear pushing the obvious forward with vivid clarity.

"Where's Jayson?" Heli demanded.

"Got the key off him, but the fool wouldn't shut up so I muzzled him with duct tape." Brigid Olander tossed her head back. Anya Runyan cowered behind her. "You were talking about me on the phone." She reached inside the deep pocket of her denim coat. "Doesn't matter now." She picked up a prescription blank with Latin symbols scribbled across the face. The paper crumpled in her hand. "You're not as smart as you think. I don't work at the Jade anymore. No severance, no benefits. Anya and me, we're blowing this town, aren't we, kiddo? But not before I get what I came for."

"Your medicine?" Heli's voice cracked with alarm.

"I don't take medicine anymore. You keep putting pills in a bottle and I get somebody on the street to sell them on the Internet. Didn't know that, did you? Stupid *in*-surance keeps paying. I make lots of money off those drugs."

"Brigid, you should be taking the nortriptyline. Stopping a drug like that can be dangerous."

"Quit telling me what to do." She whirled around. "I'm not here for the drugs." Her hand rustled in the pocket of her jacket. "You took something that belongs to me and I want it back. Hand over that painted bottle *now!*" She twisted her head. Paused for a tortured minute. "Trev loves me. We're a regular family now."

The veil clouding the mystery of Christine's death was becoming thinner and thinner as Heli began to grasp the full spectrum of Brigid's delusions. The duty-bound sister, a murderer: would she kill for a snuff jar? Dread coagulated in the pit of her stomach. Sensing Brigid's restless fingers now most certainly wrapped around a knife or maybe a gun, Heli braced for the worst.

"Run along, Anya," Heli urged in the calmest voice she could summon. "Your aunt and I have some business to discuss."

"Stay put, kiddo."

"Anya, please come with me." With her back to the counter, Heli held out her hand, never taking her eyes off the child. "We'll ask. . . Murlene. . . to put a. . .Little Mermaid band-aid on your knee."

Whether the child wriggled free from her aunt's clutch or the grip naturally loosened, Heli was too frightened to know.

"Don't hurt her, BG," Anya pleaded. Then she darted around the counter, out of sight.

"I told you to *stay put!*" Brigid's hoarse command was lost in the noontime carnival of sounds from Corner Drug.

"What have you done with Jayson?"

"Wouldn't you like to know?" Brigid's laugh had a ragged edge. "Left him bleeding in the trunk of his car."

"Why are you suddenly hurting people? Why, Brigid?" Heli inched backwards toward the counter. "I know you tampered with Buddy's meds. He could have died taking the wrong pills."

"Shut the fuck up," she barked.

"Did Buddy know something he wasn't supposed to know?"

"You don't know jack-shit about anything. Chrissy died, and we're all better off for it. 'Specially Trev." Brigid wiped her dampened forehead with the back of her hand. "Then you started snoopin' around like Buddy. Like she said, you're asking for it. Now give it to me." She pulled a revolver from her pocket and pointed the handgun squarely at Heli's chest.

"Sure, okay." Fear smelled like a corrosive chemical in the room. The Lady Rossi glistened in Brigid's hands. Sleek, hard-to-come-by, and pricier than her own Glock. Both, capable of sure-fire death.

"The snuff jar," Heli's voice quivered in a way she detested, "I'm getting it." Once she felt the edge of the counter across her back, she slid sideways, very slowly, toward the massive steel safe where the narcotics were stored. Brigid's wild gaze and the point of the Rossi followed her movements like a laser. One thought chased another through her frantic mind. How to protect herself, Murlene, Anya and the twenty or thirty shoppers in the aisles. She needed a miracle. *Ihmetapauksiini. . .* her father talking inside her head. *Hope for miracles, but do not rely on one.* The Glock was in a drawer well beyond reach. Best alternative: give Brigid what she wants. Activate the alarm ASAP with no sudden moves. She rehearsed the plan in her head, cautiously advancing along the counter.

"The snuff jar is in the vault, Brigid. I have to kneel down to unlock the safe." Her voice was steadier now. Fear can be disciplined. "Please don't hurt anyone."

From the other side of the pharmacy counter, she heard commotion. Murlene's admonishing voice: "hey, watch where you're going, hon." Then shouting. A tumbling, fall-over sound as though a vitamin display might have collapsed. More racket, louder now. Murlene's voice rising. "Be careful, hon." Glass shattering. Footsteps running. More shouting.

A female voice, close by. "What do you think you're doing?" Harsh, vaguely familiar.

"Leave me alone," Brigid yelled. "I told you I could handle this."

"Haven't you done enough, you idiot."

"Because I listened to you." Brigid jerked the point of the gun away from Heli's chest towards the shrill voice in the drugstore aisle. "Get out of here! Don't ever tell me what to do again. Get out, or I'll shoot everybody in here."

"Brigid, no more killing," Heli begged as her stomach lurched.

"Drop the gun, now," the demanding voice ordered. "Take the kid and run. I'll handle the rest."

"You said you cared about Chrissy, about Trev, even me." Brigid's nostrils flared. "Liar!"

Two rounds of fire rang through the store.

The smell of gunpowder singed Heli's nostrils. Her eyes watered. This was real. Let them be safe, she willed. Antique apothecary jars shattered on the pharmacy shelf sending streams of red liquid across the counter. She struggled to get up from the floor, only to feel the brutal force of Brigid's boot kick her flank sending another round of nauseating pain.

"The money; it's yours," the hysterical voice screamed.

"Shut up, bitch. You double-crossed me, blaming the storm and all. You knew I'd do anything for that kid. You said it'd be like before. Chrissy'd get better."

"Brigid," Heli implored, "please stop. Anya needs you."

"Everyone's got to quit telling me what to do!" Brigid shrieked as she smacked the heel of the pistol across Heli's cheekbone. "Nobody will ever sucker me into doing anything again." She fired another two rounds over the center aisle. Fluorescent lights popped and Corner Drug darkened.

Heli straightened upright through the steely pain, spun around in a daze and staggered forward, forcing her body to bridge the distance to the security alarm. Terror blurred her eyes but she managed to push the button before the second blow to her head knocked her blindly to the floor. The last words she heard were Brigid's.

"You deserve this for what you did to all of us," she screamed. "This one is for Chrissy." The gun fired into the aisle of Corner Drug and a piercing blast sent reverberations throughout the brick building. Then another. "And this one's from me."

Fifty-One

Sirens whined, announcing the arrival of Fargo police at the corner of Main and Devine at 12:41 PM.

"Over here, Officer," Murlene shouted, leading a young uniformed policeman to the aisle between the cough and cold bay and the cool mist vaporizers.

The officer wasted no time leaning into his radio device. "Woman down. Gunshot wound to the chest. Send an EMS crew stat." He looked around. "Anyone else hurt?"

"I don't know," she gasped as Anya cowered by the clerk's side. "Check Heli back in the pharmacy."

"I'm a nurse. Let me through." Donna Wadeson emerged from behind the analgesics shelf with her nursing bag. She rushed toward the body sprawled across the drugstore aisle, and dropped to her knees without any sign of pain. Multiple entrance wounds to the woman's chest had produced surprisingly little blood. Donna felt a weak arterial pulse and reached for her stethoscope

"Did anyone see what happened?" The policeman asked.

"Yes. No." Murlene fanned her décolletage, breathing in rapid frog-like breaths.

"You know the shooter?"

"Brigid Olander." Murlene pointed to the back door of Corner Drug. "Flew out of here like a bat out of hell."

The officer motioned to a backup policeman who'd just arrived in a second squad car. "Over here, center aisle. I'm checking the back alley for any sign of the perp. I've got a nurse tending the vic."

"The lungs. Listen to the lungs." Donna slid the bell of the stethoscope over the patient's left lung near the major entry wound and listened. "Good. Nice air exchange in the right lung." Concern etched her face.

Two paramedics with Lake Agassiz EMS arrived with a bright orange tackle box. "We'll take over." One medic opened the box and pulled out sterile packs of IV tubing.

"She has breath sounds in the left lung," Donna reported without budging or explaining how many times she'd seen this kind of chest trauma before—farm machinery accidents, car crashes, snowmobile wrecks. "She's bleeding into the pleural cavity, compressing the opposite lung. A sucking wound. She needs a chest tube now."

"Luke," the paramedic said nervously to the other as he cut the fallen woman's sweater with a pair of scissors, "do you recognize the vic?"

"Yup," the other gulped. "Radio the ER and tell them we're on our way."

"Double hoses," Donna shouted. "I'll start the IV in the left arm." She motioned to Luke, "you start another in her right arm. She needs lots of fluids to keep up with the blood loss. And someone get going on the chest tube. There's another wound to the abdomen. The bullet may have nicked the aorta which means we don't have much time."

The paramedic nodded to his associate, and remarked "good call, Ma'am. If Alayne Ludemann lives, she's got you to thank."

Fifty-Two

"How many fingers do you see, Heli?"

She forced her eyes to open, waiting for the roiling sea to calm. The hardwood floor, uncomfortable against the curve of her back, provided some sense of stability to the overwhelming vertigo. An acrid smell filled the air in the pharmacy as though Jayson might have left the cover off of the Flowers of Sulfur. She wanted to vomit. Cloying perfume: *Prince Matchabelli.* She turned her aching head slightly and followed the floral scent to Murlene who knelt over her, stroking her forehead.

"How many fingers?"

She saw one smooth dark hand with two outstretched fingers forming a V. Sandy's benevolent face came into focus behind them. V for *Väinämöinen,* the greatest of all Kalevala ancients and workers of magic. V for Venkata. Heli closed her eyes; opened them. One had to be alive to feel such gratitude.

"Two fingers." Heli managed to say through the pain. "Two."

Instinctively, she raised one hand to the side of her head and pulled off a 4 by 4 gauze sponge wicking blood from a wound. With the other, she stroked her stomach. Fear returned, and close behind it, confusion. She reached for the handle on the steel safe and tried to hoist herself up from the floor but the dizzying pain stopped her.

"Slowly now." Venkata reached for a blanket from the ambulance supplies and positioned the soft cotton roll under her head. "Careful. You have had a blow to the head, Heli, but you can move your arms and legs. An excellent sign."

"Possible skull fracture. Periorbital ecchymosis, too." Venkata was speaking to someone behind him.

"What happened?"

Behind a pounding ice cream headache, one detail after another ricocheted in her mind. She attempted to sit up again, but a wave of nausea pulled her down. She looked up at the wall clock above the pharmacy counter: 12:50 PM. Less than an hour ago she'd been compounding BIP ointment, waiting for Jayson to arrive. Then the flashback reared up in her mind. She looked at the ceiling to staunch the tears stinging her eyes. "Brigid? Anya? What about Jayson?" Her voice trembled. "My store?"

"Sh-sh-sh," Murlene stroked Heli's arm. "Everything's going to be all right, hon. Listen to your doctor now."

"Please follow my finger with your eyes, Heli."

She tracked the north-south, east-west movements of Sandy's index finger. Tinned ceiling overhead. A pair of black steel-toed boots near her feet. Cracked stone mortar lying on the floor to her left. Murlene in a blood-stained blouse to her right. Back to center: Venkata's benevolent eyes.

"Her extra-ocular movements are excellent, Sir. No signs yet of an epidural bleed."

Dr. Mark Lavelle came into view and squatted by her side. He examined the side of her head and shined a piercing penlight into her pupils. "Good," he said quietly, "the next few hours are important."

"Anya? Jayson? Where are they?"

"Anya's safe with Mr. Wang," Murlene sniffled. " We tracked Trevor down and he's on his way."

"And Jayson?"

Officer LaDuke looked down at her with pursed lips. "Found him in the trunk of an '88 Camry in the parking lot of Riverside Park," he said, thumbing through a small spiral-bound notebook. "According to the registration card, the car belongs to Ada Olander of Muskee, Minnesota."

"Brigid's mother," Heli explained. "Jayson's all right?"

"Roughed up some," LaDuke said. "A little sore but still exercising his vocal cords. Not that I understand a thing he said—something about 'spinning the news all over the blogosphere,' whatever that means." The officer had a wrinkled smile like Linus in a Peanuts cartoon. "His grandkids are going to get real tired of that story."

"And Brigid?" Heli squinted to trap tears in the well of her cheeks. With Venkata's assistance, she sat up on the floor. His touch was warm, smooth.

"We put out an APB on her right away. Murlene gave us a good description. We believe the perp acted alone and is on foot. We'll have her in no time."

"Please don't hurt her." Heli remembered the wild-eyed, canine look in Brigid's eyes. "She's confused, and . . . ill."

"Yeah?" LaDuke stopped writing. "Seemed sharp enough to fire a gun. We found a Rossi in the dumpster behind Corner Drug." He flipped through his notepad again. "Registered to one *Alayne Caroline Ludemann*, 1442 Kennedy Court here in Fargo."

Alayne Ludemann. A door of recognition flew open and an image of the perfectly glazed woman she'd encountered at Swedish Hospital appeared. Arms crossed in resistance, cardinal red fingernails, smug smile of power. And the voice: higher pitched and urgent. The same voice she'd heard before the gunfire.

"Alayne Ludemann was in the store. I didn't actually see her but I'm certain it was her voice."

"She walked in, all right," LaDuke said, "and rolled out on a gurney, toes up. Shot in the chest with her own Lady R. Died in the ER twenty minutes ago."

"That's enough, Officer," Lavelle interjected. "Give Heli a minute to recover from the shock."

Seated on the floor with her back against the cool steel exterior of the narcotics safe, Heli closed her eyes and gave full rein to the news. Alayne, dead. Brigid, on the run. She touched the tender area under her left eye and imagined a gentian violet shiner developing.

"Dr. Lavelle is right," Venkata squeezed her hand. "You must try to rest."

"I'll need a statement from you," LaDuke continued, "the sooner, the better. Nothing about this makes sense. The perp breaks in, shoots a customer, leaves without narcs or a hostage. We're hoping maybe you heard something to add to the story."

Lavelle cast a contemptuous glare at the voice of authority. "Can't you see that she's not prepared to make a statement?"

Accepting Venkata's arm to steady her wobbly legs, Heli struggled to rise up from the floor. Finally someone was ready to listen. "Brigid came for the snuff jar." She turned her head to Dr. Lavelle. "It has to explain . . . the murder of Christine Runyan."

"The snuff jar," LaDuke repeated. "Did the perp leave with the snuff jar?"

Details were coming home to roost in her mind. Claudette Lavelle's information. The noon-hour phone call with Venkata. She tried desperately to keep herself mentally afloat.

"No. Brigid pointed the gun at me," she said, remembering her crazed look with bone-chilling fear. "Someone approached the pharmacy, I couldn't see who it was, but Brigid's focus changed then. The two women were shouting at each other. Brigid must have fired at least six shots across the pharmacy counter."

"That jibes," LaDuke nodded, looking up from his note pad. He listened to a dispatch coming over the radio. "Say again?" The Officer was speaking into his radio microphone. "Who? The vic's brother? Yeah, all right." To Heli he said, "A call I have to take. Someone from the North Dakota Insurance Department."

Venkata twisted off the cap from a bottle of spring water and gave it to Heli. "You must drink this." He removed another sterile 4 x 4 sponge from its wrapper and placed the bandage on her head wound. "Excellent! The bleeding has nearly stopped."

She did as she was told. The water revitalized her.

"Listen to me," Heli said to the two physicians while LaDuke was taking his call, "and don't interrupt. Brigid DC'd her nortriptyline. I think she's delusional." Heli tipped the water bottle up again for another gulp. "I'm certain she was in your home Thursday evening, Dr. Lavelle—your wife will confirm this—and stole the snuff jar from your foyer."

"Why take a worthless piece of junk? If this woman was desperate for money, she could have pawned something more valuable than a cheap import."

"It wasn't about money."

Lavelle turned as pale white as the bismuth powder scattered across the pharmacy counter. "So, it was a plot to set me up for the death of Christine Runyan, after all."

"You made it easy."

In the distance, she heard Murlene sweeping up shards of glass. An aluminum garbage can groaned as it scraped the floor. The overhead lights were still off and the phones, quiet. Thursday afternoon at Corner Drug had become a crime scene.

"So," Lavelle cleared his throat, "the snuff jar traveled from my home to the Runyan apartment. . ."

"With a stop at the Jade Garden," Heli added.

"The Jade Garden has an aquarium, Sir. Aquarium water might explain the pathological findings in all four samples."

"Isn't this a rather sophisticated crime for someone of her abilities?"

"That's for Brigid to explain." Heli paused to quell the uneasiness in her stomach. "I think Alayne Ludemann coached her."

"So Ludemann plots the crime," LaDuke stepped back into the conversation, "and Brigid Olander takes the bait." He scratched his chin. "Sounds like a woman's crime all right, but what's Brigid's motive?"

"The larger question is what motivated Alayne," Lavelle asked, demonstrating that he was always one step ahead of the group. "What did she gain by the murder of Christine Runyan?"

"Perhaps Alayne Ludemann and the husband, Trevor Runyan, were romantically involved," Venkata suggested uneasily.

"A rather odd pair if you ask me. What would a woman like Alayne Ludemann see in a penniless ruffian like Trevor Runyan," Lavelle hesitated, "unless there was some money involved."

"Money, love or vengeance." Once again, the scratchy radio voice came from LaDuke's lapel. "Right, right. The Feds? Jeez! When will we know? Spell that for me. v-i-a-t-i-c-a-l. Got it. I'm on my way." He returned his attention to the trio. "This case is getting real interesting. Bohley was onto something, all right. The Feds *are* after Bryan Ludemann, the vic's brother from Texas, on drug charges and some kind of global money-laundering ring fronting as an insurance company. Weird stuff. They've been keeping an eye on the rest of the family, too. When Alayne Ludemann's murder hit the wire, the Feds jumped on it right away." LaDuke squared his shoulders. "I'll get the privilege of talking to the big boys behind the dark glasses."

"Insurance company?" Heli jumped on LaDuke's news. "Wait a minute. A private investigator came by Corner Drug on Tuesday asking me about a viatical insurance company. Remember, Sandy? 'Provisions for a journey.'"

Venkata shuddered. "Very difficult to forget, yes."

"I have the guy's name somewhere." Heli reached inside a drawer and found Roger Kenney's card. "Said he was working for the MidAmerica Life Insurance Company, investigating a death benefits claim on Christine Runyan." She rubbed her brow as if to draw forward more details of the conversation. "He mentioned your name, Dr. Lavelle. Claimed he had a copy of a letter from you stating that Christine would be dead in two years."

"I signed no such letter." Lavelle clenched his fists. "I know it, and Bohley knows it." He slumped onto a rolling stool.

"The letter," LaDuke pulled out his notepad again. "Was it to the Eastern Shore Life Insurance Company?"

"Bohley must have suspected it was Alayne Ludemann who forged my signature, and didn't tell me. She has to be at the center of this murder."

Lavelle swiveled on the stool, deep in thought, while Venkata rechecked Heli's head wound.

"How could Alayne Ludemann possibly have known about my involvement with GEM?" Lavelle asked incredulously.

"From Trevor, I imagine."

"But you and I both know Christine's final infusion came from the hospital pharmacy," Lavelle countered.

"Which explains why Alayne tried to implicate me, and Swedish Hospital. Maybe that's when Bohley stepped in and started asking questions. What he may know is probably quite important."

LaDuke closed his notebook. "I need you down at headquarters for a formal statement, Heli. Sooner rather than later."

"Out of the question," Lavelle rose from the stool. "She has a head injury, and although it doesn't appear life-threatening, we'll want to keep her under observation overnight in the hospital."

"Exactly my thoughts, Sir."

"No." Heli crossed her arms defiantly. "Under no circumstances will I be admitted to that hospital. My store is in shambles and patients need their prescriptions. Jayson is obviously in no shape to come in. Besides, I feel fine."

"The ER, then." Dr. Lavelle turned to the Chief resident. "We seem to have a recalcitrant patient on our hands."

"*SISU.*" Venkata explained as he reached for Heli's coat. "I think it is Finnish for 'hard-headed.'"

Friday, April 7, 2002

Fifty-Three

Friday's Northwest flight from Minneapolis arrived on schedule at 10:40 AM, surprising Lavelle and others who waited behind the security gate. When the first class passengers deplaned from the Boeing 757, he pulled the sleeves of his starched white shirt down until each cuff debuted properly, then adjusted the knot of his Brooks Brothers tie. The charcoal suit he wore hung loosely on his frame. Dropping eight pounds in one week had quashed the finest efforts of his tailor.

"Mark, old fellow, good to see you." The prominent jaw of J. Edward Mancino cut through the crowd. "I've been to many places in my life but never have I seen anything so utterly flat! You could roll dice from here to Montana."

Lavelle led his Philadelphia attorney to a generic grey conference room on the second floor of the terminal. Thanks to Phyllis, a pot of coffee and a plate of warm sticky buns waited under foil. Ceramic mugs celebrating Fargo, the All-American city, were arranged neatly in the center of the table. Mancino took a chair while Lavelle fidgeted with a dial on the wall to silence the Muzak.

"Much has happened since we talked on Tuesday," Lavelle said cautiously. "You might say the plot has thickened."

Mancinco retrieved the inevitable legal pad from his leather briefcase. He flipped through the pages, nodding, as if his notes provided an answer as to why he'd traveled all morning to get to flat Dakota.

"What should I add to my previous entries?" The lawyer looked up over his bifocals. "1) threat of malpractice from the husband of your deceased Crohn's patient, 2) allegation of harassment by a Swedish Hospital employee(s) and 3) inappropriate participation in research activity with Averill Pharmaceutical resulting in the loss of credentialing privileges at Swedish Hospital. The plot has thickened, Mark? How is that possible?"

Lavelle drew a composing breath. "My Crohn's patient, Christine Runyan, did not die of natural causes. She was murdered."

Mancino laid his fountain pen on the conference table attentively.

"For reasons I cannot explain, the deed was carried out in the early morning of April 1 in such a way as to implicate me." Lavelle paused. "Yesterday, a nursing administrator from Swedish Hospital was shot in a local drugstore. The police are detaining Brigid Olander, the older sister of my deceased patient, on suspicion of murder."

The lawyer pushed his chair back from the table. "Does this story, by chance, end with a wood-chipper scene?"

The arrogance of the remark made Lavelle snap. "Save your wisecracks for the old bulldogs at the Rowing Club. I'm paying you an exorbitant fee, and I expect to receive your professional advice purged of stale, insensitive humor."

"Continue, Mark. I'm truly fascinated."

"Regarding Christine Runyan's death, there is some evidence to suggest that her sister may have injected polluted water into an IV bag infusing through my patient's central line. Christine became septic and died twelve hours later in the hospital." Lavelle raised his eyes in a half-query. "Fortunately, the shackles are relaxing since I no longer appear to be under suspicion for improper care."

"But if you are no longer under suspicion, why have I made this urgent trip to Fargo?"

Lavelle cleared his throat. "My problems are not entirely behind me." He poured coffee for himself, anticipating the cheap slurry in the thermal pot to be more palatable than the story he was about to tell. "I suggest that you start a new page under the heading of 'GEM Pharmacy.'"

***

Officer Tim LaDuke sat at a small table across from Brigid Olander and her court-appointed attorney, Myron Blaznek, in the interrogation room at Fargo Police headquarters. He was hungry. Crabby, too. With any luck, the interview would be over by noon, and he could get over to Ralph's for a burger, then back to HQ for an afternoon of paperwork marking the end to one crazy week. He rocked on the back legs of his chair. What in hell was this world coming to? Across the country perps sat in airless rooms like this and lied. Lied, despite all the evidence, no matter how many witnesses lined up against them. Their dog-breath lawyers cooked up feeble defense strategies, or depended on some mishandling of evidence to get their clients off while the perps kept lying. Go figure. In the end, he supposed the perps must either be trying to convince themselves of the truth, or taking a chance that the courts, with weak prosecutors and ninny judges scared shitless of an appeal, might jumble up the lies with a few facts and an occasional mistake in a closed-door deal that could be packaged and sold to the public as justice. A strange and twisted version of *innocent until proven guilty* that he'd learned on the street in his fourteen years of policing.

But this case seemed too damn strange to believe. Like most perps, this one was careless. Dumber than most. Fleeing on foot made for an easy nab by a squad car cruising Riverside Park within an hour of the 911. But she was no meth-head with a fried egg for a brain. Not a *God-told-me-to-kill-my-children* Bible thumping fanatic or a psychotic demento hearing voices. This Brigid Olander, not too high up on the IQ totem poll, confessed to everything. The most disgusting means of murder he'd ever heard of, amazing even the medical folks from Swedish. Heli, too. Without her, the investigation wouldn't be this far along. If the Feds were on to something, the motive was as complicated as it was bizarre, involving some kind of ambulance-chasing insurance fraud by a ring of Texans. He'd had to draw it out on a white board just to figure out how and where the insurance money was supposed to flow to get into the hands of the crooks. An employee walking the halls of Swedish Hospital looking for patients to sign over their life insurance policy. Then murdering them so some investors—probably unsuspecting senior citizens in Texas—get a quick financial return while the crooks at the viatical company send the cash off-shore. On the life of his sainted grandmother, he'd never heard of anything sicker, more warped, than the murder of Christine Runyan. Blood spilt in Fargo tied to money wired to Thailand? How can the middle of nowhere suddenly become the dead center of everything?

LaDuke got up from the chair and rolled his shoulders in a lazy sinuous movement. "Let's go over this one more time, Brigid." He depressed the start button on the tape recorder. "Did you kill your sister, Christine Runyan?"

"You don't have to answer that," Blaznek countered.

"The medicine didn't work this time." Brigid hung her head.

Like a damn drooping dog, LaDuke thought, with a cask of brandy around its neck. Except it's a snuff jar. Never heard of that word until Bohley explained it to me yesterday.

"Tell us what happened during the early morning of April 1."

"Officer, Brigid, this is totally. . . ."

"It went all wrong. Alayne said she was gonna do it with insulin. Then the storm came up and she couldn't get out. It's up to you, she said when she called me at the Jade. TONIGHT. Don't have insulin, I said. Use anything, she said: toilet water. Gross; I'm not sticking my hands in the toilet. Then I had this idea. Fill the bottle with water from the fish tank. That wouldn't be as dirty as toilet water."

"Officer, Brigid, this is totally. . . ."

"What happened next?"

"Filled up the syringe exactly like Alayne showed me. Slid the needle in the tubing just like we practiced. Chrissy never woke up. Then I heard the apartment door open. Heard a voice. I got scared. Trevor would wonder what I was doing there in the middle of the night. Threw the stuff in the waste basket, my perfume bottle, syringe and all, and ran out the back door."

Blaznek shook his head and jotted notes on a legal pad.

LaDuke was no longer hungry. His lunches at the Jade Garden were over.

"Why did you go to Corner Drug on Thursday noon? Were you going to hurt Heli Harri?"

"Maybe." Brigid pinched the space over her nose between her eyebrows as though she were trying to think. "Alayne said to clean up the mess I made. 'Get the glass bottle back,' she said. 'Here, take my gun, use it if you have to. Just don't get caught.'" Brigid dropped her head and whimpered. "That perfume jar was special to me. Chrissy got drugstore perfume from Trev. Alayne got drugstore perfume from Trev. Maybe someday I'd get perfume from Trev, and I'd put it in that bottle." She looked up, childlike. "Tricking a kid like that druggist did to get the bottle back: that's bad. But I didn't kill her because Anya said not to. Okay, I said, anything for you, kiddo."

"How much longer do you intend to interrogate my client?"

"Just a few more questions. Alayne Ludemann died yesterday afternoon in the ER. Do you understand that you could go to jail for the rest of your life for murdering her?"

"I didn't do anything wrong. She double-crossed me."

LaDuke grabbed a chair and straddled it. "What makes you think that Alayne double-crossed you?"

"You're not obligated to answer any more questions." Blaznek's face was red as a watermelon in July.

"Things didn't get better, did they? The hospital couldn't save her this time. Chrissy died, and the next thing you know, Anya won't have nothing to do with me. Trev mopes around, hardly talks to me. Tells me things gotta change. Start over, he says, move on. Alayne said she'd see to it that they'd blame the doctor and the hospital for Chrissy's death and we'd make even more money from the insurance. Nobody would ever think it was family." She leaned forward across the table. "You know, I'm not stupid. I figured the only way the killing was gonna stop was to kill the one who started it all."

"Right." LaDuke kicked his boot against the table's leg. "Twelve noon. Interview concluded."

***

J. Edward Mancino III reviewed notes on his second legal pad. The coffee was cold and the sticky buns had developed a hard sugary crust. Lavelle switched from coffee to ice water to soothe a raw throat from talking so much.

"To properly defend you," Mancino opined, "at a minimum, I will need legal experts in health care law, forensics and a criminal defense team to advise me. Your problems are very serious, Mark, and obviously go well beyond malpractice, employment law and an ethics violation. That your name is mentioned in the context of murder and viatical fraud is a grave concern. The Feds will surely notice that point." The lawyer sighed, checked his watch. "My plane leaves for Philly at 4 PM. I don't know how much of a legal strategy we can pull together in a few hours."

"Assess my options, please." Lavelle was as colorless as the grey threads of his suit jacket.

"An outpatient of Swedish Hospital is murdered under the direction of a hospital employee, now also dead. This places the hospital in a very vulnerable position legally. Surely Trevor Runyan will find a clever lawyer who will see a judgment in the millions from a sympathetic jury. You will be dragged into the suit as well. In addition to levying specific charges against the hospital, Runyan will testify that his wife's outpatient care involved your referral to GEM Pharmacy for infusion services." Mancino removed his spectacles and cleaned the lens with his handkerchief. "My opinion is that you would not survive professionally if your financial involvement with GEM becomes public."

"No." Lavelle's palms slapped the table. "There has to be a way out of this. There always is."

Mancino began to replace files and legal pads back into his briefcase.

Lavelle paced around the room. "Bohley will deal." He consulted his TAG Heuer. "We'll meet with him today. I'll demand that he come to the airport within the hour. Here's what we'll offer. I'll disassociate from Averill and turn over the research dollars I've earned to the Swedish Hospital Foundation. He's that desperate to see his name on a building. I'll finish my anger management classes and I'll write lugubrious apologies to whomever I've offended in exchange for immediate reinstatement on the medical staff. I'll be at Bohley's disposal when hospital legal beagles prepare their defense. And I'll drop any charges against the hospital for the actions of its employee, Alayne Ludemann, who he knows forged my name on a letter to the Eastern Shore Life Settlement Company for the purposes of insurance fraud."

Mancino bounced his head around as though he were evaluating the merits of the proposed idea.

"And your nasty problem with GEM Pharmacy, Mark? How will

you escape incrimination there?"

"I'm thinking." Lavelle shot back. "I'm thinking."

"Who in Fargo knows about your financial involvement with the company?"

Lavelle winced. Realized the worst. Felt the manacles close around him.

"A pharmacist. The same woman who produced the snuff jar that initially incriminated me in the death."

"Can you charm her, or otherwise persuade her to keep quiet?"

Lavelle uttered a strangled laugh. "Heli Harri has made an art of being disagreeable. An absolute warden on matters of moral turpitude. Holy indignation boils out of her like lava."

"To the point of reporting you to the authorities, say, the Board of Medical Examiners?"

"She'd report me for jaywalking if it violated her sense of justice."

"Then you have no choice but to take matters into your own hands and plead forgiveness."

"You're not serious, Ed."

"I am very serious. While you were in the john, I called my office and had a paralegal check out the status of GEM Pharmacy. It's as I expected. Their problems are largely regulatory compliance issues—not filing the right form at the right time. The matter will be tied up with the Louisiana Board of Pharmacy for months." Mancino closed his legal pad. "My advice, Doctor? Establish a beachhead. File a statement with the hospital's credentialing committee acknowledging that you naively agreed to assist an old friend with his pharmacy business by introducing your medical staff colleagues and your patients here in Fargo to a convenient source of mail-order infusion services. You had no knowledge that you were violating any kind of state or Federal law. You had no intention of profiting from this advice, and when you were compensated, you passed along a large portion of the money directly back to your patients to relieve their staggering drug bills. Since you have learned of GEM's nefarious business dealings, you have decided of your own accord to bring the matter to the attention of your peers at Swedish Hospital to expose GEM Pharmacy in the hope that others in the profession will learn from your example. You will turn over any fees paid by GEM for your services to the Swedish Hospital Foundation in the form of a charitable contribution. And you will assure Byron Bohley, his Board of Directors and Ms. Harri that you have completely severed any ties with GEM or any other pharmaceutical, medical device, supplier, vendor and/or marketing company that has courted your professional favor. Not so much as a free drug-sponsored donut for you or any members of your staff. Am I quite clear, Mark?"

Lavelle walked over to a window that overlooked a runway where a Boeing 757 was taking flight. The sight fed his escapist fantasies. Leave, start over, a new beginning, no baggage. He watched until the plane was out of sight in the expansive glass-blue dome over Fargo. Then he resumed his seat at the table and asked quietly, "will the handcuffs come off if I do all of this?"

Mancino closed his briefcase. Said nothing.

In the long silence that followed, Lavelle heard the roaring creaks and terrible groans of a glacier calving in a cold, ancient world. He grabbed the sides of the chair to steady himself.

Epilog

With hands gripped on the steering wheel, Venkata's eyes bounced between Heli's crudely drawn map and the winding Minnesota roads. Driving east into the morning sunlight caused him to squint. The passenger seat held a shopping bag filled with buttermilk scones, tandoori chicken, cucumber-mint raita, dates stuffed with goat cheese and a respectable Pinot Noir from the Willamette Valley. Sunday's edition of the *Frontier Press* lay folded with its headlines face-down.

He turned off NPR and rolled down his window to absorb the early morning sounds. Tires crunching gravel. The squealing, slurred whistle, *ka-whee-oo, ka-whee-oo* of marsh birds. Seeing no one in his rearview mirror, he braked, then pulled the Audi onto the road's narrow shoulder. Such mesmerizing beauty was not to be missed. He stepped out of the car to morning air that was sweet, organic, invigorating. His eyes made a slow arc over the horizon where a broad domed sky, unblemished by cement or steel, covered dormant fields. So much space for so few people! The modest charm of this unspoiled landscape seemed to be taken for granted by most Midwesterners.

When you reach Fish Lake Road, turn north, her note read. It had not occurred to him that Heli's directions transcended GPS navigation. He returned to the car and veered slowly onto a single-lane dirt road. *Continue straight ahead for 10-15 miles until you see a grove of cottonwoods near a red barn with loons painted on its door. Turn right onto a narrow path (careful, it's hard to see) and follow the trail through the forest for another several miles until you come to a spectacular patch of white nodding trillium on your left near a fallen birch trunk. Turn in and look for my Saab in the clearing ahead. You can walk the rest of the way.*

Walk? The dashboard read 9:20AM; the temperature, forty-six degrees. Where might this journey take him?

When he finally spotted her car twenty minutes later, a much-relieved Venkata turned off the Audi's engine and grabbed a green fleece jacket bearing the Swedish Hospital logo. He slipped a backpack over one shoulder and stuffed the rolled newspaper into a side pocket. The shopping bag was heavy with enough provisions to easily feed six. Surrounded by a forest of budding trees he could not identify, he paused to watch sunlight flutter through the canopy of branches overhead. This was Heli's world and it was splendid.

After he'd walked ten minutes, the semblance of a path veered right. He consulted her map. *Swerve to your right but mind your step—Lady Slippers under foot. I've been watching this patch for years, waiting for a sign of pink moccasin petals. Maybe June, around Father's Day, if we're lucky. Nature will not be rushed.*

Venkata tunneled along the damp woodland trail through a thicket of birch trees. Patchy snow still clung to the frozen earth. Wherever he was at the moment, so quiet and mystical, and completely out of cell-phone range, seemed very far from his frenzied weekend at Swedish Hospital. He worried momentarily about the high CO_2 levels of a chronic lunger on his service, and the possibility that a first-year resident might mistakenly increase the oxygen and kill the patient. But Dr. Lavelle, now properly reinstated on the medical staff, had promised to look in on the old gentleman so the chief resident could spend a day with Heli.

When he detected the scent of burning wood, Venkata hastened his stride, brushing low-strung branches out of his way and snapping fallen twigs with his boots. He must be close after an hour of trekking. In the distance he caught sight of a weathered structure, too small to be livable, with smoke billowing from its roof. At closer range, he saw a rustic cedar hut with exposed logs and a single dwarfish window above a small veranda. On the front porch sat Heli, bundled in white, rocking serenely.

She leapt from the rocker with a smile that matched his joy. The backpack dropped from his shoulder and he returned her welcoming hug with such fierceness that he wondered if he might have added to her bruises. So soft was she, smelling wonderfully fresh of pine needles and eucalyptus. Over the past four days, her skin had lost its waxen mask and the heme pigments under her left eye had deteriorated, causing the ecchymosis to look like pesto.

"You look very beautiful in this light."

"I can explain." Her cheeks colored, red on green. "Finns believe a woman never looks lovelier than an hour after sauna. I've at least thirty minutes before the glow fades."

"Let me be the judge of that." Venkata smiled, then turned a full 360 degrees to take in the panorama of tall pines, birch-barked trees and a mesh of green growth poking bravely through the brush.

"I'm glad you found old Tapio's hideaway."

"The directions lacked your typical precision, yes." He smiled. "But no dangerous abbreviations."

"I thought you could use some windshield time to make sense of the past week."

Each time he looked at her, he saw something new, fresh—the natural curl of her wet hair, the mole near her wrist. But Heli was wrong about his mental wanderings during the drive. He'd paid no attention to obvious matters—murders, lawsuits, gram negative rods, police statements, hospital tensions, not even Dr. Lavelle's latest setback—learning that his office clerk has been embezzling funds from his medical practice for months. Nor did the chief resident give much thought to his impending move to North Carolina. Or to the difficulties needing attention in Mumbai. His imaginings had been entirely focused on Heli who now stood in front of this curious smoking hut that jutted out over a frozen lake.

"Come, Sandy." She led him up the plank steps to the porch. "Did you bring the newspaper?"

"Yes, here in the backpack."

"Read to me, then."

Trouble seemed so far away at the moment that he was reluctant to carry news of the outside world to this quiet place, yet he unfolded the newspaper. Maybe this time he might comprehend what was being reported.

New Details Emerge in the Ludemann Death

The death of a Fargo woman, Alayne Ludemann, 36, on Thursday has attracted the attention of the Federal Bureau of Investigation, the Fraud Division of the Texas Department of Financial Services and the North Dakota Insurance Department.

According to police, the dead woman's brother, Bryan Ludemann, 31, of Austin, Texas, is one of six men in three Texas cities charged with fraudulent activities with Eastern Shore Life Settlement Company, a viatical company based in Baltimore, Maryland.

In a statement released by the US Attorney for the Northern District of Texas, prosecutors for the Federal government allege that six defendants were engaged in organized fraud, grand theft and insurance fraud relating to the marketing of fraudulently obtained policies to investors. The authorities also allege that the defendants operated a large-scale money-laundering conspiracy involving substantive violations of mail fraud and interstate transportation of money obtained by fraud. The object of the alleged conspiracy was to obtain money from investors by representing that the Eastern Shore viatical contracts were on terminally ill patients and that the investors could not lose. The prosecution also alleges that the named individuals arranged to launder the fraudulently obtained funds and remove cash to overseas locations to conceal and disguise the nature, location, source, ownership and control of the funds.

North Dakota Insurance Commissioner, Ned Malone, explains that the scheme "targets elderly, mostly snowbirds in the Rio Grande Valley, who invest in life insurance policies sold as viaticals to make a quick buck. They had no idea their money had been pooled with other investors and transferred overseas with little chance of ever getting a return on their investment."

Bryan Ludemann, originally from Baker, Minnesota, is a financial planning consultant in the Mission, Harlingen and Austin areas. Ludemann has a prior criminal record for possession and sale of controlled substances, a fact his attorney and brother, Daniel Ludemann of Boise, Idaho, claims is "completely irrelevant to the present charges."

According to Fargo police, Federal authorities are now interested in the role Alayne Ludemann, a manager in the Emergency Department of Swedish Hospital, may have played in the solicitation and sale of life insurance policies of patients, including the policy on Christine Runyan, 28, who died at Swedish Hospital on April 1. Trevor Runyan, the deceased woman's husband and beneficiary, has admitted to police that he sold a life insurance policy on his wife, issued by MidAmerica Life Insurance Company, Minneapolis, to the Eastern Shore Life Settlement Company in February, but denied any knowledge of a conspiracy or wrongdoing.

Byron Bohley, CEO of Swedish Hospital has been unavailable for comment.

Fargo police have arrested Brigid Olander, 33, on a second-degree murder charge for the death of Alayne Ludemann and is also a person of interest in the murder of Christine Runyan. Against the advice of her court-appointed attorney, Myron Blaznek, Olander confessed to shooting Ludemann on Thursday in Corner Drug.

Blaznek insisted that Olander's confession was illegally obtained by the police and will petition the court for a psychiatric evaluation of his client.

"This is a good person with a history of mental illness, tormented by her sister's illness and misguided by prescription drug therapy that ultimately failed her," Blaznek said. "The evidence will prove that the

side effects of a potent antidepressant drug underlay a series of poor decisions by my client over which she had little control. She is an innocent, tossed about in a medical haze. The entire healthcare system is to blame: inadequate psychiatric facilities, negligent caregivers, and shameful health insurers with an eye on profits, compounded by a society that turns its back on the problems of mental illness."

Olander is scheduled to appear in District Court on Monday.

Venkata folded the newspaper. "No one will ever know that patients of Swedish Hospital had less to fear from an infectious agent than . . ."

"Greed." Her voice had the energy of flint on steel. "Greed fueled by too much money. Blinding the eyes of the wise and scorching the lives of the innocent." She drew a deep breath, held it, exhaled slowly. "And, a young mother's death will hardly change much. What will it take?" Her head dropped as though pulled down by the weight of the prospect. "I need this place to regroup. Listen."

He had never experienced the gravity of such profound silence.

"Sometimes I can almost hear the sap bubbling up the maples. The earthworms snorting through the soil. A lady slipper gasping for light. It's good to be here, Sandy. It's good to share this with you."

Wordlessly, she led him up the plank steps to a door with a wood-burned sign overhead:

enter the sauna as you were born

He hung his backpack on a peg jutting from the rough cedar wall and followed her through the windowless door into a very, very warm room. Once inside she loosened the tie of her robe and he watched as it slid off her creamy shoulders to the floor. Heat from the sweetly scented burning wood mellowed him like a tranquilizer. Heli ladled water from a pine bucket and poured a stream over heated rocks. Precious drops sizzled on the hot smooth stones, sending a spray of steam and a fresh, earthy essence throughout the dimly lit room. For a moment, Venkata forgot about his nakedness. The thermometer on the cedar wall climbed to 150 degrees Fahrenheit.

"Sauna is about letting go. Here we do not rush about, answer emails, listen to iPods, or worry about the stock market. Here, we let nature heal." Heli climbed to the upper shelf and reclined on the slab of cedar. "Here, we reflect on something larger than ourselves."

He had never seen her so transported, so . . . spring-softened. Sweat seeped from his pores opened wide by the heat.

She ladled more water over the stones. Once again, the droplets danced and steam curled around the room, penetrating the century-old cedar logs.

"Smell the birch leaf, Sandy?"

Venkata drew in the scent. "Oil of wintergreen, yes?"

Then, with her face tilted at a curious slant, she finger-raked her hair back and looked at him as the strange words flowed from her mouth. "*Saunassa viha viilenee, Saunassa summuu sappi.*"

Venkata wondered if the expression had anything to do with the dried birch whisk hanging on the wall.

"'Anger cools in the sauna, resentment fades away,'" she said. "It's time for Christine to rest in peace."

Venkata bowed his head reflectively as he felt the past hurtle into an uncertain future.

"In a month my residency will end, Heli. My family in Mumbai will arrive in Fargo for graduation ceremonies." He reached for her hand. "Please be at my side. As a first step, they will insist on meeting you."

She dropped her gaze and rubbed her bruised cheek. "I may not be what they're expecting." A smile tugged at her lips.

"Of course, we will take this one step at a time. Confront the obvious challenges: the separation, the distance, our careers."

She squeezed his hand as if to slow his racing thoughts. "You know that my life is here at Corner Drug, Sandy—my own safe hollow in Fargo."

What he saw through the mist was a tender smile embedded in the iron certainty of her intentions. He tucked a stray strand of hair behind her ear.

"Someone has to keep pushing the rock up the hill," she said simply.

Like a shaman, she lowered the dipper into the pine bucket and poured another cup of aromatic water over the stones. The stones hissed.

"*Löyly.*"

Together, they breathed the moist air in virtuous silence while the tiny drops sizzled on glacial stones made smooth by centuries of heat and cold, grinding and icing, without ever crumbling.

About the Author

    After careers in pharmacy, health administration and insurance, Ryn Pitts turned her attention to mystery writing, fiber arts and exploring her Scandinavian heritage. She lives with her husband in Fargo, North Dakota, one block away from the Red River of the North, where she is currently writing her second novel, ***Placebo.***